THE QUICK ADIÓS (TIMES SIX)

The Alex Rutledge Series

The Mango Opera
Gumbo Limbo
Bone Island Mambo
Octopus Alibi
Air Dance Iguana
Hawk Channel Chase

ALSO BY TOM CORCORAN

Key West in Black and White
Jimmy Buffett—The Key West Years
Key West Point of View (Photo DVD)

THE
QUICK
ADIÓS
(TIMES SIX)

TOM CORCORAN

DREDGERS LANE, LLC
LAKELAND, FLORIDA

ISBN-13: 978-0-9844566-0-4
ISBN-10: 0-9844566-0-0

Dredgers Lane, LLC
PO Box 5828
Lakeland FL 33807

Visit the author's Web site at www.tomcorcoran.net

Cover photograph © 2011 Tom Corcoran

Printed in the United States of America.

First Edition

For Martha Corcoran and Carolyn C. Inglis

For assistance, support, wisdom and time,
  I offer my heartfelt thanks to:

Katie Wagner Lockwood, Elsie and Jerry Metcalf,
Marty Corcoran, Carolyn Inglis, Dinah George,
Nan Kitchens, Nancy Harris, Les and Dona Bernier,
Eric Christensen, Peter and Sheila Badal, Cathy Keller,
Richard Badolato, Franette Vaughn, Mike Eden,
John and Laurel Boisonault, Doyle Smith,
Margo and John Frinzi, Alan and Cindy Bickford,
Bob Cruse, Brian Bradley, Ammie Machan,
the Eden House Hotel...

  and Stuart Kaminsky.

THE
QUICK
ADIÓS
(TIMES SIX)

1

I STUDIED THE PAINTING on the restaurant wall. The reclining nude stared back at me with distrust. A red ribbon held back her long black hair, and two plates in the painting floated above the blue tablecloth next to her right arm. The larger plate held a key lime pie, minus one slice. That fat slice, topped with meringue and a lime wedge, filled the smaller plate. A mixed-breed husky with sad eyes stood guard at the woman's left hand.

Perhaps, I thought, she is finished with me and is sending me away. I couldn't make out the red object she held and I wondered why she had no knife or fork.

I would have given her anything from our table.

Cathy, our server, came to the table and blocked my view. "Quit staring, Alex. Ready for your bill?"

Sam Wheeler pulled two twenties from a flap pocket on his olive green fishing shirt. "Who was the yakker that brought us our coffee?" he said. "He was not up to Pepe's standards."

Cathy held out her hand. "We just hired that kid."

"Where's our friend?" said Sam. "Greg with the face bling who never talks?"

"He, for two days running, is a no-show," said Cathy. "Which is bullshit if you ask me and you didn't. For the past... however many years, he's been on time, willing to work extra. Now, the second week of tourist season... He could have phoned."

"We miss Greg." Sam gave her his money. "Maybe he's out jewelry shopping."

Sam was in a mood. His light-tackle client had waited until seven that morning to cancel. He waited on the dock until nine, hoping for a walk-up, but failed to salvage his day. He called me to suggest a late breakfast. I wasn't hungry but accepted for the company. I had nothing else to do but pay bills and water my porch plants. And Sam offered to buy.

The early crowd had left behind a stack of newspapers. We had studied them in silence while we waited for our food and as we ate. When Sam was having one of his introspective mornings, he usually was thinking his way out of a problem. Once in a while he was deep inside himself, wrestling snakes. Given his military service, and I knew that he had seen far worse than he had done, I understood the latter. His lovely housemate of the past few years, *Key West Citizen* reporter Marnie Dunwoody, once said that we knew each other so well we could finish each other's sentences, but we damned well couldn't start them. Or else we knew not to try.

Sam and I have saved each other's sanity over the years, and each other's life as well, episodes we don't discuss much. We had tried to schedule lunch once a week. Either of us would assure you that we met no fewer than thirty times a year. With Sam's short-notice charters and my out-of-town photo work, it was closer to once a month, maybe less.

It took a few minutes to get Sam's change. Cathy had to wait her turn behind the confused newbie at the servers' register. I tapped my finger on page 2 of the *Citizen*. "Fifty years ago this very day," I said, "a twenty-two-year-old woman was arrested after she removed her clothes at the foot of Duval Street. A large crowd gathered before police arrived."

Sam finally grinned. "Why didn't the cops arrest the fool who called in the damn complaint?" His smile faded as he flipped the page and tapped the day's headline. "Did you see this lead article?

It's a lame-ass puff piece about a wannabe politician. Thank goodness the woman I love didn't write it."

"Small island," I said. "Reporters have to take what they can get."

Sam looked me in the eye. "That worries me, Alex. I mean, big-city newspapers are struggling. How much action can this town generate? Marnie's great at what she does, but if she gets fed up, she might quit. On the other hand, they could run short of cash and show her the door."

"Then what?" I said.

Sam has strong opinions and rarely shrugs. But he shrugged.

Cathy reappeared with Sam's change. I nudged her arm and pointed at the nude woman on the wall. "What the hell is that red thing in her hand?" I said.

"I've heard a hundred different guesses," said Cathy. "Everything from a personal massage device to a Bic lighter to a giant radish. Run with your imagination. Make it what you want it to be."

"You have to see it every day," I said. "You make the choice."

"Fair enough," she said. "I'll think about it."

"Just so it's not pepper spray."

A RICH BLUE, CLOUDLESS SKY and a warming January breeze awaited us on Caroline Street. Sam gazed toward the docks as if trying to decide what to do next. I began to unlock my bicycle, which was chained to a signpost. My phone, set to silence, vibrated in my pocket. I checked the incoming ID.

"The cops are calling," I said.

"Give her my regards," said Sam. "Tell her Marnie's talking lasagna for Friday night." He crossed the street toward his Bronco.

Key West Police Detective Beth Watkins doesn't like to mix personal matters with her career. She rarely calls during the workday, but she had attacked me three hours earlier, forced me to commit sinful kisses. I hoped that her call was an invitation to a rematch. It wasn't even close.

3

"It's going to be a bad Monday and an ugly week," she said. "Ten minutes ago we got a report of bodies in a condo, at The Tideline out on Bertha."

For some reason, cynical me took command. "Is one of them a young guy named Greg?"

Beth responded, but a passing delivery truck muffled her words. Only her angry tone came through.

"Whoa, pretty lady," I said. "I couldn't hear you."

"In that case, love of my life, I'll ask you once again. How the fuck did you know his name?"

I explained the conversation about Pepe's missing waiter.

"You blurted out a victim's name as a joke?"

"Nerves, Beth," I said. "A call from you during business hours..."

For the past few years any call from the Key West Police Department or Monroe County Sheriff's Office meant a request that I shoot crime photos. I have earned my living for years in advertising and magazine photography, but freelance work is never a predictable source of income. The first few crime scene jobs boosted my finances, saved my ass at the bank. Later the gigs became dangerous or depressing or both. The ugliness was undermining my love of photography, so I tried to avoid the work. Plus, my tech background is non-existent. My work was always non-forensic "back-up" stuff. A few detectives had found my work useful in solving cases, but usually I had to keep clear of the trained on-scene pros who resented my presence.

I said, "Please don't beg me to..."

"I'm asking, but I'm not begging," said Beth. "The city needs your expertise before the sheriff's office decides to pull this out from under us. Having you on hand might help me hold on to the case."

"You just made it impossible to refuse."

"Thank you, Alex. I just got here and I'm still outside the building, debriefing the first responders. But I've been warned, so I'll warn you, too. We'll have to postpone our dinner date."

"It's not even noon. We can't finish before sunset?"

"Someone has been dead at least forty-eight hours, so we'll both smell bad. Wear trousers and a shirt that you can toss in a Dumpster. The city will compensate you. I'll burn my clothing, take three showers and sleep at my house."

"Who identified Greg?"

"The first cop in the door knew him from Pepe's."

"Are you sure he's not another suicide in paradise?" I said.

"No, it's a murder, for certain, Alex. Please bring your big camera, the Nikon." Beth half-covered her phone, spoke to someone, said, "Gotta go," and hung up.

I tapped Marnie Dunwoody's quick-dial cue in my phone.

She took the second ring: "I already know, but thanks for thinking of me."

"They've identified that fellow Greg who worked at Pepe's."

"Aw, shit," she said. "That real cute guy who rides the Captain Outrageous bicycle?"

"I don't know and I don't know."

"Damn," said Marnie. "He was a nice guy. He helped a friend of mine move into her apartment. He wouldn't let her pay him, but I think she found a way. Have you been summoned?"

"I couldn't think fast enough to decline."

She laughed. "You, my friend, are a slave to the pudding."

I RODE MY BICYCLE up James Street against the wind, feeling dust in the air. In the winter months we tell visitors it's not just sunburn, it's also sandblast. Midway up the block a renovation crew in flannel shirts, shorts and work boots pounded nails and rocked out to Springsteen. In a couple of months someone would have a new home on the rock. People come and people go. Most moved to town to live their version of the dream life, but every departure was for a different reason. Marnie Dunwoody and Sam Wheeler, if they left Key West, would be searching for consistent income. I had known them for years, had counted on their friendship and advice. Their departure would leave a huge gap in my day-to-day life.

I turned off Fleming, coasted down Dredgers Lane. I didn't recognize the ratty bike near my porch door, didn't see anyone outside the house, and I couldn't see through my screens. I kept my eyes forward, kept rolling toward the lane's end. I don't like surprises, especially when they arrive on beater bicycles.

Taking a moment to think, I checked my phone. I had missed a call and message from a local number that I didn't know. As I hit the prompt for voicemail retrieval, another call popped up from the same number.

I pressed the green button. "Who is this?"

"The dude drinking on your side porch," said Dubbie Tanner, a faux-bum and suds addict I had known for years.

"Asshole," I said. "I thought I had a burglar in my house."

"Not my style," he said. "I watched you cleverly bypass your own yard. Could you turn around your costly bicycle and come open up? I only brought one beer, and it's down to the last... there it went."

Tanner, for years, had lived out of his car and bummed beers, sex and hot motel showers from tourist women. I was one of three people in town who knew about his handsome income from past business pursuits, surprisingly legitimate ones. Dubbie knew the bar scene as well as anyone and kept his ears and eyes open. He always had made sure that bartenders were tipped so that his welcome remained intact. In past years, he had helped me assist the police in solving several crimes, but I wasn't sure that I wanted to welcome him to my home.

THERE WERE TWO OF them. Dubbie Tanner, the taller by at least six inches, wore baggy once-black shorts and a sky blue tank top that broadcast Fairvilla in cursive script. With him was Wiley Fecko, a residentially challenged gentleman whom I hadn't seen in years. I doubted he cared that his green plaid trousers failed to match his maroon plaid sports shirt, though the pants almost matched his Kermit-green, nubby-textured running shoes. We shook hands like old fraternity brothers. Instinct told me to go wash, but my hand came away feeling remarkably clean.

Before they could reclaim their seats, I said, "Sorry to cut short this swell reunion, but I got a call. I have to leave in three minutes."

I took Dubbie's Natural Ice empty and waved it at Fecko.

Wiley shook his head and showed me a Styrofoam cup. By the container's size I guessed it was café con leche from 5 Brothers Grocery. "No thanks on brew," he said in his bright tenor voice. "I'm currently, perhaps permanently, off the sauce."

Not sure how to react to that, I unlocked and went to fetch a cold one for Dubbie. I found the last Beck's Light in the fridge and returned to the porch.

"Your shirt smells like you just ate breakfast," said Tanner.

"Your yard smells like fruit blossoms," said Wiley Fecko.

I looked out, saw no blossoming trees, but had to agree about the scent. "You guys are all about details."

"It's our calling, such details," said Tanner. "Mister Fecko, here, is my new senior partner."

I checked out Wiley's wino duds. "The word 'senior' works fine," I said, "but am I supposed to match the word 'calling' to either of you?"

"We've made a huge change in our lives," said Dubbie. "We're the co-managers of a limited liability corporation. Your own State of Florida has certified us to be private investigators."

"And now you two are on your way to a Chamber of Commerce meeting?"

"We live inside our camouflage," said Fecko, brushing his shirt front. "To the town's population, we're two more street persons in a town long known to harbor society's fringe elements. We're the scum that everyone ignores. They look right through us, deny our existence and hope we won't get in their faces. Who would suspect us of doing surveillance and following people?"

"Your corporation has a name?" I said.

Fecko raised his coffee on high. "Southernmost Aristocratic Investigations."

"The Aristocrats," said Tanner. "Gnarly but clean is our motto."

My cell phone buzzed. The window identified Marnie Dunwoody. I took the call. "Yes, ma'am."

"Two things Alex, and I have to talk fast. Have we got a good connection?"

"You sound fine to me."

"Okay," said Marnie. "I'm standing right outside The Tideline at the north corner of Bertha and Atlantic. My camera's lens is stuck open and the shutter won't click. I need exterior pictures for this article but the newspaper's regular salaried guys are doing photo ops at the Naval Air Station and a Tourist Development thing."

"You need to borrow one of my point-and-shoots?" I said.

"Have you got an extra?"

"I have my big Nikon and two pocket-sized Canons."

"I need to borrow one, yes," she said, "but I need you to press the button on my behalf, too. I've got fifteen things to do, and they want me inside now. I promise not to bring your name into it. Get me some outside images and I'll give my name for the photo credit."

"What's the second thing?"

"I talked to a building resident and got this far. Greg and a slightly older woman were caretakers for absentee owners. At least two condos in this building and more homes on the island. They showed up regularly, paid household bills, checked the air conditioning filter, whatever maintenance people do. I need the woman's name and the name of their business. All that is shit I have to do and it's not the second thing."

"I'm with you so far," I said. "What's the..."

"They haven't told me squat, but this might be larger than they're letting on. Beth has three city scene techs with her plus a county detective with an audio bud in one ear. They're keeping a lid on what they're divulging, and I have yet to see another reporter. If this story goes big, Alex, I need it. I can sell it to the online wire services and update my resumé."

"Okay," I said. "You stay there and keep digging. I will see you in fifteen and give you a camera with a charged battery and an empty card. After I give it to you, ignore me. I'll make you digital copies of everything I get, unless it's classified as evidence. I think I can find someone to help you with the caretakers' names and their business license, if there is one."

"Ka-ching," whispered Tanner.

Fecko victory-pumped his arm.

"Hug," said Marnie. "And a dinner before the weekend, Alex."

"First one's free," said Dubbie, before I shut off my phone.

The two men looked rational and determined. It might work, I thought, with a certain wonder. I hoped it would not become regret.

"You've got three hours max to deliver," I said.

"Our first deadline." Fecko shook his coffee cup hoping for a last ounce. "I have to take this as a good sign."

"Unless it bites us in the ass," said Dubbie. "If we go hunting background on a murder victim, won't the cops come back on us?"

Fecko smiled. "Don't sweat that, partner. I've got skills in dealing with cops."

I explained Marnie's dilemma, gave them our scant details and gave Tanner fifty bucks for "expenses." They gave me their cell numbers, pledged themselves to secrecy and went away. With their concept and preparations, The Aristocrats stood a chance.

I had an odd, illogical feeling that they would deliver. At least for a while.

DRESSING DOWN TO BLEND into the scenery was fine for The Aristocrats, but I went inside and changed my shirt. Even in Key

9

West, looking respectable has a positive effect on crime scene access. I installed fresh batteries and memory cards, and put back-ups for each of those plus my digital recorder into my big camera bag. Behind my cottage, I locked the bicycle in favor of the quicker ride to the island's south side.

My '70 Triumph Bonneville lives in a backyard shed custom-built to protect it from storms, floods and lowlife. I rolled it around front to find a FedEx van stopped in the lane. The driver waved an envelope at me. I set the stand and walked over to accept a large, flat packet from Sarasota. I didn't recognize the sender's name.

Inside the packet was a heavy manila envelope labeled, "Quote Request. Prepared for Alex Rutledge Photography, Key West, Florida." I took it as a bright launch of the year for my one-man enterprise. I didn't have time to read it just then. I reopened my house, tossed the proposal on a chair and locked up.

Driving out of the lane, I speculated on Marnie's warning about the scene being bigger than they were letting on. Right away I came up with three big ideas. A tie-in to other murders, local or else-where; dead famous visitors; or dead wealthy locals.

My mind was open, but my curiosity was under control.

It was not my gig, my problem or my style.

2

I CROSSED GARRISON BIGHT Bridge stuck behind three snowbirds on fume-spewing rental mopeds. Their pace past Houseboat Row let me slow my brain and collect my thoughts. Crime scene rules that applied to me, the civilian with connections, ranged from heavy-handed to loose and trusting. It depended on the presence of news media and which cops I dealt with. I knew not to foul evidence or contaminate a scene. I always knocked out quality work, but I refused to be upset the few times the cops asked me to leave. They had their reasons, and I had already swapped my ego for their fee. This time I was out to help two close friends at The Tideline condo. I would face disparate tasks on arrival, but I didn't want to disappoint or embarrass either one by being shown the door.

Beth Watkins was after clues, hard evidence and respect from her fellow officers. Marnie Dunwoody, to syndicate her news article, needed photos that told of urgency and human suffering. Images to pitch tragedy and horror to the masses, but having little to do with forensics. My twin objectives made me wish that I was barefoot back on my porch, reviewing the elegant quote request from Sarasota, counting in advance the welcome boost to my bank account. Slugging down the beer that I had given away to Dubbie Tanner. But I had promised two friends...

The mopeds turned left on Roosevelt, and I ran down First, trying to dream up fly-on-the-wall vantage points for Marnie's estab-

11

lishing shots. She could use views of the condo exterior, cops in uniform, their vehicles, and crowd control. I didn't need the outside officers to take me for a gawker with YouTube aspirations. And I had to get inside quickly to help Beth Watkins fend off the sheriff's investigators and hang on to her case.

MOMENTS LATER I WAS no one's white knight. On the only direct route between downtown and the airport, a green and white Crown Vic straddled the centerline of Bertha Street next to the Shanna Key Irish Pub. Why was a county vehicle working inside city limits? Why was there a roadblock for an incident three blocks away, inside a building?

"...bigger than they're letting on."

I foresaw no access at all.

Luck came through, for the moment. I recognized Chris Ericson, who knew that I had worked for his boss, Sheriff Liska, and for several detectives at the city. He also knew of my personal link to Beth Watkins. Like so many law officers, Deputy Ericson came to the job size large. Big neck, huge forearms, strong hands. In his Kevlar vest he looked like a sculpted robot with a tight-leash attitude. Scowling, his arms crossed, his butt pressed to the rear fender, he was a perfect roadblock. I stopped next to his cruiser's rear bumper with my Triumph pointed toward the crime scene. I switched off the motor and removed my helmet.

"I got a call twenty minutes ago," I said, "Do I need a wristband?"

"You might be out of a pay check," said Ericson.

"Did the city tell you to turn me around?"

He shook his head. "Ten minutes ago Sheriff Liska secured everything inside a five-block radius."

"Well, shit," I said, thinking more about Marnie losing her scoop than my being out a pay check.

"Look, Rutledge," said Deputy Ericson. "I'm just the messenger."

"How about residents of the area?"

"Let me guess," he said. "You live on Josephine."

"Let's keep going with that."

"You're going straight home with medicine for a sick child."

I nodded my acceptance of his little blue lie. "I was told a double murder. Why all the security?"

"They didn't share their reasons," said Ericson, "but it's probably just crowd control. From what the office told me, it's your typical drunk tourist bang-bang kind of deal."

"I got that, too," I said. "As if Key West has anything typical."

"Water puddles everywhere, that's typical," he said. "Plus, in this town, sooner or later, everyone fucks up." He waved to direct a motorist down Truman then turned back to me. "I mean everyone. Minor or major, local or visitor. You're going straight to a private home?"

"Exactly what I had in mind."

We both heard my cell phone buzz. I glanced down at my vibrating pocket.

"That's your pretty boss looking for you," said the deputy. "Don't piss her off by dawdling. She might run over your foot with her slick motorcycle."

Months earlier Ericson had come within a minute of busting Beth Watkins for a speed run on Cudjoe Key. She had bumped her Ducati well past 130 mph on Blimp Road, then departed for Key West after being summoned to a crime scene. I had been left behind with my antique Bonneville to deny all, to suggest that the deputy must have heard a passing jet. Ericson knew that planes weren't allowed near the blimp. He also knew of Beth's reputation for riding a powerful café racer. Out of respect for a fellow officer, he had let his query slide. But all three of us knew he was owed a favor in return, yet to be determined. Now I owed him another.

I thanked him with a silent nod, replaced my helmet, started the bike and rode away under the shade of a single cloud.

THE TIDELINE CONDOMINIUM, ONLY 1,000 feet from the Atlantic side of the island, was built in the 1990s, directly across the street from the first major development in Key West, 1800 Atlantic. When "1800" was built in the mid-'80s, it drew boatloads of criticism, but it was legal and opulent. The place filled quickly and inspired similar projects on the island's south side, including The Tideline with its ground-level protected parking, two residential levels, royal palms and peaked roof. I had heard that its condos were smaller but more luxurious than those of its larger neighbors.

The side street where I parked, by chance, behind Marnie Dunwoody's Jeep, was quieter than I expected. I was only three hundred feet from The Tideline, perhaps three hundred yards from the ocean. The air carried beach smells, a musty odor of damp seaweed. I locked my helmet to the Triumph's handlebar then, answering to habit, to assure myself that the camera was working, I removed it from its bag and pointed it south on Josephine Street. I clicked off several pictures without aiming or framing. Perfect exposure, fine focus. I was good to go.

I walked east on Atlantic Boulevard toward the crime scene. Most boulevards have medians, a line of trees, green grass or left-turn lanes. Atlantic is a skinny two-lane close to the beach, prone to flooding in storms. I once noticed on an eighty-year-old map that it used to be called Ruth Street.

Right away, for Marnie, I wanted an overall shot, the ground-level parking area around two sides of the building and three residential floors. I needed some altitude to see over the condo's surrounding shrubs and give my shot perspective. An idea came to mind that was interrupted by the buzz of my phone. The missed-call screen told me that Tanner, not Beth, had rung while I chatted with Deputy Ericson.

"Yo, bro," said Dubbie.

I didn't respond.

"Okay," he said. "I will never say 'Yo, bro,' again. Greg's last name is Pulver." He spelled it for me. "We found pictures on Facebook. I've seen the guy around town."

"How about an address, his partner's name?"

"No home address yet. Wiley knows someone to ask at Pepe's. Best we can tell, from Facebook remarks, he's also employed by a woman named Ocilla."

"Hot damn," I said, "I think your detective agency's on track. Can you check him out, see if there's dirt on the street? See if Greg was having affairs with his clients?"

Dubbie ignored me. "Wiley is running Ocilla through the search sites and, right away, having no luck. In order to better follow your orders and deplete your expense cash, I will report to the Green Parrot, the Bull and Whistle, Schooner Wharf and similar iconic saloons to learn more about Greg Pulver's habits and associates."

"A work ethic to which we all aspire," I said.

Tanner hung up. It rang again.

"Change of plans, Alex" said Beth. "We won't need your help after all. If you've left the house, you can turn around and go home."

"I've left the house," I said.

"You probably can't get in here. Your friend the sheriff just set up a five-block perimeter. No vehicles in or out."

"Why can't my friend make one exception?"

"The response teams are crowding out into the roadway. The traffic issues..."

"Beth, am I fired because their scene techs don't want... ?"

"Essentially, yes," she said. "Sorry, I've got to take this incoming."

The call ended. I had been dropped into the out basket, but my promise to Marnie Dunwoody still stood.

DODGING ONLOOKERS ON FOOT, a few bike riders taking curiosity breaks, I made my way to the in-line skaters' Southernmost Hockey Club, across Bertha from the condo. Though I had walked less than three hundred feet, I found the sea breeze carried even more pungent odors of beached plankton. A five-foot chain-link fence surrounded the vacant rink. I had no ladder, so a shot from its roof was out. With every cop in sight distracted by the headline crime, I saw no risk in light-duty trespassing. The club had mounted their home team sign on twin posts near the fence. With my camera bag strap around my neck, using gaps in the chain-link and stupid bravado, I managed a toehold. I hoisted myself, planted my feet on the top bar of the fence, and hung one elbow over the sign top.

The perch gave me a five-foot advantage and did wonders for the Nikon's point of view. I framed the condo's east wall and the cars in the near lot, then went back and forth for panoramic effect. I zoomed into the 1800 Atlantic parking area across the road, then photographed sidewalk onlookers closer to me. By the spectrum of attire, from T-shirts, sweat pants and flip-flops to dress shirts, shoes and sun dresses, the sidewalk group appeared to be Tideline condo dwellers evacuated on short notice.

I had a bitch of a time climbing down without snagging my ass on fence barbs or breaking my ankles. On my way to solid ground I noticed the sound of a low-flying single-engine aircraft. Someone else with the point of view I really needed.

I wasn't sure that I had taken helpful photos, but my larger task would be getting a camera to Marnie. I crossed Bertha, stepped through a landscaped border into The Tideline parking lot and took a half-dozen random shots, cars and vans, only for the satisfaction of pressing the shutter button. Marnie would find the photos useless. And I was stuck. She was going to get scooped by a reporter in a small plane, and my first attempt at online journalism would end in failure.

Closer to the yellow incident streamer around the police command post, I finally saw a photo I wanted. A few cops stood around wearing MCSO and KWPD jackets, but no one noticed me. I pushed the button five times as I panned left to right, then pushed my luck, aimed the zoom toward the open rear door of the county's forensic truck, shot several more. I knew that my camera's sensor wasn't capturing what I could clearly make out in the van's dim interior light: a scene tech moving around, sorting gear, placing objects on a work counter. He was preparing for something, either to carry supplies inside or to receive evidence from inside the building. Digital pictures are free; I kept shooting.

I had been in that van on two occasions in the past four years, so I knew what it meant when the tech reached into the cabinet that held body bags. His arm moved twice from the high shelf to a hefty-looking backpack, confirming the two deaths that Beth had mentioned. He then raised his arm once again to the cabinet and placed a third black bag in the backpack. I hit the button several more times as the tech climbed out, slammed the van's rear door and walked into the building.

Focusing on the technician's chore, I had paid too little attention to the crowd around me. A city cop in a group of onlookers must have seen me snap the last few pictures. I didn't recognize him, and he didn't know why I was there. He keyed his shoulder mike and beckoned me with his free arm. Not wanting to get trapped in a long explanation, I put my camera into its carrying pouch, faded across Bertha Street and took out my cell to call Marnie.

My phone vibrated in my hand. The window read: B WATKINS.

I promised myself not to lie and pressed the button.

"Alex," she said. "Why are you taking pictures out in the street?"

"Long story, but I'm doing someone a favor."

"You're not doing me any."

I scanned The Tideline, saw her standing on a third-floor balcony. "It has nothing to do with you."

"You're wrong, Alex," she said, sounding like a cop. "A lot of people associate the two of us. If one of my colleagues, one of the wrong ones, spots you taking pictures, I'm under the bus, and we already promised Marnie a photo op. Please go away."

"Her camera crapped out on her..."

Again Beth spoke sharply: "She needs to borrow yours."

"That's why I'm here," I said.

"She's in a briefing room. I'll send an officer out to get it."

"What officer won't associate the two of us?"

"I've managed to find a few friends at work," she said. "Please stay where you are for a minute or two."

I didn't want to have my gear confiscated, lose the pictures I had taken. I waited a few seconds, took advantage of a sago palm, and stepped out of Beth's line-of-sight. It took me fewer than fifteen seconds to swap an unused data chip into the Nikon and place the chip with photos in my pocket. I moved sideways so she could see me again, but she had gone away from the window.

The group of evacuees had pushed back a few yards closer to me. I approached a man dressed in striped shorts and a tank top. A brush cut and excellent earlobe-level sideburns.

"Excuse me." I pointed to the southeast corner of the third floor. "Do you know what apartment number that is?"

He turned toward me, looked puzzled, and shook his head. He nudged a woman near him, mumbled in what I took to be Russian. She also had a brush cut and tank top plus a colorful dragon tattoo on her left shoulder. I believe our planet now has more dragon tattoos than pickup trucks.

Pointing again, hoping for better luck, I posed the question to the young woman.

She looked at the building then turned and stared at my chest without focusing. It took her about ten seconds to consider her answer. Without lifting her eyes to mine she said, in a crisp military voice, a perfect midwest accent, "Three-zero-two, sir."

She looked away and didn't respond when I thanked her.

Someone tapped me on the shoulder.

The shape of a linebacker, my height, the officer wore a white polo shirt over a white T-shirt, black shorts, no hat or hair, and opaque sunglasses. His neck was as big around as his bald head.

His belt carried an array of restraints, communication equipment, weapons and chromium hardware. We backed away from the clutch of silent onlookers.

"You popping for tabs?" he said.

"Come again?"

"Paparazzi for the tabloids?"

"No," I said. "I don't shoot crime scenes for money."

"Why do it?" he said.

"The same reason as you. To stop or solve crimes."

The officer shook his head and laughed. "Shit, bubba, other people do that crap. My gig is to react, not stop or solve. The more crimes I react to, the more job security I nail down. I'm out here for rent plus my family's health insurance, and it keeps me out of the bars."

"And you get to carry a gun." I pulled one of the small Canons from my pocket. "The power is all yours. Are you going to give this to Ms. Dunwoody?"

He adjusted his swagger, looked unsure how to react to my "power" remark. He let it slide and took the camera from my hand. "I'll deliver it personally, Rutledge."

"Why would the tabloids have an interest?" I said.

"I don't know how those fuckers think. But even more I don't know why a civilian would want to waste time taking pictures outside of a crime scene."

I was stumped for an answer that made sense to either of us.

"I'm supposed to watch you go away," he said. "Orders from the female detective, through me to you."

"Great job you got," I said.

"Whatever," he said. "Guess we know who wears the gun in your house."

He hadn't let it slide after all.

I WALKED NORTH ON Josephine away from Atlantic Boulevard and away from the breeze. A January day, and my ballcap was damp

19

with sweat. I wished for a cloud to pass above me. I heard another small plane, then a chopper, and knew that people with better views and video had scooped Marnie on visuals. Her best hope was the story behind the story. Stopping in front of a porch filled with colorful Styrofoam trapline floats, I tapped Dubbie Tanner's number on my cell.

"Apartment 302 in The Tideline," I said. "Try to compile a diagram of condos to either side of that one and any others on the third floor. Check ownership, mortgages and liens, current and past tenants, property tax status and previous owners. See whether those names show up as owners of other condos in the building. Also, see if anyone from that group has been recently arrested for disturbing the peace, domestic violence, DUI, or narcotics possession."

"Or manslaughter?" he said.

"Anything at all. Parking tickets. If you can manage it, I want names to go with the crimes."

"Got it," he said. "We already have this. The business that employed Greg Pulver is Acting Chief Execs, LLC. The sole owner is Ocilla Ramirez, and it's located at 490 Crawford Street on Big Coppitt."

"Great. Keep rolling with it. A client list would make our day."

"I'm beating the bushes," he said.

"Beat away, Dubbie," I said. "Try to restrict it to one beer per research location."

THERE I WAS AGAIN, behind the backdrop, half in the fog, playing two-bit snoop in the wake of horrible violence. Drawn into another tropical puzzle, and I had failed at least one and maybe two friends who expected better of me. The worst part was being reminded that my patch of paradise—sea breeze, sand and palm trees included— was no less evil than the rest of the nation. Bad as I felt, there were people in this country who walked among gray buildings and bare trees dodging sidewalk ice, slush and snow drifts, swearing they would give anything to be in my sandy, tar-stained Nikes.

Two ideas appealed to me. The fuel value of my Pepe's breakfast had dropped to zero, so I needed a meal. I called Saluté at Higgs Beach and ordered a shrimp salad sandwich. Rick, the owner, said he would set me up at the bar. He assured me that there would be no yellow crime scene tape strung around the beer cooler.

After the hubbub had died down, I needed to connect Marnie Dunwoody with the Aristocrats. If I made them a team I could make myself scarce. That trio could chase her three-body-bag story up to Pulitzer level without me.

Or so I thought.

3

A BLOCK FROM THE Tideline I felt removed from evidence, solutions and rivalries. Distance is good but overrated. Four blocks farther along I hit a new roadblock.

Two wide-shouldered city cops at Atlantic and White ordered me to halt. They demanded my ID, registration and insurance chits, and wanted to know where I was coming from. Each had his right thumb hooked in his tactical utility belt, right next to his quick-action holster. I don't begrudge their wariness, but the hostility gets old.

I pulled out my phone, pressed two buttons. B WATKINS popped into the window. I showed it to the officer nearest to me, then looked him in the eye. "I'll dial and you talk, okay?"

He looked away, told me I could proceed. He made it sound like a favor that ran counter to his fine judgment. I wondered if he acted like a prick when he talked to his kids. To be fair, I had snapped at him too quickly, and Beth had enough problems. I didn't want a testy exchange to come back on her as bad office politics.

"Thanks," I said, trying to sound appreciative. "Guess that ugly business down the road got to me a bit."

He stared at me, a tilt to his head, a sneer and no response.

I made sure to exceed the limit in the last two hundred yards to the restaurant.

THE MEAL AND COLD Beck's Light at Saluté restored my strength except I faced the liquor racks instead of the shoreline. My request, my fault. The TV flickered down by the door. The Weather Channel showed Kansas City snow drifts and Buffalo's famous Vehicles on Ice Ballet. I perused inshore waves in the mirror just above the rum rack. An outside table with an ocean view might have tempered my thoughts on personal work ethic and lives ending ahead of schedule.

A voice I didn't know stopped me from memorizing my beer bottle label.

"Alex, Mr. Rutledge, how you doing?"

A stocky man stood near the restaurant's west exit. Bright daylight shone behind him. It hurt to look.

"Sorry, do I know you?"

"Sure," he said. "Justin Beeson." He approached to shake my hand. "We were introduced on New Year's Eve. You and your beautiful detective friend. We talked about your classic Shelby and restoring old Ford Mustangs."

I didn't recall Mr. Beeson's face, but something rang a bell. "You had a Nightmist Blue, sixty-seven fastback with a four-speed and a 390?"

"Still have it, Alex, garaged, climate-controlled and maintained in Sarasota. I would love to show it to you, give you a ride. Did you receive my proposal today?"

It took me a second. "The FedEx?"

"What did you think?"

I explained about leaving my house in a hurry.

"I apologize for presuming your schedule," he said. " I hate rudeness, and here I am..."

Justin Beeson looked about fifty, well dressed, like a tennis player who shopped Brooks Brothers. He was about five-ten and had thinning blond and silver-streaked hair, overdue for a trim but no issue in the Keys. Light khaki trousers, a blue oxford cloth shirt, tassel loafers, and the forearms of a carpenter.

"Can you give me a preview?" I said.

"Sure," he said. "If you have a minute."

"All afternoon, Mr. Beeson."

"Justin, please," he said. "This might sound glorified, but it's an architectural job in Sarasota, two full days at the most, if the weather cooperates. My cover letter suggested we meet to discuss it at your convenience, though I expect to leave town..." He checked his watch, a slender Patek Philippe. "I'll be leaving two days from now, almost to the minute."

A striking brunette as tall as Beeson, perhaps fifteen years his junior, strode from the doorway to his side. A dark brown linen top, gold bracelets, gold earrings, and a gold Rolex accented her light tan. Beeson introduced her as Anya Timber. With a casual elegance Anya removed her sunglasses, nailed me with her baby blues and stuck out her hand to shake mine.

I said, "Should we move to a table and..."

Beeson shook his head. "We've got a mess of errands that can't wait."

Anya slid her hand under his elbow, gave him a subtle hip bump, an affectionate "hurry-up."

"My cell number is in the letter," he said. "We should be back to our house on Olivia in ninety minutes. Call today or tomorrow. Whatever's convenient. I'll leave it to you."

After Beeson and I shook hands, they hooked arms and walked outside.

A minute later Rick, the owner, walked in from his parking area. "That fellow you were talking with has a nice..."

"Her name is Anya."

Rick grinned. "I meant his car, Alex, but she's fine, too."

"Mustang?"

"No," said Rick. "Not many people know the '99 Riviera. They look dated, but they're supercharged and your friend has the Silver Arrow Edition. One of the last Rivieras ever built."

"You're into collectible cars, too?" I said.

"All of us rich guys like beautiful women and fancy automobiles." He stuffed his hands into his trousers, pulled out his empty pockets and laughed.

I PAID MY BILL, walked to the parking area and checked back with Dubbie Tanner. He wanted to meet me on the bench outside of 5 Brothers Grocery.

"What's wrong with my cool, shaded porch?" I said.

"There's a cop on the porch and his car's out front," said Tanner. "It's your badge buddy, Sheriff Liska. He's hunched over, working on his laptop. Probably poaching on your wireless network."

"He never shows up without a plan," I said. "He wants to fuck with my future."

"Could it be tied to your past?" said Dubbie. "I'm a fine one to talk."

"Give me ten minutes."

The phone buzzed as I clicked it off. It was Malcolm Mason, the boat broker who had hired me a few days back. He had wanted photos of pre-owned pleasure craft in open water. Work on the ocean can be tough and unpredictable, especially in winter, so I suggested that he use the original manufacturers' brochures to sell the glamour. To speak more effective nitty-gritty to buyers of used boats, I took drydock shots of intact hulls and framework free of corrosion. Malcolm wasn't sure at first but he went along with my idea.

"Success on this end, Alex," he said. "We sold two of the six where you took detail photos, so your approach was perfect. One buyer said it was the first time he had ever bought a boat based on pictures of the bilge."

"That's a relief," I said.

"For all of us, Alex. We just grabbed two more boats from a foreclosure deal, and my sales rep is freshly inspired. Any chance you can shoot them today?"

The money would come in handy. "It'll have to be after four o'clock," I said. "But it gets dark early this time of year. No way we can do it tomorrow?"

"We bow to your expertise," said Malcolm. "The sooner the better."

I PARKED IN A scooter space on Grinnell around the corner from 5 Brothers, locked my helmet to its keeper, and walked around to the outside bench that faced Southard. Tanner handed me a café con leche in a short Styrofoam cup. He sipped from a tall can of beer stealth-wrapped in a brown bag.

"You summoned me," I said.

With a smug look on his face, Tanner handed me a business card. I couldn't fault his pride. Finding a card for the housekeeping company, Acting Chief Execs, was a splendid investigative coup. Only their first names, Ocilla and Greg, were printed above the phone number. The stylized letters ACXX formed their logo with a wiggly arrow drawn through them. The graphics of a fourth-grader. Their font choice made the lettering look like an obscure rating for a skin flick, not that I was an expert. It was the first card I had seen in years without a web site or email address. It gave no clue to the nature of their business.

"Greg was quite the horndog, I'm told," said Tanner. "He played the snaggletooth twilight rodeo. Went by the slogan, 'Ugly girls need loving, too.'"

"A dogcatcher?"

"One of the first to head home each night, never alone. People in the bars called him Dregs instead of Greg. If he ever said 'boink,' you knew it rhymed with 'oink.'"

"Do we know that his business partner was not a love interest?" I said.

Dubbie shook his head and finished his beer at the same time, an admirable feat. "Not with certainty." He chucked his empty can into the trash barrel, removed a fresh one from a plastic bag, placed

27

it in his narrow brown bag and popped it.

"How about Greg's background?" I said.

"We're getting there." He pulled out a three-by-five card covered with notes. "We have conflicts in timeline and two Gregs from the same area. One in Murphy, North Carolina, and one in Blue Ridge, Georgia, thirty miles apart. Both have varying birth dates and high school graduation dates. One's been married twice, the other never. Wiley thinks it's probably the same guy doing an identity dance."

"Could they be cousins with the same name?" I said. "Let's see if the given name on each is Greg or Gregory. And see if they have the same middle name."

"We'll get it nailed down."

"How about Ocilla Ramirez?"

"She registered the name Acting Chief Execs with the state three years ago last month with that legal address on Big Coppitt. She has to re-register each year, and inform them of changes, but public records show it's still at that address and still a sole proprietorship."

"Two names on the card, Greg must have been her only employee."

"Looks like it," said Tanner. "People say he rides a bike to the bars and to work, so he must live in town. I'll drive out to Big Coppitt this afternoon, bang on the door, see who's home."

"Ocilla's background?" I said.

"We're diving in, approaching with caution."

MONROE COUNTY SHERIFF FRED "Chicken Neck" Liska sat at my porch table, a white porcelain-enamel relic that had stood up to weather for years. The liquid in the tall clear plastic cup next to his laptop could have been iced tea or dark rum and ginger ale with lemon slices. It was the middle of his working day. I hoped it was tea, but his face looked drawn, his eyes weary. Even his hair appeared tired and thin. He wore dark blue trousers and a floral polyester shirt reminiscent of his past affection for disco-era clothing, back when he was a hot-shot Key West city detective. No one complained when he began, upon being elected sheriff, to dress like a grown-up.

He closed his computer, stared through the screening. "You've been where?"

"We had a major crime in town, as you know" I said. "I was summoned to the scene then brusquely dismissed on arrival. My creative talents weren't required. My legendary deductive talent was sent packing. I took myself to lunch next to a south-facing beach full of sunbathers and watersports devotees."

"Ahh, Rutledge. You complain when we need you, and you grouse when you're not asked. My best new reason to stop crime in the Keys is to stop your whining."

His words carried an attempt at humor, but he drooped slightly, bothered by something or several things. He hadn't shaved that morning, odd for Liska.

I stepped onto the porch, sat in a cushioned armchair. "What's with the polyester train wreck?"

"Laundry issues," he said. "All my presentable shirts are at the cleaners. Happens about once every six weeks, but on those days I try to stay in the office. I wore a sport coat at The Tideline but I still drew stares."

"You don't look all that good."

"I feel like a slug," he said. "Does that mean I'm sluggish?"

"Have you bothered to eat this week?" I said.

"Shit, I haven't been able to face a full meal for a month." He sat up, reopened his computer, double-clicked a file and touched a finger to the screen. "Every day for the past few months I've downed a fish oil pill, a multi-vitamin for mature people, a saw palmetto capsule, seven almonds, five walnuts, one-point-seven glasses of red wine, four ounces of broccoli, five ounces of asparagus, a sliced peach, and a banana."

"Admirable, sheriff. You might live to a hundred."

He moved his finger down the laptop screen. "I also consume a

CoQ10 softgel pill, twelve ounces of cranberry juice, a cup of plain yogurt, an 81 milligram enteric aspirin, a half-ounce of dark chocolate that's 85 percent cocoa, two cups of coffee, three black olives, a glass of calcium-fortified orange juice, two ounces of unsalted dry-roasted peanuts, and a bowl of oatmeal with rice milk and cinnamon." He lifted his finger from his monitor and looked at me. "If I'm lucky and still hungry, some tuna with Miracle Whip on whole wheat. After all that, if someone offered me a slice of key lime pie, I'd puke on my blood pressure monitor."

"Why the regimen?"

"It's the result of a grotesque tactical error," said Liska. "I showed the results of my last physical exam to my new woman friend."

"You traded in last year's model?"

He nodded. "She was the enthusiastic type," he said. "I once told her how much I enjoyed taking part in her orgasms. She said, 'That's great, sheriff, but I do okay by myself.'"

"She would rather jack off than be with you?"

Liska stared out at the yard. "That's an accurate summation. And, I might add, a king-hell drain on an aging man's ego. At that point our deal was irrevocably broken. So right away I found a new one. Will I never learn?"

He hadn't dropped in for a yak session about diet and girlfriends.

"Do we need to discuss today's event?" I said.

He sipped his tea like it was precious cargo. "It was complicated before it went down. It'll be ten times worse before it's over. I hate political implications worse than I hate walnuts."

"If Greg Pulver had out-of-state warrants, aren't they history now?"

"Rutledge, you were the first person outside of law enforcement who knew his identity. Now you know his life story?"

"You've spoken with Beth Watkins," I said.

"I spoke with her before and after she asked you to leave The Tideline. When you were trying to help Ms. Dunwoody get a story for the *Citizen*."

"I help you, I help other friends. I'm a walking democracy."

"You bet," he said, "and you get help, too. An acquaintance of yours is prowling the saloons, asking about a murder victim's habits and personal life."

He stopped and let that hang for a moment.

I shut up.

"Just so you know," he said, "my office, like the city police, receives periodic reports from Tallahassee about the issuance of private eye licenses. We want to be aware of any freelancers working in our jurisdiction. We keep their photos and basic info on file. As of last week that folder includes Mr. Tanner and Mr. Fecko, though someone in my office has nicknamed them 'The Bumsnoops,' a tag infinitely more suitable than 'The Aristocrats.'"

"I think their heads are in the right place," I said. "They're not stupid men."

"Fine," said Liska, "but let me explain the shit coming from two directions. One concerns Greg Pulver's employer. The one he had in addition to Pepe's."

"Ocilla Ramirez?" I pulled the ACXX card from my shirt pocket, handed it over. "Tanner gave this to me fifteen minutes ago."

He looked at me in disbelief. "Your Bumsnoops are quick. Why are they doing this?"

"Marnie figures she has an exclusive. She asked me to help expand her story."

"That's it?"

"The Aristocrats also asked for my help, to get their new business going."

"You're a great guy, Rutledge. A regular facilitator."

"Why is that such a big deal, sheriff? What's this Ocilla's link to politics?"

"We call her a tangential party to a scam," he said. "This mess is about to ruin a major investigation. We were helping to build a case against the people who were handling her from a couple rungs up

31

the ladder. Another agency has been funding our man-hours, what-ever you want to call it. I need to salvage this project."

"Was Greg Pulver part of the scam?"

"He had become an informant. He wasn't a cop but he was being compensated."

"That's motive for murder on a silver platter," I said.

"Correct," he said. "But we know that Ocilla hasn't been near that condo in over a week. We have to question her, and she doesn't know the strength of her own alibi."

"She didn't go around looking for him?"

He shook his head.

"I assume she didn't report him missing."

"Correct again. But she could gab her way out of that."

"You said two directions."

Liska studied the simple business card. "The Canadians were investigating the deceased condo owner for reasons as solid as our need to nail Ocilla. Some kind of fraud, and the FBI was cooperating."

I said. "It wasn't that long ago that someone killed a Fed in the Keys."

Liska scowled. "Your assistance in that case had great value."

"You really like me," I said.

He stared at my chest, then let his eyes drift to the outside foliage.

"Call me paranoiac," I said, "but I always worry about kind words from those in authority."

"I know how it is with you, Rutledge," he said. "You say one thing, you mean next to nothing. When you come through with something that makes no sense at all, we know who we're dealing with."

"I make no sense?" I said. "You've got a snitch paired up with a scam artist in a maid service business. He gets killed in a condo that's linked to another scam based in another country. I also know that you dish out abuse before you ask favors. What do you really want from me?"

He turned to look me in the eye. "Between me and you?"

"I can do that," I said.

"I'm a public official. I can't ask Ms. Dunwoody to shut up about Ocilla Ramirez, but that's what I need. Maybe you can back her away from that aspect of the story, if she hasn't already filed for publication."

"Now you're groping," I said. "She's a dedicated reporter. If either one of us tells her to back off, she'll dig even deeper."

Liska looked pensive, tapped his fingertips on the tabletop.

"Let's say Marnie agrees to go along," I said. "Isn't Ocilla going to wonder, with a dead employee, why her name isn't in the paper? Or worse, won't her associates wonder the same thing?"

"Now you're getting warm," he said.

"And you are so damned cold, sheriff. You're willing to risk her life so her bosses might show up and close your case?"

"And one last thing," he said. "I can't order your Bumsnoops to quit whatever they're doing. But please tell them to be more circumspect, if they know the word. If you stick with what you're doing, stay clean. There will be no crossing of legal lines, no blanket forgiveness."

"Stick with it?" I said. "I have no desire to be anywhere near your case."

Liska looked at me, tried to smile. But it wasn't last year's smile or his even wider one from five years ago. This attempt at smiling carried pessimism and regret.

He stood, picked up his watered-down concoction and his computer. He looked me in the eye, then cast his gaze to the floor. "I can't fucking believe I'm saying this. Maybe I can explain later. There are things my people can't do." He stepped around me to leave the porch. "Please continue, Aristocrats and all. Give me a jingle every now and then."

The screen door shut, and I caught a whiff of rum.

4

DEFINING "QUALITY OF LIFE" is like describing "medium blue." Each of us has certain requirements to get us rolling, facing ourselves in the mirror. One of mine is to never run out of beer, but guess what.

I was about to pedal to Fausto's when Marnie Dunwoody called.

"Ask me how a marionette feels when its strings are yanked," she said.

"How..."

"Jerked around, if you'll pardon my stupid humor. They put us in a vacant rental condo. It smelled like a soap store and the walls had framed paintings of fish we don't see in the Keys."

"It's tropical ambiance for tourists who don't know," I said. "Probably a shelf in the kitchen full of plastic wine glasses. Why a condo, and who is us?"

"There was a guy from Miami TV, one from local TV, both with video rigs. And a *Newsweek* guy in town on vacation. They wanted to isolate us."

"*Newsweek?*"

"Made no sense to me," said Marnie, "except he and his family were staying on the second floor at The Tideline. He saw the commotion and asked. He was barely going through the motions. In his head, he was still on the beach or in Sloppy Joe's. He had the only other still camera, so your Canon saved my day, such as it was."

"Good of Beth to send a man after it."

"That was so weird," she said. "I had been in the vacant suite for maybe twenty-five minutes, waiting for my chance. Then Beth came in and looked really shook up. Obviously, the crime scene was gruesome. To get her mind off it, I made small talk and told her I had spoken with you, and that you were bringing two cameras because mine had broken. She said, 'Alex won't be working with us after all.' Her tone of voice was angry, as if you were being punished. Then she went onto the balcony and, right away, saw you in the crowd below."

"Did they let you view anything?" I said.

"Only after a long wait to inform next-of-kin, except we didn't get names. I kept my mouth shut about Greg."

"Names, plural?" It was my turn to shut up, while I was still wondering about the third body bag, if my mind hadn't taken my eyes on a fantasy ride.

"I thought you knew there were two bodies, not one, Alex. They let us stand in the hallway and peer into the apartment. An older guy they called the resident, in a white shirt and shorts, dressed for tennis, was slumped cold on the tile floor. They think he found the other one murdered, and the shock brought on a heart attack."

"Is Beth thinking one murder and one reaction?"

"She didn't say as much," said Marnie, "but that was the gist. We didn't get to see the second guy. They said he was sliced up in the master bath with a box cutter and a dagger, and dumped in the Jacuzzi. It was the Fourth of July back there with all the official camera flashes, but we couldn't get near."

"Who was official?"

"There were three of them. One guy from the city, one from the county, and a woman I didn't recognize. No one mentioned why she was there."

"Let me guess," I said. "They showed you the dagger and the box knife."

"And staged a photo of a scene tech holding them next to a ruler."

"I was going to say that next," I said. "At least you photographed something. I tried a few but I couldn't get anything worth a shit."

"I noticed you didn't shoot anything, Alex. Unless that cop erased your photos from the memory card."

"I didn't use the camera I gave you," I said. "I grabbed a few on my Nikon. I might have one or two building exteriors right here in my pocket."

"Can you email them to me?"

"Give me about ten minutes. And keep my camera until yours is repaired. Is your article coming together?"

"I've puffed it up in my notes," she said. "Gruesome and sad. The inability of wealth to protect anyone from violence. I have everything but a headline, but you have a quick mind. Any brainstorms?"

"FATAL HEART ATTACK BLAMED ON MURDER VICTIM."

"That could win prizes if it wasn't funny."

"It would draw attention to your story," I said.

"God, those puppeteers were slimy."

I FELT SPLIT LOYALTIES in honoring Liska's request not to tell Marnie about Ocilla. At the same time, I still was puzzled by the third body bag inside the county's forensics van. Maybe I had over-employed my imagination. No one, not Liska, Beth or Marnie had mentioned a third death. Maybe having an extra plastic cadaver pouch was a new standard procedure in case of a flawed bag.

Bullshit. They could always go back out to the van.

I went inside, absent-mindedly opened the fridge to zero beer. It reminded me to call Dubbie Tanner. I pressed buttons and he took the call before I'd put the phone to my ear.

"From now on," I said, "anything further on Ocilla's background, do your research on a neutral computer."

"Like untraceable?" said Tanner.

"*Like* that, precisely," I said. "I'll explain face-to-face."

"I should lose the word 'like,'" he said.

"You're a businessman now."

"That I am," he said. "Maybe you and I could write a book about inappropriate slang in professional settings. Publish it on the friggin' Kindle."

I didn't respond.

"Oh, there I go again."

I DOWNLOADED SIXTEEN MEANINGLESS images to my laptop, copied them to a new folder, then compressed and sent the file to Marnie's personal email address.

In truth, I didn't really want a beer. I wanted a nap but knew I'd never doze off with my mind churning. The rest of the afternoon offered me the FedEx packet from Justin Beeson and, hopefully, a short wait to hear from the Aristocrats. They knew what I needed.

I DON'T KNOW WHY the funky deals all show up before 10 AM. Offers too good to be true, requests from law enforcement, assignments of a "special nature" guaranteed to go downhill on the work site or when it's time to be paid. They always arrive as morning calls. In a perfect world I would listen to client requests only between noon and four. I needed pay-on-time, straight-ahead, surprise-free enjoyable gigs. The delivery of Beeson's package fell into the realm of ideal, non-funky timing.

Beeson had come off as a decent type, too. Nothing he said in our short chat at Saluté had flipped a caution light. If anything, his opener flashed green: his schedule was flexible, his manners respectful. He had researched my work ethic and sounded ready to honor my fees fairly. He had style but he wasn't consumed by it. He was a Beemer type in a Buick. His friend Anya was stunning but not flashy.

They were, by Key West standards, normal.

I pulled the manila envelope from the FedEx packet, opened it with a steak knife, then skipped the one-page cover letter to examine the elegant report folder. On first look, first-class design. I had to wonder why Beeson would need more pictures. The folder's front photo was a late-day shot of a two-story building with a glorious cloud-bloomed sunset reflected in its entrance and west-facing windows. Under the image, in gold leaf: 23 - BEESON WAY - SARASOTA - USA.

The package made it clear why the man needed multiple brochures. His modular building had been designed so partitions and office-sized cubes could be shifted to adjust to businesses of varying size. Ideally, it would lease to a growing company that could reshape spaces to match its changing needs. A separate set of pages, distinct in their poor layout and font usage and their horrible photo quality, called it an Office Space Condominium. That suggested to me that the first idea hadn't sold. A third group of pages, laid out in sketch form, looked more like a real estate presentation. That meant the second idea had bombed as well.

Bingo.

Beeson needed new photos for a new approach. He wanted out. He was putting his building on the market, bad timing be damned. Which meant that he *needed* to get out.

Which made him, in today's business climate, normal.

The cover letter was short, to the point. The company that produced the first promo packet had closed after the death of a principal. Beeson knew that the second brochure was awful and believed that "fresh eyes" would help his situation. He had heard my name before New Year's Eve, from both a woman he met at a Mote Marine fundraiser and a Duval Street gift shop owner. Our introduction at the party had been coincidence.

He proposed a mid-day flight out of Key West, an early evening for scouting the location, the next two days shooting exteriors in the early morning and early evening hours, and interior set-ups from ten until four each day. He would pay half my total day rate in advance, provide "upscale" accommodations, a meal allowance, a vehicle and advance cash for "incidentals." He would make crews available during workday hours to move partitions and cubicles in order to demonstrate the building's interior flexibility.

The final paragraph was a short, glossed-over company history.

The package was straightforward and professional and offered what I wished of all jobs: transportation, work, delivery and pay. I called Justin Beeson. We agreed to meet at 2:00. He gave me his house number on Olivia.

I have owned the antique thermometer on the porch for twenty-five years. Its red glycol fluid has spent most of its life at the top of the scale, giving me endless reasons never to leave the Keys. A young friend once stared at it and said, "Oh, analog, cool."

It read 73 degrees. A bit high for January, just when I needed it. Given the lack of parking on Olivia Street for the past twenty years, I decided to walk the few blocks to Beeson's place.

THE HOUSE WEST OF BEESON'S was a modestly restored shotgun with chain link fencing and less-elaborate plantings. The one to the east had two white, solid doors and four windows facing the street, three of which held A/C units. Beeson's home, an "eyebrow" style Classic Revival, dominated the north side of Olivia between Simonton and Windsor Lane.

It was the showcase of the block. Three royal palms stood in his small front yard behind a four-foot, vanilla-colored picket fence. A Conch-style cottage took up the far northeast corner of the property. Two vehicles filled the short red-brick single-lane driveway, a silver RAV4 closer to the sidewalk and, in front of it, the classic Buick under a sturdy wood frame carport.

My phone buzzed. I hadn't called the boat broker.

"Malcolm, I..."

"I know," he said. "I drove past you on Fleming a few minutes ago, but I had a city truck on my ass, so I couldn't stop."

"Today's been..."

"I figured," he said. "I heard about the murder. My brother works for the county, and I know you get called in times of tragedy. Look, get back to me when you can. The work will wait for you."

I switched my phone to vibrate, unlatched Beeson's fence gate and approached the veranda. A small brass knocker, engraved BEESON, adorned the sand-colored front door. With a cedar rocker, a mailbox made from a flower basket, two planters of blue lisianthus, and several conch shells on the decking, the porch was picturesque but simple. Keeping shells on the porch was a fine detail for a non-local. Old-time Conchs thought it bad luck to bring conch shells inside their homes.

Beeson answered my knock wearing a gray sport shirt and Hawaiian print swim trunks. He smiled, shook hands, looked to his driveway, then asked if I'd had trouble finding a parking spot. I told him I had walked. He smiled again and nodded as if my willingness to exercise added one more point to his opinion of me. He led me through his house toward a backyard patio.

"Please excuse the mess," he said. "We take the word 'vacation' at face value."

Except for one *Vogue* on the floor, the place was cool and spotless. Everything inside the home beamed Keys elegance. Vertical tongue-and-groove wall planks of a width they don't mill these days. The loft stairway was reclaimed oak, the banister and sculpted post coated in white satin enamel. The front room's rattan furniture held tropical print cushions and pastel pillows. Hardcover books by a dozen or more Key West authors filled a white bookshelf. The art looked to be 1930s-era watercolors of Key West beach scenes, old sailboats and palm trees, in bamboo framing.

I noted nothing related to automobile collecting.

We passed through sturdy French doors to a screened enclosure with a full view of the yard. Subdued sunlight and shadows through twin arbors gave an illusion of a life-sized watercolor. The familiar sound of palm fronds rattling on tin shingles over the alcove gave it the comfort touch.

I couldn't help saying, "Damn."

"Thank you, Alex," said Beeson. "That was exactly the reaction I was after when I sketched out this quiet area. I say the same thing every time I walk out here."

"It proves you understand the island," I said. "A lot of people take one ride a year in their motorboat and pat themselves on the back for living in the Keys."

He pointed me toward a pair of cushioned lounge chairs under a slowly moving overhead fan. Anya Timber and a dark-haired girl perhaps eleven or twelve years old stood toweling themselves on the far side of a lagoon at the end of the small pool. Both wore modest one-piece suits. They donned robes and crossed a short arched bridge to the main patio. Anya waved before they entered the house through a sliding glass door thirty feet away.

Beeson watched his daughter slide shut the door. "Eileen is a dream, fortunately. Unlike her mother."

"Cute one," I said.

"Horribly shy, as perhaps you could tell," he said. "And brilliant, as I heard you are behind a camera. You've had a look through the firm's background and the work proposal?"

"Hell of a building."

"It's become a royal pain in the ass," he said. "I usually have better luck investing on impulse. Now it's my albatross, if you follow my meaning."

"I read the Coleridge poem in high school. Never again since then."

Anya's voice came from the French door behind us: "Anything for you gentlemen?"

Beeson smiled and looked across the pool at a palm tree. "It's time for my early vodka and soda, dear. Please make it Grey Goose and... tell you what. I will take tonic today instead of soda. Do we have a lime?"

"We have twelve," she said.

I turned to face her. "A glass of OJ would be fine, thanks."

She smiled and nodded. As she backed away from the door, her robe fell open. She had removed her wet bathing suit and chosen not to put on clothing.

Beeson didn't notice her partial nudity. "I don't drink before seven when I'm in Sarasota," he said. "I get a lot of work done in Key West, but we play by holiday rules down here."

"That's what the island inspires," I said, thinking *Thank goodness.*

"It's partly to accommodate Eileen. She's a bit of a prodigy, and that's become a problem. Anya and I try to make sure her visits are true vacations. Her mother, in Sarasota, keeps enrolling her in boutique art schools so she can rocket her through Ringling and specialty schools beyond that. She intends to turn her daughter's talent into a gold mine. As if we need money. I'm a believer in having a normal childhood."

"It's an admirable goal," I said, wondering why I hadn't seen Eileen with Beeson and Anya at Saluté. "If any childhood could ever be called normal."

Beeson took it with the humor I intended. "Too true, Rutledge. Do you still shoot film, 35-millimeter and medium format?"

I shook my head. "My film cameras are packed away with all my VHS tapes and audio cassettes. I don't even know where to get film developed anymore. My favorite was Kodachrome 64, and Eastman Kodak quit producing it in 2009."

"Did you buy a supply before it went away?"

"It wouldn't have done me any good," I said. "The film required a special process. Dwayne's, a photo shop in Parsons, Kansas, was the last place that handled that film. They stopped working with it in December 2010. The last time I looked at my old 35mm film gear, I saw mold inside two or three of the lenses."

Beeson regarded me with mild amazement. "I have to respect a man who knows the history of his profession. What about crime cases that go to court? Aren't digital pictures easy to manipulate?

Wouldn't you rather have negatives to show judges and juries?"

Anya returned to the patio with our beverages on a small tray. Her robe sash was tied but, as she handed us our drinks, we both enjoyed a view of her lovely breasts.

"Put some clothes on, honey," said Beeson, unfazed, "and join us."

"Maybe I will." She smiled again then left the patio.

Beeson drank from his vodka and tonic, set it aside. "Where did we leave off?"

"You asked about digital photos in court," I said. "I have a program that runs alongside Photoshop to track changes made to my images. They ensure that anything done to an original enhances rather than modifies. My work has been admitted as evidence in two cases. Plus, so many cameras these days have GPS locators..."

"Fine." Beeson looked relieved. "I say it again, it's great to deal with an expert."

We discussed my day rate and expectations for per diem and incidentals. A painless negotiation. I told him my calendar was open for the next week or ten days, a true statement more or less.

"We're going to borrow a friend's plane and fly up the day after tomorrow," he said, standing to end the meeting. "We'll leave at one or one-thirty. You are welcome to join us, and I'll arrange for you to fly back on Friday. We've had great luck with the Sarasota-Miami-Key West commercial route."

"I'll be ready by noon. Two bags and a tripod carrying case. Fifty pounds plus one-ninety-five in my traveling shoes."

He cracked a grin. "The pilot will appreciate having that in advance."

On our way back through the house I praised the watercolors. Beeson admitted that he had bought most of them at an estate sale. One was signed "Martha Watson." A painting by Martha Watson Sauer from the 1960s hung in my bedroom. She had been a Works Progress Administration artist who arrived in the Keys in the 1930s and married a local attorney during World War II. Though she traveled the world, she called the island her home for the rest of her life. I met her a few times before her death in 2005, but I had never seen work created so early that it didn't include her married name.

One other painting stood out from the rest with finer detail, colors more subtle. It might not have been better than the others, and I was no art critic, but it was equally impressive. I studied the signature in its lower right corner.

"Eileen, my daughter, did that when she visited here last year."

I paused to look more closely. Its shadows, the perspective of its street scene, the color blending and use of both sharpness and blurring. "Her work is brilliant."

Beeson said, "Say 'Thank you,' Eileen."

From the top of the oak staircase came, softly, "Thank you, sir."

I couldn't see her up there. Allowing her shyness, I didn't try to look.

"She goes to school in Sarasota," said Beeson. "She's taking a short break right now. I'm trying to talk her mother into allowing her down for the summer so she can learn how to fish with light tackle."

"Book her with my old friend Sam Wheeler," I said. "He enjoys beginners and inspires proficiency."

"Good to know," said Beeson. "So many of the prima donnas on the docks want experts on board."

"I don't want them to die," said the child's voice from up the stairs.

"You'll be the best kind of fisherman," I said. "The expert guides make sure the fish are returned to the water alive."

"Okay, cool," said the girl, whom I never did see.

Beeson looked pleased with our blind exchange.

I glanced at the digital thermostat as I walked to the door. Seventy-one degrees indoors. One must protect art from mildew.

Beeson stepped outside to see me off, pointed toward his picket fence. "Can you believe I paid some hot-shit wood artist to build a goddamned enclosure for my trash cans? He disguised it as a gazebo with an access gate through the picket fence. It cost me more than Anya's SUV over there."

"I've always said the island will belong to the carpenters and exterminators."

"Hell," he said. "I owe my soul to the man who cleans my pool. Enjoy the rest of your day, Rutledge."

So many restorations in Key West over the past thirty years had failed to grasp what Beeson's home had captured. Setting, history, mood and a sense of the owner's personality. Except for the aggressive air conditioning, he had nailed it. It would be nice to have that kind of money.

Two minutes into walking home I passed Poorhouse Lane. Too much irony.

FIVE MINUTES LATER BEESON called.

"We had a couple things come up, Alex, a change of plans. We fly out of here at four, less than an hour from now. I would like you to join us if possible, and I would compensate you for this imposition."

One side of my brain screamed, "Red flag," while the other argued that he was handing me an excuse to flee the rock, to distance myself from drama I didn't need. Opting for crisis avoidance, I took a moment to cover my butt for contingencies.

"I can make the flight, Mr. Beeson, but I may have to spend time on the phone this evening and tomorrow morning."

"I understand and sympathize," he said. "Can you meet us at Island City at three-fifty?"

I didn't want to leave my car or motorcycle in the airport lot, or pay tourist rate for a taxi. I asked Beeson if I could share his cab. We agreed that I would meet him in front of the Eden House at three-forty.

5

I HAD FIFTEEN MINUTES to get ready. Pack the duffel for Sarasota, water my porch plants, pull walk-around money from my stash and leave a message for Beth.

Reading my mind, the phone buzzed as I reached Dredgers Lane.

"I sounded like a shit," said Beth. "I'm sorry. Be glad you aren't here."

"Accepted," I said. "I've got to…"

"Me too. We'll talk later." She ended the call.

I stared at the cell's window. The phone knew. It vibrated again.

"The syndicate picked me up, thanks to you," said Marnie. "I get paid for every hit your headline attracts on the web."

"The murder victim caused the heart attack?"

"Pure genius, Alex. I couldn't think of anything brilliant and I knew they would change it if they didn't like it, but they didn't."

"The *Citizen* didn't go near it, right?"

"They rolled with an official city press release, which left me free to file online. Now the news service wants follow-ups, so I better damn well deliver. If too many people add tags to the story, I could lose my primary byline."

I stood on the porch, let the breeze cool me. "Did you get an ID on the heart attack victim?"

"He was a Canadian named Emerson Caldwell. The city waited to tell us until a Toronto Victim Services rep located his wife at a ski lodge near Montreal. They took care of the official notification. Did your source find anything worth a damn?"

What could I say? "They confirmed that Greg worked for or was part-owner of a house-sitting business. I asked them to search for an occupational license."

"Housekeepers must have access to all kinds of personal info," said Marnie. "Bank statements, letters from relatives, retirement plans, love affairs, drug use, you name it. Should we assume it's fraud or blackmail?"

"We should keep our minds open," I said, "and you need to celebrate this moment of high journalism."

"The first thing I'll do is nothing, barefoot, on Smathers Beach, Alex. I feel grimy for having been that close to murdered people. I won't even take my iPod. Will you keep your... what did you say, your 'sources,' working? Can you keep them nosing around?"

"Count on it," I said. "I'll have them contact you. Don't be put off by appearances. I've got to run."

...away from my own bullshit.

I CALLED WILEY FECKO's cell number. It went to voicemail.

"The name for the condo should be Caldwell," I said. "Disregard all the others unless you find out that Greg and Ocilla were employed in one of them. Or that Mr. Caldwell owns more than one condo in the building. Thanks."

EVERY CAB ON THE island drives down Bertha on the way to the airport. Perhaps I was checking my mental list to determine if I had forgotten anything. Or sliding into travel bliss, the calm I felt when a trip began and there was no turning back. But I was as surprised as the van driver when we reached the roadblock. The crime scene remained active, and Deputy Chris Ericson, looking bored and resentful, was still on duty. He scanned the van's occupants as it turned east on Truman, noticed me in the front passenger seat. His expression went from passive to puzzled to suspicious. He had to be wondering why the city's photographer was going to the airport, leaving town so soon after a double murder.

JUSTIN, ANYA AND EILEEN had only jackets and small carry-ons; they kept clothing duplicates in Key West and Sarasota. The pilot stowed my tripod case and duffel, and I kept my camera satchel with me in case I saw anything worth documenting from aloft. It was a quick load-out to the King Air 90 with no wait for take-off. Giving the weight of my luggage to Beeson had been, in retrospect, a useless detail in a plane that size. He had been gracious in thanking me and not bragging about our upscale transport. For starters, the armrest cup holders of each leather seat in the passenger cabin held half-liter bottles of both Evian and San Pellegrino water. A small central bin held bananas and small packets of nuts and dried fruit. Trail mix for the sky.

Leaving Key West by air is less fun than arriving, even in good weather, because it's difficult to sightsee from an aircraft tilted upward. The northbound turn toward the mainland separated us from island scenery within three minutes. From there on it was clouds, haze and a blue blur of salt water two miles below us.

Minding Eileen's shyness, I hadn't spoken to her in the taxi van or the waiting room of the fixed base facility. Once we had been seated next to each other on the aircraft, I handed her a booklet of color photographs called "Tropical Trees" that I had owned for years. She eyed it suspiciously, studied its front and rear covers, opened it, then settled back to study. I kept my eyes forward for most of the trip.

When we reached cruising altitude, the pilot, introduced only as Sherwin, gave us a few details on our tailwind, 12,000-foot altitude, 260-mph speed and our estimated time of arrival. That was it for conversation. I couldn't decide whether the other three had agreed not to chat while in the taxi or the aircraft, or a private chill had set in and I was not to be told why. Perhaps the mood was tied to their reason for leaving Key West two days earlier than planned. It was Beeson's flight and his rules, but I felt that their silence approached rudeness. My solace was that Anya Timber's subtle scent filled the cabin instead of words. Her perfume, no doubt, made from roses and gold.

The quiet gave me time to ponder the day's events, though I knew I was stepping into quicksand. Greg Pulver, housekeeper, Pepe's server and police informant, had been killed maybe two days ago in Emerson Caldwell's condo. Caldwell had died too, not necessarily at the same time. Who had discovered and reported the bodies in Condo 302? Had the killer left the apartment door open so that a passerby could see Emerson Caldwell on the floor? Had someone placed an anonymous 911 call?

From there my mind flooded with cop questions. Had the police drawn up a list of suspects, and was Ocilla Ramirez, the other housekeeper, already in custody? Why, exactly, had Sheriff Liska's people been investigating Ocilla? Were security cameras in use at The Tideline Condominium? If so, where were they installed and who kept an eye on their video? Which agency had responded first? Had either victim received a previous threat?

Damn... My mind spun with questions that Beth Watkins was trained to ask. I felt infected by a weird sleuth virus, and I had to remember that I been hired and fired by Beth within four hours of a tender and damn-near acrobatic belly-to-belly at my house. Then I had to witness Liska's odd behavior on my porch, an indication that something more personal than police work was bothering him. Odd misbehavior, since he was drinking on duty. If a straight line of logic lay under all that activity, it was hiding from me. But I had escaped it all in a King Air, flown away from the island pleased by the idea that none of it was my problem.

I was off to earn good money, rude company and all.

During our descent alongside Longboat Key, I glanced to my left.

Eileen held a small spiral-bound art folio in which she was drawing a tree branch with several blue and green crayons. At one point she chose one blue tone over another and swapped crayons. I'm good with colors because of my photography, yet I saw no difference between the two blues. She checked the open booklet I had given her, added a detail and saw me looking. Her mouth twitched but didn't smile like her eyes did. She made a fast thumbs-up sign and went back to her details.

Nearer the airport Eileen packed up her art gear and nudged my arm with the trees booklet, giving it back to me. I smiled and made a hand signal that it was hers to keep. I was surprised by her astonished look, especially from a girl surrounded but apparently not spoiled by the trappings of elegant living. As she tucked it into her carry-on pouch, I saw a photo, a head shot of a lovely woman.

Eileen noticed that I had seen it. She looked straight at me and silently mouthed the words, "My mom."

I smiled, raised my eyebrows in appreciation and, still smiling, looked away.

THE PILOT WHOSE FIRST or last name was Sherwin had stated shortly after take-off that we would be on the ground at Sarasota-Bradenton at 6:04. He made his arrival to the minute. We went from daylight to sunset to dusk on our descent, from seventy-five to the mid-sixties stepping off the plane.

Beeson signed off some forms while the private terminal's manager pulled a silver Ford Escape Hybrid to a slot near the office door. Anya and Eileen took the rear seat, while I rode shotgun. We drove a half-mile to another lot. Beeson stopped between two rows of cars.

Facing forward, he said, "Keys?"

I looked to my left.

Anya peered into her small handbag. "Yes. Pasta?"

"Perfect."

Twilight Zone. Next they will start speaking their own private language.

Anya and Eileen got out with their carry-on bags and walked toward a cream-colored Porsche Boxster.

Beeson waited for the Porsche's engine to start. Its rumble was deep enough to suggest an exhaust system modification. He then cued his stereo to an old Marley tune and drove away. He turned right onto the Tamiami Trail, the highway built in the 1920s to connect Tampa with Miami, a project that also launched the long-term annihilation of the Everglades. A minute later we were eastbound on Tallevast Road. After being quiet for over two hours, Beeson began to make up for it.

"I grew up in Bradenton, about six miles from here," said Beeson, "and worked construction out of high school until my twenty-fifth birthday. I saved a hell of a lot of money by sharing shithole apartments with beer-swilling roommates and by not helping them buy their drugs."

"I think we all hit a phase like that," I said.

"That's when I learned all the tricks I used in remodeling my home in Key West. But one day I stood back and tried to envision my future," he said. "I knew I couldn't be pounding nails when I was forty, or even standing out in the weather supervising nail pounders. I would have to master some other skill at a poor time in my life to be learning new ways to get along. So I looked for an alternative to busting my ass, though I didn't quit my day job."

We heard a faint doorbell as the music volume dropped. Beeson's in-car cell.

He pressed a button on his steering wheel. "Yup."

Anya's voice came through the car's speakers: "Morton's. Eileen wants a slice."

"Her mother's decision."

"No answer from her," she said. "We're latchkey again."

"Okay," said Beeson. "One is plenty." He thumbed his phone's off button and said, "One slice of pizza at Morton's is more than I ate in a day, growing up." He thumbed the button again. Bob Marley returned.

"We can look at my building while Anya takes Eileen to her mother's place," he said. "By the time we reach the house, our supper will be ready. You can stay in my guest house unless you prefer a hotel."

He gave me a fraction of a second to respond, then said, "Anyway, I didn't know what it was called back then, but I was placing venture capital on a local level. A tire outlet, self-storage units, a chain of four ice cream stands. The first few worked on a certain level. I got my money back and some free tires and too much storage and ice cream. Then I bought one more concrete block building out on 301 that was really too big for an ice cream stand. I thought it would be my downfall. But before we got a chance to move in, Hertz came along and offered to lease it for thirty years. Zap, I was golden."

"Can I ask one question?" I said.

"Anytime you need to, Alex."

"This building at 23 Beeson Way. What do we expect to see after dark?"

"You won't believe this, with my expertise in numbers," he said, "but I've never been able to remember that address. Here you are, knowing it after reading it once. Anyway, I want you to see the campus in its worst light. You'll appreciate it more in the morning. I also want to pick up my mail and check a couple of things."

We were eastbound on State Route 70. I saw I-75 a short distance ahead and feared his weird lecture might never stop. This had become far more complicated than the cushy gig I envisioned while boarding the King Air in Key West.

Beeson passed the cluster of gas stations, motels and convenience stores near the Interstate, drove under and a quarter-mile beyond the big highway, then turned right onto a multi-lane service road. We went southward, hooked back toward I-75, then south again. A minute later he pulled to the roadside, put the Escape into Park but left the motor running. It took me a few seconds to realize that we had stopped in front of 23 Beeson Way, complete with night crime lighting. The two-lane roadway was illuminated with orange-colored sodium-vapor lamps, while more intense blue-green mercury-vapor lights lighted Beeson's property. My eyes saw a toxic blend of bad apricots and two-year-old butter.

I reassessed my opinion of the photography in Beeson's promo folder. His bland building had been made to look attractive, which it was not. That may have had a lot to do with its failure rate. The prospective tenants had felt taken, as much as I felt conned by Justin Beeson's fancy offer. Thinking farther, however, if he had warned me of the drudgery, for which he would pay well, I might have agreed, if only to get off the island for a couple of days.

"This dump was supposed to be my early retirement," he said. "I figured I'd build a square-footage monster and sell the air inside of it, like selling apartments. Thanks to people in New York who didn't have to worry about risk, the economy went into the tank, and I owned expensive air. I tried to turn it into a car museum. I threw that party and nobody came."

I wanted to escape the Ford. A bright bulb lighted my brain.

"I've learned in this type of work that security sells," I said. "Tenants like sunsets and they'll tell you so, but they buy into safety. I can take some photos right now that will capture the location's after-dark visibility."

"Worth a try," he said. "I have a Maglite under the seat. Let me walk ahead so you don't fall in a ditch. Or step on a snake."

I keep a Mini-Mag in my camera kit, but I didn't want "the boss" to feel useless. I said, "Great, but I have to ask a favor. No conversation while I'm working."

"Can do," said Beeson. "I've been talking your ears off for twenty minutes."

No shit.

"Matter of fact," he said, "I've got two calls I need to make. Take my Maglite and go to it, and I'll park and go inside..."

"The photos might look better without your vehicle in front of the building."

"Not a problem," said Beeson. "I'll sit here and use my cell."

ONE ADVANTAGE OF SHOOTING digital is knowing within seconds whether you got the shot. My bonus was not having to compensate for the artificial color cast of the crime lights. Ugliness, just then, was what I wanted to show. I opened my tripod, set it in a corner of the building's parking area and took my time. With Beeson in his SUV, not tempted to direct me, I had plenty of latitude in my shot selections. I went for angles that showed available paved space, ground-level windows and the main entrance. I played the lighting, the lines of the building.

While the images fit my concept, I felt an odd sense of isolation while I worked. The sodium- and mercury-vapor lights suggested a high-crime area, and the sound track was the high-pitched whine of truck tires on the highway. I saw shapes but no horizon, ground-level movement but no stars. I worked more quickly and damn near got artsy until my cell vibrated in my pocket. It was Wiley Fecko, and the screen said that I had missed seven calls and three messages.

I glanced at the SUV, saw Beeson's raised arm, the silhouette of a man talking on his phone.

"Bad time, Wiley," I said. "I'm out of the Keys for a day or so, taking pictures. Please be quick."

"You pay your money," he said, "you get a daily summary. Full-service business."

"I can give you thirty seconds."

"Ocilla Ramirez is a no-hit Google. Even her first name gets no hits. It sounds Hispanic but we searched the hell out of it, and it came up only as a town in south Georgia. The electric, garbage and gas bills for 490 Crawford Street on Big Coppitt are paid in cash right on time every month by a short man who speaks a non-Cuban, non-Mexican Spanish. The one guess I've heard is Guatemalan."

"That makes Crawford a sub-lease," I said. "Maybe Ocilla lives in town. Hell, she could be living in another state by now."

"We'll get on that tomorrow," said Wiley. "Have I gone past my thirty seconds?"

"Take another thirty," I said. "This is good info."

"Okay, the condo at The Tideline is owned by a big Canadian holding company called Branchdale Corporation. The occupants, as you thought, are Mr. and Mrs. Emerson Caldwell. The mortgage payments and condo dues are seven months in arrears. Last year's property taxes haven't been paid, but they're not overdue yet."

"That makes me wonder if Ocilla was supposed to take care of those things," I said. "Maybe she was pocketing the money."

"We'll put that on our list, too," said Wiley. "Meanwhile, Caldwell made news in the Keys ten years ago when he was suspected of bilking an investor group. This was long before Madoff, but the term "Ponzi scheme" showed up in one news release. After about four days of bad press he proved that the deal was legitimate and no one lost money. The scam rumors were traced to a former business partner, also Canadian, now deceased."

"Where does that leave us?" I said.

"Here's the thing, Mr. Rutledge," said Fecko. "One of Caldwell's early investors was your friend, Sheriff Chicken Neck Liska."

"Oh, shit."

"We thought you might say that."

I DROPPED A FEW money shots into the bank but my creativity ran dry. I couldn't show the structure's proximity to the highway until morning, anyway. And I was sure to see a few more photogenic angles in daylight or, in this case, favorable shadows.

Beeson saw me hang the camera around my neck and collapse the tripod's legs. He drove into the lot, picked me up then rolled fifty yards to the main entrance.

"I won't be five minutes," he said. "Come on in for a preview, but please forgive the access control system."

In spite of the crime lights, I chose to keep my camera bag with me. Following him up a short walkway, I looked around, saw two video cameras aimed toward the entry alcove. The one on the swivel mount was easy to spot. The other, set into an architectural detail, was visible if you had sharp eyes and were smart enough to look. But not many B&E practitioners play on the upper slope of the IQ curve.

Grimacing, Beeson summoned his memorized list. He began by inserting a thick electronic key, then waved a magnetic smart card toward a sensor. He was prompted to enter a five-digit PIN. "They hooked me for the whole package," he said. "We had to integrate the ID devices with the video imaging, make it ADA compliant and allow for emergency egress, their term for getting out in a fire. Inside it will also catch you tailgating my authorization."

"Not sure what that means," I said.

"That's when two people enter on a single okay. Your legs will trip the infrared if I don't enter a special buffering code. The system goes haywire if someone is pulling a suitcase on wheels."

"This is what it takes to please high-end tenants?" I said.

"You bet it does, out here by the lonesome highway. They're security-conscious. It blows their socks off."

"Like the first brochure in that package you sent me?"

"Right..." he said, "but that's a good point. With no tenants, high- or low-end, I probably should re-think the whole installation."

"Does it run all the time?"

"Only after sunset these days," said Beeson. "I had to disable the daytime codes to please my real estate broker and his three sales-people."

"Who monitors the video?"

"Nobody," he said. "It gets stored for seventy-two hours, then erased unless we have an unauthorized entry attempt during that time. You want to hear the pisser? There's an almost identical installation at the back of the building. That one runs twenty-four-seven. This whole setup cost me as much as the roof."

I wanted to ask, but he interrupted my thought with the answer.

"Yes," he added. "I signed a damned lease agreement. "

The door emitted an electronic click. Beeson entered one more PIN and we were inside. He led me down a hallway past modest beige and gray offices on the left, each with twin windows to the front. Off to our right, a huge single room held an array of work cubicles. Cheap fixtures, commercial-use carpeting and fluorescents prevailed, as if someone had ordered the sterile furnishings out of a catalog. Or sight-unseen off the Internet.

I sensed that the space would not be photo-friendly.

"I know," said Beeson. "It looks like more than a full day's work.

It looks like far less, I thought.

"Our helpers can shift those cubes to different arrangements," he said. "We can emphasize fabric colors, drop-downs, modular height, lighting, privacy and corner offices."

"Flexibility," I said, already bored shitless.

"Yep," he said. "That big room doesn't exist for its beauty. It's there to generate revenue." In a lowered tone he added, "For someone. Speaking of which..."

He stepped into the last office on the left, flipped on the ceiling lights. With a key on his pocket ring, he unlocked the top drawer of his desk. He lifted out a notebook-sized checkbook and began to write.

"Let's call this your sixty percent up front, but if your bill runs higher, for any reason, you'll get no argument from me." He handed me a check for $1,500 then locked up the checkbook, flipped off the lights and led the way out of the office.

Bordering the maze of cubicles, the hall turned to the right and ended at a steel door that Beeson opened with his passcard. "These were shipping and receiving bays in our first incarnation," he said.

The workshop smelled of anti-freeze, axle grease, stale gas and Go-Jo soap. Just inside the doorway a young man in a vintage Guns N' Roses T-shirt and oil-stained Levi's sat at a parts bench. He appeared to be rebuilding a hefty carburetor. Beeson introduced him as Edwin Torres.

I guessed that Torres was in his late-twenties. He nodded and wiggled his right hand as if to say, "I'm too greasy to shake hands." He had a tattoo on the left side of his neck that resembled a hitch-hiker's thumb. I had to wonder if Edwin needed the skin art to solicit a ride back to prison. Then I reminded myself to hold back on my judgment of his appearance. The guy was working for Beeson. He could be a family man, a normal fellow.

"How are things?" said Beeson.

As if he knew he wasn't to answer, Torres returned to his task. Another young man, face-up on a flat mechanic's creeper, rolled out from under a 1955 Chevy two-door 150 with a shaved hood and American Racing wheels. "Smooth as can be," he said.

I looked back to Torres. He nodded in agreement but kept his eyes on his work and said nothing.

Beeson introduced me to Luke Tharpe, a man with a choirboy face, probably in his early twenties. He also gave me a wave in lieu of a handshake. His hair style, with its part to starboard and wave above his forehead, was straight from a 1940s Norman Rockwell painting. He wore royal blue coveralls, a gray T-shirt and greasy sneakers, and came off as the spokesman for the pair. When he stood to chat with Beeson, I thought that he and Torres might be the two slimmest men in Florida.

"There is one thing," said Tharpe. He and Beeson began to discuss re-chromed trim and bumper guards that hadn't been delivered on time. I walked away to let the men talk business without me.

"Two minutes," Beeson half-shouted to me. "I'm hungry, too."

The rear interior section of the building was partitioned under a maze of trusses and high storage bins. The rear wall had a glassed-in security access cube, less fancy than the one out front. It appeared to be a bother and a foolish expense next to three roll-up galvanized steel garage doors.

In the section given to the failed museum, old gas station signs and framed showroom placards hung on walls and partitions. One sign promoted the aftermarket installation of seat belts. Model cars, chrome fender badges and vintage brochures were arranged in glass-topped display cases. Three cars were pushed up against one wall. A '66 Mustang fastback that someone had turned into an imitation Candyapple Red Shelby GT-350H with gold stripes. The Nightmist Blue '67 fastback Mustang that Beeson and I had discussed on New Year's Eve. And a green '54 Ford Customline V-8 coupe with whitewalls, vinyl seat covers and small hub caps. Three fine cars and four antique gas pumps, all pushed aside like old ashtrays. The checkered-flag motif flooring was covered with the kind of file storage boxes you buy from Office Depot. The proud display had gone to seed.

My phone buzzed again in my pocket. I couldn't answer, but stole a look. Dubbie Tanner trying to get through.

From thirty feet away I heard Beeson bark, "Fuck him. We'll buy our manifolds from someone else."

I turned to look. He was walking toward me.

"That was my grandmother's car." He pointed at the '54 Ford. "Original Highland Green. It survived her driving right up to the day she died, bless her soul, even while the DMV was trying to revoke her license. They claimed she didn't sit high enough to see over the dashboard. These, however..." He stepped behind another partition and I followed. "This is Amanda's stable. My ex-wife likes attention."

Along the opposite wall sat a red Mini Cooper convertible, a white Mercedes-Benz SLK300 roadster, and a silver BMW 335 convertible. A trio of showroom fresh Draw-Attention specials.

Beeson called out to Luke Tharpe. "How are we so blessed? All three are here?"

Luke walked over and explained that he had come in the day before and found the Benz outside, as if it had been dropped off. He had moved it inside to its regular spot. I wasn't trying to eavesdrop, but somewhere in his explanation he used the word, "ostensibly." His vocabulary didn't match his clothing.

Beeson and I left the way we had entered. The Cubicle Wasteland turned me off even more the second time through. On the upside, some buyer might see the huge open-plan room as an inviting challenge. My view was that no photo of mine, no matter how artistic, could beautify the workplace.

As we passed back through the security "man trap" to the parking lot, I had to wonder why Beeson, with his expensive classic and modern cars needing shelter and maintenance, was so anxious to sell their oversized garage? If the building sold, what would he do with them all?

I saw the place as promise of a tough and boring day ahead of me.

I would be correct. I would also be wrong.

6

BEESON DROVE SOUTH ON I-75, west into Sarasota and south on Orange Avenue. During that time two thoughts played inside my mind. One was the quick attitude shift the man had displayed inside his failed museum. He had vehemently cussed a supplier and ten seconds later, in a respectful, wistful tone, expressed fondness for his late grandmother and her '54 Ford. That ability to transform himself so abruptly would shade my opinion of the man from that point on.

We entered a pleasant area of tall trees and lovely homes tragically devalued by its concrete speed bumps, obnoxious traffic calming mounds announced by reflective pavement paint that read, "Hump." It was a part of town similar to many in America where anyone on foot and not wearing jogging clothes is under suspicion. A mile farther, under mature, leafy trees, Beeson turned right into Cormorant Lane.

"You can't tell because of the privacy walls," he said, "but we're only 200 feet from salt water."

I asked if he kept a boat at the house.

"My pristine 2011 Sea Ray 350 Sundancer with the custom-built teak interior is owned by my ex-wife these days," he said. "With fuel prices through the roof, it's everything I could wish for her. Of course, indirectly, I pay that gas bill too."

Beeson's home looked new, Mediterranean, with arches and high ceilings, lighted landscaping worth more than my home in Key West. He parked to the left side of his three-wide driveway, grabbed his satchel, we got out. He unlocked a tall gate next to the garage and led me down a flagstone path to a private entrance to the guest house. The small bungalow was a masterpiece of indirect lighting. Its king-size bed looked like ivory-toned high-thread-count heaven. Six fat pillows rested against a stout, solid wood headboard. Dave Brubeck jazz came from speakers I couldn't see.

"Drop your bags and wash up." He pointed through the French door to a window on the far side of the lighted pool. "Please join us for drinks and supper when you're ready."

"I'll need to make one or two calls," I said.

"Take your time." He pushed open the French door, left it ajar and strode across his pool deck toward the kitchen. The bungalow door closed slowly until the last inch or so then snapped shut automatically.

Another call had come through during our drive back into town. I sat in a leather chair, practically sank to China. Fred Liska's message said, "There was something I meant to mention this afternoon, and I didn't do it. For that I apologize, and I would rather not discuss it on the phone. Please call when you can. Maybe we can sit on your peaceful porch again and chill out."

From Beth: "Okay, I'm going to hope... Never mind. I know you're not being an asshole like I was. There's a real reason that you haven't answered four times in the past three hours. I've changed my mind about not seeing you tonight, but right now I'm going to have a drink with my next-door neighbor. She wants to sit at Antonia's bar and listen to the bartender's jokes. Call if you want company."

Hell, yes, I wanted company. I wanted to yell out the door so she would be sure to hear me.

Four empty voicemails had arrived from Dubbie Tanner. Finally he lost his mike fright: "Hope you don't mind me leaving this in your message box. My partner, on a library computer, found Christi Caldwell, Emerson's wife, on Facebook. He can't get to her stats page until she accepts him as a "friend." Her profile photo, we're talking soccer mom."

Wiley may have thought that the library's computers were secure, but I feared he had a surprise in store. I felt certain that the staff required some form of ID to use the machinery. If some agency wanted to find him, they could.

I looked toward the main house, saw Anya Timber peer back at me from a kitchen window. Beeson's remark that I should take my time may not have fit Anya's idea of suppertime. Best to get inside, be a dutiful guest.

I WALKED AROUND THE pool's chlorine cloud, across a painted deck, and found the kitchen by way of a central room large enough for volleyball. Even with six or eight plates of food on the center island, I could smell Anya's shampoo and conditioner. Her damp hair was tucked behind one ear, a touch that highlighted her loveliness.

Beeson stood alongside a glass-front liquor cabinet at the far end of the kitchen. He shook a cocktail glass, rattled the melting ice in the dregs of his first toddy.

"Drink, Mr. Rutledge?" he said. "There's beer... and wine, if you'd rather."

I noticed an open Grgich Hills bottle next to Anya. I pointed at the Cabernet.

Anya poured generously into a fourteen-ounce glass. Handing it to me, she tapped the U-shaped granite-topped island that held all the food. "This is albacore tuna salad, here are two turkey reubens and that's hot beef and brie. Over there is vegetarian lasagna. This is eggplant rollatini. Please help yourself, Alex." She pointed to one empty plate. "Justin and I are light eaters."

She had bought dinner for six to ensure that I had something I liked. I sipped the wine and watched Beeson fill his rocks glass with

Johnnie Walker Green Label.

Anya understood my reluctance to dig in alone. "I can make you a plate," she said. "Is there anything you *don't* like?"

"Not on that table," I said.

Beeson and I watched as she created an assortment of salads and pasta, then slid the plate onto a teak party tray.

"Shall we adjourn to the den?" said Beeson.

I followed him out of the kitchen, spent another ten seconds in the huge central room and entered an entertainment center paneled in walnut, filled with mahogany furniture and leather chairs. Three 60-inch TV screens filled one wall, a bookcase filled another, and two sets of French doors faced the pool area. A sofa and three chairs were at the library end of the room, and eight theater seats faced the center screen on the wall. I didn't see speakers, but knew there were plenty somewhere. Beeson pressed a remote and one of the screens popped on with a movie of a real aquarium. We sat and he raised his glass in a toast to something. The task ahead or my presence in his fine home. Or for no other reason beyond habit. Then he sucked down about fifteen bucks worth of scotch in one gulp.

Anya joined us carrying a tray. She had fixed herself a small plate so I wouldn't have to be the only one eating. She sat next to Beeson on the wide sofa. With his housemate next to him, Beeson went philosophic.

"I've gone from no worries to high pressure, Rutledge," he said, "but I'm still better off than ninety-nine percent of the people in this country. I quit running around like crazy three months ago and I thought things through. I had made a series of bad decisions, I won't deny that. But I also tolerated second-rate associates. I can change that, and part of my rehab is hiring people like you.

Anya stared at the fish. "You may be trivializing the word 'rehab,' Justin."

His confident grin froze, rictus-like, and he wiggled his arm a moment, swirling the ice in his glass. "I meant only to praise a fine photographer, dear. I suppose I was bragging about leaving behind all my destructive habits."

"You paint with a broad brush, my love," she said.

Beeson looked away from Anya, didn't respond. A cold expression enveloped his face, his eyes locked on his drink glass. The liquor was gone. I couldn't tell if the topic fatigued him, or he resented Anya's making her comment in front of me. He stood shakily. "When she starts to edit my pronouncements, Alex, I know it's time for one of us to go to bed. Please excuse me."

Beeson left us in the mini-theater watching the aquarium. Anya reached for the remote, pressed it several times. The aquarium went dark and another screen began showing a movie of a beach in the Caribbean. The camera was fixed, pointed at the water, at lapping waves, tree fronds swaying to each side of the view. Other islands were visible in the distance.

"British Virgins?" I said.

"Yes," said Anya. "An old friend of mine has a home there, and he sends me one of these every month. Justin's not too wild about them. Would you like another glass of wine? Or some other drink?"

"Wine, thank you, but I can pour it."

"Good, because, I'm going for a swim."

She stood, unfastened a snap about six inches under her left armpit. Her wrap-around dress hit the floor. She removed her watch, bracelets and earrings and placed them in a small glass bowl. Beautifully nude, she opened the French door and said, "Join me. The pool is heated."

My mind filled with warring visions: her lovely derriere illuminated by the pool's sub-surface lights, Beeson in a bank canceling payment on my $1,500 check, and the rest of my pay flying away, into the night sky. A documentary on sex play of dolphins flashed through, then images of closets full of lethal weaponry in the large home of a security-conscious man. Finally a close-up of Beth with a scowl of disapproval as I told her quite innocently what had happened in Sarasota.

I stayed put, though I forgot to refill my wine glass.

Anya swam ten or twelve laps, alternating freestyle and breast-stroke, during which time I inspected the wall-sized bookcase. A lower shelf held coffee table-sized art books. The next two shelves were for Eileen's books, Harry Potter first editions, some well-worn classics, several teen thrillers and books from her elementary school days. The rest of the bookcase was filled with a collection of fairly recent mysteries and general fiction.

Looking back at the pool, I noted that Anya had switched to backstroke which I found enjoyable to observe. She took a break in the shallow end, the one closest to the open glass door. With her elbows resting on the edge of the pool she said, "Two things, Mr. Rutledge. We don't care about shrinkage here, especially when it's this cold outside. And Justin won't mind, I promise."

"It's the chlorine that gets me," I said. "I dated a varsity swimmer in college. She never understood why I wouldn't watch her compete in the natatorium."

"I guess I've gotten used to it."

Graceful in every move, she boosted herself out of the pool and leaned over to remove a towel from a lidded wood box near the doorway. Standing just outside the French door, she dried herself erotically, on display, though I didn't know why. Being human, I wasn't going to turn my head. Maybe she needed to show off; or she simply didn't care. She made sure to remove moisture underneath her breasts and trapped in her pubic hair. The hair, oddly, blonde.

She replaced her wrap-around garment.

"Your first name is kind of exotic," I said.

"Yes, I guess exotic is what I intended when I started using Anya. My real name is Tonya. I changed it when that notorious one came along in figure skating. My sister's name is Sonya."

"Does she live here in Sarasota?" I said.

"The Florida panhandle. She works in a lumber yard outside of Tallahassee, sells domestic and import hardwoods. There's a lot of pressure to be one of the guys, so she has to act tough. You can imagine the crap she gets up there because of our last name. "

"I suppose Plank might be worse," I said.

She laughed like I had told her the best joke of the year.

"Does she look like you?"

"Identical twins," said Anya. "It's one reason we have to live in separate towns."

"You and Justin must share a solid love and mutual trust."

"Trust, yes."

"I know he loves you," I said. "You don't love him?"

"When I was nineteen I fell in love. When I was twenty-nine, the man I dated for ten years broke my heart. It hurt so badly, I promised myself that I would never allow it to happen, I would never fall in love again."

"He committed a crime against your heart?"

"Exactly," she said. "He did a lot of damage."

"For the rest of your life, will you punish the victim?"

"That's not it at all, Alex. I'm protecting the victim."

"By removing love from your life?"

She laughed but looked worried. "Not entirely. But, yes, I've banned love from my love life."

"And you find romance on TV or in books or by watching other people?"

"That's it," she said. "Spectator sport. And painless."

"What was the deal in the airplane, the overwhelming silence?"

"Mister Big Deal is afraid to fly. He views small talk as a lame attempt to cover up his fear, so we've learned that silence works best."

"Born with the fear," I said, "or did he have a near-miss?"

"It's a recent addition. A business school associate of his died in a small jet crash in Arizona. The man's partner had paid someone

69

to sabotage the plane. The partner almost collected five million from an insurance company."

"It's good when bad guys get caught," I said.

"That's the first time you've voiced an opinion tonight," she said. "You've been very quiet."

"If I told you my opinions, we both would be in trouble before morning."

An honest smile. "We don't want that, do we, Alex?"

I felt my phone vibrate in my pocket. "Nope," I said. "We certainly don't."

Anya walked toward the main part of the house. I watched her go. The view was just as enjoyable with her clothing in place. I had behaved honorably. Was I required to deprive myself of one last vicarious pleasure?

Walking back to the guest quarters, I pondered Beeson's fear. Did he specifically know of someone who would like to kill him? Or was he naturally, or unnaturally, paranoid?

I called Beth and got her voicemail. A one-minute explanation of my plight and whereabouts would have to do. I was too wiped out to return the other phone calls. I buried myself in luxurious pillows and fell asleep wondering why Anya, like Beeson, felt compelled to give me details of her life story. Her best line had been, "I'm a smart woman with big boobs. Get over it."

I SLEPT WELL IN spite of a few wind gusts that caused branches to brush the guest house roof. My phone's alarm went off at 6:00. Five minutes later I learned that my quarters shared the rear wall of the garage. I heard Anya's Boxster start up with its distinct rumble, then back out and depart. Stretched out under the covers, my head deep in a huge down-filled pillow, I had the strange feeling that, having seen every square inch, or cubic inch, of Anya a few hours earlier, I might never see the woman again.

I showered, elected not to shave, gathered my stuff and zippered my bag. Call it a motel habit, I checked to see if I had left my travel shampoo in the shower, dropped anything in the bedroom, forgotten to unplug my phone charger. All clear... until I saw the white corner of an envelope sticking out from under a cabinet-style night table. It wasn't mine, I knew, but I nudged it free. It wasn't an envelope.

The photo had been rendered on a home printer. The image of Anya nude near the pool didn't surprise me after the previous evening's swim party. I thought for a moment that the other nude woman in the picture might be her twin sister Sonya. They were the same height with similar smiles and hair styling, almost identical figures. They hugged, posing for the camera, their arms behind each other's waist, and all their charms on display. Then I recognized the other woman, knew where I had seen her before and knew that it was *not* Sonya Timber.

My immediate reaction was that I couldn't slip the photo back where I found it. Anyone could come upon it. It was Anya's private business, and perhaps not Justin Beeson's. It certainly wasn't his daughter Eileen's. I stuck the print in a flat pocket of my camera bag. I would give it to Anya when I next saw her.

7

BEESON KNEW THE LINGO, didn't have to check the picture menu. Staring at his sun visor, looking fifteen years older than when he shook my hand in Saluté nineteen hours earlier, he canted his head toward the Mickey D's microphone. "Four Sausage McMuffins with eggs, two hash browns, two large coffees, black, extra napkins."

He looked at me with a questioning expression then a grimace of pain. The distress from turning his head too quickly.

"Black is good," I said.

I didn't need breakfast yet, but I hoped that the food smells would mask the stale scotch escaping the man's pores, the persistent vapors that had thrown me a second-hand buzz for almost twenty minutes.

Back at the house a half-hour earlier, hauling my duffel and camera bag into his kitchen, I had entered a culinary war zone. The coffee machine was steaming, the bean grinder a mess of dry grounds. He had readied cups, sugar and cream.

"How we doing this fine Tuesday morning?" he said. "Ready to kick ass?"

Four English muffins popped from an elaborate toaster. Burned muffins, a waste of good food, a fine toaster. He was trying to be gracious, going through the motions, but he wanted to get the show on the road. The coffee was strong on water, light on java. He put away the jam and butter, the cream. Left the mess for later. For Anya.

We passed through the central cavern, the leather odors of the huge, impersonal living room, and left by the front door. True to Beeson's outward image of fastidious wealth, his dew-covered yard and foliage had been trimmed with precision.

My phone rang. I had forgotten to switch my ringtone to silence. Three seconds later, Beeson's rang, too. I let Dubbie Tanner go to voicemail. Beeson took his call with a grunt.

He listened for a half-minute, said "Thank you, honey," and thumbed his end-call button. "Never happened before," he said, "but a very bad sign. Eileen's mother didn't show. She never came home last night. Anya's usually off to the gym by 6:45, but she had to detour to take my daughter to school. Pisses me off. I hope it's not the start of a new bad habit."

Those were the last words he spoke until he placed his food order. When the young woman at the window handed him the hot cups and open bag, he said, "Let's wait and eat in my parking lot while you dream up more good shots." He drove away and added, "We're really in no hurry. I just wanted to get the hell away from my own bedroom. Even with Anya sleeping next to me, my ex-wife, the loopy bitch, inhabits the darkness. I should have kept the boat and given her the damned house."

I saw that as a perfect moment to keep my mouth shut. A mile northward on I-75 a white polyethylene bag floated forty feet above the roadway. It skidded, dove and lifted, pushed by drafts from the truck and car traffic. It reminded me of sea gulls that play winds above bridges in the Keys. I had been gone only fourteen hours, I thought, and a plastic bag was making me homesick.

Eight miles farther he took Bradenton Exit 217, went east a few hundred yards. Just past a Burger King we turned onto Ranch Lake Boulevard and followed the curving road back to the south, parallel to the Interstate. A minute later, parked in the road in front of 23 Beeson Way, we each took one or two bites of lukewarm McMuffin and dumped the rest back into the bag. The coffee was a lifesaver for me. Beeson was toughing it out, fighting his way through nausea.

Daylight told the story. The forest combined slash pine, sabal palms and oaks, with ferns and saw palmetto dominating the ground cover. Beeson had clear-cut several acres of dense Florida scrub to pave his slice of property. The rich hammocks to either side remained mercifully undisturbed. I had to wonder how he got permits for his project. "Beeson Way" had to be the stubby driveway that connected his property to the boulevard.

"Is there a web page that lists the building for sale?" I said.

"My real estate slackers showed me something," he mumbled, "but it's not my department. They scanned glamour shots from that first brochure."

"I think you need to stress utility. You could have a map showing your proximity to big trucking depots and the Sarasota airport. The site could link to a slide show of my photos, inside and out. It also could highlight your state-of-the-art connection to the Internet."

"I don't know about that. Every last one of my ex-wife's emails comes straight to my desk. But state-of-the-art, I can't promise..."

"You must," I said.

"Why didn't I call you two years ago, Rutledge? I've got one of the boys coming in to help you this morning. He should be here anytime."

In the closed vehicle, his stale odor was overwhelming the bagged food. I grabbed my camera bag with one hand, the door handle with the other. "The light is about to be right," I said. "I could knock out a few sun-up exteriors to stress function."

"That window to the left of the entrance?" he said. "That's my office. Tap on the window when you want to come in. I'll buzz the door for you. But don't tap with anything metallic. You'll light the place up like a county fair."

"Can you do us both a favor, and park around back?" I said. "The photos might look odd with only one vehicle out front."

"Done."

"Also, do you have the building's original plans? Or anything else official to show its elevation? We can scan whatever you have..."

"Wonderful, Rutledge. My real estate geniuses didn't think of that. And we built high because this area is known for flooding. I'll find you something."

AFTER HE DROVE AWAY I checked the message. In a calm, business-like tone Dubbie said, "We have good background on Greg Pulver, but we haven't found a reason for his murder. We confirmed his birth in Murphy, North Carolina, near the Georgia state line. He didn't graduate from high school there, but he has shown a false diploma to get several jobs. He also obtained a fake high school diploma thirty miles away in Blue Ridge, Georgia, probably to establish Georgia residency. Starting in 1998 he held a real estate salesman license in Blue Ridge. He let his license lapse four years ago. We have him married twice and, a true miracle, divorced three times. He's been in Key West almost three years, working part of the last two years at Pepe's and some of that time with Ocilla.

"Here in the bars he has claimed to be a former charter sailboat crewman and a leasing agent for road-building equipment. He also bragged that when he first arrived he drove a truck for Toppino Construction. That lasted six weeks until he got caught for drunken driving. The HR woman at Toppino is an ace with names and she can't recall him. If Pulver's ever had a DUI, it wasn't in Monroe County. Maybe he just wanted to hear himself talk. Key West bars are full of the type. Image is not their agenda. They just want to fill the air with words and see tomorrow. More to come on Ocilla Ramirez. Give us a call."

Odd, I thought, to be bragging about an arrest. Greg Pulver didn't care if his lies were ups or downs. Unless, of course, he was trying to build bad-dude cred to mask his informant status.

I walked to the road, aimed south, then shot westward toward I-75, and again to the north. Looking into the morning sun, I took three of Beeson's building. I knew as I kept pressing the button that my pictures showed very little and had no pizzazz. I wondered again how I had duped myself into thinking this was a dream assignment.

I heard a vehicle approach, stepped to the shoulder to give it space. A dark green Ram pickup slowed to a stop, its passenger-side window sliding down. Beeson's slick, talkative and barely awake mechanic, Luke Tharpe, gave me a thumbs-up sign.

My phone vibrated again. I checked Tharpe's ride, gave him a puzzled look.

He reached out, patted his dashboard. "I work on old rattletraps. Doesn't mean I have to own one."

"You here to lend me a hand?"

"Help you move partitions and furniture, and set up lighting," he said, no doubt repeating the instructions he had received from Justin Beeson. "I took a sick day at my regular job."

He looked the part with watery eyes, reddish nostrils. Substance abuse from the previous evening or the previous hour? He wore an unbuttoned, checkered flannel workshirt over a gray T.

"Is there a tall step ladder inside?" I said.

"Give me three."

I checked my voicemail while I waited.

This one from Beth: "Yes, I wanted your advice. Yes, you are in Sarasota. Where on my wish list was a Mystery Man? Is this still Act One of the play? Would you walk on the wild side and give me a fucking call? Love and kisses."

LUKE RETURNED WITH A heavy-duty ten-foot ladder in his truck bed and stepped out of the vehicle. "You can set it smack on the center line," he said. "This is a dead-end service road with no traffic." He made no move to help.

"I'll be through here in ten," I said, lifting the ladder, setting it on the pavement. "If you can start inside, I'll need a couple of shop lights with clamps, so I can position them anywhere. If you can find a pole lamp with a flexible top section, I can use that, too. And please check the cubicles. Find one that still has a monitor and a keyboard. I'd like to shoot a couple that look like they're in use."

He handed me his keys, started toward the building. "Try not to scratch my baby when you load that sucker," he said. "You can park up by the front door. I won't be going around back today."

Twelve feet off the ground, I ran again through the string of cardinal-direction photos. I found a hole in the tree line to the west through which I snapped long-lens shots of semis on the Interstate. Thin scraggly Spanish moss hung off trees like an aging rock star's facial hair. My east-facing views still fought harsh sunlight and shadows. Boring, except for losing my balance, almost tilting the ladder, but the best I could get. I loaded the ladder and drove Tharpe's truck to a far corner of the parking lot. Standing in the pickup's bed so I wouldn't have to fool again with the ladder, I aimed northward, caught an oblique angle and captured one. Not a winner but close enough.

I parked next to Justin Beeson's Escape. He saw me coming, probably had been keeping an eye on me, and met me at the security door, watched as I ran the gauntlet. His security sensors didn't complain about the camera hung from my neck strap.

"Do we have spectacular exterior photos?" he said.

"Nope," I said. "We scored a few points for truth in advertising."

He looked me in the eye, swiveled his head to stare at the far wall, then turned back to face me. "I get it," he said. "Anya told me I owed you an apology. This isn't the glamour job that I oversold you in Key West. I may need a miracle to sell this structure, but I don't require magic from your photo gear. All I need is an honest day's work."

"I'm fine with that," I said. "I look at every job as..."

We heard a horrifying guttural moan from back in the cubicle farm. It had to be Luke Tharpe, and I couldn't fathom the agony that would produce such a drawn-out, low-pitched wail. Beeson and I started down an aisle between the cubicles. With a series of deep grunts, Tharpe crawled from a workspace into the aisle, holding his hands to his eyes, vomiting on himself and the carpet. My first thought was that he had been sprayed with acid or poison, had kicked open an unused bug bomb.

Tharpe lowered his hands. His eyes bugged out filled with terror. He pointed into the space he had fled, said, "Amanda," then threw up without aiming downward.

Beeson ran ahead of me, slipped in a puddle of spew, and went down. Pivoting on one knee, he leaned around the corner, recoiled in shock then pulled himself up and lunged forward, almost slipping again.

I followed, stepping carefully, giving Luke Tharpe room to crawl to another workspace. The woman's arms were spread, her wrists duct-taped to uprights in the cubicle wall, her ankles taped to the opposing casters of an upside-down office chair. An elegant, unbuttoned silk blouse was all she wore. A stubby dull orange blob, perhaps five inches long, hung from her mouth. Finger-length narrow orange worms drooped from her nostrils.

"Call 911," cried Beeson. "Call 911!" Bracing his fist against the dead woman's shoulder, he grabbed the orange shape and pulled it from her mouth. It took him two rough tugs and it came out with a sucking noise and a rush of dark brown fluid.

I realized I wasn't really watching Justin Beeson. I was seeing him through my camera's viewfinder, taking pictures as fast as I could. Pictures of the entire space, the man in a panic, the woman strangled by the kind of expanding foam sealant used for building insulation and bug-proofing. I was documenting the desk, the keyboard she sat upon, her body slouched to her left, held up by a stack of empty wire mesh filing trays.

Who has time to parse differences: reflex, instinct, constructive panic? Give it a hundred names. I took pictures. Out of habit, or some other name for it, I took some with flash, some without. I changed lenses, stepped sideways carefully, clicked and moved two steps backward...

...and, I thought, no hurry with the 911 call. But when I looked Luke Tharpe was gone. Then I heard his voice in Beeson's office, stammering nonsense, trying to give someone bad directions, arguing left and right turns.

Describing the trio of luxury cars in the building's workshop the night before, Beeson had said, "This is Amanda's stable. My ex-wife likes attention." Beeson, the bitter ex-husband, was on his knees, sobbing, hugging his ex-wife's legs. Indeed, I had seen her before. She was the woman posing with Anya in the photo I had stuck in my bag ninety minutes earlier. The "mom" of the photo in Eileen's backpack.

My work was done for the day.

Amanda would see no tomorrows.

Who was I to tell Justin Beeson not to destroy evidence? He owned enough TVs. He understood such things. I put away my camera and walked to the office.

Luke knew he was babbling. He handed me the phone.

"Alex Rutledge speaking," I said. "I assume you have Automatic Caller Location. Three of us arrived here to find a dead woman in the building, an apparent murder victim. No one else is in the building. There is no need for paramedics."

"We send them anyway," said the dispatcher. "All three of you, please leave the building, wait outside for officers to respond."

I gave her my cell number.

Luke was slumped in the office chair, making volcanic noises. I was still catching my breath when I got a call from "PRIVATE NUMBER." I guessed what it was, correctly.

Detective Glenn Steffey identified himself. "Right now, how many people are in the building?" he said.

"Three," I said. "Please bring bottled water and Rolaids. One man took ill."

"Were you told to go outside?"

"Yes, we were."

"You don't have to leave," he said, "but stay in one place and away from the body. The whole building is a crime scene, so don't touch diddley and don't anyone leave. Got that?"

I WALKED BACK BETWEEN the cubicles and found Justin Beeson sitting on the floor, his back against a temporary wall, his face in his hands. He was shivering.

"The sheriff's office is on their way," I said. "They said we could stay inside but asked us not to touch anything."

"Will they arrest me for hugging my murdered wife?" he said and went again to tears.

She's your ex-wife, Beeson, and you've already contaminated the evidence. No matter what they find, your fingerprints will be part of it.

I found Luke pacing the hallway that led to the car maintenance area. When he saw me approach he tried the door, found it locked, shook his head. He started back toward me looking trapped, turned away again.

"Luke," I said, "a sheriff's office detective called back and asked us to stay in one place. He asked us to keep away from... the scene."

"I'm trying to calm myself here," he said. "You want to fucking back off?"

"Here are your truck keys."

"Put them down somewhere, Rutledge. I'll get them later. Put them anywhere. I'll pick 'em up."

"You bet, Luke."

TWO SQUAD CARS ARRIVED, one deputy in each vehicle. The officers remained in their cars and hawk-eyed the front door, obviously not considering the rear entrances. Six minutes later three detectives from the Manatee County Sheriff's Office showed up, followed by a quartet of EMTs who rushed to the door with a stretcher, a medical box and a defib kit. Finally an oversized white van with green sheriff's markings and the words "Crime Scene" on its front and back.

After assessing the scene, sending away the EMTs and showing us their IDs, the detectives launched their formulaic game plan. They separated us.

Detective Steffey, treating me like a long-lost friend, took me to the office next to Justin Beeson's. He patted the single chair in the room, indicated that I should sit, closed the door and left. I fought the urge to review the photos on my camera. I did not want to revisit the discovery of Amanda or Beeson's short period of intense grief. But I didn't want to be accused of stealing evidence or trespassing a crime scene. Or taking pictures for the tabloids. I would hand them over when I found an investigator I trusted. To save time when the detectives got around to me, I removed my driver's license from my wallet, placed it on the desk.

Ten minutes later Steffey returned, the picture of calm. Again, he motioned for me to sit. He probably was about my age, about four inches shorter, and he looked like a heavy man who recently had lost weight. He wore dark slacks, an open-collar blue button-down shirt and a rumpled tan sport coat. The color of his sagging facial skin suggested that he was a sailboater or a fisherman.

"Happy to stand," I said, knowing that he wanted the psychological advantage of height.

He pulled a small yellow box of Chiclets from his shirt pocket, offered me some by rattling the gum inside. I declined and he helped himself to three pieces. He said, "My occupational hazard is I sit all day long, unless there's a tragedy."

I sat in the chair, gave him his upper hand.

He picked up my driver's license, studied it for a moment and handed it to me. "Key West, eh? Bet you're about ready for your breakfast beer. When did you get here this morning?"

"Can I say something first?" I said. "In case no one has mentioned it, Beeson has a young daughter who should be notified. I believe she's in school right now, and I think the deceased woman is her mother. Her name is Eileen."

"Oh, fuck," said Steffey. "No one said a damned word. Thank you." He used his cell to pass the info to his supervisor.

When he shut off his phone I gave him the larger details of staying at Beeson's home on Cormorant Lane, hearing Anya Timber leave at dawn, my ride with Beeson by way of McDonald's and Tharpe's arrival shortly after that.

"How long were the two men inside while you took pictures?"

"Ten, fifteen minutes max," I said. "Probably closer to ten."

"Camera in that bag, with the pictures intact?"

I nodded. "No time and date stamp on the images, but Nikon attaches that info to each digital file."

"Yep," he said, "my kid's cheapo Walmart peashooter does that, too." His first attempt at attitude. Here come the hardballs, I thought. Along with curves and sliders. Good thing I didn't kill anyone.

"Before this morning, when was the last time you were in this building?"

"Last night around seven PM, my first time here," I said. "Beeson, his daughter, his lady friend and I had just flown in from the Keys."

He pulled a ballpoint from his pocket, looked around for a scrap of paper. "What airline?"

"Private plane," I said. "Beeson said it belonged to a friend of his."

"Where did you disembark?"

"Silver Wings Aviation. Both Beeson and Anya had their cars parked nearby. She and the daughter went home. Beeson and I came here."

"Was anyone else in the building when you arrived?" he said.

I mentioned Tharpe and gave him Torres's name, explained I had no address or phone info. He didn't appear interested, made no moves to track down Edwin of the neck tattoo.

"You and Beeson talked, I'm sure," he said. "Did you discuss his ex-wife?"

"He made a few remarks. He doesn't like her approach to raising their child. This morning he complained that he should have kept his boat and given her the house."

"What brought on that statement?" said Steffey.

"He said that even with his lady friend next to him in bed, his ex-wife... what did he say... inhabited the darkness. He called her a loopy bitch."

"Present tense?"

"I suppose," I said. "He didn't say that she *used* to be loopy."

"Okay, maybe he didn't know she was dead," said Steffey. "Saying crap like that, he sounds to me like a million other divorced guys."

"I don't know," I said. "I've never been..."

"Don't tell me," said the detective. "I'm a two-time loser."

"Or winner, depending," I said.

Detective Steffey stifled a laugh then stared, narrowed his eyes and sized me up. "That's a sick mess out there, and you're pretty calm," he said. "You've been through this kind of shit before. Are you a cop or a serial killer?"

I shook my head. "My girlfriend's a Key West detective. I'm a photographer. I've worked a few times with the Sheriff's Office down there."

"Fred Liska?" he said. "How's Chicken Neck doing these days?"

"He's worried about getting older. I didn't know that his nickname had escaped the Keys."

"A handle like Chicken Neck in this state?" said Steffey. "Bound to travel. I knew Fred when he was humping for the city, before he ran for sheriff. He's a good man."

I opened my camera bag. "You said the magic word, you win the prize." I took the 8-gigabyte chip from my Nikon and handed it over. "Four or five shots on that card will interest you. The rest I'd like back."

The detective held it in the palm of his hand, stared at it, stared back at me.

"Beeson's first reaction to seeing her dead," I said.

Steffey kept staring as if evaluating my character or deciding whether I knew in advance that Luke and Justin would find Amanda. He sat back, inhaled, dropped the data card into his shirt pocket and said, "Calm and collected."

"Not always."

"Would you have kept these pictures if I hadn't spoken of Liska?"

"I would have given them to someone," I said. "In a sense, they're evidence. But I prefer to deal with people I can trust. For all I know, you're Justin's best friend and Luke's cousin and Amanda's lover."

"But I passed your test?" he said.

I nodded. "Did Beeson explain his alarm system?"

Steffey nodded. "Yeah. We love the fact that it's disabled in daylight hours. But we'll review the past week's tapes just the same."

"Week?" I said. "What did he tell you, seven days?"

The detective raised his eyebrows.

"He told me they got erased every seventy-two hours," I said. "I assumed he meant that the past three days are saved while the previous three are cleared, but I don't know how those things work. I know for sure he said it was seventy-two hours. He also mentioned that the cameras and security system out back run around the clock. They don't shut off for the real estate visitors."

Steffey phoned back to his office. "We could use that forensic intern who knows how to copy video surveillance tapes," he said. "If he hasn't left early for his lunch at Applebee's. Or... especially if he has."

He ended his call, stared at me for a moment then said, "Why is there a Ziploc bag sticking out of your pants pocket? Your shorts, whatever. To hold and protect the drugs you're out to score? Or are you already carrying certain products that might get you busted?"

"No. I carry it in case of rain. That baggie is just big enough to hold my phone, my wallet, my car keys and one point-and-shoot camera."

The detective cold-eyed me again for ten seconds. "Shit," he said. "Why didn't I ever think of that?"

With that, he lost interest in me. Or so he appeared. He sniffed and cleared his throat, fiddled with the ballpoint pen, wiped non-existent sweat from his upper lip. After sitting still for no more than five seconds, he reached down to scratch his ankle, then stuck an index finger in one ear and fished around for wax balls.

Holding his disinterested expression a while longer, he said, "Let's go back to when you woke up this morning." He let that hang without asking me anything. It was an invitation for me to open up, spill all.

I finally said, "I'd like to do that. Rewind the reel."

"You didn't see Anya Timber leave."

"I heard her car back out of the garage. She was probably parked within twenty feet of my warm, expensive pillow. But, no, I didn't even open my eyes."

"No offense, Mr. Rutledge," said Steffey, "but are we likely to find evidence that she was near that poufy pillow?"

"No offense taken," I said. "It sounds like splendid fun, and my honest answer is that I don't know. One assumes clean sheets when offered a guest room, but she may have used the bed on some prior occasion. You certainly won't find any evidence of my having par-taken of Anya Timber's splendid fun, if you get my drift."

"You mean no come stains, drool, fashion lubricants or latex con-dom residue?"

"You guys love details," I said.

"Chicken Neck didn't tell you?" he said. "Details solve more cases than drift."

8

UNDER THE ROOM'S GREEN-TINTED fluorescent lights, I felt somewhat trapped in the vinyl office chair that Detective Glenn Steffey had insisted I occupy. I turned off the light switch, let calming slivers of daylight ease their way through the blinds. All I needed was Norah Jones right there in the room, playing her electric piano, singing about raindrops. With the sounds of only a few subdued conversations outside the door, my mind let me think larger, see things less through a microscope and more from a distance.

First clues first. If the Boxster had departed in the middle of the night, I would have heard its engine. If Anya had left the house between the moment I last saw her and the minute I heard her Porsche start that morning, she either had called a taxi or had access to another vehicle, or someone picked her up and brought her back later.

But then... bullshit. In the bigger picture that line of logic didn't play. Amanda Beeson's body had flexed, actually wiggled, when Justin yanked the lumpy orange mass from her mouth. I was no death expert, but from articles I had read, her body had already progressed to a late stage of rigor mortis, of diminishing rigidity. She had been dead at least twenty hours, so why was I trying to work Anya into complicity? The body probably had been in that cubicle when Beeson was writing me a check the night before. Thank goodness for air conditioning.

Where had Amanda Beeson been killed? Had she walked in the building's front door during the hours of reduced security? If she had been in the tiny trunk of her SLK300 when Luke Tharpe moved it inside two days earlier, she had to have been flexible in order to fit. Either way, there would be no video record of her arrival. But her murderer had to be someone who knew how to dodge the security system.

ANOTHER DETECTIVE SHOWED EDWIN Torres into the office. The collar of the dark brown work uniform hid his neck tattoo. He sat on the desk, let his legs dangle, then unbuttoned and removed his shirt to relax and adjust to the room's stuffy air. The tee he wore read MADE IN AMERICA WITH CUBAN PARTS.

"Just get here?" I said.

"Hell no." He rubbed his right thumb against the now-visible tattoo. "They sent a green-and-white to fetch me at work. My boss scoped the deputy and I felt my job go up in smoke. I've been out back saying, 'I don't know,' to three of those officers for the past twenty minutes."

"United Parcel?"

"I load trucks from 5 AM to 2 PM. Then I moonlight here three evenings a week, for a couple hours, and at least six hours on Saturdays."

"Those four cars need that much work?" I said.

"Oh, he's got other cars in a storage building he rents. An '03 Mercury Marauder, an '86 Mustang SVO, a '94 Ford Lightning pickup, and a '68 Camaro.

"And his ex-wife has three cars?"

Torres shook his head. "She went by moods, whatever she felt like driving on any damn day. Used to be, she might show once a week to swap cars. With a few sunny days ahead, you know she loved that roadster. Then, I don't know, maybe four, five months ago, she started calling for home delivery. Some days I would take her a clean one and bring the dirty one back. Some days Luke would make the run."

"She live far away?" I said.

"Thirty-six minutes, round-trip."

"Must be fun," I said, "working on classic cars."

"It keeps me sane," he said. "One of these days I'll have a street machine."

"Which of Beeson's cars would you own if you could?" I said.

"That fake Shelby, someday," said Torres. "I mean now, right here..." He twirled his finger to indicate our surroundings. "These cars have a nicer home than I do."

"It's a well-done GT-350," I said. "Too bad it's a fake."

"I'd stroke it, put a roller cam in it, make it scream. Mr. Beeson says he'll buy a real one if he can sell this building. How about you?"

"I got lucky and bought a real one when normal people could afford them. It's also a former Hertz rental car."

"What color?" he said, his disbelief poorly hidden in his nonchalance.

"Black with gold stripes when it was new, but now it's in primer. The guy who sold it to me installed a fresh T-10 four-speed."

"A true Hertz car?" he said. "What's your VIN code?"

"It's 6S1900, delivered originally somewhere in Ohio."

He still didn't buy my story but he opted for diplomacy. "Hey, you're the expert. Why primer?"

"The previous owner drove it all over the country, even on race tracks in regional events. It was pretty dinged up. I was having it painted to look original, and the shop went broke halfway through the job. I decided to keep it looking rough. I want people to think it's an old beat-up Mustang instead of a treasure. I drive it all over the Keys and no one suspects that it's worth stealing."

"Did you ever find out the original Ford VIN code?"

"Got it years ago from SAAC, the Shelby club," I said. "Where does your partner Luke work his day gig?"

"Some office," said Torres. "He works high finance on a computer." He paused then said, "He ain't my partner, really. Really, he's a butthole, a prime butthole. He thinks he's a snappy mechanic, but I believe he'd cross-thread his own toothpaste." He paused in thought then added, "That thirty-six-minute round-trip I mentioned? Some days it took Luke an hour longer than it should have."

I SAW MOVEMENT OUTSIDE, checked through the blinds. A smaller EMT vehicle had arrived. Three men were shifting a gray body bag from an ambulance stretcher onto a short platform inside the vehicle. Amanda had left the building.

Had I really just seen a gurney with whitewall tires?

Justin Beeson poked his head into the room, a grim expression on his face. With grief combined with his hangover, he appeared to have aged ten years in two hours. "The county people out here say they don't need you anymore," he said. "I've got to get Eileen out of school, spend some time with her. A lot of time, actually, for the rest of her life."

Surprised to see him, I was stuck for words.

"Anya made reservations for you on a six o'clock," he said. "She can take you to the Tampa airport in an hour or so. Please mail me an invoice for two days and your travel minus that check I wrote last night."

I nodded. "I'm sorry about your…"

"And hold on to those pictures you shot this morning. We'll sell this place another time."

The door closed and he was gone.

Just as well. I wasn't sure what I would have said next.

Edwin Torres shrugged. I pulled out my phone, called information, and got the number I needed. I had missed breakfast and wasn't sure I would have time to eat before rushing off to the airport. I ordered four large pizzas and a dozen soft drinks for delivery. The law enforcement people would appreciate the food, now that the body was gone.

Two hours later, in Anya's Porsche Boxster, I felt fifty grand richer for not owning the car. It wasn't because it sat too low to clear cracks in the road, or smelled of skin lotion and perfume. Nor did I object to Oscar Peterson's jazz piano. I simply didn't fit in it. My head, legs and shoulders begged for acreage.

I was, for certain, fifteen hundred bucks to the good. I had asked Anya to use the drive-thru at Beeson's bank so I could have "travel money" in my pocket. She knew, of course, that I wanted to make sure the check was good. I also wanted to cash it before Beeson had to spend all his money on lawyers. Given the circumstances, that amount was sufficient for my time and efforts. I would invoice him later for the cost of my air ticket and Key West cab.

Anya drove northward on I-75, at one point passing through a short, intense rainstorm without slowing down. "So much for our brief tease of warm weather," she said. "January's coming back to us. It'll be cold tonight, but I like brisk air. My little secret."

Among several others, I thought, but I kept my mouth shut. I was comforted by her driving ability. On the surface streets she had timed lights to minimize braking, changed lanes often but carefully. On the Interstate she used the vehicle's power but anticipated the moves of idiots around us. All rare skills in the general population.

"Sorry, Alex," she said. "I walk around showing my bare ass last night and now I discuss the weather."

"It's okay," I said, thinking ass plus other attributes. "It's a tough time for small talk."

We rode in silence for a while on I-75 then crossed the Sunshine Skyway. Two hundred feet above Tampa Bay, and I couldn't enjoy the view because of the safety railings. Not that the misty seascape would cheer me up. I kept thinking about the morning's events at 23 Beeson Way, trying to force one particular impression to the surface. It finally came to me. Edwin Torres was a car enthusiast while Luke Tharpe resented having to work on "rattletraps." Did Torres hold any resentments?

I wondered if Edwin resented Luke's extra-long trips to Amanda's house.

A CLIENT WHO PICKED me up at the Tampa airport six months earlier told me about the free Cell Phone Waiting Lot. You can pull into the lot, sit in your car and wait for arriving passengers to call. You don't have to drive in circles or fight for a space near the baggage claim. I had plenty of time to check in for my 5:55 flight, plus check and return some messages. I asked Anya to turn into the free lot and stop for a minute.

She shut off her motor, stared for a moment at a car similar to hers, then looked straight at me, almost daring me to break the silence.

"How long have you been with Justin?" I said.

"Two years, last week," she said. "The woman you were with on New Year's Eve, have you been with her a long time?"

"Less than a year."

"Is she the reason I couldn't seduce you last night?"

I said, "Yes," and thought, even the beautiful ones want to be wanted. I let my answer settle for a moment then said, "You're already Eileen's trusted friend. Will this notch it up a bit?"

"That would be up to Justin," said Anya. "I know she'll look to me for comfort in the short run. Beyond that..."

"You'll need each other," I said. "You lost a friend, too."

"How is that?"

"Amanda."

She held back for a few seconds. "How could you possibly know?"

I handed her the photo.

She studied it, considered it. I could tell by her face that the sight of it brought her immediate calm. "Thank God," she said.

"It was stuck under a cabinet next to the bed I slept in. I thought it was something I had dropped, so I lifted it up and..."

She nodded. "I didn't miss it for two or three days, then I couldn't find it. Eileen never goes in there, but if she had found this... God, it would be dreadful."

"That's the possibility that crossed my mind. I planned to give it only to you. And no one else. Why was it in the guest quarters?"

"I sleep there some nights when Justin's insomnia affects us both. Nights when I've had too much wine to drive home. There was a night when I wanted the picture with me."

"You have your own place," I said, more as a statement than a question.

"My pocket of calm. It's a condo on Longboat Key. My boyfriend's parents loved me more than he did. They had loads of money and were generous after he broke off our love affair." She offered the photo back to me. "It was taken with my camera. The original is on my computer. Do you want to keep it?"

What the hell? Was she coming on, tempting me? Or handing me a clue to help solve a crime? Either way, hell hath no fury...

I accepted the picture, put it back in my camera bag.

"Is that all you wanted to say?" she asked.

"Please accept my sympathy."

"I accept, thank you." She started the car, drove from the Cell Phone Parking Lot to the Blue Zone departure gates, and stopped next to the curb.

"Thank you for the ride," I said. "Take care of Mr. Beeson."

Anya nodded sadly. "I have a big task ahead," she said. "He really loved her."

So much that he called her a loopy bitch.

Three sides to every story, minimum.

MY RESERVATION REQUIRED ME to change planes. It was too late to book direct. I'd spend more time in the Miami North Terminal than

I would in either aircraft. But I would be inside my cottage before ten PM, cured of my impulsive desire to escape the island, at least for a while. And, while I carried my camera bag aboard, Justin Beeson was paying the rip-off baggage fees for my duffel and tripod. Assuming, of course, that he would honor my invoice.

On arrival in Miami I found nothing in my voicemail. Ominous, though I felt thankful. The phone had thrown me nothing but trouble for twenty-five hours. I elected not to call from the terminal but to wait for face-to-face chats to reassure Beth and find out how Marnie and the Aristocrats had fared. I had time to eat some half-decent grilled chicken, then found a small saloon selling large mojitos. My wait involved far more people-watching than drudgery. When I walked outside to the "regional carrier" gates, my phone buzzed twice. Two calls hadn't made it through while I was inside. Both callers had left messages.

The first was a quote request from someone I had never met. Friend of a friend, or so he said. I was inclined to wipe the voicemail, then thought it best to hold off. It could turn out to be a decent job, and I hate to turn down moneymakers. The second message was from Detective Glenn Steffey in Manatee County. He gave his number and asked me to call when I got a chance. I decided to wait until I reached Key West so he couldn't turn me around, boogie me back north for more questions I couldn't answer. Especially with Anya's beloved cold weather coming back in.

A diverse group of island-bound passengers milled about in dim lighting, waiting to board. I recognized only one as a Key West resident, a real estate broker I never had cared for. Several people smelled of fabric softener, and someone should have chomped an Altoid after smoking a jay. As usual in crowds that size, one man had a loud mouth. Within a minute of his arrival I knew his name was, "Robert Fonteneau, call me Bobby."

"French name," someone said. "Louisiana?"

"Canada, but I'm about as French as Bruce Lee," he proclaimed.

"I'm like a Cuban named O'Reilly."

Or more like a teenager yell-talking in a mall. Don't hear my words but be damn sure to notice me. Still, Fonteneau made a couple remarks that proved he had a good sense of humor. He stood about 5'-9" with a thick neck and medium build, and looked like he had combed his brown hair with the flat of his hand. He wore a heavy white sweatshirt under a Navy blue sport coat, pressed blue jeans and new Nikes. Sweat streamed down his face. It was a January evening in south Florida, but to him it had to be worse than summer. Another northerner giving the tropics a try.

BOARDING WENT SMOOTHLY EXCEPT for a flight attendant's demand that a musician's guitar go to baggage. After a woman offered to give up her seat to the instrument, a crew member relented and placed the Martin case in a hang-up locker. The woman, it turned out, was assigned the aisle seat next to my window slot. I traded and gave her my view of Miami's night lights. Aloft, I fell asleep, nailed down a solid thirty-minute nap.

Awakened, of course, by the voice of Fonteneau three or four rows behind me. He was bitching about Canadian weather, having to shovel a path to his car that morning to get to the airport on time. Then came the all-encompassing brag medley: "I got a friend who did this;" "My best friend did that;" "I got a friend who'll let me use his..." I pitied the man's seatmate until I realized it was the broker and I didn't care. I could tell by his disinterested grunts that he wanted out of the conversation, wanted Robert Fonteneau to shut up. The Canadian finally took the hint, left the broker and the rest of the plane's passengers to their own thoughts.

I remembered reading, in a Beat Generation novel, about a "rambling man" who kept a packed duffel behind his living room sofa. Always ready for the fast departure to anywhere else. When younger I believed that constant motion was a fine, romantic idea—right up to the year I hit Key West, saw the island, unpacked and grew roots.

With most out-of-town trips, I felt hell-bent to get back to the island, back to my own home. This time I had mixed feelings. I was escaping my second crime scene in two days, neither of which had anything to do with me. They were like passing news items except that everyone around me was sucked into tornados of grief and investigation, guilt and regret. I've always believed it was bad luck to assign myself imaginary negative traits. I didn't want to think I was a shit magnet, but I was sure as hell archiving shit at a record-setting rate.

AFTER OUR LANDING IN Key West, a flight attendant held up the Navy blue sport coat. "Mr. Fountain-ooh, please identify yourself."

Oh, don't get him started, I thought.

Bobby corrected her pronunciation with, "Fawn-tone-oh," but kept quiet as our fellow passengers filed off to the tarmac. While we waited our turn to leave the plane, the broker told the visitor to have a great time in paradise.

"Actually, it's a sad visit," said Fonteneau. "A colleague of mine died here in town, died of a heart attack two days ago. I'm here to settle his affairs."

Emerson Caldwell was that colleague, I thought, but offered no reaction. I left the plane just ahead of Fonteneau, and hurried to the Baggage area, hoping the chatty man would go straight to a taxi. I didn't want to be his next victim. But that backfired when he and I were among the last people waiting for luggage. When my tripod box finally appeared, I walked outside and pointed at a taxi driver. He waved me toward his vehicle, then pointed at someone behind me.

"Sure," said Robert Fonteneau. "La Concha Hotel, eh?" He turned to me, stuck out his hand and reintroduced himself as "Bobby." Up close he had an unreadable face. He could have been a Little League coach or a Russian mob assassin. He had what Sam Wheeler called bi-polar eyes. That meant he could be a softy or get mean-angry without warning. But his smile looked genuine. He repeated what I had heard him tell the real estate man, the sad reason for his trip to the island.

"Can you recommend a good local attorney to handle this kind of situation, to get past all the red tape?"

"I can recommend restaurants and fishing guides," I said, "but lawyers, I really don't know. Pick one who's been in town a long time. It may cost the estate a little more money, but the veterans know how the machine runs."

"Every town has a machine," said Fonteneau.

"And it takes years to learn how to navigate..."

"Well, it's been years since I set foot on this island," he said. "Is Captain Tony's Saloon still in business? And the Green Parrot?"

"Tony sold the bar back in '89," I said. "He died in 2008. And Jim Bean, the man who co-owned the Parrot, died in 2010. But the bars are still there, almost the same as always."

"Good," he said. "No matter what I have to do, to take care of my friend's affairs and final wishes, I will spend tomorrow afternoon in Captain Tony's and the next day at the Green Parrot. I'm in a mournful mood and booze will hurry me to my personal rock bottom." His grin looked more evil than sly or sad. "Maybe it'll take me to some young lady's soft bottom, too."

Full circle, and the cab delivered me back to the curb in front of the Eden House. Fonteneau wanted to shake hands again. I pretended to fumble with my camera bag and not see his outstretched fingers. I wished him luck and closed the cab door.

IT WAS GREAT TO return to tropical scents, the sea breeze, the muffled sounds of cars over on Eaton Street, the flickering of streetlights through the canopy of palm trees. Familiar old architecture of homes on Fleming, so different from anywhere else in Florida. I wondered how many times I had walked that patch of pavement, how often each year for all of the years I had lived in the lane. Even the pebbles under my shoes felt familiar.

The last time I had come around the corner, less than thirty hours earlier, I was returning from Beeson's home on Olivia Street. Hurrying back from the meeting where he had asked about the legal status of digital photos.

"What about crime cases that go to court?"

Why had he used the word "crime" instead of "civil?"

He had followed that by using the words "judge" and "juries."

Had I been blinded by his style, his approach, his money or his woman?

THE FIRST THING I noticed in the lane was the Mercedes SUV with Illinois plates owned by the Neighbor I Didn't Know. He had bought the house a year earlier. He came for six weeks in winter and three weeks in summer and never said hello or waved. In October two workmen had placed paving bricks over a patch of marl in front of his house. Now he had a precise, perfect spot for his Benz. That was all I knew about him, except that he always dressed like he was still in Chicago.

I surely didn't know why a committee awaited me. I didn't even notice their cars until I had to walk between them to reach my house. I opened the screen door and found Dubbie Tanner standing on the porch. Sheriff Liska, Beth, Marnie and my close friend and neighbor, Carmen Sosa, sat staring as if shocked to see me appear at my own home.

"Everyone has Liska's eyes," I said. "What's with all the long faces?"

Liska smiled, shook his head. "We weren't exactly expecting you back tonight."

I looked at Beth. She cast her gaze at the porch decking for an instant then raised her eyes to me. We were locked eye-to-eye but I could feel everyone else's gaze upon me. Could feel their eyes sorting my expression, reading my doubt.

"What?" I said.

Beth's eyes held pure sadness. She bit her upper lip between her teeth, released it and said, "As a group we have failed your friendship."

Far too quickly I said, "Who's dead?"

Her shoulders sank and told me that my guess was correct.

"At The Tideline condo, another person. Someone we all knew, but you…"

"Oh, shit," I said, dreading her news. "Please just say."

Beth shuddered and barely whispered, "Teresa Barga."

9

My eyes had caught it, with help from a telephoto lens.

The third body bag at The Tideline crime scene.

Teresa Barga had ended our short-term relationship several years ago. For eight months we had spent almost every night together at her Shipyard townhouse or in my cottage, depending on our moods and schedules. I probably had loved her. She had not closed out our affair gracefully. Her head was turned when an old college boyfriend showed up in town. He was a scam artist and a loser. Worse, not long after recapturing her heart, he was murdered by a woman he had been blackmailing.

After that mess Teresa and I kept our distance until a complication no one could have foreseen. Tim Rutledge, my younger brother, hit town in a swirl of typical Keys misbehavior. In the first week of his drunken visit, he met and charmed Teresa in a restaurant over breakfast. I viewed their intense, short-term romance with certain opinions regarding their motivations. Events forced me into acceptance before the couple's inevitable split and Tim's departure for the mainland.

Since then Teresa and I had run into each other only three times, odd for a small island, and especially since she was still the KWPD's Public Information Officer. Our meetings had been short and cordial. I was happy to discover that my bitterness over our breakup had vanished. I wished her well each time and I had meant it. And, for some reason, I remembered each encounter.

Everyone on the porch stared at me. Carmen, Beth, Marnie, Liska and Tanner. I could tell by their faces that Teresa's death had been violent. I had been given the story's ending but no grisly details. Oddly, I felt little grief at first. Dozens of images and ideas swirled in my brain, including the fact that the bad news could have been worse. The death of Carmen Sosa's daughter, Maria, or my brother, Tim. Or any close and loyal friend on the island. Of course, there is no way to prioritize tragedy. Just as there is no standard form of grief.

I was unsure how to respond, had no words adequate to the loss. I offered only secondhand gossip: "I heard last summer that she was living in New Town with some city cop."

"Officer Darrin Marsh," said Beth. "On the force for six years. They moved from Fogarty Street to The Tideline last fall. They lived fifty feet down the hall from the murder condo. Her body was found in Emerson Caldwell's kitchen."

I thought I had escaped the mess, washed my hands of everything, left it to Beth and Marnie and the Aristocrats. Now, for sure, I was sucked back in.

WITH THE SAD NEWS aired, everyone but Beth left the porch. Dubbie Tanner went first, Carmen and Marnie offered hugs, Chicken Neck shook hands but couldn't look me in the eye.

I sat in the chair that he had vacated. "First, let me explain Sarasota."

"I know," said Beth. "I got your message. I wasn't sure how to answer it."

"Why this group, this mini-summit meeting?"

"We expected you back, your message said tomorrow. We were deciding how to let you know by phone. We knew it would be in tomorrow's *Citizen*."

"Did you draw straws to pick the bearer of bad tidings?"

"Don't be that way, Alex. I wasn't sure how or when, but knew I would tell you. I wanted to include the others in my decision."

"I'll have to call Tim."

"Has he made new friends up in Florida?" she said. "Did you meet anyone while you were there, someone who might stand by him if he needs reassurance?"

"I met two of his pals and a women he'd been dating. I didn't feel them out for emergency hand-holding. I don't think he was going to meetings or anything like that."

In October my brother Tim had found a job in Orlando, which we both needed. I had paid his motel bills for several months until he got situated. Finally a searchlight company hired him to tow a beacon and generator rig all over central Florida. His assignments were sparse. There weren't many grand openings in a tough economy, so his money was tight. Of all people, the perennial rambling boy had sounded lonely the few times we spoke on the phone. Just before Christmas I borrowed Beth's new Audi A5, drove up from the Keys and stayed well north of the Disney-Universal mess. I survived a cheap motel and six restaurant meals. After Tim and I shared a farewell lunch at a Bonefish Grill, I drove back to Key West in crazed and urgent holiday traffic. I felt like sleeping for four days. To my surprise, he had mentioned Teresa Barga a half dozen times. Now I would have to ante up brotherly duty a second time.

"LISKA WAS HERE YESTERDAY, full of one-liners and praise," I said. "Did he come to tell me about Teresa?"

"He assured me that he was an old pro at breaking bad news," said Beth. "When he was face-to-face with you, right here on the porch, he couldn't do it. He meant well. Both he and Marnie felt bad about not saying anything right away."

"It wouldn't have changed what happened," I said.

"It would have changed one major factor," she said. "I owe you an apology for taking away your fun yesterday."

"Excluding me from forensics?" I said. "You know me better than that. I would never view a crime scene as entertainment."

"I wasn't saying that. I know that murder starts ugly and goes downhill."

"Where does fun fit?"

"When a detective asks you to help out," said Beth. "You get the power to say, 'No.' It's flattering to be asked, and it's strong to turn it down."

"Wrong and wrong, my lovely friend," I said. "It's a pain to be called and a relief to decline."

"What needs relieving?"

"I hate being the outsider," I said. "Every time I get dragged into a case, I'm surrounded by trained scene workers. Aside from you and Liska and one or two other detectives, I can see the looks in their eyes. I'm worse than a pain in the ass. I'm a civilian intruder who could molest evidence and undermine their reputations. I'm no better than a TV cop show fan living out his dreams."

Beth nodded, took a sip, then shook her head. "That's not what law enforcement people say about you."

"Not to mention," I said, "my presence confuses a situation that needs clarity, not turmoil. It makes mockery of their training. Even you have to sense that, right?"

She looked at me and said nothing.

"Who would take time to talk about me?" I said.

"Believe me, out of the public eye, they talk about everyone and everything. A few resent that you don't think like a cop. The majority say they like your approach. You have a way of clinging to a case."

I wasn't sure how to react so I shut up.

"They all respect your results," said Beth. "A lot of veteran detectives would like to have your case closure rate."

"You weren't around the first couple times Liska talked me into it," I said. "I had reasons to cling, as you call it. There was someone close to me that drew me in and kept me on it. With this case, I'm a true bystander. I have no stake in the outcome."

"Amazing bullshit."

"Okay," I admitted. "I'd like to bring down the bastard that killed Teresa."

Beth walked around my chair, lifted my shirt, began to massage my upper back. One of her habits that I most enjoyed.

"If Teresa lived down the hall," I said, "how did she..."

"She was strangled and her neck was snapped. The strangling killed her."

I fought to keep the picture from my mind. "I didn't mean that," I said. "Why was she in Caldwell's condo? Was she having a fling with the late Greg Pulver?"

My shoulders were tight as bridge cables. Beth's thumbs were up to the task.

"According to her boyfriend, Marsh, that wasn't the case at all. He and Teresa had taken the day off. They were lounging around, having their coffee, deciding where to go for lunch. She went to drop garbage down the chute and to get something from her car. She may have found Caldwell's door open, or heard a cry for help and looked in. She may have walked into a crime-in-progress."

"Shall I bet that she was found by Officer Marsh?"

Beth eased her massage. "Yes, but it's not your job to speculate."

"Will you do me a favor and talk me through Darrin's story?"

"Okay," she said, "but let me say first that her T-shirt, sweatpants and flip-flops fit the idea that she was having an easy morning. Enjoying coffee and the newspaper on her balcony."

"Let me guess. She didn't return and Marsh went looking for her?"

"After about twenty minutes he wondered, but he figured she was caught in a conversation with a neighbor. After forty minutes he called her cell phone, but it rang in their bedroom. So Darrin went looking, found Emerson Caldwell's door wide open, saw the man on the floor, then found Teresa in the kitchen. He called 911 from Caldwell's land line and backed out of the crime scene. He didn't venture far enough into the apartment to find Greg Pulver in the master bath."

"Did Teresa or Marsh know Caldwell or his wife?"

"He said they didn't. They had seen the cleaning crew come and go, but never an occupant. They even discussed hiring the cleaners."

"Well," I admitted, "it's all logical. Except he put his fingerprints on the phone before he backed out to preserve the crime scene. He probably left his prints on the kitchen floor, too."

"He did," said Beth. "And about six other places, too."

"There's bound to be a civil rights question. Will the Feds see Marsh as a person of interest?"

"They questioned him for three hours yesterday afternoon. They've got two agents watching him, not that they informed us of that fact. We know that he's acting mopey but he's going through his day-to-day motions. One of them said he was a person of boredom. Naturally, they're curious about that, too."

"Nothing like normalcy to set off a bureaucrat."

She quit rubbing my neck, walked around and sat opposite me, grim-faced. "One other thing," she said. "His service pistol is missing, and he can't account for it. He thinks it was stolen from his pickup in The Tideline parking lot."

"So... he's a sloppy cop. How could that matter in this case? No one was shot."

"Greg Pulver was not carved up with sharp knives," she said. "We decided to put out that story to thwart false confessions. The hollow-point bullet that took out Pulver entered his lower jaw and went upward. One of my sicker colleagues called it a brain smoothie."

"I hope someone had the presence of mind to search for Marsh's weapon."

"Oh, yes," said Beth. "One of the sheriff's guys ordered a search of the condo grounds and adjacent properties. When he expanded it to halfway up Smathers Beach and back down to White Street

Pier, I shut down the search."

"You countermanded him?"

"He bought my logic. Darrin Marsh is a cop. He knows about evidence. He could have shot Pulver, driven less than two miles in any direction but south and dropped the bastard off a dock. No one would ever see it again. Looking around The Tideline is fine. It accounts for the panic of a murderer. But anything else assumes lack of cunning, becomes bogus by the infinite possibilities."

"But he didn't have time to drive anywhere... Oh, okay," I said. "He ditched the gun, came home and found Caldwell's door open with the man dead on the floor."

"Except maybe Teresa found Caldwell first, then found Greg Pulver. When Marsh returned she may have been calling 911. So he hung it up, killed his girlfriend, then called 911 himself."

"Two calls?"

"A hang-up, which is guaranteed to generate a police visit. Then Marsh's call."

"He could have wiped her prints off the phone then put his own all over it."

"That would be nice to prove," said Beth. "Impossible, but..."

"Is there any kind of security video?"

She nodded, sighed deeply. "Inoperative since 4:00 am that morning."

"Was her garbage located at ground level?"

"Hauled off by Waste Management about the exact time Marsh called 911."

"Coffee in her stomach?"

"Yep. All bases covered."

"I'm afraid to react," I said. "This is going to take some adjustment. Will the Feds come in because of this Marsh, the cop she lived with?"

"Yes," she said, "there's a civil rights question. Which is one reason you couldn't come near this case, but that was not why I sent you away. Your relationship to the victim, no matter how long ago it happened, could blow our chance for prosecution."

"Not if I was a work-for-hire employee."

"Especially for that reason. They'd take one look into your work history and my job would go blooey." She sat back, stared at the far wall and exhaled. "Which might not be so bad. This whole thing sucks out loud. I questioned two condo dwellers who were angered by the inconvenience. I guess they thought their daily routines were more important than violent deaths in the building."

"They pay big bucks for those apartments," I said. "A few think it insulates them from the street, from the rogue crap that the human horde creates."

Beth looked back to me. "Now you sound like our people when they're out of the public eye. One woman, I asked her if she heard anything that morning. She said, 'Screams.' I asked if the screaming included words that she understood. She shook her head and said, 'No, just normal screams.'"

"Like normal gunshots?" I said.

"So I asked her if the screams could have come from children at play."

"Don't tell me."

Beth nodded. "She remembered it was kids running in the hallway. But it might have been the night before, the dingbat bitch. One witness was a true eagle-eye. She described a man with his hair done up in 'spring rolls,' wearing sleeveless jammies with calf-length bottoms and shoes with zebra stripes. We determined it was a black man who had delivered pizza two nights before the deaths."

"Speaking of normal gunshots," I said. "Did no one report hearing gunfire during the time frame when Pulver could have been killed?"

She shook her head.

I had exhausted my limited investigative brilliance. My mind went purposefully blank, fogged with grief. We listened to several sirens on Eaton Street and White Street. They sounded like they converged about four blocks south and east of us.

"Jesus," she said. "It's the usual time of night for domestic violence. I do not want my phone to ring."

Beth stood and came around behind me again to raise my shirt and resume my massage. Half the time she administered relief, her massages led to other activities. My favorite clue to the next step was when she rubbed her breasts against my back. The absolute giveaway was when she removed her top and lifted her bra and tickled my shoulder blades with her nipples. Which is exactly what she did.

"Did you think about this in Sarasota?" she said.

"You bet I did. The client's girlfriend tried to get me to fuck her. She engaged in flagrant solo skinny-dipping after he had gone to bed. I'd have been a fool to turn her down if I wasn't coming home to you."

"Please follow me to your bedroom, Alex Rutledge. Your perfect answer deserves a reward."

It was a reward we both redeemed, using bedpost leverage, multiple fingertip exploration, laughter and deep breathing.

Before we zonked out, just before I blew out the candle, I brushed a strand of damp hair from Beth's eyelashes and whispered, "I like your approach."

I EASED AWAKE TO faint daylight, Beth Watkins's smooth leg against mine, one of life's great natural luxuries. Except it was a queen-sized pillow, and I had been fooled by a high thread count.

She had slipped out early, a relief to my conscience. In spite of our lovemaking hours earlier, I had been virtually unfaithful just after dawn, ninety-eight percent asleep, dreaming of Teresa Barga.

Nothing exotic or erotic, at least by my interpretation, but who knows the true meaning of dreams? She sat across from me at an art deco-patterned Formica table in a loud restaurant full of neon signs, a sly expression on her face. Her low-cut top and high-end bra put lovely tan skin on display. With all the shouting, rock music and clattering, I couldn't hear what Teresa was saying to our server. He looked charmed. She pointed at me then at something in the bar area, and they laughed. I watched her squeeze his forearm. Were they sharing a little secret?

I shouted above the din, asking if the joke was on me. Teresa waved her hand as if to say it was inconsequential, that I shouldn't worry about it.

BETH HAD LEFT A note in the kitchen: PRESS THE BUTTON. THE ONE TO MAKE COFFEE, MY LOVE. She had prepped the filter and grounds, poured the water.

I pressed, went to brush my teeth, and my cell phone rang.

The readout: PRIVATE NUMBER. I hoped it wasn't the Police Benevolent Association. My guess wasn't that far off.

"Glenn Steffey here, Mr. Rutledge," he said, "from Manatee County."

"Morning, detective," I said. "How can I help you?"

"You know the term, 'BOLO,' I'm sure."

"I've heard it used on television."

"Well, we need your help there in Key West. Would you be on the lookout for the people we dealt with yesterday?"

For the second time in thirty-six hours I envisioned hundred-dollar bills flying off into the sky.

"All of the people?" I said. "Are they missing?"

"Just Beeson and the mechanics. None of them are answering their cell phones. We found Anya Timber at her condominium on Longboat Key. She told us that she hasn't seen or heard from any of them."

"Surely Beeson picked up his daughter at school yesterday," I said.

"Yes, then failed to return to our office for more discussions, as planned. "

"Was he driving that Escape?"

"The last time we saw him," said Steffey. "Ford named their product well. None of his other cars have left the crime scene building."

"Maybe you don't know this," I said, "but that mechanic, Edwin Torres, told me that Beeson keeps several other collector cars in a warehouse up there somewhere. He may have traded the Escape for... shit, if I can remember..."

"Did he say what models were stored?"

"I'm trying to think. I know he mentioned a Mercury Marauder and a mid-90s Ford Lightning pickup truck."

"Marauder?"

"It's a glorified Grand Marquis," I said. "It has dual exhausts and sporty wheels, more horsepower and monotone trim. It looks like those sneaky-ass stealth cars the Highway Patrol uses these days."

"Gotcha," said Steffey. "I'll access his state registration records, start looking for everything he owns. I'm looking at a photo of a Marauder on my laptop right now. It looks like a perfect alternative escape."

"I don't know where his ex-wife lived, but..."

"We checked it out completely, and placed a deputy in the neighborhood."

MY CELL RANG FIVE seconds later.

"Mr. Rutledge, sir?"

"You don't always have to say 'Sir' to the man with the cash, Mr. Fecko. What's up?"

"Time for a couple visitors? Newcomers to the local business community?"

"Coffee?" I said.

"Mountain Dew for me, if you have it," said Wiley. "Otherwise black coffee for both of us, thanks."

10

FECKO AND TANNER MUST have called from seventy-five steps away. One minute later, Dubbie softly rang my brass bell one time. I invited them onto the porch and asked Tanner if he would rather have beer than coffee.

"I've already had two," he said. "If I do three before ten in the morning, I lose count come evening. I get into too much trouble in the wee hours when the drink count goes haywire."

"Legal trouble?" I said.

"A general reduction in standards. Guys who don't deserve the drinks I buy them and women as ugly as the guys I bought drinks for."

"No fights?"

"Against my religion," he said. "When the knuckles come out, I crawl to the exit."

Dubbie wore ratty plaid Bermudas and a blue T-shirt that read, SPECIALLY DESIGNED TO PRESERVE FRESHNESS. Fecko looked more respectable in clean-looking jeans, a Blue Heaven ball cap and a blue striped sport shirt. He carried a manila folder with loose pages sticking out.

I carried out three tall cups of sweet, black Bustelo. Wiley sat in the chair I had used two days earlier when Liska was working on his computer. Dubbie chose to stand, so I sat at the table. On the wall above Wiley's head was a yard-long section of driftwood I had found years ago on Boca Grande. Water and wind had shaped it to resemble a bird's wings in graceful flight. I recalled that Liska's eyes had drifted up to study it several times during our talk. I always had thought that the natural sculpture offered an image of absolute freedom. I wondered if Liska had seen it the same way, if it had added to his distraction.

"What brings you two out so early?" I said.

"We're in a bind, procedure-wise," said Wiley. "Something's funky with Ocilla Ramirez."

"Is she dead?" I said.

"I have no knowledge of that. But a county detective dropped by our secret hideout an hour ago and read me the riot act."

"Let me guess," I said. "Your web search two days ago, before I advised Dubbie not to use your own computers."

"In so many words, that's what he told us," said Wiley. "We lifted a red flag on a county surveillance. Which means the woman is a heavy hitter with ongoing history. How did we rate a warning instead of a bust?"

"Sheriff Liska called you the Bumsnoops."

It took Fecko about five seconds. "Of course. Our new status. Tallahassee told him that we had been granted our license."

"The city knows, too," I said.

Wiley and Dubbie exchanged glances, raised their eyebrows then nodded at me.

I felt like I was running a two-man domestic spy ring.

Hell... I was.

I had no idea how far Marnie had progressed with her news scoop, or if she was still chasing details. "I'd still like to have Ocilla's client list and work schedule," I said. "But if the sheriff is monitoring local Internet traffic, you may need to limit your time in the library as well. Or not use it at all."

Wiley waved his hand to indicate no sweat.

"I thought you had to show a library card," I said. "Sign up to get in line to use their equipment. Can't they trace these queries right back to you?"

Wiley's eyes showed pity. "Four things you carry in your wallet," he said. "Your driver's license, a credit card, a library card and your VA card. Correct?"

"I have those," I said. "I also have a discount card for B.O.'s Fish Wagon."

"Damn," said Fecko. "That's better than being mayor."

"Better than mayor means Buddy Owen buys you a beer. He does that only when your name is Buffett."

"That's okay," said Dubbie, "a friend's a friend."

"Back to my explanation," said Wiley, "the four items a homeless person needs are a welfare card, a Florida ID card, a VA card and a library card. Welfare and VA speak for themselves. The one from the state is almost identical to a driver's license but, with the photo, it identifies you to cops you haven't met yet. That can save trips to the Concrete Hotel because they know you're not some out-of-state scumbag hiding from warrants. You're just a local wino looking for a bush to sleep under."

"Gotcha," I said. "How does that..."

"The library card is important for two reasons," he said. "First, the library is the Great Escape from cold and rain and sunburn. It's the place to find air conditioning on hot summer days that'll ruin a man who is two-thirds ruined already. And, like last week, it wards off hypothermia during a cold snap."

A world separate from my own, not by far. All I could do was nod my head.

Wiley went on. "Second, the library is county property and the sheriff's deputies earn overtime there. Their job is to keep bad cases from ranting or nodding out, or pissing on the sofas and chairs. Mostly the pissing. If you have a current card, they're less likely to boot you if you stay awake and look busy. With me so far?"

All I could do was nod the affirmative.

"When one of our kindred souls catches the westbound," said Fecko, "goes to hide in the Alley Up Above, the first things harvested from the body are the cash, the ID and the library card. Bear in mind, it's usually a man who would want it that way. He surely doesn't need those items anymore."

I felt like I had just attended a college seminar. Wiley's pity had been for my lack of street smarts. "You're packing a supply of library cards?"

Wiley shrugged. "I trade cigarettes for them."

"What if they're watching you surf as you go?" I said. "What if that deputy taps you on the shoulder while you're deep in your research?"

"I tell him I was looking up old football scores and the computer reverted to the last person's Google search. If you mention the root kernel in directory mode, you really twist their heads."

"You guys are going to be good at this," I said.

Dubbie Tanner grinned broadly but said nothing.

"Can I ask more questions? I said. "Such as, this 'hideout,' as you called it. Where the deputy knocked on your door this morning. What's that?"

"I graduated," said Dubbie. "I quit living out of my Chevy Caprice and bought a three-bed, two-bath on Staples."

"And paid cash," said Fecko. "His secret wealth's no secret anymore. We have slummed-down New Town which is the stone opposite of gentrified. I'm his low-rent tenant and we have impressive office space in the third bedroom."

"I'll need adjustment time to picture you two as suburban roommates," I said.

"He's an okay guy with weird habits," said Wiley, "but it works out. On a week-to-week basis I smell better for having regular showers. The only drawback is that my business partner would rather buy Natural Light than toilet bowl cleaner."

I withheld comment. "Okay, what does it take in the State of

Florida to become a private eye? Two days ago you mentioned certification."

"Fecko," said Tanner, pointing at Wiley, "this guy over here, long
ago, had phone company experience. Before he sidetracked himself
to cheap bourbon blends. He was doing undercover snoop work on
line-hookup fraud and possible sabotage. The work required security clearances and tech schooling. His career was documented by
what was then called Southern Bell. So he provided the state with
the old documentation, and they waived his two-year requirement
of a limited license. He went straight to a full-boogie manager's
ticket. I'm a licensed intern working under his supervision."

"What do you have for me?"

"First," said Dubbie, "I want you to know something. I wasn't
part of that silent conspiracy last night. I came by hoping you were
home. They were all sitting here on the porch and they told me
why. It wasn't two minutes later you appeared. Hell, I knew Teresa,
too. And I know you two were ancient history, but I'm sorry."

I nodded a thank-you. "It was a bad surprise. But it gives us even
more incentive to chase down whatever the cops can't find."

Fecko rattled through his sheaf of papers. "I printed out a bunch
of shit in the office last night, if I may..."

"Please."

"The late Emerson Caldwell started Currie Forms in Toronto
almost twenty-five years ago with two partners. Their first products
were knock-offs of Igloo coolers and ice trays that made cubes
shaped like pyramids and half-circles and wiggly worms.
Eventually they found their first real money-maker, a flexible,
zebra-striped, multi-speed vibrator."

"Why not human necessities like yo-yos and wax lips?" I said.

Fecko stared without saying a word.

"Sorry... the pressure," I said. "Go ahead."

"Currie Forms parlayed their earnings into better designs for
boat hulls, hot tubs, shower enclosures and motel ice buckets, all of

them manufactured in China. That's when things began to escalate. Twelve years ago Emerson Caldwell bought out his minority partners and sold Currie to the Canadian conglomerate called Branchdale. He also agreed to stay on as CEO for seven years, but Branchdale bought him out of his job after three years."

"Sweet deal," I said. "He made money twice, on the sale and the buyout."

"And he escaped a shitstorm," said Fecko. "Currie Division is struggling because China closed two of their plants, allegedly due to PVC pollution of rivers. From what I've seen online, China likes to close foreign-owned operations after stealing their designs. To make matters worse, a company based in Valdosta, Georgia, is producing competing products with lower prices and shipping costs. Currie is hurting."

"It's amazing there isn't more violence in the business world," I said.

"It's no different than the rest of society," said Dubbie, "except it's white collar crime when the honchos do it. And the stress at the top brings on strokes and heart attacks."

Wiley handed me a one-page printout. Its logo identified a cardiology clinic in Toronto. Its summary made out Emerson Caldwell to be a ticking clock. He was off the scale in several risk categories, close to danger in all the rest.

"Bad report card," I said. "Aren't records like this supposed to be private?"

Fecko agreed. "That's what tipped me to keep digging. It wasn't my genius that spit this out of my printer."

"Your modesty is your new bad habit," said Tanner. "You are smarter for sure than the people who can poison someone and make police in two countries think it was a heart attack."

I eyeballed the two of them. They were about to deliver big.

"The cardiology report is fake," said Dubbie, "planted online to fool anyone who might be nosing around. There's a clinic with a similar name in Montreal and it has a great reputation. But that

Queen Street address in Toronto is a fish-and-chips joint in an area called Little Portugal."

"And who would look around," I said, "but the badge boys? You think they were the main target?"

"Seems like a lot of work, doesn't it?" said Tanner. "Why not just hack him to bits like the other stiff?"

The stiff that had been shot, not stabbed, I thought, but I kept quiet on that. I dug out my phone, found Beth Watkins's name, pressed the prompt.

She took it on three rings. "Is Superman just waking up?"

"Hours ago," I said. "He kicked off his booties and his feet got cold. Where's your Emerson Caldwell about now?"

"*Mine?*" she said. "Someone else's Caldwell is chilling at the funeral home on Kennedy Drive. Waiting for his cremation and paperwork to fly home to Canada."

"You have every right to order an autopsy, correct?"

No response.

"Please do it," I said. "Nothing ventured, nothing gained."

"The medical examiner signed off. The county and the Feds both came up with reports on his medical history. There's nothing inconsistent with a heart attack."

"Did you personally verify those report sources?" I said. "Because if this deal goes sour, it'll be your failure before the other agencies throw their babies to the wolves. That's one of the bennies for bottom cop in the hierarchy."

"It will piss off my boss and Caldwell's family members," said Beth. "And the piss will come straight down to me, the bottom cop. Along with a lot of shit from the Feds, Liska, and the media."

Something in her words pulled a string in my brain. I motioned for Dubbie and Wiley to listen up as I spoke to Beth. "In our focus on Teresa last night, I forgot to tell you a piece of trivia from my trip home. There was a man on the Miami-to-Key West flight, the gregarious type, and we shared a cab from the airport into Old

Town. His name is Robert Fonteneau and he mentioned that he had come from Canada to tend to the affairs of a friend who recently died of a heart attack."

"Thank you for the warning," she said. "He'll be in the vanguard of those who will be pissed at me. What prompted your suggestion that I insist on an autopsy?"

"I don't know, maybe an old TV show or something."

Dubbie motioned with his hand and whispered, "Potassium injection."

"I heard that," said Beth. "Are your snoops obstructing my investigation?"

"I'll take all the blame," I said. "Just trying to help."

"Thank you, Alex, for caring about my career," she said. "An autopsy was in the back of my mind, but my mind was overruled by professional pressure." She clicked off her phone.

"We anticipated this path of inquiry and resistance," said Wiley. He held another page printed from the web and read aloud, "Canadian consular staff can request a local investigation in the event of a crime or death, if there is evidence of suspicious circumstances. Consulate General of Canada, 200 South Biscayne Boulevard, Miami. With a phone number and an email address."

"Will they accept anonymous tips?" I said.

Wiley smiled. "Can't hurt to try."

"And why this guy Fonteneau," I said, "instead of Caldwell's wife?"

"Her schedule may be full," said Dubbie. "She finally accepted Wiley's 'friend' request on Facebook. We haven't had time to dig deep, but our first impression is they've been 'kinda married' for the past seven years."

"Emerson is a Key West kind of guy, eh?"

"Probably, but we need to do more work on her," said Tanner. "There's a chance that Christi Caldwell is an anywhere kind of cougar."

Wiley extracted a four-by-six photo print from his envelope.

"Christi Caldwell is a lovely woman. She could attract partners wherever she wished. We pulled this off of Facebook."

For about ten seconds we looked at the picture in silence. The collar-length light colored hair, the high cheekbones, cute chin and straight nose.

I finally spoke. "She could be Beth Watkins's sister."

"I thought the same thing," said Tanner. "Damn close and spooky."

Wiley put his papers on the table. "I'll look into her when I can't chase Ocilla."

"Can I ask you one question, personal as hell?" I said to Fecko.

"The personal side of my life has been on public display for eight or nine years," he said. "Why would I worry about one question?"

"What caused you to sober up, all of a sudden?"

"Fair enough," he said. "Two reasons. I was panhandling on Front Street and a passerby threw a handful of pennies on the sidewalk. I was scrambling around on the hot concrete, sticking my hands under the sandals of tourists, burning my fingertips to grab pennies before anyone else could get to them. I mean, picture it. Pennies. Fucking pennies."

"Gotcha," I said.

"And the second reason dips into the extra-personal," he said, "but you asked."

I waved my hand. "It's not a requirement."

"No, it's part of my rehab," said Fecko. "Part of baring my soul. Or my previous soul."

"Okay," I said.

"You might regret this," said Dubbie.

"I woke up still drunk one afternoon in July," said Wiley, "and grabbed the wrong tube from my kit. I brushed my teeth with hemorrhoid ointment." He shook off his mental image of the memory. "I couldn't eat or drink for a day and a half."

I admired his decision, but I wasn't sure how to react to his story.

I smiled but held back my laughter.

Dubbie Tanner kept a remarkably straight face. "He couldn't talk, either," he said. "That was the best part."

Then we all had a laugh.

I extracted my wallet, pulled out four fifties, handed them two each. "Keep on doing what you're doing," I said. "Both of you. I think we've hooked a fish here. The trick will be to play it right."

Fecko stood, stretched proudly, put a hundred bucks in his front trouser pocket and bum-shuffled toward the door. "We'll boat it," he said.

AROUND 11 AM MARNIE'S bright orange Jeep stopped in front of the house. I wasn't ready to face her. If she had found out that I held back info as a favor to Liska, she would literally kick my ass. While she had cut back on karate recently, her skills were genuine.

But it was Sam behind the wheel. "Fish sandwich, Square Grouper?" he said. "I'll drive."

"Splendid," I said. "My turn to buy."

By the time we hit Stock Island I was no longer in the mood for a 45-mile round-trip. "Hogfish Grill?" I said.

Sam veered down Macdonald Avenue. "Your call, I'm good with it."

He wove his way around to the funky restaurant, past dozens of ancient cars with faded paint, mismatched tires, duct tape repairs, drooping headliners. Unlike years ago, most of the trailer homes in the area were in better shape than the cars.

Sam found a parking slot down toward Fishbusters. Climbing from Marnie's Jeep we were greeted with a thunderous fly-by, four Navy jets in formation. Inside, every table was taken, so we chose stools on the far side of the bar. Creedence Clearwater Revival sang about looking out a back door, and electric fans on tall stands provided a blanket of white noise, put the restaurant chatter in the background.

Sam asked for a Beck's and a cheeseburger. I ordered a hot

Bloody Mary and a Pork Poor Boy.

The server winced and scratched her shirt collar.

"Changed my mind," I said. "Shrimp Poor Boy, instead."

She smiled, wrote it down.

The Creedence song faded into "Ophelia," by The Band, and I heard Levon Helm sing the line, "Ashes of laughter, the ghost is clear..." and my thoughts whipped back to Teresa.

"Was she in the *Citizen* this morning?" I said.

Sam knew who I meant, and nodded. "Her mother died of a stroke last year, and her natural father went down to diabetes a month later. The FDLE finally found Paulie Cottrell vacationing in Aspen. Once he was informed, the cops gave Marnie the go-ahead to publish. She said that City Hall is like a funeral parlor. There's a black ribbon on her office door."

I hadn't heard that Estelle Cottrell had passed away. Paul Cottrell, Teresa's stepfather, the city's zoning inspector for years, had retired a while back. He dabbled in real estate for about six weeks, said "Screw it," and took his retirement seriously.

"I guess Marnie had success with her story," I said. "Does that give her a bit of job security she didn't have a week ago?"

"Neutral effect," said Sam. "She sold the piece to an online syndicator, then the *Citizen* editor asked her forgiveness before insisting that her follow-ups stay local. They also assured her that the paper's financials were in fine shape, no danger of shutting down. Now she's her own biggest problem. Her passion is print journalism. On days she doesn't feel like writing, she imagines she's burned out on Key West. That might be the truth. It's not the newspaper, her colleagues or her boss. She's suffering Rock Fever, as we called it years ago."

The server brought our food. We concentrated on stuffing our faces for several minutes. I wasn't sure why she had steered me away from the pork, but the shrimp was the rare type that hadn't been to Miami and back in a reefer truck before being served in the

Lower Keys.

"Has Marnie considered leaving town?" I said.

"She talks about independent city newspapers, medium-sized cities, like they're the last American pinnacles of truth and high ideals. I try to remind her that news is everywhere, but my income flows best in warmer climates."

"What options do you have?"

"Hell," said Sam. "I can hustle charters anywhere there's salt water. Every year I spend a little more time in south Alabama. I could build a clientele, talk some of my regulars into fishing the Panhandle and Mobile Bay, the Mississippi coast. She could look around Pensacola and Mobile."

"Okay, let's say you take her to Alabama. There's no guarantee that the papers up there are solvent enough to promise her a future. While you're out making a living, she might have to sit around at home, bored."

"We'll cross that bridge when we run into it."

"Are you sure you want to see that bridge?" I said. "She's done well these last few years. She could go back to hard time on the sauce."

"Oh, shit, we don't need to go backward."

"What do you think will happen first?"

"What do you mean?" he said.

"The world runs out of newspapers or the ocean runs out of fish?"

11

I LEANED AGAINST A fish-cleaning table, studied the water behind the Hogfish Grill and watched foot-long fish more skilled at begging handouts than the city's ubiquitous street people. It was too early in the year for silver king tarpon, the creature I preferred to observe, though I hated that they had learned to beg. The air was sticky with marine moisture cooked out of the L-shaped boardwalk by the tropical January sun. Several sailboats, nosed to the dock like horses to a hitching rail, bobbed between pilings a few yards west of where I stood.

I became fixated on small items. Styrofoam flecks, off-white paint spatters, gull droppings, nylon fishing line, strands from old dock lines. Out of all that, for some reason, came the memory of my first lunch with Teresa Barga, our first date, years ago. We had stopped for sandwiches at B.O.'s Fish Wagon. Afterward, like sneaky teenagers, we had kissed in her city-owned car, a ratty ancient Taurus not worth the tires it rode on.

Escaping my renegade memory, I returned to the bar where the lunch crowd was leaving, mostly locals headed for business offices or back to their homes. Sam started to pay the tab when the server took our food baskets, but I stopped him. It was my turn. Pocketing his wallet, he wisely and generously ordered two more drinks. I went for an Amstel Light, not wanting to push my limits with noon vodka.

"You blew town," said Sam. He hadn't mentioned my trip until then.

"Gainful employment."

"What's Sarasota like?" he said.

"I'm sure there are plenty of wonderful folks there."

"And the ones you met?"

"They're apparently into over-eating, sport-fucking and classic cars."

"Where do they find time for cars?"

I told him a condensed version of my twenty-four-hour Sarasota Saga. The chance encounter at Saluté, the chat on Olivia Street, my agreement to work for Beeson, the change of plans, the quiet flight, and the awful building full of exciting muscle cars. I dropped in the back-story of Eileen's gift for art, then Anya's strip tease and aquatic ballet, the naked photo I happened to find in the guest bedroom and Justin Beeson's morning hangover. Finally my exterior photos, Luke Tharpe's godawful discovery of Amanda's body, the procedures of the investigative team.

Sam nodded as if he understood everything, which meant he didn't. "You left without telling anyone? Not even Carmen?"

"Things happened quickly. It was a cash job offer."

"Beeson knew all about you beforehand?"

"He asked around town. My name came up. He heard good things."

"Why didn't you back out when you saw his building? Have you no shame? They rent cars in Sarasota, right?"

"It was a fat paycheck," I said. "Then I saw the man's car collection and I hoped my assignment might expand. Pictures for insurance companies, show entry forms, what have you. I love to shoot cars. All you need is sunshine. You don't have to wait for them to smile."

"And now this joker's disappeared?"

"The detective bitched because Beeson wasn't making himself available. Those were the words he used."

"Big money and flash cars," said Sam. "A foxy girlfriend, high-end child support and an expensive ex-wife. Now this boy needs to sell a building because it's flopped a couple of concepts. Can we assume cash crunch on all fronts?"

"Maybe not current," I said, "but impending. I hope it's not current. He still owes me expense money."

"You think the fox and the ex-wife were sporting around?"

"I don't know if the women were an item. I don't know if that picture was taken before or after the divorce. But they sure looked like close friends."

"Okay," said Sam, "check me on this. You have talked about Justin, Anya, Eileen, Amanda, Edwin and Luke."

"Correct." I drained my Amstel, balanced the cardboard coaster on top of it so I wouldn't get served another.

"For my money," he said, "the four adults all did it. They brought you in as the confusion factor. Beeson knew your reputation as a photographer but also knew that you had worked with the cops, and not just in this county. You have credibility up the wazoo. You are what they call impugnable, don't let it go to your head."

"Don't even say it, Sam."

"Already did, Alex. Think about it. Forty-eight hours ago you didn't know any of these people. They were total strangers. Now you know one hell of a lot about all six. Beeson set you up to be everyone's alibi, discounting the daughter. You haven't heard the last of this nervous little drama."

WHEN I GOT HOME I faced up to a task I dreaded. I called my brother Tim's number in Orlando to let him know about Teresa.

"Hey, old man, what's poppin'?" he said.

Right to the nut, a family tradition: "Teresa's dead."

"Hmm. Well, I suppose I could have used better news. But if it had to be anyone... Did her cop boyfriend take her out?"

"What makes you say that?"

"Well, our time with the girl more or less overlapped, so I got a feel for where he was coming from. From a distance, I mean."

"Well, there are no suspects so far."

"Truth is, from what I heard, she did me like she did you. She lets her gents down hard, as they say."

"Everything cool?" I said.

"Cool as no school," said Tim. "Thanks for making the call. I know delivering bad news is not your favorite pastime."

I hung up relieved that Tim had taken it well. He was dealing with his recently acknowledged alcoholism, doing his best not to slip back into the sauce. There was always the chance that shit news might tip the teetering balance.

AN HOUR LATER I walked the aisles in Fausto's Food Palace, greeting half the town's residents and filling my basket—not forgetting Mountain Dew for Fecko. All of life's necessities. The weight of my selections told me it was time to pay up. I had to carry them all on the Cannondale.

I chose the shortest checkout line, not that anyone in line or working the register might be in a hurry. A woman in front of me said, "Talking the other morning at breakfast, it was a shame we didn't know Greg was in trouble. Have they questioned all of his girlfriends?"

I hadn't noticed that I was in line right behind Cathy, our server at Pepe's.

"All of them?" I said.

"There was the older woman, the Latina who dropped him off for work every so often. She came in one time, drunk, demanding to know where he was. It was his day off, I remember."

"You know for sure she was Hispanic?"

"She had a first name... You know, it sounded like..."

"Ocilla?"

"Just like that," said Cathy. "There was also the woman who

taught art at the college and the girl who bartended at Irish Kevin's. Then there was the bubbly doll from up north who would come to town every so often and hang with him."

"How far up north?" I asked.

"Funny accent. Long vowels like, maybe, New England."

"Did the Latina come in to look for him after he quit showing up for work?"

Cathy shook her head. "Nobody did."

"Busy dude, Greg Pulver."

"Always on time," she said. "What a shame."

MY BICYCLE BALANCING ACT could have been a featured routine at Mallory Square's Sunset Celebration. Fausto's policy of no plastic bags added two degrees of difficulty. Beer, soft drinks, crushables in two bags. I wanted to make the light at Fleming and Simonton but didn't quite.

A jogger on the sidewalk pumped her legs in place while she waited for the green. She looked fortyish and fit, wore a Nike exercise monitor on one arm, an orange iPod Nano on the other. Neon green wires ran to her translucent earbuds and she carried small barbells in each hand.

A kid in his late teens wearing shorts and no shirt coasted slowly by on a bike. He grabbed the woman's left butt cheek, gave it a mean squeeze and began to turn south on Simonton. Without a word she whirled, wound up like a major-league pitcher and threw a strike. The barbell clocked the kid in his upper back. One of his feet slipped off its pedal. He slumped on the bike, ran over his foot, fell and skidded under a parked delivery van, whacking his head on its rear bumper. He tried to stand but slumped again, then threw up next to the curb.

The woman skipped in a circle and yelled, "I waited two weeks for that, you sick ass grabber. Now you will stop fucking with me!" She ran toward the injured young man, retrieved the tiny barbell, called him a dipshit, took a deep breath and jogged back toward Duval Street. Not a single bystander offered to help the punk until a woman who hadn't seen what happened stopped her car, got out tapping hurriedly on her cell.

AFTER STASHING MY GROCERIES I checked for messages on the land-line phone I keep for faxing quotes. The number is listed, so I get a few local calls. Four messages from friends who had read about Teresa and knew that she and I once had been a couple. Sympathies, wishing me well, "thinking" about me. One, behind the times, offered me strength in my time of loss. Said I was "young enough" to find someone else when the time was right. Down deep, I wondered about strength and why I felt compelled to avenge the death of a woman who had dumped my ass like a cold Conch fritter.

I called Dubbie Tanner's cell and it went to voicemail. "Our mystery woman, Ms. Ocilla, may be a bar-hopper," I said. "You might do just as well on the rum telegraph as your partner will online. In fact, why don't you ask him to back off that library card trick for a day or two and save it for when you really might need it? Also, are we okay in regard to your fees and expenses? I threw around that cash yesterday, but I have no idea which of us is getting screwed."

FIVE IN THE AFTERNOON and it took my ripe T-shirt to remind me to shower. Time to make my daily visit to the one-month-old, all-weather loudspeakers. I put on the re-mastered edition of "There Goes Rhymin' Simon," set it to start with the four acoustic bonus tracks, vintage songs-in-progress and a lesson in songwriting. I already had shampoo in my hair when it cycled to that verse of "Kodachrome" that mentions all the girls Paul knew when he was single. Teresa jumped back into my thoughts, in the place where she and I had played games and made love in better days. Why did this memory clip keep looping? Was I going to be haunted by the ghost of a woman I had stopped loving years ago?

I TOWELED OFF AND found a message from Beth Watkins on my cell. "I'm your local stinger, staked out with Pete Trainor. We're waiting in an upscale home to bust the dude responsible for a mess of break-ins near the Casa Marina. Lieutenant Trainor baited the trap on Facebook. He posted as if he was the home's owner and told the whole world he was in Ocean Reef for the day. I don't know how long this might take, especially if it works. If you see me tonight, it will be a fine surprise to both of us."

While shaving I failed to hear a call from Marnie Dunwoody. Her message said, "Wanted to thank you again. I just got a late boost to my story on The Tideline. I happened to take a call at my desk from a Toronto newspaper. They wanted a local statement regarding the Canadian Consulate's request for an autopsy of Mr. Emerson Caldwell. The consul's refusing to talk about it, but such requests are made only when there's a high probability of foul play. So I got to refile my piece and double-dip on my flat fee and royalties. I owe you a shrimp remoulade, my great enabler."

I didn't know if Wiley was Fecko's nickname or real name. It sure as hell fit.

I called Beth back, trusting that her phone was set to vibrate. She answered with a muffled, "Unh-huh."

"I know you can't talk, so I'll be quick. Make a formal request for the autopsy. It's got to happen. Trust me on this."

"Umm, okay..." Her voice went quiet for a moment. "Action here," she whispered. "Don't call back to explain."

I drank a beer and went to meditate.

MY DREAM-FREE NAP WAS cut short by the slap of metal against metal. Carmen Sosa doesn't like the volume of my brass bell. She wraps her hand around the bell's flare and rattles the clapper. It sounds like someone smacking two glass jelly jars against each other.

Bleary-eyed, scratching my belly, I stumbled to the porch.

131

She laughed at me. "You need to perk up. Drink a Red Bull." She wore dark slacks and a pale blue top, on her way home from work at the post office.

"Blech," I said. " I've had only one of those, ever. It tasted like I was drinking a cheap brand of floral air freshener."

"Be like me," she said. "I killed a Fat Bastard last night."

"Pardon me?"

"It's a wine joke."

"Got it," I said. "It's also an admission of loneliness."

"Maybe. You don't have an open red, do you?"

"I will make it happen," I said.

Carmen Sosa has lived for years with her daughter, Maria Rolley, at the end of Dredgers Lane. Her father, Hector Ayusa, and her late mother, Cecilia, had lived across from my home since my arrival. After Cecilia died, Carmen swapped homes with her father to give Maria, a teenager, more space and to distance Hector from a houseful of sad memories. More than a former lover, Carmen is my closest friend, my inner strength and a font of humor. She holds my house keys, computer password, most of my secrets and the ability to read my mind. I keep my '66 Shelby GT-350H in the garage she rents to me. I have always thought of Maria as the daughter I had never had, though cranky moments in her teen years have forced me to retreat for safety's sake. I love them both and depend on their friendship.

I returned to the porch and handed Carmen a glass of J. Lohr Cabernet.

"I apologize for waking you up," she said. "You've had a rough couple of days."

"You're forgiven. Teresa's death is awful, and my trip to Sarasota was gruesome."

"Actually, now that I think about it," she said, "I retract half of my apology. I'm not one to speak ill of the dead, but Teresa was an idiot. I hope they play 'Lyin' Eyes' at her funeral."

"Rough words," I said.

"She fucked you over so badly, she deserved that boy she ended up with."

"Ended up?"

"You know, in the sense that no one ever 'goes out to eat' at Denny's. They 'end up' at Denny's. He was, to my mind, a squeeze of last resort. He was the only place still open, and greasy as well."

"You know Darrin Marsh?"

"Not in the Biblical sense," she said, "but it was a near miss."

"Do tell."

"Not a proud moment, in fact scary. He kept showing up at the post office, sending small packages to people named Marsh, so I assumed they were gifts for family members. He'd crack jokes, tell me he liked my hair, my eyes. This was before he became a cop. He was an electrician. He worked four days a week for a company on Ramrod. One afternoon he asked if I would meet him at La Tratt for a margarita. I forget why, but he picked the right goddamn day. I was so ready for a margarita, I could have chewed the glass."

I raised my wine to her. "That's the woman I know and love."

"Except, after we split a dinner and left, he was so ready to get his hands on my big titties, he could barely kiss without drooling. If these charmers had been Cuban bread dough, the way he kneaded them, we could have made sandwiches for fifty people."

"I recall that I have been guilty of the same crime," I said.

"Alex, in case you don't know, you possess a subtlety that is scarce in the modern male. You didn't squeeze. Your hands felt like they were molding silk purses full of gold dust."

"Why is this the first time I have heard this?"

She waved off my question as if I had asked about her shoe size. "Anyway, we were parked on Whitehead at the time, so I told him I wasn't comfortable with the neighborhood. I wanted to go home."

"Did that become a problem?"

"No, he took me home for one last wrestling match. But first he had to show me his arsenal, show me I didn't need to be afraid of the natives, as he called them."

"A gun under the seat?" I said.

"No, it was in this compartment, like a console some cars have between bucket seats. Except this was on his headliner, between the sun visors. The thing was locked solid, but he twisted a key in the slot and out dropped a nasty-looking little gun. I was on the edge of a massive freak-out but he popped it right back in its hiding place and closed the compartment. Brought me back here to the lane, massaged the girls for a half-minute before I pretended I was sick and might puke in his truck. He didn't even wait to make sure I got into the house okay. I had no problem turning him down the next six times he asked me out. He finally got a clue."

"Well, that clue at least," I said.

"To her credit," said Carmen, "Teresa almost redeemed herself when she was nice to your brother. But that whole situation reeked of ulterior horseshit, too, so I don't know..."

"I've been nice to you for years and these postal service shirts, I can't even scope the cleavage. I can't remember what you looked like upside-down."

"Which is one view you never got anyway, best as I recall," she said. "But if you need an ego boost, there have been nights in the past year when I wished I could have walked across the lane in my jammies and crawled into bed with you. Just to hug, be next to a warm body. Nights when I missed my mother, and nights when I would sit awake wondering if I'll die of cancer, too. Plus, it was so much easier to be single when Maria was little."

"Is she Miss Eagle-Eye?" I said.

"I can barely date, she puts me under so much scrutiny. She analyzes everything, sees every event on multiple levels. She knows what I expect of her in her friendships, and she, of course, expects the same of me. Which is why I will not have the second glass of wine you are about to pour for me. Oh, wait, just one more."

Before I could add to her glass, Carmen changed her mind and went home to spend time with Maria.

AROUND SEVEN O'CLOCK MY house phone rang. I didn't recognize the Caller ID, but the 941 area code suggested that it might be Detective Glenn Steffey. But no, it was Edwin Torres, the mechanic from Beeson's operation in Sarasota.

"You're back in the Florida Keys," he said.

"You just called me here, Edwin. What can I do for you?"

"Look, I need a favor. It would make life easier for me, if you ever come back this way, if you didn't repeat what I said, you know, me bad-mouthing Luke. Of course you can tell me to go straight to hell."

"I have no reason to repeat any part of our conversation," I said.

"Well, you never know," said Torres. "I thought I'd ask... I mean, I would really appreciate it."

"You got it. Everything okay up there in your part of the world?"

"I guess," he said. "Those cops kicked me loose after you left, and I ain't heard from them anymore. My boss at UPS was cool with me missing hours, after he heard what happened. I was afraid I'd have to go back to work at Midas, replacing exhaust systems."

"How's Justin Beeson doing?"

"Fuck him," said Torres. "He hasn't called me like I hoped he would."

"Why would you want that?" I said.

"Well... shit. Why else? To find out if I still work for him. Thanks for that favor. If I ever get to the Keys, I'd love a ride in your car."

I DIDN'T RECOGNIZE THE vehicle that pulled into the lane and stopped in front of the house. Through the half-shut blinds I saw the illuminated car top pizza delivery sign.

Then I heard Beth's voice: "My treat, I'll get it."

I pulled plates from the cupboard, set out trays.

She did the transaction and carried in two pizza flats. "I called the order while I was walking here. I had a feeling you wouldn't want to go out."

After we inhaled our first couple of slices, I asked about her B&E stakeout.

"We arrested a housewife from Sugarloaf, where the county also has a backlog of daytime break-ins. This babe was truly retro, trying to facilitate an old-fashioned diet pill habit. In fairness, I should give her credit for being clever. We caught her with twelve digital cameras, seven portable hard drives, a duffel full of iPods and iPhones and three laptops set up to create counterfeit prescription orders. She created bogus email accounts for a dozen doctors between here and Key Largo. As of five o'clock today, every drug store and grocery store pharmacy in the Keys will send follow-ups to doctors' certified email addresses before dispensing drugs."

"That should pull down some respect from Chicken Neck's boys."

"Remains to be seen," she said. "Did you call your brother?"

I told her it had gone okay, and repeated Tim's question about whether Darrin Marsh might have killed Teresa. "Before I forget," I said, "didn't you say that the security cameras at The Tideline were out of order when Marsh found the bodies?"

I caught her with her mouth full. Her eyes opened wider and she nodded.

"Carmen told me this evening that Darrin Marsh was an electrician before he became a cop. Here comes the other shoe. She went out with him once and never again. He didn't threaten her, but he had a handgun stashed in an overhead console in his truck."

"Lieutenant Trainor and I talked about Darrin today. He called him a 'piece of work' and made it sound ominously close to 'piece of shit.' Said he'd had to work with him for six years. Then he said, 'Six years too long.'"

We finally quit eating and sat quietly, not talking for at least five minutes. I had no idea where Beth's thoughts had gone until she said, "I love it when my job goes well, like it did today. I love it less when it gets complicated and jumbled up, but I don't really blame you as much as I sound like I do."

"You weed your way through the complications, lovely lady," I said, "you'll be proud again on the far side of the mess. Every so often you take risks. Calculated risks, I hope. You do it with your smarts and instinct, the payoff's even sweeter."

"Are you up for an early night of it?" said Beth. "I have to slide out early for two meetings at the county."

"Yes," I said. "Next question?"

"Care to dance?"

I loved the idea. "Tango colchón? Rumba reclinada?"

"Call it what you like," she said, "but we're going to be barefoot."

We took turns making footprints on the ceiling.

12

BETH WATKINS'S PHONE ALARM chirped before dawn. She turned on a light in the bath to find her clothing in three different rooms. I watched as she dressed in near-darkness then whispered a few words about being careful out there, and she kissed my forehead. The next time I opened my eyes the walls glowed with sunlight dappled by crotons in easy motion outside the window. The bedroom smelled great. The rest of the house smelled of day-old pizza. I opened windows.

More than allowing in fresh air, the open windows informed me that someone over on Eaton Street was using a gas-powered tree trimmer. The racket inspired me not to make coffee at home. I pulled on yesterday's shorts, a fresh shirt and flip-flops and walked 200 yards to Azur on Grinnell for their "Morning After" breakfast.

As I approached the restaurant, a silver BMW X3 wagon backed out of a space near the entrance. The driver was E. Carlton Gamble, an attorney whom I had met several times over the years. His passenger was Robert Fonteneau, Canadian estate rep and pro yakker. Fonteneau fixed his eyes on me, said something to Gamble and pointed. I wondered whether Fonteneau knew of Caldwell's business history—or if he was part of it. At least he had taken my advice on finding an established lawyer.

To my surprise, Gamble pulled back into the parking slot, lowered the windows on both front doors and introduced me to

139

Robert Fonteneau.

"Bob says you shared a cab last evening," said Gamble. "I appreciate the advice you gave him regarding representation."

"And I thank you for your friendly welcome to the island," said Fonteneau. "It was a positive way to begin a mournful duty."

"That's the way Alex is," said Gamble. "Maybe that's why he dates one of the most lovely women in Key West, city detective Beth Watkins."

"I look forward to meeting her," said Fonteneau, "and seeing you again soon."

Even better than fruit and granola was the quiet restaurant's solitude. My cell was muted. For the first time in three days, no one could find me. I lingered over coffee and a side-order croissant, and thought about how I might spend the fresh cash in my pocket and the additional money if Beeson honored my expense invoice. Maybe take Beth to the British Virgins for a week of nothing but sleep and air. I read the *Citizen* headline piece about the sting-arrest of a woman who was linked to a dozen breaking-and-entering complaints. She had been tagged "Scratchity Sue" by Stock Island neighbors who knew of her drug habit. Lieutenant Pete Trainor received credit for the bust, an obvious goodwill gesture on Beth Watkins's part. I didn't recognize the name of the KWPD's "interim" spokesperson—Teresa Barga's replacement.

On the verge of ordering a breakfast beer and blowing off the whole morning, I paid up and hiked back to the lane. A weather-worn bicycle leaning against the screen door warned me. Dubbie Tanner stood inside my porch door. He wore a Scrub Club ball cap and a faded plaid madras sport shirt. He sipped from a can wrapped in a small brown paper bag.

"I like hosting parties at my house," I said. "I never have to drive home through cop stops and roadblocks. What's up?"

"Ocilla Ramirez," he said. "Your call last evening at cocktail hour..." He raised his beer then continued. "You asked that we delay Internet and hit the streets, right?"

I nodded, fearful that the Aristocrats had run afoul of Sheriff Liska's observers.

"Fecko and I were a step ahead of you. We drove out to Big Coppitt at lunchtime yesterday. I gotta say, it's getting cute out there. Bunch of townhouses alongside the highway, pastel all to hell like Necco Wafers."

"Whoa," I said. "Didn't we already decide that Ocilla sub-leases?"

"Right, we guessed... correctly. But my associate and I speculated, as private eyes will do, that it couldn't hurt to look around."

"Ignoring the sheriff's office warning to keep clear of this woman..."

"We checked for surveillance from a block away," said Wiley.

"But on Big Coppitt?" I said. "Even the sheriff can afford to pay a homeowner to mount a camera in the bushes. They could be watching Ocilla's property around the clock."

Dubbie agreed. "We thought of that after the fact," he said. "That's part two of the story."

"Out of curiosity," I said, "what color is Ocilla's house on Big Coppitt?"

He didn't have to think about it. "Stale yellow jelly bean."

"Gotcha."

"Continuing here," said Tanner, "we went to her so-called address and eagle-eye recognized a food thief. In his tough times Fecko used to buy stolen pork chops from the guy."

"Wiley was a food fence?"

"No, he bought them for himself," said Dubbie. "Even winos have to eat. But don't ask about his Night Train marinade."

"What did this thief have to say?"

"He was the actual tenant's cousin. He washes dishes for a living, in four different restaurants. The actual tenant's brother works in five other kitchens. They're all from Nicaragua, not Guatemala, and nine family members share the house."

"Where's this going?" I said.

"Immigration looks hard at restaurants, so kitchens stick to hiring legals for their shit work. People with up-to-date papers, Social Security numbers, people they can put on the books. Once these people are hired, the kitchen never sees them again. But someone always shows up for work. Always. It's the most dependable labor on the island."

"The jobs are sub-leased?" I said.

"Our actual tenant on Crawford has his green card, or white, whatever it takes to please Immigration. He's the actual employee, too. He takes his cut across the board, gets a paycheck, pays taxes, and pays his relatives in cash. He's the one paying the utility bill."

For the second day in a row I felt like I was being schooled, reintroduced to Key West. "And the guys without documents sell pork chops clipped from restaurants?"

"Their jockstrap discount," said Tanner.

Not a pretty picture. "Does this put us closer to Ocilla?" I said.

"Wiley called the cousin to the car, slipped him ten and asked in Spanish how to find the landlady. Wiley speaks the language like a champ. Because of that, we got an address on Seidenberg which brings us to Chapter Two."

"Call it what you want," I said. "But we keep away from Seidenberg."

"We know that now," said Tanner. "We bum-cruised the block and saw the dudes with fresh sunburns posing as cable repair techs. Wiley thinks they were pretending to replace a power supply on a repeater. But they were really swapping out the video transmitter."

"So that's where they have their twenty-four-seven surveillance," I said.

"Either way," added Tanner. "Wiley spotted their safety infractions and improper tools. There was an olive-green Honda Element wedged into the yard. It looked like there were broomsticks inside its back windows. We kept on rolling."

"A handy work vehicle," I said.

"And there's one last thing," he said. "A blip or two in her social life. I'm not sure they pertain to matters at hand."

"Blips tell tales," I said.

"She might be a one-woman escort service." Tanner drank from his beer. "This comes from a bartender at the Casa Marina who shall remain nameless. Except her name is Holly and she happens to drink at the Bottle Cap. Anyway, Holly went home one night last year with a wealthy local man who has since gotten married to a shrew from Dallas. He owns a well-disguised mini-mansion on Riviera. Holly and wealthy man were into a robust Round Two the next morning when his housekeeper, Ocilla Ramirez, walked into the bedroom. Ocilla made a few jealous remarks, so the guy invited her to join in. That's how Holly came to know Ocilla."

"Not the first three-way on the island," I said.

"It was a first for Holly, but to quote: 'I wasn't going to tell her to stop.' A couple of months later Holly saw Ocilla with an elderly tourist fellow at the Casa, doing the leg rub and chug-a-lug routine. Ocilla either didn't recognize or pretended not to know Holly. The drunk pair left together, headed for the elevator. Couple of months after that, the same routine, in the Casa Marina bar, with a middle-aged woman."

"That's a significant blip," I said.

"Not really," said Tanner. "Not on this island. But Ocilla sounds like she'd do a snake with its lack of ears no problem."

"How do you stumble into these tidbits, people like Holly?"

Dubbie scowled as if he disliked analyzing the process. "You've taken pictures for so many years, you know this town, right?"

"I thought I knew it well. I guess I do, visually."

"You know about morning and evening light, blue or cloudy skies, cheerful and depressing colors. It's all in the light and shadows."

"Okay," I said. "It's second-nature to me now, but that's about right."

"While you master the scenery," said Dubbie, "I do the social end, the highlights and the dark side, especially the shadows. I understand the street scene and what happens in parked vans and behind frosted jalousie windows. It's part of the reason Wiley and I are going to succeed."

"May I ask how you mastered your expertise?" I said.

Dubbie shook his head. "Nope, you can't. For a long time I had to live by my wits. That's all I'm going to say. How was your fancy breakfast?"

I asked by raising my eyebrows.

"I figured you'd gone to 5 Brothers for con leche. Worth the walk to find out." He lifted his beer-in-a-bag. "You weren't there, I played the possibilities and looked in a window at Azur."

"One last thing," I said. "Have Wiley look around for five more names, whatever he can find. First off, Justin Beeson and the late Amanda Beeson out of Sarasota. The other three share the last name Timber, what you yell when you chop a tree. Their first names are Anya, Sonya and Tonya." I spelled all three. "To relieve you of undue confusion, Anya and Tonya are the same person."

"On it, boss," said Tanner.

He read my face.

"You are 'boss' no longer." He crushed his beer can in his hand. "And, I suppose, 'sir' is forbidden, too."

TEN MINUTES LATER MY cell rang. Chicken Neck Liska, Monroe County Sheriff.

"When you're out this way," he said, "do me a favor. Drop by my office for a minute."

"Stock Island isn't one of my regular routes."

"You never know," he said. "Lunch at Hogfish, yesterday about this time. Drinks and beers, whooping it up, living your carefree

144

life. Anything's possible. If you could make it today, all the better. In, say, forty minutes." He hung up.

A paperless summons. A cheap notice that he could find me, or I couldn't hide, anywhere in his county. I decided to ride the Triumph. I was in no hurry.

He called back. "All right, El Siboney, but you buy."

"And your healthy diet?"

"Oh, shit," he said. "Make it the salad aisle at Publix."

"You win. El Siboney in fifteen."

WE LONG FOR THE days when El Siboney on Catherine was a quick, cheap meal for locals. The place has "gone snowbird," but the food is still close enough to true Cuban fare to please everyone. I might need a yardstick to confirm this, but El Siboney could well be the Cuban-American restaurant nearest Havana. If you ever see them use that line for an ad slogan, you will know it came from the addled mind of Rutledge.

I got there early enough to avoid waiting in line. I asked for a back room table so Liska wouldn't have to schmooze every bubba who came through the door. The place smelled of fish, plantains and grilled pork chops. It was packed with large tourists in golf clothes. I ordered espresso and sangria for each of us and asked the server to keep an eye out for *El Jefe*.

You play by unspoken rules in El Siboney. The servers are all third- or fourth-generation Conchs who never slow down. They ration their patience, speak Spanish to each other and pretend that they don't speak English. They own their homes. A few have put their kids through colleges in Tampa, Gainesville, Tallahassee and Miami. One or two own nice boats, plush cars they don't drive to work. They got it all through hard work. If you want good service, you cater to their moods and pace.

Three minutes later Liska walked straight to the table. He wore brown trousers and a floral shirt that looked like a Beall's Outlet markdown. He sat, slammed the coffee, up-ended the sangria and held out the cup and glass to our server for refills.

She took them and paused, maybe two seconds.

"*Dorado a la plancha*," said Liska. "Yellow rice, *plantanos*."

So much for his health-food regimen.

She looked at me for two seconds. It was the wrong time to admit that I wasn't hungry.

"*Puerco asado, white rice, pantanos, por favor.*"

She disappeared for ten seconds then returned with a plastic basket full of warm buttered Cuban bread wrapped in white paper.

"Give anything for that kind of efficiency in my department," said Liska.

"You're the sheriff," I said. "Go back to the office and fire somebody. The others will perk up."

"Paperwork until next Christmas." He pulled the bread basket closer and dug in.

I began to bounce back another one-liner of questionable wisdom.

"Look, stop right there," he said. "There's a reason for this lunch. I'm not in the mood for distractions."

I nodded, reached for my sangria. "I'll shut up."

"I've had to rethink something I said to you two days ago. Hear me out on this and please let me finish what I have to say. Agreed?"

I knew what was coming. I shrugged and nodded simultaneously.

"To launch this tirade," he said. "I want to make sure you understand that Greg Pulver's murder was a cold execution. It was not a crime of passion, an unpredicted moment of rage. It was an ugly and quick adiós. His killer planned that he would get a bullet up through his chin and out the top of his skull."

He paused for effect. I looked around. People at nearby tables had noticed Liska's intensity, his choice of words, his focused tirade. I splayed my hands, palms down, to shush him.

He resumed speaking with his teeth clamped together, his eyes squinting with hatred, his words coming out as hissing sounds.

"After he was shot, Greg Pulver was kicked in the balls. It was a grotesque post-mortem injury that targeted his genitals, broke a pelvic bone called the ischium and came directly from hatred. We have little choice but to see it as revenge. Tell me your take on that, five sentences or less."

"Not many women wear shoes capable of cracking bone."

"Good, Alex, so follow this logic. We don't know if the killer was one person or several. It could have been a man or a woman or one of each, but I'm using 'he' for this discussion. We don't know if *he* is still in town. We're all running around pushing paper, talking shop, reporting to each other, but we're not finding shit. Have you got me so far?"

I nodded again and kept my mouth shut.

Liska retreated into his thoughts, began fiddling with the paper packets of sugar substitutes. "Let's say a murderer is still on the island," he said. "If said killer believes that any of us is close, he has no choice. He will act to protect himself. And we have no idea what he will do or how to stop him because we can't identify where he's coming from. When I say 'we,' I mean 'we the cops,' which starting right now no longer includes you or the Bumsnoops."

"Little late in the game to change the rules," I said.

"Have you any idea who will catch the next bullet?"

I shook my head and put a finger to my lip, reminding him again to tone it down.

"Do you want to put your private eye rookies at death's door?" he said. "Draw bad guys to your doorstep? Endanger your girlfriend? Count the bullet holes through your porch screening?"

"No."

"When I was a city detective, Rutledge, some shitbird came within two seconds of piercing your forehead with a large, ugly hunk of lead. Since I've been sheriff, you've had your house torched, been in a car wreck, taken a beating that required a hospital stay, and been run down by a car near Fausto's. Am I forgetting anything?"

Half the restaurant was staring at me. I felt like a misfortune magnet. Like a freak on one of those TV shows where people eat roaches and gargle with snakes.

Again Liska lowered his voice. "Your Bumsnoops rode past Ocilla's place this morning and took their damned time checking out my surveillance team. Please understand, that team is not just watching the woman. She was Pulver's business partner. For all we know of the killer, Ocilla could be his next target."

"You want that to happen, right?" I said. "To identify the shooter by drawing him to the woman?"

"Make no mistake," said Liska. "I want the process to begin, but not to the point of murder. My men have orders to protect a probable scam artist from being killed herself. We will take down the sharks, if they appear, and we can't have sloppiness. I can't have amateurs wallowing around on my turf. Argument?"

"Your words are well taken."

"You're a fine photographer," he said, his words quieter. "I've been a good cop for years. Everyone has talent, and you've been a great help to me in the past. But you're not a deputy. You have no weapons training, no body armor. And, for once, I suspect, no comeback at all." He went silent.

I took his pause as an invitation to rebuttal.

"I have a minor critique," I said. "Please don't take this personally. Wiley Fecko, prior to being a street person and a licensed investigator, worked for years at a major phone company. Your 'cable' guys were blowing their own cover. They were using the wrong tools for their job and ignoring safety regulations. If Fecko can spot them, who else can do it?"

Our food arrived at the table. Liska excused himself to step outside to make a call. After he returned we picked at our meals, spooned beans into the rice, passed the hot sauce. Liska's fish sat there looking fresh-caught. My roast pork smelled like heaven, but I was still full of fruit and granola.

Liska crumpled his paper napkin, dropped it on his food. "I am glad to note that I have not wasted my time and words."

"What have I done to transmit that message?" I said.

"I've never seen you not finish a plate of Cuban food."

"I had a big breakfast."

"One other thing I need to tell you about," he said. "I got a call from an old friend in Manatee County, and you'll get one too. Glenn Steffey will play dumb with you, but don't fall for it. He told me he's hasn't seen a better crime scene photo in years. He said you kept your cool, didn't lose your shit at the sight of a mutilated corpse. He's a fine detective, so that's high praise."

"Still not my preferred line of work," I said. "I was glad to turn my back on that situation."

"I can sympathize," said the sheriff. "But my take on his words is that you might want to anticipate a call from their grand jury. Thank you for paying the tab."

OUR FAIR WEATHER VANISHED while we failed to eat our lunch. The sky was overcast, Catherine Street a strip of washed-out colors, the palms on Margaret more purple-gray than tropical. I guessed that rain was a quarter-hour away, maybe less. I reminded myself of the cliché that never fails: a stormy winter day in Cayo Hueso beats every option north of Tampa.

Feeling pleased that my delivery of Wiley Fecko's tech critique had inspired a corrective phone call, I replayed our little chat in my mind. I quickly realized that I had never seen Sheriff Liska so animated, or heard such gravity in his words. For years he had dealt with danger. Monroe County is a haven for those who stray from "normalcy," whatever that is, and thank goodness. But it's a magnet for dysfunctional strangers who want to misbehave under palm trees rather than snow drifts. It can be, on occasion, a volatile social scene, and that is when most law-abiding citizens of the Keys leave worry and dread to others. Cops and deputies, each of them an employee of those citizens, have a two-word job description: Confront It. They all know that evil doesn't take breaks.

I CAME AWAY FROM the meal with a ball cap that smelled of fried plantains and a mind full of worthwhile advice. His warnings had been genuine this time, not a ploy. Not a mind game.

13

THROUGH SHORTAGE OF TIME or lack of money, I have been my own shrink for years. I have been known to pool my resources for self-medication. I felt it was time to take my full belly, caffeine and sangria to a therapy session. That always meant a ride next to the ocean.

Key West is a four-by-two-mile island halfway between Puerto Escondito, Cuba, and Marco Island, south of Naples, Florida. It's attached to America by a constricted hundred-mile asphalt umbilical cord, and it's smack in the middle of nowhere except the Gulf of Mexico.

My '70 Triumph T120R Bonneville is a 650cc twin rated at forty-six horsepower. It has a four-speed transmission and weighs 600 pounds with me aboard. When new it would do better than 100 MPH. I baby the old beast these days and try to keep it under 85. I store its original seat and carburetors in a box in the house. I've added turn signals and fresh rubber, but I kept the drum brakes and wire wheels. It rarely fails to jack my mood, blow dust from my brain.

I stupidly ignored the fact that a trip to Smathers Beach would take me past The Tideline condos. It wasn't as if I could have worn blinders, and Beth might forgive the image from the past:

For some reason Teresa and I started early one morning. She worked five days a week. I tried never to schedule clients before ten. On the day that came to mind, our best shot to beat the clock was to share my outdoor shower. As lovers will, we messed around, did everything we could dream up to make ourselves late. It was her idea to put her feet on the bench seat and face away from me. She got hers first then tried to get fancy. It worked like she knew it would. When my knees buckled we both went down like playing cards in a failed stack. We spent more time laughing than we did having sex. I can't recall if either of us got to work on time.

Maybe, when he found time, my budget shrink in the mirror would explain my desire to sift through brambles and barbed wire to find the thoughts of Teresa that most effectively crushed my heart.

My restorative ride took me to the smells of distant fish and coconut skin lotion. Folks quitting their beach time carried over-sized towels and folding chairs from the sand back to their vans. Hot dog vendors were packing it in for the day. A young couple leaned against their car and dumped sand out of their shoes. A die-hard paraglider headed ashore. License tags on parked cars were from Michigan, New York, Delaware. The island joke: What do you call people who swim in January? The answer: North Dakotans.

The city derives great income from vista gawkers who creep above thirty. This was not a race against the clock. I rolled slowly eastward. I kept to the left lane to avoid chuckholes. Salt spray, cops and thousands of gawkers have played hell with the slow lane's surface. I scanned the horizon, let my mind drift. A bad idea on a motorcycle, but traffic was light.

"Have you any idea who will catch the next bullet?"

Leaning through the bend where A1A curves to the north, I passed the stretch of waterfront where the original Houseboat Row lost its fight to Hurricane Georges in 1998. I rode by the hotels and condos built since then, buildings whose scenic views would have been spoiled by a line of funky houseboats. Many islanders would prefer, of course, the houseboats, but we cannot argue with the weather. Nor the passing of time. I couldn't remember the last time I had seen a shrimp boat in the main harbor. I wished I could hear Captain Tony say one more time, "All you need is a tremendous sex drive and a great ego. Brains don't mean a shit."

My thoughts about Key West dodge the maudlin, for the most part. I have felt for years that my future holds promise for experiences equal to those in my past. Not the same events, which risks boredom, but fresh ones. Not the same me, either, which I can accept most of the time.

Nostalgia has its moments. The trick, I believe, is to shed regret.

LISKA HAD GUESSED CORRECTLY that Tanner and Fecko were answering to me. And he was right about the danger of not knowing our adversary. Until law enforcement could determine the killer's identity or a hint of his motive, the Aristocrats were at risk. But I couldn't see how any trail might lead back to me. I was simply a messenger boy. The sheriff also had skipped over, practically swerved to avoid the fact that Greg Pulver hadn't died alone. Emerson Caldwell and Teresa Barga had died in the same condo the day Pulver was found.

The sheriff had no real reason to discuss Caldwell. There was nothing messy and threatening about cardiac arrest or, from what I knew, death by poisoning. But he hadn't described Teresa, how she looked after being strangled and having her neck snapped. His silence sent the exact message he wanted to plant in my brain. He knew that my photographer's mind would provide sufficient impact and horror. He also believed that his left-field approach would keep me from acting the rebel, tracking mud into his department.

Chicken Neck was a detective at the city when I met him. He didn't promote his own reputation. He didn't have time for that. It grew from his crime solutions, case closings and convictions. I had worried that he might slack off after his election, get discouraged by the office routine and supervisory chores, get caught up in politics or human resource flaps. But as Monroe County's sheriff, he had proved himself effective and worthy.

Maybe his health-food regimen was making him smarter. He set up our lunch chat as a one-sided debate. Having armed himself with details, he delivered his barrage, pushed procedure, stayed away from jerking tears. He had tried to bully me into backing off.

He almost made it work, but he left me with two huge questions. What could we do to screw up his investigation? How could we endanger ourselves or his officers? We weren't out pounding the streets, walking solo in iffy sections of town, cruising bad alleys at night. We were gathering data. Well... Wiley and Dubbie were out gathering data while I was going around in circles.

Maybe Liska was trying to keep us clear of the FDLE or the Feds.

I PULLED OVER AT the east end of Flagler, made a call.

"What was the address, the house number?"

It took Wiley a moment. "Sixteen, thirty-three."

Six minutes later, just west of the dogleg where George intersects Seidenberg, I slowed the Triumph to absorb the view. Gone were the fake cable company van, the deputies with their hard hats and toolbelts. Without making myself obvious to the neighbors or lens, I checked a nearby utility pole. A thumb-sized video camera was poorly hidden among a half dozen steel boxes and cylinders. I looked away before I entered its field of view. Ocilla's green Honda Element was in the yard, tucked into a leafy car cave. Nothing outside the house offered a clue to the resident. The only other vehicle in sight, parked across the street, was a bronze Hyundai four-door. Something about it, perhaps its cleanliness, made me think it was a rented car.

Except for confirming my guesses, I learned nothing from the drive-by. With no pressing appointments, even with incoming weather, I wasn't in a hurry to return home. In the past three days my porch had hosted too many odd meetings, suffered too much bad news. Photographers are accustomed to rainy holidays.

I RODE DOWNTOWN AND juggled my choices for skulking off. I needed anything but food. Almost anything. I didn't want noise beyond rain on the roof. Nor loud music or a majority of tourists or, God forbid, video games at skull-splitter volume. I would suffer a beverage or two, or more. There was the former Che Che's, now Don's Place, on Truman. Too many TVs to suit my mood of the moment. The Bottle Cap had the clattering pool table, and more nostalgia. The fine photo of the old bar on the wall. Virgilio's would smell too much like dinner prep at La Trattoria. Schooner Wharf was guaranteed to be too raucous for what I needed. The Green Parrot stood a chance of being peaceful but I would think about nights I danced there with Teresa. I might get busted for sniveling.

I had argued myself into the second-story Tower Bar at Turtle Kraals.

I found a parking spot on William, just south of the Red Doors Inn, an off-plumb pillar of Key West history. In the shrimping heyday of the '40s and '50s, the joint knew flailing cue sticks and thirty-five-cent beers, knives in the boots of fishermen. Women who earned piecework wages deheading shrimp in the stifling heat of slimy waterfront processing plants, women who waited ashore for their men to show up with slim paychecks, and women who waited for men who never returned from sea.

The air smelled of rain and the Calda Bank flats. I hurried northward past West Marine, admired again the undersea mural at the former Waterfront Market and hoped it would survive transition. Wind gusts warned me, started a clatter in the rigging of sailboats along the bight's south docks. Crews on charter boats hustled to stow ad placards and clean-up gear. Sailors in ponchos snapped covers onto their inflatables at the dinghy dock. Heavy, cold raindrops hit my shoulders and arms, made quarter-sized splotches on the boardwalk.

I climbed the Tower Bar stairway, worked my way to the back side of the bar, the leeward end of the action, and took one of four vacant seats.

"Hey, Alex," shouted Elizabeth Ann, a bartender I had known for years. She was swamped by customers anxious but too late to beat the storm. The downpour slapped loudly on the bar's roof. The fair weather drinkers scrambled to settle their tabs and leave. At mid-mêlée Elizabeth Ann deserted them, walked toward me with her eyebrows raised. She knew that I sympathized, and servers on the island know the drill. Locals put extra green in the jar.

"Barbancourt, soda, please," I said, knowing she would pour with a high elbow. "Piece of lemon."

Where the hell had that come from? I had intended to stick to two, maybe three beers, but my mouth had overruled me. Bad enough that the Triumph was parked in salty rain. I don't slash my wrists and I don't ride with rum in my system. I would have to figure a way to get the bike home.

By the time I had been served and the register was quiet there were only four or five people under the roof. Except for the lovely Elizabeth Ann, I knew none of them. Half of my drink had gone down in the first sip. If I had any tension left in me after the beach ride, it vanished when the rum hit home. I was about to zone out staring at a rain-splattered neon beer sign, wondering why it wasn't shorting out, but I thought of four calls I wanted to make, a couple of errands I had let slip. Why the hell did my mind jerk into gear when my body went slack?

As skilled saloon ambushers will do, he waited until I had taken that second gulp and placed my glass back on its coaster. I saw him coming, a typical lonesome tourist. He would tell me about his gas station in Ohio. Ask about the best boat to charter for shark fishing, or where we locals chased pussy after midnight. He wore a plain black form-fitting T-shirt that showed off his muscular build.

"Rutledge?" he said. "We've never met. I expect it's inevitable. I'm Marsh."

Darrin Marsh, the cop boyfriend. He must have heard Elizabeth Ann call me by name. He held an almost-empty Corona bottle, didn't offer to shake hands. Right away his body language offered clues to his grief.

"My sympathies," I said. "I'm sorry for your loss."

"She was a keeper," he said, "but who am I telling? You've been there too."

His statement didn't require a reaction. I faced him and waited. He showed his empty to Elizabeth Ann, ordered another. She didn't look happy about it.

"They did her right in the *Citizen* yesterday," he said. "Loyal city employee and all that. They get some of her background from you?"

I shook my head. "Probably Paulie, her stepfather."

"Maybe so," he said. "She sure had a nice ass."

Oh, Darrin Marsh, you're a class act, I thought. It was the first time I had heard a woman's derrière discussed in memoriam within hours of her tragic death.

"Teresa kept herself fit," I said. "She looked younger than her age."

"She once told me that her boyfriends were like paper towels," said Marsh. "They could only absorb so much of her. She knew when it was time to rip off a new sheet."

"She never told me that one," I said. "You must have been up to the job."

He shrugged. "She wasn't always a walk on the beach."

I thought, *Don't say a fucking word.* He looked like a poster boy for high blood pressure. He brought to mind a boss I had in the Navy, an Academy grad who bullied himself out of his dream career. I heard at some point that he died of a stroke before he made forty.

"You don't agree?" said Marsh. "No walk on the beach?"

His body language had shifted to aggression. I had misread Marsh's posture from the get-go. He hadn't been grieving, he had been bluffing. Working himself up even before he told me his name. I needed to calm the asshole before he got out of hand. I needed to remind him he was a cop.

"If I hadn't started with a high opinion, Officer Marsh," I said, "I wouldn't have spent time with her."

"Right on," he said. "It was her opinion of you that ended your deal."

"That a fact?"

Darrin inhaled deeply, went for flex effect. I wondered about the testosterone content of the sweat dripping down his face. I looked around in hope of spotting someone I knew. Two men at the far end of the bar were paying attention but they were strangers.

"Lot of humidity this afternoon," I said. "Strange for January."

"Fuck weather talk. I know what you're all about."

"I can't imagine she sat around and discussed me," I said. "What did you do, Marsh, read her diary? I know she kept one."

His face told me I had nailed it by chance, with a wisecrack. I saw a disconnect in his eyes, his pupils the bulging cue balls of a meth freak. His nostrils ballooned from narrow ovals to full, dime-sized circles.

He spoke with a sneer. "She said you got a brass bell outside your house."

I wished I could retract the diary remark.

"You got brass balls, too," he said. "Your high opinion of yourself, being much too good for everyone else."

I would need to think about that. Again, no need to respond.

He put his empty on the bar, didn't notice that Elizabeth Ann had yet to deliver a fresh one. He began mouth breathing, working his jaw as if he was chewing his thoughts. A city cop would have to be worse than stupid to bust me up in public in broad daylight.

"No comeback on that, Mr. Rutledge?" he said.

"Put it this way," I said. "It's a quality-of-life thing. It's sometimes tough in this town, but I like to keep my distance from disagreeable people."

"You ignored my size? I could do you horrible damage with my bare hands."

"Is your threat supposed to change my mind?" I said. "What's wrong with my having strong beliefs? Looks like you've got your share."

Marsh turned to his right to flick away sweat. He also telegraphed his punch. I saw it coming, stood to avoid catching it smack in my face, tightened my stomach muscles. That saved my teeth but brought ungodly pain to my stomach muscles.

The men at the far end of the bar yelled, "Back off, buddy!" and, "Whoa just a minute, mister."

"You're out of here, Darrin," shouted Elizabeth Ann. "I'm dialing right now."

I knew that fistfights take a toll on finger bones. There would be no whoa in the action. Marsh rocked back on his feet to assess the damage he had caused me, and I aimed the heel of my left hand at his upper lip, the lower part of his nose.

He answered with his left, an open-hand slap that almost turned out my lights. With my vision blurred I didn't see his incoming right-hand shot to my solar plexus. The next punch almost pulped my shoulder. He went sideways, kicked backward, and broke out two or three slats under the porch railing. If I had thrown a punch at that moment, I would have hurt myself more than him. Or missed.

A gust of wind scattered napkins, straws, plastic cups. The champ was getting his ticker-tape parade. Marsh backed off, crouched and grabbed a railing spindle, a two-foot section of one-by-four. My mind slipped into slow motion, but I couldn't figure out a way to grab the slat without taking hundreds of splinters or snapping my wrist. Marsh raised his arm, wavered a split second, then struck downward. I jammed my head against his chest just as the slat hit the top railing hard enough to split it into drumstick-size wands. He whirled and flung away the pieces still in his hand. I heard them land in the yard behind the restaurant.

I wasn't sure what had crossed Marsh's mind, made him quit the fight. Then I heard the sirens that he must have heard first. Marsh shook his head, spoke to no one. Blood streamed down his chin. He turned to the bar, peeled open his wallet and counted out four hundred-dollar bills. He disappeared down the stairway to ground level.

"Nice meltdown," said Elizabeth Ann. "Are you okay?"

John Wayne would have had a snappy response. I had a bar napkin stuck to my elbow and nothing to say. I felt like crap, probably looked worse, and Elizabeth Ann didn't press for an answer.

The two men that had shouted down Marsh were gone. The neon beer sign went fuzzy for an instant, then returned to normal. Next to it I saw Dubbie Tanner, his camera at chin level, probably still filming a video record of my losing battle.

Shouts came from ground level, heavy footsteps on the wood stairway. I signaled Tanner to hide his camera. He got it into his pocket as the police arrived.

When the lead officer questioned the 911 call, Elizabeth Ann had an answer for him. She proved why top bartenders are valued. "Our power went out for a minute," she said, "and my register got stuck open. This schitzo guy at the bar was checking the cash drawer, scaring me, I mean really piss-scaring me, so I called. He blew out of here, like, two minutes ago. Bad-looking dude, so thank you for responding. I was shitless for, like, three or four minutes."

"Which way did he go?" said the officer. "Did you notice?"

She pointed at the stairs and tilted her finger downward.

Another cop stood next to the broken railing. He held a bouquet of wood splits. "Anything you can tell us about this, ma'am?"

"Must be from last night," she said. "It was there when I came to work and I've been slammed, until it rained. I forgot to call our maintenance man."

The cop nodded slowly, half-believing her. He sized up my dazed appearance then took a long look at Dubbie Tanner. "Everything else okay here?" he said.

"Perfect," said Elizabeth Ann. "Wish all my customers could be like these guys. You boys come back when you're off duty, you hear?"

THE RAIN HAD STOPPED. The harbor came back to life, boat engines rumbling, yacht crews calling back and forth. The episode ended my worry about riding the Triumph home with rum in my system. I was cold sober. I also hurt too much to ride.

Liska had warned me of hidden dangers. Or perils made worse by the fact that we hadn't identified the bad guys. For my money, Darrin Marsh had just placed himself in that category, but I suspected that my big mouth hadn't brought on the slug party. His rage had carried more than grief and frustration. His mood had been festering for a while and he had been waiting to act on impulse, to use someone's upper body for a punching bag. He hadn't come looking for me. I was a target of opportunity. My arrival had offered him a timely recipient. If deep-rooted anger was running his agenda after her death, he must have been a charmer beforehand.

When would I see him next?

I finally turned to Tanner and asked a question of him.

"I was sitting on a lady friend's sailboat when you walked past looking glum," said Dubbie. "I saw you come in here. Figured I'd come over and cheer you up."

"You arrived just *not* in time."

"The first punch he threw, I was too far away," said Dubbie. "I felt powerless, but you took it okay. It ended quickly."

14

ELIZABETH ANN GAVE ME a generous rum roadie for my pain, dropped in a lemon wedge that stung the inside of my mouth. I would have to check later for wobbly teeth and new purple skin tints.

Dubbie Tanner helped me walk the Triumph home. He didn't have a motorcycle license endorsement and I wasn't sure I could turn quickly or hit the brakes if I had to. He pushed the bike up Caroline, and I tried to keep up without spilling. Rainwater dripped from trees near Pepe's and balcony overhangs farther along. Wet leaves filled curb gutters, mist rose as cars hurried by. Nearing Margaret Street we watched a taxi round a corner, hit a puddle, splash brown muck on four people holding cameras and fresh drinks.

What I saw next took me a few moments to absorb. A silver SUV angled into a parking slot across the street from Harpoon Harry's. A slender man in a Hawaiian shirt and Ray-Bans got out, clicked his key remote to lock the Toyota, then walked toward the restaurant. He paid no attention to Dubbie or me. I looked back at the vehicle, but couldn't read its tag. I held the bike vertical while Tanner ran over to look.

"Sarasota County," he said. "Your old stomping grounds."

I winced.

"Sorry," he said. "You know the car?"

"I know it from here," I said. "It pertains."

I had just watched Luke Tharpe park Anya Timber's RAV4.

Hanging back by Los Cubanitos marine hardware store, I scrolled through the messages I had received in the past two days. I clicked on the number that Detective Glenn Steffey had given me—only to reach a switchboard. Steffey wasn't available, and the man on the line wouldn't give me a cell number. I offered my name. He sounded as if he might find time to write a note for Steffey.

I entered Harpoon Harry's as Tharpe seated himself in a booth next to the east wall. I approached him, trying not to look like I had been pummeled by a muscular schmuck. Tharpe canted his head, slowly recognized me, and looked puzzled to see me somewhere other than 23 Beeson Way. He raised his chin, as if that meant "hello," then looked down to scan the menu and ignore me.

His hair was disheveled but the gel told of intended messiness. He wore an authentic-looking piece of eight on a neck chain. This was not the choirboy I had met in Justin Beeson's auto maintenance shop. Nor was he the reluctant morning helper in his Ram pickup, or the man vomiting in revulsion on finding a trussed-up dead woman. This was version number four.

"Good to see you here at the southern tip of Florida," I said. "Who's watching the classic cars up north?"

He scratched the two-day stubble on his cheek, raised his eyes just enough to see my neck. "You're a photographer, that's it, right? That's all you do, take pictures?"

"Yes," I said. "That's what I do."

"Beeson said something about you working for the cops, too. You a cop?"

"I get hired now and then. But I don't have a badge. I work for myself."

"Huh." He glanced away as if a passing gnat had snagged his interest. "Do me a favor and go away. I don't need your frigging pictures."

"I also do art shots," I said. "I like to combine objects to contrast texture or age. Like a Google Earth photo truck passing in front of a 100-year-old Conch house. A Maserati on a dock with a beat-up shrimpboat in the background. I also love to show objects in unlikely settings, such as your face next to that silver RAV4's license tag. Think I could sell that somewhere?"

"You're bigger than I am, Rutledge," said Tharpe. "But don't judge this book by its skinny-ass cover. I mean what I say. You don't want your balls to live in a new home up behind your belly button, stay the fuck away from me."

I had lost fights to bigger men in the past hour.

"My pleasure, Luke," I said with a touch of volume. Even louder I said, "Thanks for the great advice about my scrotum."

Every head in the place turned. Kelly Finnegan, a server and island resident for years, said, "Oh, don't shave it, Alex. It'll look like a squashed tennis ball with pepper sprinkles."

The laughter in the restaurant drove Luke Tharpe out the side door and around to Caroline and the Toyota. Subtract one more name from my list of best friends. When Tharpe drove away, I looked around. People still were laughing at Kelly's one-liner. And again, there was Dubbie Tanner, small camera in hand. I squinted and raised my eyebrows.

He read the question, smiled and patted the camera.

Walking down Grinnell, Tanner said, "Did he really use the word frigging?"

WE LEFT THE TRIUMPH in the backyard. The rain had gone away and I wanted to wash it, but I didn't have the energy. An alternative reason: the pain between my cranium and waistline outweighed my desire to be neat and clean.

Before he walked back to Key West Bight to retrieve his bicycle, Dubbie let me duplicate his camera memory card. For future reference, each of us would have a copy of his movie features, my short fandangos with Marsh and Tharpe.

"One more small assignment for your partner," I said. "I learned last evening that our boy Marsh was once an electrician. Please ask Wiley to find and download the schematics for the security system at The Tideline condominium."

Tanner was less than a minute out the door when I heard my name being called from the bedroom. It was a low, tempting growl. It was the mattress crying out for company, reminding me that my body needed to heal. My two-hour slumber was almost dream free.

Just before I woke, I reviewed the lunch I had bought for Liska. By not mentioning Teresa, the circumstances of her death, he had done nothing to keep me away from a murder investigation. He had put fear in me, but not enough. The depression he had inspired was not quite cured by a beach tour and the Haitian rum. The motorcycle ride was eclipsed by the scene in the Tower Bar.

Smart as I thought I was, however, I had missed part of Liska's message.

He had wanted me to keep away from Darrin Marsh.

My nap ended with a call from Malcolm, the boat broker. He didn't want to "bug" me, but the rain had blown eastward and the next few days' weather would be great for documenting the boats new to his inventory. With a twinge of guilt I promised him a morning call and a fresh photo session within twenty-four hours.

UNDER MY MANGO TREE, under a violet twilight streaked with fading reds, with an upbeat Tom Petty song playing in the house, I wiped salt residue from my Triumph and locked it away. Its shelter had been repainted inside and out several months ago and, for good reason at the time, a deadbolt installed.

My phone buzzed. As usual I wanted to ignore it but succumbed to curiosity. To my delight it illuminated: B WATKINS.

"It is our dutiful, beautiful civil servant," I said.

"Alex, what are you doing?"

"Playing with it and thinking of you."

"You are so dependably subtle and romantic. Do you want help?"

"Only if it's you."

"That better not be a smoke screen, mister. See you in ten."

I didn't check the clock but it felt like ten minutes to the second. Enough time to turn on some lights, open wine and switch the music to a low-stress Jim Hall jazz guitar session.

Beth flicked her fingernail on my brass bell and stepped in off the porch. I bowed and handed her a cool glass of St. Supery Virtu, her favorite white meritage. I raised my own glass to recite a short toast to our having two nights in a row.

She raised an index finger—a silent "wait"—while she put her glass on a table, hugged me with both arms, kissed my lips with a subtle pelvic bump, then returned to her wine for a solid sip.

"You smell like you had an hour in the shower," I said.

"Why did you flinch when I hugged you?"

When I shook my head I felt a new ache in my ribs. "I attended a short anger management seminar three hours ago."

"Oh, shit. Were you at the Kraals? I heard the radio call for a disturbance."

I pictured the scene in the bar, the banging around, my barstool scraping on the deck, Elizabeth Ann's threat to call 911. Did I remember correctly that two men at the bar also yelled at Marsh? When the dust cleared those two weren't in sight. How did they get down the stairway past the arriving cops? Dubbie's digital movie would settle the question, but I didn't want to put Beth in an awkward place by watching it immediately.

"You may want to steer clear of this story," I said.

"Allow me, for a few minutes, to separate my concern for my lover from my duty as a law officer."

"I will allow you anything," I said. "Will a judge do the same if you have to testify in court?"

"I can cross that mine field when the time comes," said Beth.

"Right now there's no field and I don't know a damn thing. Just to be safe, are you about to admit to me that you broke the law?"

"I broke none that I know of, today."

"Sorry I hugged you."

"You can do it again if you'd like to."

I pulled a second chair to my desk, woke my laptop and opened Dubbie Tanner's first movie in QuickTime. The first eight or ten seconds were unfocused, blurred. The sound was obscured, perhaps by a thumb or finger over the pinhole openings of the pocket camera's microphone.

Beth said, "What are we..."

I held up my hand to ask for patience. As the image brightened the soundtrack became clearer. I heard Marsh say, "Fuck weather talk," and I could see the top of the Tower Bar stairway. Tanner was shooting from hip level so as not to draw attention to his camera. I heard my distant voice say, "...diary? I know she kept one." The camera steadied, auto-focused on several empty barstools then panned left. Its lens caught the men in dark colored shorts and shirts at the north end of the bar, and I heard, "...brass balls, too." More loudly, Elizabeth Ann said, "Ready for another beer, Darrin?" Words I hadn't heard when things were happening fast. A question to calm my attacker, defuse the craziness.

The camera's point of view lifted and the image grew as Dubbie zoomed. Marsh set his empty beer bottle on the bar, and I thanked my luck that he hadn't clocked me with it. I watched myself say, "I like to keep my distance from disagreeable people." Marsh said something I couldn't make out, then I spoke in response. Every movement from that moment forward was news to me. I moved my rum drink away from myself as I stood to take Marsh's first punch. I saw a blur in the background.

When male voices close to the camera shouted, "Back off, buddy!" and, "Whoa just a minute," the zoom pulled back. One of the men started to go around the bar in Marsh's direction. The other grabbed his friend's shirt and pulled him back. When they faced each other, the second man shook his head one time. Their heads turned in time to see Marsh nail my left shoulder. At that instant a wind gust sent bar cups and napkins airborne.

Again Tanner zoomed. His microphone caught the kick that knocked apart the wooden railing behind Marsh. The wind eased and the faint siren could be heard, its doppler warning of its approach. Marsh's arm rose with the splintered slat. I head-butted his chest as he banged it down on the railing. I saw blood dripping from his nostrils. I watched myself push my barstool backward, then droop down onto it.

I promised myself not to forget that head-butting is an awful idea.

While Marsh counted money from his wallet to the bartop, Tanner pulled back on the zoom and dropped his camera to belt level. He caught the two men in dark shirts going for the stairway. But they weren't fast enough. They had to stand back to allow Darrin space to go first.

By the timing of their exit, they must have encountered the uniformed officers at the base of the stairs. Maybe six or seven seconds later the first policeman's head appeared. An instant later the "home" movie ended.

Only one explanation. The feds had flashed badges and told the city officers that the problem was still up top.

Beth looked exhausted just from watching it. "Can I see it one more time?" she said.

I traded seats with her, set the video clip to play again. She hit the space bar twice to pause the action, catch her breath. I saw nothing that I hadn't seen the first time. When it reached the end, she closed the laptop.

"If those two are the ones keeping an eye on Darrin Marsh," I said, "they sure as hell chose not to blow their cover."

"I don't recognize either of them," she said. "If they're his babysitters, they had to know that a Key West cop was in a bar fight. They're carrying badges, so by choosing not to interfere, they became Darrin's accomplices."

"Is it a civil rights violation if the cop isn't on duty?" I said.

"Tricky," said Beth. "Did he tell you he was a cop?"

"No, he introduced himself. He said his name. Of course, I already knew he was a cop."

"I hate to say it," she said, "but that scores points in his favor. If he had claimed to have official power, then slugged you, he'd be a goner. Just his name... that's a big gray area."

"Not that I would report it, anyway," I said. "But someone should bust him for saying that Teresa had a nice ass. Even if he said it just to rile me up. That's a real touching memory of his lover."

"Did I see it right?" said Beth. "He threw the first punch?"

"The first, third, fourth and fifth, but I can shut up. If the feds have to ignore my discomfort to nail Teresa's killer, I'm all for it."

"With this video in hand," she said, "whatever we do about Marsh, we don't have to hurry. Please copy this to a thumb drive for me."

TEN MINUTES LATER WE were more relaxed, sitting in the main room.

"Thank God I made detective," said Beth. "There's so little these days that street officers can do. They have to think like lawyers. It makes me long for the days when a cop could slap a kid upside the head and tell him to stop stealing. It worked a lot of the time. These days punks thumb their noses and get away with it. Even if they're hauled downtown, two, three days later they're back on the sidewalk. It's a vicious circle. At least I get to use my brain."

She returned to her wine glass and raised her own toast. "Enough about Darrin Marsh, the screw-up cop. Last night I came here to apologize. This evening I've come to thank you."

"For letting you call the dance last night?" I said. "I recall that you favored the Bone Island Mambo."

"Yes," she said, "and you fell asleep five minutes too soon, but I understood your fatigue. Let's move to another subject. On your insistence, I requested an autopsy of Emerson Caldwell one hour before the State Department ordered Monroe County to do it. The feds acted on a request from the Canadian government. I beat everyone to the punch."

"Do you get to wear a feather in your hat? A star on your forehead?"

"Chief Salesberry was copied on the message, as was the district FDLE supervisor. Salesberry was overjoyed to report back to all recipients that Detective Watkins of his department already had taken the initiative. He told me that a letter would be placed in my permanent file. It would include the words 'professional' and 'foresighted.'"

"Did he question your ordering an autopsy on a simple heart attack?" I said.

"He did," she said, "but he gave me slack, probably because of my case-closure record. I explained that it made no sense for us to order autopsies on two victims and not the third since the deceased all were discovered in the same condo. If we catch a killer and go to trial, a defense attorney might toss a wrench by demanding to know why we hadn't treated each body identically. It might not be a strong point, but then it might put a cloud on the prosecution. Best to play it safe."

"Has the autopsy been performed?" I said.

"Yes, but Homeland double-jumped me. Their guy said he needed first look because another Canadian died from a potassium chloride injection less than a year ago. Also in Florida."

"Piss you off?"

"Not really my case, anyway," said Beth. "But if they start seeing the whole scene as a single crime, I might lose the little I have."

"Would that piss you off?"

Beth swirled her wine, up-ended the glass, swallowed and smiled. "Not if it gave me more time with you."

She must have detected my involuntary wince.

"After you heal, of course," she said. "Two of my rules. It's not smart to ride a broken motorcycle, and it's no fun to ride a lame horse. I can be very patient."

15

LATER THAT NIGHT, AFTER Beth had gone to sleep, I sat down to edit my photos of 23 Beeson Way in Sarasota. I couldn't expect to be paid expenses if I didn't provide the man with product. I wanted to trash the bad ones and burn a disc of high-resolution pictures to mail in the morning. I also needed to charge my batteries and format data cards so I could start fresh with Malcolm Mason's boat detail photos.

My computer came to life and an email arrived through my web site, my business-only address. It almost went the way of obvious spam. But the sender's address looked like Manatee County. I guessed—correctly—that it was from Detective Glenn Steffey:

> "My apology for the hardass who would not patch you through. If you saw Tharpe in town, we are on that solid. We connected with Mr. Beeson, more or less. Other ideas, call me. Don't print this or you will learn tetherball the way we play it in our jail. Kidding."

He signed off with his personal cell number. I saved it into my phone.

Halfway through my Beeson folder, I found a problem in an image that I took the morning of his liver-twisting hangover. Wanting to show the building's nearness to transport, I had shot from the ladder that Luke Tharpe brought me in his high-riding, high-dollar pickup. I had aimed through a tree line to catch semis rolling northward on I-75.

In the only image that showed two trucks nose to tail, the smudge caught my eye like a lens flare. It was probably no more than a pale rock next to a foreground tree, but it killed the photo's impact. From past experience, I knew how to remove it with Photoshop's clone stamp. I bumped the image to twice its actual size and, looking more closely, I could see that it wasn't a rock. It looked like a road bum's rucksack. Still, it was a distraction.

Just before I worked my digital magic, a thought came bouncing into my skull. I pulled a dozen bad shots back out of the "Trash," opened them in Photoshop and found what I wanted. In that moment when I lost my balance and almost tumbled from Tharpe's ladder, I must have pressed the button, so here's to auto-focus. The "rucksack" was, indeed, a wad of clothing or a yellow bandanna wrapped around a jacket or a pair of trousers. An odd package to see in the scrub weeds, too far from either the Interstate or the service road to have, perhaps, fallen out of a truck.

Nothing to lose. I reduced the image to a size more suited to email and sent it to Steffey. I told him what the clothing wad looked like to me and explained where and why I snapped it. I suggested that it might be of interest so close to a murder scene.

Exhausted, I made two thumb drive copies of Dubbie Tanner's Tower Bar debacle video, then shut off the computer.

BEFORE SHE WENT TO the bedroom, Beth elaborated on Darrin Marsh's background. I assumed that her info was a blend of office gossip, his confidential personnel files, and the news release from his first week on the force. There wasn't much to it beyond clues for a two-bit run at analyzing his outlook, hangups and screw ups. He had been an average high school student but a star football and baseball player. His scholarship to a small college in upstate New York hadn't led to playing first-string in either sport. He went from majoring in business to history and finally to law enforcement sciences.

In two years of police work in his hometown, Marsh had rescued two women from a flooded car and talked a suicidal teenager off a river bridge arch. An "office romance" led to his only reprimand. During a vacation in Key West, he had gone to the new police station and applied for a job. Someone found mention of his heroics on the Internet, and the city hired him pending state certification. He moved to Key West, took a training course and pinned on his badge.

Teresa Barga met Darrin Marsh in the course of her efforts as the KWPD's Public Information Officer. Accusations of police brutality, specifically naming Marsh, had been published in a weekly paper known for its grudge against cops. It turned out that the story fed to the paper was bogus. Marsh was wrongly accused, and Teresa helped clear his and the city's reputation. Their romance began shortly after that. There had been four complaints since then about Marsh's handling of arrests and investigations. He had dodged reprimand each time.

That was it. Nothing stuck.

ON MY WAY TO the bedroom, I was again reminded of each injury from my guest role as Darrin Marsh's punching bag. It hurt to brush my teeth. It hurt to change my T-shirt. For the first time in our romance I was glad that Beth didn't sense my arrival and try to snuggle. My aching chest assured me that the morning would be a special adventure.

ABOARD SHIP IN THE Navy, at sea in the Atlantic, I learned to listen in my sleep. When I first came aboard, it took me time to adjust. Certain sounds always were there. The rhythm of the propulsion system, echoes of waves striking the hull, distant sonar pings, the keel pounding in rough weather, leather soles on steel ladders, hatches being opened or secured. I heard new sounds as threats though most were filed in my sleeping brain as shipboard normalcy.

I knew when the midwatch was chasing an unidentified submarine. The ship's roll told me the bridge was preparing for a dawn refueling from an oiler or carrier. I'm sure that I wasn't alone in blending noise into my dreams. The second to last thing any sailor wanted to hear was General Quarters at four AM. The worst thing he could hear was splashing water.

Since my release from active duty, I have been a light sleeper. I never have felt burdened by my alertness. It allows me to close windows before rainstorms, hear vehicles in the lane at the wrong time of night and flip on my backyard light to send a prowler to easier pickings. On the other hand, I worry when I miss noise inside my house. The sounds of Beth Watkins dressing and leaving at sunup. Or of Chicken Neck Liska setting up his satellite office on my front porch before a rational human might think of starting a day's work. How had I not heard him arrive? Was I that exhausted from Marsh's pounding? At least the sun was shining, the air warm for mid-January. Probably the reason Beth left the door open.

"Coffee, sheriff?" I said.

"Been there." He looked away from my T-shirt and skivvies. "Nice pajamas."

"I'm fresh out of donuts. If your schedule's out of synch, I can microwave a Marie Callender's chicken teriyaki dinner."

"You're a laugh a fucking minute, Rutledge."

"Minutes are a toss. I take the hours seriously," I said. "Like the two more of sleep I'm about to miss. We've got to stop meeting like this."

He stared at the tabletop as if it had committed a heinous crime. I went to pull on shorts and start a pot of Bustelo. When I returned to the porch, he was reading his horoscope on the web.

I said, "Have you been upstaged in the ordering of an autopsy?"

"Minor blip," he said. "I've got an inbound shitstorm that's got nothing to do with work."

"Your financial connection to the subject of the autopsy?"

It took him thirty seconds to raise his glazed eyes, lift his jaw, close his mouth and figure out how I knew. "Does this mean I have to be civil with the Bumsnoops?"

"Take the big leap and lose that name," I said. "If you can't bring yourself to say 'the Aristocrats,' their first names are Wiley and Dubbie."

"To be precise," said Liska, "their names are William B. Tanner and William B. Fecko."

"I didn't know that. They're good, eh?"

"They may not even know that about themselves," he said. "Who else knows?"

"No one," I said. "They're discreet, too. No axes to grind, no downtown agenda. They told me because they knew we were friends."

"That could become ancient history," he said. "Are they good enough to remove it from the online search engines?"

"I can ask, but it was in the news years ago."

He nodded. "When I worked for the city. No one believed it was true because I had so little money. Of course, my lifelong poverty was the reason I rolled the dice with Caldwell, the douchebag. At least I got out when there was something to get."

"Leave you with a spoonful of bitterness?" I said.

"Bitter takes too much time. If I had the luxury to be pissed about anything, it would be my choice of women for the past twenty years. They've cost me more than I ever would have lost with Caldwell."

Maybe, I thought, he chooses misery because that's where he's most comfortable.

"What's next on your list?" I said.

"This Canadian link, the Feds are breathing down my neck," said Liska. "They're in touch with the governor's office and everyone wants fast results."

"It's been four days since the murders. I don't even know which case is yours. Do you?"

"I'm sorry," he said. "I'm not authorized to discuss the investigation."

I kept my mouth shut. I wanted to leave the story-telling to Liska. He hadn't come to my house to keep his mouth shut or to bad-mouth old girlfriends.

He closed his computer. "The deaths of Pulver and Teresa belong to the city. The FDLE took Caldwell and his autopsy off my hands yesterday, which I don't mind at all. But I'm still stuck with Ocilla Ramirez, for two reasons. Her cute housekeeping business, Acting Chief Execs, specialized in cleaning homes of the vulnerable. We aren't sure yet whether she or Pulver, or both of them, accessed some of their clients' computers. Their scam didn't go after current cash. They would hit medium-sized retirement accounts, lightly. They targeted money that people look at once or twice a year. Or never, in some cases. Their odds of success were huge."

"So your priorities are with money crimes instead of murders?" I said.

"In effect, yes," said Liska. "The murder investigations are covered by competent people, including your friend Beth. And we're back to the joint ops case I mentioned to you several days ago. There may be, in fact, an additional ongoing scam involving these people. My people are doing the legwork to keep federal agencies out of the equation. If Ocilla's handlers suspected fed involvement, they might close up shop. We can always arrest Ocilla but we'd never get near the crime managers."

"You have to work on the FDLE 's deadline?" I said.

"It's always somebody's deadline. They think the scam will tie together two of the three murders. When is there time to do a job the right way?"

"You know what race drivers say?"

He studied the driftwood on the wall. "Will this be useful to me or just to you?"

"They tell you to drive your own race," I said. "Focus on your job, not on theirs. Don't let the guy on your bumper dictate what you do in the next corner."

PISS AND MOAN MUSIC felt right at the time. I sang along with Gram Parsons and Emmylou Harris in the outdoor shower, tried to recall the quick sling of words to "Ooh, Las Vegas." I harmonized elegantly on "Hickory Wind," and felt more on top of things when I emerged as the new improved me in slide sandals and a towel. The yard was a wash of post-rain color, and the bright sunlight threw off my vision. It took me a moment to adjust to the shaded porch.

There sat Anya Timber in extreme cut-off jean shorts and a red plaid farmer-girl top, gold loop earrings, the Rolex, but no bracelets. Her dark hair was tied back at the nape of her neck, and she was toking on the slimmest joint I had ever seen. She must have worn a jeweler's loupe to roll it.

A truck with a salt-rotted muffler rolled up Fleming. Its raw noise reminded me of a detail that had nagged my thoughts since Sarasota.

"Edwin Torres told me he used to work at a Midas shop," I said. "Did he install those hot-sounding tailpipes on your Porsche?"

"You've been holding that one in your brain for how many days?" she said, offering me the doobie. "I thought you would want to discuss Luke Tharpe."

I declined the smoke. "All my poisons are liquid, thank you," I said.

Her eyes dropped to my chest. "Did you walk into a door?"

"I got hit by an asshole. Speaking of Luke, I almost suffered a double."

"I knew we would get to him sooner or later."

I leaned against the door jamb. "Do you call him your pet chameleon?"

She didn't reply, smile or frown. We stared at each other for a few seconds. Her gaze drifted off to the screening, and I realized she was watching a prowling lizard.

"Let me start over," I said. "I'm sorry about the loss of your friend."

"Thank you." She nodded. "I think I'm hurting even more than Justin is. And Eileen, for now, is the strong one."

I agreed. "But her remarkable eye for detail, her ability to paint subtle light and tone shifts. That could easily translate into her view of our adult world. Could be she dwells inside herself with too much comfort. Please make sure she isn't masking too much."

"I will do that, if I see her. She trusts me, and I couldn't bear to let her down."

I nodded, dropped my eyes from her face to the floor, allowed her legs to register in my thoughts.

"Did you enjoy looking at my pussy four days ago?" she said.

"Sure," I said. "Don't we all enjoy watching a lovely sunset, a classic sailing yacht underway?"

"Well, your eyes sort of tended toward that region. Justin was still awake when I went to bed that night. For some reason he wanted me to shave myself before I came to bed. I trimmed it a little." Anya unbuttoned and unzipped her shorts, pushed them down an inch or so. "Do you think too much?"

"I can't see from here," I said, "but it's really none of my business."

"We're not talking business, Alex, we're talking about the absence of pubic hair."

"And tailpipes and a murder."

"So," she said, "that night in Sarasota, we didn't make love."

I stared through the screening at a croton bush. "Correct."

"Can we say that you and I put one in the bank? A night of unfinished business, snug in the safe deposit? It could be ten years from now, but we'll see each other, somewhere in the world, and we'll both know."

"Like, we'll always have Paris, except we haven't had it yet."

"And maybe we'll shake hands and smile and walk away."

"Probably so," I said. "Can I ask a question off the subject?"

She tilted her head and squinted.

"Why did Justin change his plans so quickly? Why did we all fly to Sarasota two days earlier than he said we would?"

"He mumbled something about Amanda's bullshit. He said that only when they argued about Eileen. I could tell it wasn't a good time to press for details."

"I'm going to put on shorts and a shirt," I said. "Can I get you anything? Water or coffee, a glass of wine?"

Anya went back to studying my bruises. She began to speak, then stopped and shook her head. "I don't fuck Luke, just so you know."

My turn to shake my head. "Again, none of my business, Anya. I am not the guilt god or the bed police. When I sit in judgment, it's usually on saloon singers or pizza delivery service. A negative rating means I could do better myself. That's not saying much."

"Can I have two more minutes?" she said. "Then I will leave. You can put on your clothes and shoes and get on with your day."

"That's what all the girls say to me."

It took her no more than three seconds to register my words. Then she went on a laughing jag that lasted nearly the whole two minutes. I was afraid every neighbor in the lane would come around to hear my joke. I have no idea why I cracked a tired old one-liner, except that I was weary of murders and recriminations and intrigue. I wanted to change the channel, kiss off the scammers and power geeks, the mystery women and pro victims. I felt like I needed another shower.

Anya pulled herself together. She made sure the joint was out, flicked off the ash then rolled the remaining sliver into a capsule-sized pill and swallowed it. "As you know," she said, "Justin found you by asking around the island for a photographer. When your name came up, I overheard several people discuss your ability to... also to... make things right. Is that a good way to say it?"

"It sounds fine," I said, "but it's half right or half wrong, and that depends on how you look at life."

"I'm looking back at death, Alex. Five of us need your help, because none of us knows who killed Amanda. I don't know, and I'm certain that Justin couldn't have done it. Amanda lived apart for the sake of the child. She also did a few things to boost her dismal self-esteem, things Justin and I couldn't help her with. A few people who knew about us didn't like the idea that we were a trio. We could give you a list of possible..."

"You're getting to the heart of my selfishness," I said.

"What does that mean?"

"Every time I've ever unraveled a knotted story, it was because someone close to me had been hurt. And, yes, I can focus. Once in a while I can help. But I can't solve all the problems in the world."

An angry expression crossed her face. "You sure as shit couldn't solve mine four nights ago." She stood and stormed off the porch, her lovely legs all the way up to her shorts.

Blame it on the second-hand smoke. I caught myself wishing for one last look at her bare ass. Then I told myself not to test a shark's friendliness by sticking my hand in its mouth. Or something like that.

She wasn't accustomed to being turned down.

MALCOLM MASON'S OFFICE MAY be the most luxurious land-based 600-square-foot space on Stock Island. A few yachts in marinas equal its precision cabinetry, wall art, earth-tone tile flooring, and the touch and scent of its teak furniture and leather upholstery. But his oasis of affluence amazed everyone who set foot inside the place. It was the sizzle that sold the burgers. Every cubic inch helped to market used yachts. Ironically, his small building looked like a bait shack in a foliage-free "transition" neighborhood of trailer homes, rusted-out sedans and ten-foot chain link fencing.

I arrived to find a tray of chilled seafood. Conch seviche, steamed shrimp, salmon mousse, thin-sliced ahi tuna, smoked fish dip and water crackers.

"Let me guess," I said. "A promising client arriving in twenty minutes."

"Yes, but help yourself," said Malcolm, sitting behind his desk. "Hors d'oeuvres to sustain you in the elements."

"I could call it breakfast, knock down a bottle of Pinot gris, take a nap and do the shoot tomorrow."

He grinned. "Then I'd have to charge you restaurant prices."

Malcolm let his office speak louder than his attire. He was dutifully laid back in shapeless Levi's, white Nike Airs, and an aqua-toned Columbia shirt. I knew he was in his late thirties, so I guessed that his hair was cut short to mask premature gray. "Key West Point of View," a 40-minute Key West photo DVD, played on an HDTV monitor above Malcolm's chair. The aquarium DVD I had seen in Justin Beeson's home in Sarasota filled a smaller screen on the opposite wall.

"I've seen that movie before, the fish," I said. "Must be popular enough to warrant a sequel."

"This boat I need you to document, they could shoot a few DVDs right where it sank," said Malcolm. "Because it went down so close to the reef, it was easy to get salvage rights. But it was a huge chore to refloat it. We brought it here to the yard, and I subcontracted the hull, the fittings, all the wiring and the interior finish and glass work."

"Why salvage rights?" I said. "Why didn't the owner refloat her?"

"The owner panicked and drowned. We raised it on his wife's okay."

"How could a boater panic?" I said. "I mean, the requirements for safety gear. Who doesn't have the sense to pull on a life vest?"

Malcolm shook his head. "You're right. Even children have that going. His three passengers kept calm and lashed together everything that floated to the surface. They made themselves a raft of trash. They even took turns sleeping on furniture cushions. One of the survivors said the owner's last words were, 'I can't think of what to do next.'"

"Then he used it like a car," I said. "Turn the key and go. He didn't have a plan. He didn't think through the possibilities ahead of time."

"Right you are. Like the leak he never discovered and the three bilge pumps that he ran off one instead of three separate breakers."

Not one to micro-manage, Malcolm sent me outside to work alone. He trusted me to pick the best combination of flash and sunlight to show the boat's design and quality materials. He knew I would capture the important details of seaworthiness and safety. Malcolm was the type of client I enjoyed most, the kind I had hoped for in Justin Beeson four days earlier.

Back outside, the southeast breeze was no warmer than my porch had been when I found Liska in his funk two hours earlier. The southeast wind carried a familiar scent. I wondered how many current Key West residents would know the smell and sound of diesel shrimpboat engines. The shrimpers, as a species, had been moved to Stock Island years ago so Key West could go into the marina business. The city could rent dock space by the foot and ambience by the week.

Alone with my gear and static subjects, I felt an almost Zen removal from five days of confusion and tragedy. I was alone with light, shadows, my camera and the boat's internal structure. I had brought my Mini-Mag flashlight and a white parabolic umbrella to bounce flash and to filter the odd ray of sunlight that might sneak below. Sounds from the nearby shipyard were muffled, and my Triumph was locked safely inside Malcolm's tall, barb-topped fence. This insulation from the world, the fact of the boat owner's death and my proximity to the boat's keel took me again to the past.

During my Navy days I had been sent to numerous single-day training schools. Two stood out in my mind. One was Buttercup; the other was the helo-dump.

The USS Buttercup is a shore-based mock-up of critical spaces below sea level on a Navy ship. Sailors attend class then go "aboard" to be subjected to a "missile attack." Buttercup's operators pull levers and flip switches that mimic battle damage at sea. Bulkheads split and pipes spring leaks. Teams must use anything they can find to keep their ship from "sinking." I remember scrambling underwater, trying not to swallow the brackish cocktail, patching hull splits with mattresses, plywood and loose timber. We all learned that, in a real situation, our lives depended on teamwork and timing and ingenuity. We had to be inventive. We learned quickly, and I can't believe that any of us would forget it.

In the "helo-dump," also a shore-based contraption, two sailors are strapped into the "cockpit" of a helicopter that is dunked into a deep, cold pool then flipped upside down. The trick is to keep your cool, hold your breath, release your restraining belts, make sure your dunk partner is free, then get out of the sinking chopper and find the surface. You do it once with lights on, then again in near darkness. You know it's an exercise, but it gets your attention. Even the strongest of us had to admit to moments of apprehension.

I heard a knock on the hull. It was not a torpedo.

"You can quit work on this one," said Malcolm. "I really could use photos of the pale blue hull at the end of this row."

I threw him a puzzling look. I would have been done in ten more minutes.

"I just sold the damned boat," he said. "The man inside the building paid my list price without coming out here to inspect the damned thing. Please invoice me for this one as if you had finished up."

IT TOOK ME LESS than an hour to finish photographing the pale blue Bertram.

I checked my phone. I'd had a call from Wiley Fecko so I called him back.

"We've been getting frantic messages from Marnie Dunwoody,"

he said. "How is that, and what's she talking about, writing a book?"

"I gave her your numbers," I said, "but this is the first I've heard of a book. Do what you want, but trust her. Anything else?"

"We should have a sit-down meeting," said Fecko.

"I hope it's because you found Ocilla Ramirez's client list."

"Let's give your porch a break," said Fecko. "It's your private place to relax but it's suffered a rash of meetings."

"Rash?" I said.

"It's turning into Mallory Square," he said. "Come over here and see our company campus."

"That sounds strange to me."

"Don't worry. It doesn't smell that way."

16

THE CO-OWNERS OF SOUTHERNMOST Aristocratic Investigations were
the last two men I expected to find living in the New Town section
of the island. Especially so close to Bible hours and potluck dinners
at Grace Lutheran Church. Wiley Fecko had given me their address
on Staples, told me where to turn off Flagler. Fenced yards jammed
with SUVs, vans and boats made it tough to find house numbers. I
drove past it once, dodged a rain puddle at 11th Street, U-turned
and found their place shaded by a huge sea grape tree.

The telling clue was Dubbie Tanner's old Chevy Caprice in the
carport. The beast had been his primary residence for years, his
downscale Caroline Street crib before the city put parking meters
east of Margaret. The new home was concrete block and stucco with
fresh siding, a new roof and storm-proof windows. Dubbie had
spent his money wisely. Except for its height above sea level, this
structure was where I wanted to be during a hurricane. Fecko saw
me arrive and opened the front door. He wore a lavender Tri-Delt
sweatshirt. I doubted that he was up-to-date with his sorority dues.

I parked on the concrete walkway that ran to the porch, but
Wiley motioned me around to the carport.

"I was watching the radar," he said. "A big green blob is heading
our way."

After he helped me cover the Triumph with an old tarp, I carried
in my camera bag. Two empty Dion's chicken boxes sat on a table

made out of an interior door slab. I couldn't tell if it had been their noon meal or supper the night before.

The only furniture in the main room was a quartet of plastic-webbed lawn chairs and a five-foot television. Three Monkey Tom driftwood paintings hung on the wall opposite the TV. Sliding glass doors in the rear wall led to a screened lanai that also held four cheap yard chairs and a makeshift table. On the upside, the prevailing odor inside their home was that of fresh latex paint.

Dubbie pointed down a hallway. "Want to know what we have? My associate will escort you to our office."

"What's wrong?" I said.

Their expressions went from gross innocence to dueling shame. Rain began to fall outside, quickly becoming torrential. It was the first time in five days that I had seen Tanner without a beer in his hand.

"Why do I feel like I should be pissed off about something?"

They stared at me wondering how I had guessed.

"Come on," I said. "You wanted this meeting and you wanted it here. Why?"

"We might have fucked up," said Tanner.

"Why 'might have?'" I said.

"Consequences unknown at this moment."

The rain made it hard to hear. "Pardon me?" I said. "Might have... ?"

"We won't know for a while."

"Was it on the computer?" I said.

"Not at all," said Wiley. "It started with luck and what we thought was first-rate sleuthing."

"Your good intentions took you to... ?"

"Ocilla Ramirez," said Wiley. "I rode my bike to the library this morning to spend time researching her background. They open the doors at 9:30, so I timed my ride to arrive a minute early. I was tooling down William Street and there she was, parallel parking her moss-green Honda Element, going to a client's home."

"You're sure it was a client?" I said.

"She made three trips back to her car to carry in cleaning gear."

"Let me guess," I said. "You were challenged by the deputies that watch her?"

Wiley shook his head. "Didn't happen. I rode my bike down that block twice. Then I sat on the porch of a closed-up home across the street and down a couple houses. Except for a mother with two kids headed for the library and typical traffic, there was no sign of humans—walking or in parked vehicles."

"Why do you think you screwed up?"

Tanner picked up the story. "Ocilla never came out," he said. "Wiley called me to come and help. My first task was to look for the surveillance deputies. I didn't see anyone, and we thought, if they were hidden somewhere on the block, why weren't they worried, too? If she had come back out, we would try to follow her to her next job and start to fill out that client list you want so bad. We took turns riding our bikes and walking on William Street, but she never appeared. Her Honda never moved."

"Maybe she saw one of you and outwaited you both," I said. "Or fell asleep and is just now waking up?"

"I rang the damn doorbell," said Dubbie. "I was going to pretend I was trying to buy a sewing machine advertised in the paper. No one came to the door. I walked around back and knocked on the door. No answer, but I checked and it was unlocked. Let's just say I found all of her cleaning gear and confirmed her absence. Then I saw the gate in the back yard fence. It opens to the yard behind that one, leads to a house on Elizabeth Street."

"The Honda Element?"

"It was still parked on the street when we gave up and came home," said Tanner. "Our problem is we don't know whether she spotted Wiley and he scared her off, or she planned to split before she even went to work. I mean, the house had an escape hatch, that gate in the rear fence."

"You think she planned ahead, chose that William Street house on purpose?"

"Logical," said Dubbie. "It was pure luck that Wiley saw her, so she probably wanted to ditch the deputies."

"But they weren't there," I said.

"Not in the two hours we were around," said Fecko.

Tired of standing, I sat in one of the living room chairs. "Go back to page one," I said. "What inspired you to go to the library, to look into Ocilla's background?"

"Another touch of good luck," said Tanner. "A friend of mine knows a woman named Janice who takes care of rich people's homes. It's the same kind of service that Ocilla's little company, ACXX, provides, except that Janice has been on the island for thirty years and has a great reputation. It went from there."

"From there to where?"

"She agreed to talk with me, but refused to name names. She admitted that 'a few' customers had hired her after firing Greg and Ocilla. They all fired ACXX because of 'trust' issues. Some of the words that Ocilla's former clients used to describe her were con artist, hooker and old-fashioned grifter. One said that Ocilla tried to steer her toward an investment counselor. Turned out the guy had a shady past."

"Caldwell?"

Dubbie shook his head. "I asked. Janice wouldn't say, but she didn't act like she recognized his name."

"Question?" said Wiley.

"Fire away."

"You've wanted her ACXX client list from the first day of this mess. What are you thinking of doing with it, once we find it?"

"I know where you're going with this," I said. "You want to break the news to me that Liska has the entire list because his men have been following Ocilla."

Once again I inspired silence in the room.

"I've lived in town for a long time," I said. "I thought that if I knew someone on the list, that person might open up to me more readily than to a cop. What I want is insight to why Pulver was killed. Knowing motive might help lead us to a murderer. Identifying his murderer might lead us to the person who killed Teresa Barga. That's the crime I want to solve. Greg and Ocilla are my route markers."

"That answers my question," said Wiley.

"Good," I said. "Now what else?"

"More on Ocilla," said Wiley. "Maybe this more than Janice inspired my trip to the library. I told you four days ago that Ocilla's not a valid Hispanic first name."

"It's a town in Georgia."

"And now we know that that's her home state. Playing the source of her first name, I found the web site Georgia Felon Search and paid their fifteen buck fee."

"Instantly traceable," I said. "You put it on a credit card."

"Except the cops get that info for free," said Wiley, "so they're unlikely to come across my transaction. Or even think to look for it. Anyway, you can search by known aliases. Her real name is Ameebah Dobbins, also known as BeBe."

"Ameebah?" I said.

Wiley spelled the name for me. "There are people making babies in this nation who don't know about dictionaries."

"But, Ameebah?"

"Her mother probably heard the word in class the day before she dropped out of school."

"BeBe had a real felony?"

"Ameebah boogied out of south Georgia in 1999 after serving almost five years for first degree cruelty to a child."

"What form of abuse?" I said.

"Malicious and excessive mental and physical pain. Beating, bit-ing, starving and isolation. Ameebah claimed she did it to make her daughter more tough."

"Where is that poor child today?" I said.

"No surprise, on Facebook, with no home town listed," said Wiley. "I found a note posted by Angel Baby Dobbins that said, 'If you ever see my unnatural mother, who now calls herself Ocilla, kick her in the pee hole for me. Tell her it's a love tap from her little Angel.'"

"And that's it?" I said.

"Yep, it is. No links to Ocilla, so she must not worship on the social network."

"Links to and from Angel Baby's friends, nothing?"

"Zip. End of story," said Fecko. "Or all we know so far."

Dubbie raised his hand so I could call on him.

"Two other things that Wiley discovered," he said. "Your new customer Beeson? His late ex-wife owned the building you photographed."

That explained Beeson's skimpy knowledge about the real estate broker's selling strategies.

"What else?"

"The late Amanda was his second wife."

"Damn, that was never mentioned," I said. "How long ago was his first?"

"Twenty-one years ago this month his first wife was murdered, but he was not a suspect. He was in Costa Rica when she was killed. One of the investigating cops, a veteran Bradenton detective, got his ass in a sling because of a wisecrack he made to a reporter. He said that she might have brought some side action to the house while her old man was out of the country. The reporter printed it, and the cop was forced into retirement."

I was inside the home of two former street people, learning background facts late in the game. I felt an odd vertigo, a disorientation. I felt like I needed a blackboard or a huge dry-erase white board to diagram the week's events. An old college friend used to say at crowded parties, "You can't tell the players without a seating chart." Out of all the confusing pairings and break-ups and hookups, I needed one that was three-dimensional. My brain was failing to sort and keep track.

"This is a lot to absorb," I said.

Wiley patted himself once, solidly, on the shoulder. "All in a day's work."

"This twenty-one-year-old murder, did you find an old news item on the web?"

"I printed it out," said Wiley. "It's back in the office."

Dubbie pointed. "Last door on the left."

Their office was a geek's dream. A large iMac, two new laptops, two external hard drives and a Canon scanner-printer occupied a sheet of plywood. Their "desk" was laid across a pair of short file cabinets. A cheap, assemble-yourself bookcase was filled with Keys-related reference books, old phone directories and software boxes. Their office chairs probably cost more than the rest of the furniture in the house. A large cork bulletin board held a scattering of Office Max receipts and three-by-five cards covered with cryptic notes. Most surprising was the five-foot tall safe.

I knocked on its door. "Weaponry?"

"Wardrobe, for now," said Tanner. He turned the massive handle and eased open the safe. Inside was a collection of shirts and trousers that a Salvation Army collection center would quietly stuff under the table and send off to the Dumpster. The clothing was clean, however, and wrinkled but hung on hangers. "We'll adjust our storage should we acquire some firepower."

Above the computers was an Internet printout of four scruffy-looking gentlemen "Wanted" by the sheriff's office.

"We get around in this town," said Dubbie. "We see all kinds. We also see more clearly than citizens who don't take the time to look at faces."

"These people aren't just deadbeats or stupid or down on their luck," said Wiley. "Look at this guy, he's still a kid. Aggravated battery with a deadly weapon. And this guy. Possession of a weapon by a convicted felon, firing a weapon in public and carrying concealed. Don't get ahead of him in line at the grocery store. They're all scummy louts and, if we see one of them, it can't hurt to butter-up the big boys."

I stepped over to the bookcase. "What's this?"

"It's exactly what it appears to be," said Fecko. "A book."

"The Complete Idiot's Guide to Private Investigating?"

"You will note," he said, "that it stands among a number of fine books in our growing professional library. It's a valid source for knowledge and research. If we questioned its validity because of its title, we wouldn't be true investigators."

"Can I use your laptop for a minute?" I said. "I need to send an email."

"Use mine," said Tanner. "It's already booted up."

I sat, opened the browser and entered my access password. I had to think for a moment to recall Detective Steffey's email address. He hadn't mentioned Beeson's first wife, and I thought it was an important fact to pass along. I wrote a quick note, short, to the point.

Just before I clicked the SEND button I said, "Wiley, have you got that old news article?"

He pulled it from a stack of loose papers next to the printer, handed it to me. I read the first paragraph then jumped to the ending. I was glad that I looked. The veteran cop who had blabbed to the reporter was Detective Frank Steffey. He could have been an uncle or a much older brother, but I would bet that Frank was Glenn Steffey's father. Glenn didn't need me to remind him of that earlier case.

Jumping to the present tense, I had to wonder how it would affect his handling of Amanda's murder.

I quit the webmail program, closed Dubbie's laptop then noticed a photograph on the desk. It was a picture of Ocilla's Honda Element printed on copy paper.

"I forgot to mention that," said Wiley. "There's the house she disappeared into, and that's her Honda where she left it."

The picture was pixilated and the color too blue. But there was something in it I wanted to see more clearly. "Have you got this image in one of these computers?"

Wiley waved me out of his seat, sat and opened an iPhoto folder of pictures from William Street. Parked two cars in front of the Element was a bronze Hyundai four-door. I tapped my finger on it.

"If you see this," I said to Wiley and Dubbie, "and I think it's a rental car, try to get a tag number. It was parked on Seidenberg yesterday across from her house."

"Do what we can," said Tanner.

"If you could call me a taxi, I'll go away and let you keep working," I said. "I'll come back for the motorcycle when the rain stops. How do we stand for the time clock and expenses?"

My question cost me a Franklin. I gave them the names Luke Tharpe and Edwin Torres, but asked Dubbie to keep digging on Darrin Marsh. "Before I forget," I said, "is there any way to remove Sheriff Liska's connection to Emerson Caldwell from the online search engines? That one feat could be worth endless brownie points."

Their faces widened into broad conspirators' grins.

"Anything yet on Anya or Tonya and Sonya, the Timber twins?" I said.

"We got three hits," said Wiley. "Sonya works for Novak Hardwood Lumber in Leon County upstate. Anya Timber has a Longboat Key zip code. Tonya and Sonya graduated from a high school in Lake Forest, Illinois. I've just scratched the surface on that assignment. Should I make it a priority?"

"Get it when you can," I said.

Dubbie's phone began to buzz. He took the call.

Wiley offered to show me to the door. Out in the hallway, he pointed into a room on the right. "Walk fast here," he said. "We call Tanner's bedroom 'Baghdad.'"

I ignored Dubbie's minor slum but looked into the bedroom across the hall. It was clean, organized. Wiley looked ill at ease, perhaps embarrassed by his room's meager decor, or still not used to be sleeping in a house rather than a tent.

"This is good for me," he said. "I'm getting older and I was getting bitter. Nothing like a roof over your head to brighten your day."

There were only two wall decorations, but they caught my eye. It was a shrine to the man's former life. Fecko explained that a county official had taken the Polaroid photo of his old Stock Island campsite when the camp was active, during some bullshit campaign to rid the Keys of indigent hobos.

"That old tent of mine is the tarp we threw over your motorbike," said Wiley.

Next to the picture was one of Wiley's cardboard panhandling signs. The message in thick black ink said, "HAVIN' A NICE DAY? I'M NOT."

"Good sales pitch," I said.

He shook his head. "It's on the edge of self-pity, but I call it nostalgia."

"Don't beat yourself up over that," I said. "Couple of hours ago, I swam in that muck myself. It's therapeutic if you don't overdo it."

Wiley looked me in the eye. "It's a damn good reminder of where I don't want to go next."

MY PHONE BUZZED. It showed J BEESON.

I took the call and waited on the porch for my cab.

"I have a favor to ask," he said.

"First, Mr. Beeson, I have a question," I said. "Why did you hire me for a job that any decent photographer in Sarasota could have done?"

"Frankly, Alex, I did it to build my reputation in Key West. You're known on the island, and I thought that I would look more important if I hired you. Plus, Anya was intrigued by your reputation for helping to solving crimes. I understand you spoke with her earlier today."

"We had a puzzling mid-morning chat, yes," I said.

"All women are puzzling, Alex. Every last one of them. There's also that classic rule that someone, somewhere thinks every woman is a pain in the ass. Anya could well be the exception."

I chose to let him bask in his belief.

"What's your favor?" I said.

"The Manatee County prosecutor is considering the idea of calling a grand jury in regard to my ex-wife's murder. I can't imagine a more painful ordeal for my daughter to witness and endure. I would like you to fly back here, at my expense, for a meeting with my attorney and the county prosecutor. I want to convince the legal eagles that I couldn't have been involved in the crime."

"Why would my presence have any bearing on their decisions?"

"I don't know how they think or work," he said. "But you're the only non-family member that I have to confirm my timeline and my state of mind. Your being there may make the difference between a difficult situation and an unbearable one."

I couldn't imagine being a character witness for someone I had known for only four days. I was, however, being asked to tell the truth, not to tell lies.

Beeson sensed my hesitation. "I would compensate you for your time as if you were here working, of course. Per diem expenses, you name it."

That was good news but he had misjudged my silence.

"I'll get Rodney, that same pilot, for you, Alex," he said. "Round trip this time. Come in the morning, you can be back home before sundown."

"Tomorrow is Saturday," I said.

"Yes it is, but I need to act quickly. We discussed the hour between eleven and noon."

"I thought his name was Sherwin."

"That's right," said Beeson. "Rodney's last name is Sherwin."

"Please give him my cell number. I'll want to know Rodney's schedule before I go to bed tonight."

"Thank you, Alex."

I've made plenty of mistakes in my life.

17

Dᴜʙʙɪᴇ Tᴀɴɴᴇʀ ᴊᴏɪɴᴇᴅ ᴍᴇ on his porch, sat on a sun-bleached shellback chair. Still no beer in his hand, but I refused to take the bait and mention it. The downpour sounded like a hot griddle and smelled like Garrison Bight. My cab hadn't shown yet.

"Ameebah Dobbins is a long way from her dirt patch hometown," said Tanner. "She must have found a first class tutor in prison."

"And now, as Ocilla Ramirez, she's abusing grown-ups," I said. "Maybe they can deal with it better than her daughter did. I still can't figure out what makes her such a premium target for surveillance. How does she rate her low-rent immunity?"

"They see her as bait fish, that's all," said Tanner. "Cops tolerate minor bullshit when they're after serious felons."

"A multi-agency task force is more than just cops," I said. "She may be the tail end of the dragon, but something brought down Greg Pulver's murder. That's a huge step up from minor."

"Look at the major menu, Alex. The sex trade, financial fraud, dope smuggling, dope sales, illegal aliens and terrorism. Or mix and match. It's heavier than jacking up 7-Elevens, also a felony."

"Play with it," I said. "You're the new snoop."

"Okay," said Dubbie. "Sex would rate attention if she was pimping immigrants. Women from Eastern Europe or Central America who had overstayed their tourist permits. Or came to practice their trade in a safer country. This town has no shortage of women call-

199

ing themselves dancers. And she had illegals staying in her home on Big Coppitt. She knows how to play the invisible economy, the men washing dishes and women polishing knobs."

"Do you think she owns on Big Coppitt, or she rents and subleases?"

"It's my bad I can't answer that," he said. "We plain forgot to check public records for ownership. But own or rent, it doesn't really matter in the scope of things, unless, say, it's owned by someone linked to the rest of our puzzle."

"Good start," I said. "Give that one four stars."

"Dope makes sense paired with a housekeeping business," he said, "but no sense in a town full of small-time dealers. Big-time crooks don't trust druggies."

"Two stars," I said.

"If Ocilla Ramirez was a terrorist, she would already be in Guantanamo."

"Correct. Zero stars."

"She had access to clients' computers, online bill-paying accounts and incoming mail deliveries."

Right there Tanner echoed Liska's remark about Greg and Ocilla cleaning the homes of the vulnerable.

"She tried to steer a client toward one particular investment counselor," I said. "And Liska suggested that she's been pilfering her customers' retirement funds. But I can't believe she's engineering a big city Ponzi scheme. Financial fraud looks like four stars."

"She could be selling that access to the whole world," said Tanner. "Big money's part of the mix," he added. "Pulver's murder is proof of that."

"That puts us up to five stars. Check on that home ownership. And, what the hell, find out where she banks, carefully."

I ASKED THE TAXI driver to pull into Dredgers Lane and give me one minute inside the house. I wanted to stash my camera and grab a legal pad and a couple of felt tips before heading to my next stop. I had just walked into the kitchen when my landline rang. If I had been in another room, I might have ignored it. I picked it up without checking the Caller ID. One day I will learn.

Darrin Marsh identified himself. I didn't respond.

"I need to talk with you Rutledge," he said. "I didn't want to knock on your door without calling ahead."

"I'm not at the house, Marsh."

"I'm calling your house."

"Call forwarding?"

"If we could just get together," he said. "I don't care, wherever you are... Talk for a few. No rough stuff, you got my word. Your choice of location. You call it."

Rough stuff? A new legal term for assault and battery?

I looked at the plain, round plastic clock on the wall. It read 1:55.

"What's in it for me, Darrin? You want to pour out your soul, go to church. Or the gym, wherever you worship."

"I want to say to your face that I'm sorry, and ask you a favor."

He hadn't answered my question. I didn't say anything.

"You're right," he admitted. "It's all about me. But we have one thing in common, and her murder is unsolved. We owe it to her to be in touch with each other."

It was a good line, but I couldn't buy it as genuine.

"I'm up the Keys," I said. "I'll be back in a couple hours."

"Like I say, you call it. Her stepfather's useless. He claims she ignored him, shut him out after her mother died. I need to start thinking about a funeral or memorial service."

Much as I hate funerals, that was a better line.

Anywhere but this house, I thought. I wanted witnesses, but I didn't want to be seen with the hothead, at least by locals. If Beth ever decided to tell Internal Affairs that Marsh had slugged me, I didn't want to beat her case at its outset. My mind ran a fast tour of Old Town. I wanted neutral ground where we could talk without being overheard. Out in the open, with people around. He still had first punch advantage, but if it happened again I would use the witnesses.

"I'll be in the mood for a beer when I get back," I said. "How about the pool bar at the Southernmost Hotel?"

"Next to South Beach?" said Marsh.

"No, the Pineapple Bar next to the swimming pool, between South and United. How about you show up in uniform?"

"Then you'll be the only one drinking," he said, "but I follow your reasoning."

"Four-thirty?"

"That's when I write my shift report," he said. "Ten of five okay?"

"I'll call you back if I change my mind, Marsh."

THE BLACKFIN BISTRO, DIMLY lighted, vegetable art and wine posters on the walls and every table taken. People forced indoors by the rain took their time eating as the weather lifted. Servers tapped their feet waiting for credit cards to wave. During the cab ride from Staples Avenue to Dredgers Lane to Duval Street, I craved a yellowtail snapper and avocado sandwich. I blamed my urge on the elegant seafood in Malcolm Mason's office. I wanted that sandwich.

The rain had just quit when I reached the restaurant. I looked out the back door to the small, walled patio. Not a soul. I borrowed two towels from behind the bar and walked out to my choice of tables. There was a vacant wine bar with a tin roof, two picnic tables with benches under a palm canopy, and a short upright fan. Antique bird cages hung from what looked like a rare long stem acacia tree. A candelabra was suspended from a tall sapodilla. I had stumbled upon a hidden corner in Key West, Internet jazz included. I chose a table big enough for four, asked my server to turn down the exterior speakers, and ordered the fish sandwich and a glass of Pinot gris.

My visit with Wiley and Dubbie convinced me that I was dealing with an overload of facts. Escape helps. If every object in sight, especially in my house full of my stuff, distracts from a project, it's time to flee. I sympathized with Chicken Neck Liska's use of my porch as a satellite office. I counted on the Bistro patio to open my brain, lead me to simpler ways to view the ongoing storm.

The wine, the legal pad, the pen. Think large, underline and draw arrows. Write down possibilities, create an outline. Ponder the concept of a grand jury summons. I wished I had brought pens of two different colors. Visual drama promotes alertness.

"Your wine, sir."

"Thank you."

"Your sandwich should be up in five."

He wanted another "Thank you," but I was already listing a cast of characters. Everyone met or mentioned during my Sarasota trip: Justin Beeson, Anya Timber, Eileen Beeson, Luke Tharpe, Edwin Torres, Amanda Beeson, Detective Glenn Steffey, Rodney Sherwin, the pilot, and Sonya Timber, the twin sister.

Then came the questions, theory upon theory, no favorites allowed. The Rutledge grape-induced scientific method. Starting with just one sip.

What really had changed in Beeson's schedule that required his quick departure from Key West? Had he known we would leave that day when I was at his home on Olivia? He had told Anya it had something to do with Eileen. I knew that school was in session because that's where Anya had taken her the first morning in Sarasota. Had Amanda insisted that Eileen attend her classes?

Or was Amanda already dead? If he knew that his ex-wife was dead, only two people could have told him. Someone who found her body, or the murderer. But if someone had found Amanda, why would they call Beeson instead of the cops? If the murderer had informed him, Beeson had hired her killer. Along that line, perhaps Anya had hired the killer, received the "mission accomplished" call, and made up a reason for them all to leave Key West immediately.

Still, why would he go to 23 Beeson Way straight from the airport yet not find her body until the next day? He had done nothing in the building that evening except write me a check, introduce me to Tharpe and Torres and talk with Tharpe. He could have talked to him by phone and scribbled my check the next morning. Was it part of his plan to take me to his building—and *not* find her? Had he planned all along to let someone else make the discovery? The mechanic that didn't kill her?

Just a theory. And a moment to remind myself to slow down. I had written so quickly, I could barely make out my own handwriting.

Luke Tharpe and Edwin Torres were an odd pair. The money they made couldn't have been great, and both had day jobs. Torres had expressed his appreciation of the older, collectible vehicles. Tharpe had called them rattletraps. They were men with different lives and tastes. Tharpe's day job was in an office; Torres did manual labor. Either could have found another place to moonlight. Edwin had suggested by his car-delivery timeline that Luke and Amanda were an item. Had he tossed that out in an attempt to steer the investigation toward a culprit or away from himself? One day later, when Edwin Torres called me at home, he had sounded afraid of Tharpe.

Were both mechanics having affairs with Amanda?

New approach. What did I know about Amanda? She had a check mark tattooed where a tuft of hair once had grown. Beyond that, I had no idea where she was from, how she lived her life. But maybe my restricted viewpoint would help me find insight without post-judgment. From the moment that Anya stated that they were a sexual threesome, I wondered why Justin Beeson had bothered to get divorced. Unless the split was Amanda's idea so she could also be with other partners. Perhaps it was her idea to leave Justin because it was her money that he was throwing away.

Who had the best motive to kill Amanda? Why was she murdered?

Justin, for the money. He could save on alimony and inflated child support, and inherit, as Eileen's custodian, Amanda's home.

He could get back his beloved boat and sell Amanda's shiny two-seater cars to buy himself that real Shelby GT-350 that Torres said he wanted.

Anya was free to marry Beeson, so she might already know that his cash was getting tight. If Beeson's financial outlook improved, Anya's would lift on the same tide. Maybe she had become tired of their ménage à trois. Perhaps the divorce had turned each of them against marriage.

If there was a pattern in there, it hadn't burst through to me. I couldn't force it, either. I put my thoughts elsewhere. I tried a different approach, a back-door look.

Who had the fewest reasons to kill Amanda?

I could start with Eileen. She would have no reason or capacity to kill her mother. Next, if he didn't stand to inherit a thing, was Justin, who needed his sugar ex, his bankroll. Next was Anya if, indeed, she and Amanda had been close friends as she had claimed—if the love triangle was truly free of jealousy and hidden hatred.

One of the mechanics, or both perhaps, had a good deal going. An unsupervised job, work performance measured primarily by maintenance of status quo, and a dash of sport sex now and then with the boss's ex-wife. Maybe the employees' animosity came from conflicts in scheduling Amanda visits.

How many different, or how few, ways could Amanda enter the building? Who had the capability of entering with her or meeting her there? Had she come on her own only to be ambushed at the pass? Was she stalking one of the mechanics? Did she suspect that Luke and Anya were messing around behind everyone's backs?

She had been bound and disrobed. Why was she put on display? Was Amanda having sex with someone in that cubicle? If she had been caught having sex, and her killer wanted revenge, he or she would have had to murder two people, so that idea wouldn't work. Had the tableau been merely a diversion tactic?

Shift gears once again, my mind open wide. Two questions have been raised after the fact. Why did Luke and Anya come to Key West, or was Beeson in town, too? If Luke and Anya wanted to duck out of sight, there was always her condo on Longboat Key near Sarasota. Except for the possibility that Beeson had a key to the place.

I was getting almost scientific in my little wine-fueled inquiry. I could nail this down by building to a crescendo then...

I had forgotten to turn off my cell phone.

Detective Glenn Steffey. Was he monitoring my inner thoughts?

"How you doing down there in the lovely Florida Keys?"

"My parade is suffering intermittent rain," I said.

"I might have continuing clouds for you, Mr. Rutledge. We'd like you to return to Sarasota for a crime scene reconstruction. Let me add that this is prior to your being summoned for a grand jury proceeding. It would be voluntary."

"What a coincidence," I said. "I'm going to be there anyway."

"Why would that be?"

"Beeson's flying me up in the morning to sit in his dugout. Some kind of sit-down with his attorney and the prosecutor."

"I may sit in on that meeting," said Steffey.

"What am I supposed to do?" I said. "Be on his side of the table while the county's asking questions, and be on your side when he responds?"

"It's informal at this point, Alex. You can sit next to him the whole time."

"What do you need me for?"

"Something we can do later in the day," he said. "Beeson's narration of events hasn't convinced our prosecutor of his innocence. Your photos suggest overacting rather than typical grief."

Steffey's phrasing reminded me of Beth Watkins's witness at The Tideline. The woman who heard "normal" screams then decided that they came from children at play.

"Is there a reference book on typical grief?" I said.

He ignored that one. "We noticed that Justin's attorney has his own doubts as well. The phrase he used with me was, 'The idea of working out a deal is premature,' which suggests that it could mature in the future."

"Do you have plans to induce this maturation?" I said.

"Our thinking is that he may have orchestrated the body's discovery, with or without Tharpe's knowledge. The red flag in the timeline was Luke's finding Amanda within moments of your entering the building. It could be perfectly legit, but it feels too scripted. We want to use your photos as a guide while he walks us through his story one more time. And we want you to verify the scene as we go."

"Why my pictures?" I said. "Why not take him back to that cubicle at 23 Beeson? Set it up with a mannequin."

"We're afraid they might claim emotional prejudice or some such legalistic horse crap. We like solid evidence like the parcel you found last night in your photograph."

"That object that looked like a rucksack?"

"Right," said Steffey. "We found it twenty yards south of where you described. It's a real teaser. Amanda's skirt wrapped around her underwear, two canisters of spray insulation, a pair of cotton work gloves and an empty Carta Blanca beer bottle. You must have been on a ladder or something. Standing on the road, we never would have found it, but one of our guys volunteered to ride on top of the crime scene van. We're lucky we got to it when we did. Two wild dogs were dragging it away. We've found no prints or other clues so far, but we sent the bottle off for DNA analysis. Thank you."

"Kill the dogs?" I said.

"No, we bleeped them with the siren. Any other questions?"

"I just wrote down about forty of them."

"Read them to me," said Steffey.

"You serious?"

"If one out of forty goes somewhere I haven't been, it might be Clue One," he said. "How about your top four?"

"Did Anya Timber have her own key pass to the building?"

"Got me," he said. "I'll have to find that out."

"Has the coroner determined cause of death and is there a toxicology report?"

"Both confidential," said Steffey. "That's two questions."

I used silence to fight back.

He relented. "The alcohol, cocaine and valium did not contribute to her death. She was strangled during or after having sexual intercourse."

"Then dressed up to look like she had choked on that orange goop."

"I would tend to agree with that," he said.

"Did the surveillance video show Amanda coming inside the building?"

"Nope."

"Did you see either of Beeson's mechanics bringing his personal vehicle into the garage area for, say, an oil change or new spark plugs?"

"That's good, Alex," said Steffey. "In fact, they both did. The day before you got to town."

"What does Torres drive?"

"An old Camry sedan. And, yes, we've already executed a warrant. Its trunk is clean. We're waiting to execute on Tharpe's PT Cruiser. We need to find it first."

"Tharpe drives a fancy Ram truck," I said. "I saw him driving it the day he found Amanda."

"We'll check with the DMV again," he said.

Steffey sounded full of good intentions. I didn't want to slam him with the fact that his father may have tainted the murder case regarding Beeson's first wife. But I wanted to plant a seed so the fact of that death might enter into this case.

"It's a long shot," I said, "but has Beeson ever had an employee involved in violent crime, a perp or a victim? Or someone with a criminal past who may have held a grudge against the man or his business?"

"Another fine one," said Steffey. "I've lost count, but throw a couple more at me."

"How many real estate sales people had access to the building?"

"Sales people? It's for sale?" A moment of quiet. "Oh, shit. Thank you."

"Why does Beeson have such an elaborate security system for a building that's just a shell?"

"I asked essentially the same question, Rutledge. His explanation was that bums and winos live in the woods around there, off the Interstate. Hobos and bail jumpers from up north. Which is true. One of our deputies found a local man hiding from his family, back in that hammock. Beeson said that when they were putting up the place, they caught them sleeping in construction huts and inside the building. He told me it was worth the price if it kept one vagrant from sleeping in his grandmother's classic Ford."

"I don't buy it," I said. "Nobody needs that much gear to fight off trespassers."

"I'll ask him again and phrase it differently," said Steffey. "When you get here, where are you staying?"

"Beeson said I'd be back in Key West by sundown."

"We can arrange a motel," said Steffey.

"He probably booked the pilot for a one-day round-trip," I said.

"I'll look into the pilot's fee and a second room. I can't guarantee you much more than two pillows, free shampoo and twelve channels."

"I've slept aboard sailboats in raging storms and called it Paradise."

"Call me when you get in."

18

THE TROPICAL PATIO AT Blackfin Bistro stirred up a lot of ideas. The fish sandwich restored my faith in the wonders of nature. The empty bird cages were spooky but quiet. That's what helped. And the second glass of wine. Before leaving my private think tank, I called Sam Wheeler at his home on Elizabeth Street.

"Captain Wheeler's office," said Marnie. "May I tell him who's calling?"

"Both of you at home at four in the afternoon," I said. "Would I be out of line to suspect an enhanced nap?"

"What makes you think that, pervert?" she said coyly.

"He would have answered if you were working, and you wouldn't have answered if you two weren't taking a dance break. Don't worry, I'm not your boss."

"Sam!" she said only a few inches from the phone. "A man on the line wants to know about our sex life."

Muffled by distance: "Tell him our best photos are on the World Wide Web."

"How was your walk along the beach?" I said.

"Which one?" said Marnie.

"Five days ago, after the mess at The Tideline. You were going to leave your iPod at home."

"It helped, but not much. I've taken two walks since then. Here's Sam."

Sam agreed to dress like a European tourist and have a frothy piña colada around four-forty at the Southernmost Hotel Pineapple Bar. My short-term care insurance.

I STEPPED OFF THE patio, and entered the restaurant to pay my bill. I could barely see in the reduced light. While I waited for my change, I looked at a few of the late-day customers and glanced quickly at a couple in a far corner engaged in an intense conversation. I didn't want to snap my head back around and draw their attention, but what was Beth Watkins doing here? Why was she sharing a bottle of wine with E. Carlton Gamble, the attorney I had seen a day and a half ago with Robert Fonteneau? What was so important about their meeting that she hadn't seen me walk inside from the back patio?

Slowly, not wanting to appear combative, I turned again to regard the two of them. The relief I felt almost buckled my knees. My memory of the photograph shown to me by Tanner and Fecko saved me from approaching the table, causing a scene when my silence was the only alternative. The woman with Gamble was Mrs. Christi Caldwell, a grieving widow just in from Canada.

Outside on Duval I called both Wiley Fecko and Chicken Neck Liska. I reached voicemail in each case, and informed them of our visitor. I also asked Fecko to find out if Gamble had represented Emerson Caldwell during his financial troubles in the late 1990s.

I REACHED THE PINEAPPLE Bar early, wove my way between several square columns decorated with pineapple sculptures, and grabbed two web-backed barstools at the east end. I heard several languages spoken by people in the adjacent pool. A woman lounged in the shallow end reading a paperback titled *Kald Mig Prinsesse*, which I took to be Swedish or Danish. I ordered an Amstel from a genial bartender who told me his name was "Tim, the surly bartender." He asked where I was from. I told him I lived on the island.

Tim looked bewildered. "Don't see much of your kind in here," he said. "Except for my girlfriend, you're my first local this year." He ducked away to make blender drinks for a German couple.

Like aquarium DVDs, the tourist scene at the Southernmost Hotel pool is a world away from anything we Key Westers might experience. Or else we experience it in the company of other locals, and the tourists are stuck with other tourists. When I travel, anywhere in the Caribbean or the States, I prefer to blend in with residents, eat their foods, stay in small hotels, walk their streets.

Still, it was the middle of January. The children couldn't romp in a backyard pool in Omaha. Their parents couldn't sip blender drinks barefoot in snow or listen to Bob Marley in an outdoor tiki bar when it was fourteen below. Each visitor looked happy and fulfilled, and I reminded myself that we all choose our own approach to time away. These people were getting their money's worth.

Sam Wheeler looked to be basking in luxury. With his hands wrapped around the tall umbrella drink on the bar, he looked prayerful, lost in his own world a million miles away. I hoped he would be able to hear clearly from ten bar stools away.

If DARRIN MARSH HADN'T been in uniform, I might not have recognized him. There hadn't been time in the Tower Bar to consider his features, to react beyond blurs of clenched fists, flaming eyeballs, blood flowing from his nose. Here, with his bright white shirt and fresh military haircut, he didn't look like the ripped barfly that had jumped me thirty hours earlier. He walked into the Pineapple Bar with that typical swagger they learn early to remind us that they're wrapped in Kevlar and carrying gear they need to stop crime. This time I was ready for Marsh's menacing glare, but it took him a few moments to look me in the eye. He asked Tim, the friendly surly bartender, for a Coke then eased his posture to look more relaxed and less official.

Perhaps his work shift had tamed the monster.

"Thanks for seeing me, Alex."

"Lots to talk about," I said.

"Where I come from, people didn't open up much. We were taught not to discuss the awkward topics."

"Which ones were those?"

"Sex, politics and religion," he said. "My family added divorce, mental illness and bankruptcy."

Not to mention police brutality, I thought.

Marsh looked away, checked out the people at the bar. Checked Sam and three tourist couples farther down. Sam looked to be memorizing objects behind the bar, the hot dog griller, popcorn maker, convection cooker and cash register. Marsh didn't recognize Sam as a local.

"Of course, in this town," Marsh added, "sex, politics and religion are primary points of discussion."

"Where was it you grew up?"

"Binghamton, New York, the north side," he said. "It wasn't the rich part of town, so knuckles made a difference."

"You got out alive."

He looked bored by the idea but inhaled, puffed up his chest. "Lucky and big. By ninth grade even seniors wouldn't mess with me."

"Cuba's got a law you might like," I said. "The cops there can charge a man with Social Dangerousness if he looks like he might commit a crime. Emphasis on 'might.' Talking potential for bad behavior, that's it. An offender gets an automatic two-year sentence. If this island had that law, every badge could be the town bully."

Darrin shook his head, stared at his untouched soft drink. "Yesterday worries me, Rutledge, I'll admit that," he said. "I can count on one hand the rookie cops who weren't thugs-in-training in high school or pushy jocks in college. But we find out fast. We tone it down or blow out of the job. Those who are meant to be cops learn rules and respect. We maintain an air of authority because we have to show that, sure. But in this city, at least, very few of us are power freaks after a couple years of police work.'"

"Let's go back to the part about respect," I said.

"I didn't act like myself. What the fuck was I doing? I don't whup on people."

"Could've fooled me."

"I'm sorry," he said. "If it would help convince you, I'd say it a hundred times."

"No thank you," I said. "We came here to talk about Teresa."

Marsh inhaled, puffed his cheeks, blew out air. "Look, I want you to know, a few months ago, one Sunday morning over coffee, Teresa and I were talking about high points in our lives. And regrets. She said that she was the bad guy in your relationship. She told me her biggest regret was the way she ended things with you."

I shook my head, bewildered that she would discuss me with her lover.

"She never told me about the guy she left you for, Alex. The one who died."

"The old college boyfriend?" I said. "He was a hustler and a blowhard. I think she was entranced by the situation's nostalgia more than him."

"Variation on the old Keys saying, 'Arrive on vacation, leave on probation?'"

"Like that, but worse," I said. "His case was, 'Arrive on the island with money to burn, leave the Keys in a custom urn.'"

Marsh laughed but I wasn't convinced that I'd humored him. And hearing myself say "urn" didn't do much for my mood, either.

"She didn't tell me your name, by the way," he said. "I figured that out for myself. I also, pretty much, figured out how she had misbehaved."

"So, you..."

"Yes, like you said yesterday. I found her stash of diaries, including the one from when she was with you. I was stupid to pry into her past. But, at the time I did it, she was Miss Attitude, and I was worried that she was having a fling behind my back."

Oh, what a perfect time to shut up. I sneaked a glance at Sam. He was holding his drink with one hand, picking his teeth with a business card, staring at a convection oven behind the bar. Marsh was sweating. If I mentioned it, he would blame it on the post-rain humidity. I didn't mention it. I wanted him to keep sweating.

"Fling?" I finally said.

"Yep, she spent an afternoon with some tourist, but it was history, over and done. I guess I picked up delayed signals. I wouldn't have stayed with her if I'd thought she was still... If I knew for certain."

"Ask her about it?"

He shook his head. "I was afraid of her answer. There were days and nights when I told myself that I hadn't been this happy or contented in my life. I was also afraid what she'd say if she knew I had scoped the diaries. She had days when she was no walk on the beach."

"We all have those days," I said.

"Did she have any quirks, habits that bothered you?" said Marsh. "Anything that got under your skin?"

Tread lightly, I thought. "One thing she did, no other girlfriends have done it. Whenever I was reading a good novel, she would get this message in her brain that told her when I'd hit the last two pages. She would interrupt and ruin the ending. I can't tell you how many times it happened, like ugly telepathy. Maybe a half dozen paragraphs to go, and there she was, asking if I'd taken out the garbage or turned off the yard light. I would have to force myself not to toss books in the trash can right there and then. But other than that..."

"By the way," said Marsh, "when I was telling her my biggest regrets—at least biggest since I arrived in the Keys—she warned me that you and Carmen Sosa are close friends."

"That we are. Neighbors and friends."

"Carmen and I had drinks and dinner one night, years ago,

before I started work with the city, and I acted like an ass."

"Maybe you should tell her someday that you're sorry for that."

He shook his head. "She doesn't want to see my face."

"You tried and she blew you off?"

"No, I screwed up that one solid. She's like the girls from junior high who think you're an asshole for the rest of your life."

Marsh signaled Tim and ordered an Amstel and another Coke.

KEY WEST IS A SMALL island, and you hear almost every siren in town. You know which street they're on and have a general idea where they've stopped. I hadn't heard one all day long.

"Puros Reynoso," said Marsh. He pointed to a cigar vendor display among the bottles behind the bar. "They're excellent, from the Dominican Republic. A friend of mine said they used to roll those between the thighs of virgins."

"That's been an urban legend for 150 years," I said.

"Well, I can't smoke in uniform."

"That's right, you're a cop, Marsh, a professional," I said. "Have you worked up any theories? Made a list of who might have killed Teresa?"

"One and only guess," he said. "Wrong place, wrong time."

"Nothing more scientific?"

"That's what detectives are for, that science. If I got in their way, I'd never hear the end of it. One of them could write me up for obstructing. Screw my job, maybe end my career, no reflection on your lady friend."

"It sounds like a reflection. Are you saying she's vindictive? Maybe she would appreciate your insight."

"All of us, we have our jobs to do," said Marsh. "If we do them well, we don't step on each other's toes."

I wasn't so sure of that. If I was in love with a murder victim I wouldn't fucking care. I would tromp on toes, obstruct my ass off, force action, find what other officers couldn't find or refused to find. Hell, I had pushed Teresa out of my life a while ago, but I was adamant about solving her murder. Why was Marsh complacent?

Why was there no hair on his arms? I didn't want to know.

"You have training in this stuff," I said. "On the job or did you go to school?"

I knew the answer. But I didn't want to tip him to the idea that Beth had dug up his background info.

"College major, not that I'll brag my GPA. Then I had to take a few courses at the college here to get my Florida certification. That was when I paid the bills working construction, installing electrical equipment, re-wiring old office buildings."

"You were with Teresa how many minutes before she died?"

"Hard to tell," said Marsh. "Probably less than twenty minutes."

"And the most sensible concept is that she walked into a crime-in-progress. The perp was still inside and she became a liability."

He nodded. "Just like on television. She walked into a neighbor's condo. The only possible reason was because the door was open. She saw Caldwell on the floor, she went in to help him."

I wondered if Marsh was smoke-screening, trying to funnel an alibi through me to the investigators that counted. The people who could make him an accomplice or the sole perpetrator. But I didn't know him well enough to separate truth from his lies. I had had a busy day and he'd had several days to write his own script. Also, he could be innocent as hell and still building a CYA wall around himself.

I quit the silence: "Wouldn't she come and get you first, before she went into the condo?"

"I think her first reaction was compassion," he said. "She saw a man slumped on the floor, or watched him fall, and had no way to know that a man had been shot in another room. She went in to help Caldwell and, somehow, saw the murderer. Or she tried to dial 911 and the murderer grabbed her from behind before she could speak. He killed her and left quicker than he wanted to, left the door wide open."

"A man shot?" I said.

"Fuck, I thought you knew," he said. "I found him and saw the head wound, but the detectives told me to stay quiet about it. They put out the false fact that Pulver had been cut to shreds. It was a way to filter out fake confessions."

"I'll be damned," I said, playing dumb. "I will have to speak to my girlfriend about that. Did either of you know Greg Pulver or Emerson Caldwell?"

He shook his head. "I sure didn't. I never heard Teresa mention them."

"Ever heard of Ocilla Ramirez?"

"After the shit went down," he said. "Never heard her name before this week."

"Me, too," I said. "Are you worried?"

Marsh twisted his head to face me. "Why would I be?"

"Come out of the fog, Darrin," I said. "You discovered three bodies when you were off duty. I hear there's the issue of your missing gun. You went to college for this shit. You could be anything from a grieving boyfriend to a bad apple to a true suspect to a cop-abuse civil rights mudbath."

"What about you, Rutledge? She's not your first ex-girlfriend to be found dead, to be murdered."

Success, Darrin, I thought. You landed a mental gut punch I didn't see coming. Teresa must have told him about Julia Balbuena, not that I was ever considered a suspect.

"That was the first time I ever worked for the county," I said, "for Sheriff Tucker, the weasel. When Liska was still a city detective."

"It must have been after he got tangled up with Caldwell."

Red flag. Play stupid. "Liska and Caldwell?" I said. "Tangled?"

"They were partners in a Ponzi scheme fifteen years ago," said Marsh.

"Bullshit," I said. "Liska was the lead detective in Key West. When would he have time to rip people off?"

"This isn't new scuttlebutt from the city, Rutledge. It's bounced around the police department since I started there. Probably for a few years before that. I'm surprised you never heard. Whatever went down, it went backward for Liska. Caldwell ripped him off for his life savings, and no one got arrested. All Liska could do was eat shit. Now he's hanging in the wind because he could be a suspect for revenge motive."

I had to think about that for a moment. Liska's twin statements from earlier days informed me that he wasn't involved. "Please stick with it, Aristocrats and all." Then later, "Do you want to put your private eye rookies at death's door? Draw bad guys to your doorstep? Endanger your girlfriend?"

"I'm surprised that didn't come out when he ran for office," I said.

Marsh shook his head. "Before my time."

"Did Teresa say anything about burial or cremation?"

By changing the subject I stalled his train of thought.

Marsh took another look around the bar. Fixed his gaze on Sam again, but didn't flinch and turned back toward me. "She wanted her ashes spread around that Little Hamaca Park behind the airport," he said. "She didn't want a church service. I figure we can have a gathering at The Chart Room or, well, shit, she used to love PT's, but that's history. Kind of like she is, and there's nothing we can do to bring her back."

"With all her fellow city employees who'll want to attend, a restaurant might be better than a bar," I said. "A Sunday afternoon at one of the hotels. Make it easier for the non-drinkers to show their faces. And maybe we shouldn't discuss Little Hamaca except between us. I don't know if we'd need a permit or anything."

"Good thought." Marsh thrummed his fingers on the bar, signaling that his part of our chat was concluded.

"One last item." I handed him the thumb drive that held the video record of our altercation.

He studied the plastic form without expression and finally

guessed. "Pictures of Teresa?"

"It's a full-color clip starring you."

His lower lip drooped with his jaw, a perfect mouth-breather frozen moment.

"A friend in the Tower Bar gave it to me," I said. "You'll be only the third person to watch it."

"Where you going with this, Rutledge?"

"There's no reason for it to go viral," I said. "Isn't that the YouTube term?"

"Do you intend to blackmail me?"

"I'm not looking for cash, Officer Marsh. But you assaulted me, which was illegal. Am I supposed to run to higher ground? Can't I do something illegal in retaliation?"

"What do you want?" he said.

"A simple guarantee. Fewer fists and knees and makeshift weapons."

"Did you put some bad word on my ass, Rutledge? Is that why I'm being followed?"

"Don't let grief cloud your perceptions, Darrin. If you're being followed, it's not the city or county, and it started before yesterday."

He polished off his soft drink, surely from nervousness, turned to leave. "Fuck," he said. "Now I get to mourn two things. My woman and the only job I've ever come close to liking."

"Your call, Marsh."

SAM GAVE HIM TEN yards then followed him out toward United Street. Alone, I looked at the canopy over the bar, then the white posts with their mid-relief ceramic pineapple sculptures. I had concentrated so much on the conversation, I had almost forgotten where I was. The sun had disappeared and the air had gone chilly. A few chain-smoking diehards remained at the bar. They all wore jackets or sweaters. The German swimmers with their blue-striped towels had retreated to their rooms and left me a cold wind down from Hamburg. I was warmed only by the piped-in music, and a song I recognized called "Buoyancy."

I walked out to United Street where Sam waited in his Bronco to drive me home. The wind had eased and the moon, not quite full, rose above the Santa Maria Suites on Simonton. I heard the strong, low horn of a departing cruise ship and I thought about my faith in the wonders of nature.

BACK AT THE HOUSE a FedEx packet sat on the porch table.

A check from Beeson. The expense money he owed me, plus a $500 bonus. Why the extra money? I could draw up another endless list of possibilities.

After two Amstels at the Pineapple Bar, I didn't need another beer. I found the open bottle of J. Lohr Cabernet and took it to the porch to ponder my abrasive chat with Darrin Marsh. Unlike my brainstorm session at the bistro, no insights came to mind. I had given Darrin his soapbox, he talked himself up, made his plea, and I had shitcanned his apology with a QuickTime movie on a thumb drive.

A rare occasion to appreciate today's most overused cliché: Whatever.

Rodney Sherwin called. I confirmed that I had talked with Beeson, and Sherwin said that he had promised to have me in Sarasota by ten-thirty. Could I meet him at the airport by eight-fifteen? Again not wanting to leave a vehicle in public parking, I asked for and was assured a ride.

"Are you in trouble up there, or something?" said Sherwin. "I got a call from a cop who wants me to hang out, bring you back the day after."

"If they make it worth your while," I said, "it's your choice. Just don't fly south without me."

WHEN BETH WATKINS ARRIVED, around nine-thirty, the wine bottle still held enough to quench her thirst. Right away I made her promise not to discuss Marsh. We sat on the porch and listened to traffic on Fleming, a thumping, distorted reggaeton tune on a passing car's stereo, the John Prine CD at low volume inside the house.

"I think the absence of leads tires me more than having too many clues," she said. "This vacuum of information is sucking me dry. Too many days have passed. Every day I worry that something I missed gets farther away."

"Can we think for the next two hours that something will turn up?" I said.

"We can try," said Beth. "You work on suspects and I'll imagine that I'm watching a million-dollar lottery ticket float into my wallet."

"An event that would prompt you to keep your job and buy a faster Ducati."

"Me? A lightweight Panigale?" she said. "Moi?

The knock at the door was timid, as hesitant as the dimly lighted face outside the screen.

"Can I help you?" I said, knowing immediately who it was.

"Look, I know there's shit flying all about me. But I didn't kill Greg and I didn't kill my client. That's not how I do things. I'm not a model citizen, but I don't ever do very bad things."

I had thought that a woman named Ocilla Ramirez might have, at least, a hint of Hispanic in her facial features. Her lank hair mixed dark brown and bronze. Her face was gaunt, almost haunted.

I came back with a tentative, "Okay…"

"Not talking to you, mister. Don't know who you are. I'm here to tell the lady cop a thing or two."

Beth didn't turn to look, didn't move at all. "I'm listening."

"Someone's been watching me. I don't know if it's the county or the state. They even had phony cable guys on a utility pole in front of my house tapping my phone or putting a camera up there to watch my come-and-go, and my visitors. I know we got murders, but they are plum wasting time on me. If it's any help to your case,

I think Mr. Caldwell, he liked to blow Gregory."

I recalled Dubbie's words: "She'd do a snake with its lack of ears no problem."

"Thank you for finding me," said Beth. "Or following me, whichever."

"Well, I just need a good night's sleep," said Ocilla. "Thought this might help us both. Be seeing you."

We watched her silhouette as she walked back toward Fleming Street.

"That was weird," I said.

"Worse," said Beth. "It bugs me that I didn't know I'd been followed. That fact scares me almost more than a gun."

We put together enough snack food to call supper, then discussed methods of pleasure that would aggravate my fight injuries less than "doing it." Two of the arrangements were well worth the pain. Lo and behold, the best pleasure came from the method we had tried to avoid.

Beth is hellacious fun to watch when she is on top.

19

I woke to watch Beth put on her panties and bra. My eyes have seen the glories, the goosebumps, the elastic and adjustments. I wished her a safe day on the job, as I always do, and she reminded me that it was Saturday, so she didn't have to work. She was going in to finish some paperwork, then quit by noon. When I climbed out of bed to make coffee, I found no filters, but I had time to walk to 5 Brothers for high octane cafe con leche and a sugar bomb guava pastry to fuel my day.

Anya Timber walked out of the grocery as I began to cross Southard Street, no surprise as I already knew her to be an early riser. My thought from ten yards away was that she must have spent money in a hair salon since visiting my porch. Her hair looked shorter, a little lighter. My second thought was that I didn't want to get into another horny or spite-filled conversation.

I approached and offered a harmless, "How are things for you today?"

She looked at me oddly and said, "Pardon me?" with a southern accent.

I saw the subtle differences. The shoes more utilitarian than stylish. The muscle tone in her forearms and a lack of gold jewelry. A surprising sparkle in her eyes. This one, Sonya, had solid moves. Her athletic grace made her the more beautiful of the two.

"Sorry," I said. "I've met your sister and I mistook you for the other twin."

"It happens." She turned away, walked toward Duval.

They were nearly identical, and each had a solid steel core. Fifty yards down the street Sonya climbed into the passenger side of the silver RAV4. I couldn't see the driver but assumed it was Luke because the vehicle's departure lacked the authority of Anya's Boxster-inspired lead foot.

TOWELING OFF NEXT TO the yard shower, I remembered. My motorcycle was not in its mini-garage. It was safe in the Aristocrats's carport, and I would ask the pilot to drop me on Staples when we returned—if I hadn't been slapped into the Manatee County jail for failing to register as an amateur sleuth.

Inside the house, in long sleeves and trousers for Sarasota's cooler weather, I had twenty minutes to meet Rodney Sherwin for my ride to the airport.

My phone buzzed. The Caller ID announced: TIM RUTLEDGE.

"How's life in Orlando?" I said.

"Count this as a fact," he said. "She was cheating on her cop."

"Is that your insight for the day?"

"For the whole week, Alex. I can't get it off my mind. Given all the possibilities, all the crap every one of us gets into during our lives, it boils down to misbehavior. I'll bet you my life savings it was the jealous boyfriend."

"Life savings right now," I said, "or when he's convicted?"

"There you go brother, playing the future. It always paid off for you. Have a good one. It's cold here, since you asked. I gotta go to work."

I packed lightly and pocketed a point-and-shoot Canon before I walked to meet the pilot in front of the Eden House. For once I was able to break my travel routine and leave my heavy camera bag at home. Less to carry, but I paid the price. It was the first time in years that I traveled without that bag. For the next hour I couldn't shake the feeling that I'd left something back at the house.

RODNEY DROVE A KIA sedan shaped like the weird love child of a budget BMW and a Focus four-door. Design aside, I couldn't fault the legroom. I blamed myself for not preparing in advance for rolling again past The Tideline. The condo would be there for the rest of my life. I needed to put it behind me, chill its association with Teresa Barga's demise. Seeing it, however, reminded me of Tim's arm's-length indictment of Darrin Marsh. Also that I had forgotten to follow up with Wiley and Dubbie regarding schematics for the building's security system.

Ten minutes later Sherwin placed the card on his dashboard that allowed him to park inside the private flight facility's chain link fence. Before we left his car, he said, "I know I look rough, but I'm fine. I say this because you're trusting your life with me in the air, and my appearance is simply a laundry issue. My wife has been in Toledo this month tending to her dying daddy."

"I wasn't alarmed," I said. "Key West is not a place where you judge threads."

"Well, I also hope I smell more like Old Spice than a bar. I was in Captain Tony's at 5:30 last night, all set to party late, when Beeson called me. I paid my tab, went home, ate a frozen dinner and slept well. This morning I found out that this shirt from yesterday was my only one that wasn't clumped in the hamper. Ready to fly?"

INSIDE THE AVIATION OFFICE, Sherwin signed a fuel chit and did the paperwork that pilots do. We walked fifty yards down the tarmac, and I stood aside while he circled the aircraft and reviewed his exterior pre-flight check list. As he went about his task, he recited a standard charter pilot intro, "Our King Air 90 runs a Rockwell Collins Proline 21 avionics package. Our twin turboprops pull a cruising speed around 260 miles-per-hour, a maximum speed of 311. Horsepower to spare."

"I felt that power when you left Key West five days ago."

"You bet," he said. "This King Air will fly fine on just one engine."

"Like a glider if both engines quit?"

"No, altitude and a calculated glide slope can bring you down easy, improve your odds. Like any airplane, sure, if you lose control speed, it drops like a piano. That's unlikely to occur during my career, but I've trained for it, of course."

"Why would it happen, bad fuel?" I said.

"No, that's rare. More like not enough fuel, which would be pure pilot error."

"Don't gas gauges ever give false readings?"

"It's possible," he said, "but I keep a fuel log with pencil and paper, my own brain, my own hand. I trust me."

"Best way to be."

"You were pretty cool that last time you flew with me," he said. "Guess you don't mind small planes."

"I learned to fly a Cessna 170 when I first moved to Key West."

"You're a pilot?"

"Never licensed," I said. "When I first arrived in town I was in the reserves, so I joined the Navy Flying Club. I logged about thirty-five hours, did my touch-and-goes here on runway nine back when there was no traffic at all. I flew my cross-country to Tamiami and Sebring. Hell, lessons were only twenty bucks an hour. My instructor flew for Air Sunshine, and moonlighted as an instructor."

"After all that prep, why didn't you get your ticket?"

"I was right next to broke. I couldn't afford to go to Miami for the cram school. I couldn't afford the motel, I couldn't pay for the school. I sure as hell couldn't rent a plane whenever I felt like it."

"But that license is freedom."

"I had nowhere to go, no reason to leave," I said. "I already lived here. I moved to this island on purpose."

"I see your point," said Sherwin. "But all knowledge is good, whether it's riding a bike or mastering long division."

"It was fun at the time," I said. "These days I'd be better off with a road map than an air chart, but I remember the basic principles. Do you mind if I ask the name of Justin Beeson's friend, the person who owns this plane?"

Sherwin looked baffled. "It's owned by four plastic surgeons in Palm Beach. I doubt that he knows any of them. They lease mostly to people who write off their charters for business reasons."

"Does Beeson fly with you often?"

Rodney made six or seven check marks on his clipboard then said, "Too often. Justin's an odd bird."

"Afraid to fly?"

"Petrified," said Sherwin, "but even more afraid to admit it. I guess he thinks fear is unfashionable. I've always believed it's what keeps me alive."

Sherwin hauled down the left-side swingdown door. We felt a rush of warm air escape the closed-up cabin, sun-heated on a tropical January morning. Inside, he pointed at the right side bulkhead. "That cabinet holds bottled water and snacks, should you care for any. That emergency exit handle? It's number one on Beeson's list of forbidden mentions. The last time we flew I kept quiet, but the girl and the woman knew how to use it. No one wants to spook Mr. Beeson."

He motioned me forward to the cockpit, asked me to take the right seat. Once he buckled in, he handed me a light headset with a mike on a skinny boom that looked like a knitting needle. "You're welcome to wear this," he said. "Your voice goes only to me. It's not patched into broadcast."

I positioned my headset, and Sherwin said: "You've done pre-flight before, Alex. Check me for accuracy?" He handed me a copy of his check sheet.

Hooked like a barracuda: "I'll try."

Fat damn chance.

The real dazzle began, and I tumbled through three harrowing

229

minutes inside a fast, baffling video game with no control stick in my hand. The Cessna I had learned to fly was the equivalent of a Ford built in the 1930s. The King Air cockpit was a maze of high-tech gauges, buzzers, clashing chimes and multi-colored lights. Sherwin ran a new check list reciting aloud, "Left, right boost pumps, on. Master switch, on. Right engine start and ignition. Low idle."

I heard whistling to starboard, the gradual increase in RPM.

"Starter off," he said. "High idle. Right generator, on for a gen-assisted start. Low idle. Left engine start and ignition. Left starter off. High idle. Low idle, left. Inverter on. Avionics master on. Fuel transfer pumps on. Fuel crossfeed, auto. Fuel control, both on. Fuel vents, both on. With me so far?"

"Maybe the first third of that," I said.

"We're out of here soon. I saved our flight plan to my route list the last time we went to Sarasota."

He flipped a switch and two dozen gauges and LED screens came to life. Lights flashed along the rim of the dash. He worked through another list, pressing buttons, double-checking. I heard the tower, but couldn't tell when the controller was talking to other aircraft instead of us. Sherwin answered every fourth or fifth query.

When he asked for a weather report from KEYW, a speed-talker answered in five seconds: "Wind one-one-zero at seven, visibility more than ten, sky condition few at two thousand; temp two-zero, dew point one-seven; altimeter three-zero-one-six and steady."

How did he remember all that? He requested departure and set his altimeter.

The tower said: "Zero-six-foxtrot-foxtrot, to Runway 9 and hold short."

"Six-foxtrot to Runway 9 to hold short." Sherwin powered the engines and we began to move forward, then swiveled left and started westward on the taxiway.

He reached the end, swiveled right and said, "Ready on 9."

"Roger. Check for incoming, then clear."

Sherwin rolled to face east, pushed on the King Air's power and focused on the runway's center line. I felt like I was sitting on a bar stool perched on the nose of a dragster. Halfway down the runway Rodney eased back on the yoke. All three wheels lifted at once. With a solid, deep hum, we were airborne. Moments later I heard the soft squeal of hydraulics raising the landing gear as we left the broad air field and went to the realm of big water and small land.

From the tower: "Six-foxtrot-foxtrot, turn zero-two-zero and climb to 4,000." The voice gave him a frequency, instructed him to contact Miami Center and wished us a good flight.

"Thank you," said Sherwin. He tuned his radio for Miami, called and was granted a cruising altitude of 10,000 feet. From that point to altitude he watched his gauges more than the road ahead. It wasn't until we reached about 5,000 feet that I realized that the morning had been hazy back on the island.

Passing through 8,000 I pointed at weather to the northwest.

"Too far away to affect us," he said. "We'll have clear air all the way into SRQ. It might get lumpy closer to land. Heat of the day."

I gave him thumb's up, listened to the engine sounds, the constant, pulsing hum. I let my mind drift back to Key West, to the front door of 5 Brothers Grocery and my encounter with Sonya Timber.

I had left Sonya out of my Beeson Way crime scene analysis. While logic told me that, with Anya's help, she could have had access to the building, I couldn't guess a motive for Sonya to hurt Amanda Beeson. Unless the twins had expanded the love making, turned it into a trapezoid. Or maybe Sonya wanted to reshuffle the triangle, cut Amanda out of the affair and form a scissor-sister arrangement that allowed her to quit working in a lumber yard. The more I thought about her, the more she fit. I wanted to suggest to Glenn Steffey her possible link to Amanda's death. I pulled out my cell phone.

"Good luck," said Sherwin. "A cell tower in the Gulf of Mexico?"

I looked down at my useless phone. A screen note told me I had a text message from Wiley Fecko that must have arrived while we were still on the ground, while Sherwin was revving his turboprops. I rarely initiate a text. The concept makes the phone companies look far too brilliant. They sell us a phone that sends and receives free email, then charge us extra to send typed messages over their phone line. What am I missing?

> "Found bronze Hyundai still on William St. Got tag number. Leased 5 days ago to R. Fonteneau of St. Petersburg, Fla. Same dude you described to Det. Watkins on phone 3 days ago. We will ramp up our look."

An opening, finally. A link between Ocilla Ramirez, the boss or business partner of murder victim Greg Pulver, and Robert Fonteneau, the man who had shared my taxi from the airport four days earlier, the Canadian who had come to the island to settle a dead friend's affairs—presumably Emerson Caldwell's—and who apparently showed a Florida ID to rent a car. Beth Watkins and Fred Liska needed this.

"I pretty much know the answer in advance," I said, "but is there any way to send a message over the radio?"

"If it doesn't pertain to operating this aircraft or reporting an emergency," said Sherwin, "the FAA would not approve. Nor would the message be delivered."

Out of touch with the world and my mind had turned into a fountain of clues.

I THOUGHT BACK TO my lessons with Del, the Navy Flying Club instructor. He loved to fly west to Ballast Key, Woman Key, Man Key and the Marquesas. He claimed it was for stall training but he loved to sightsee. Every so often he would take control to dive low and chase sharks which I thought was stupid. At twenty bucks an hour I didn't complain. I also hated practicing stalls though I knew it was fundamental to flying safely, but I loved the car that Del drove to the airport on our lesson days, an antique Chevy hardtop with a Corvette engine. It was a sleeper, a plain-looking car with hidden muscle. My enjoyment of cars like that since high school inspired me to own and drive the '66 Shelby that I had disguised as a beat-up Mustang.

"Damn," said Sherwin. "I've got port engine temp up, oil temp up, oil pressure down." A scarlet LED on the dashboard lip triple-flashed at him. He pressed a button under it and the light flashed three times again. He pressed more buttons, pulled his procedures manual onto his lap and opened it to a tabbed section. He ran his finger down one page then a couple others. "This isn't right, to overheat. The damned oil cooler must be leaking, but that's next to impossible."

"Meaning what?" I said.

"This is going to be an expensive trip, Rutledge, but not for us. The question is, do I let the engine run itself to death?"

"If it really lets go, could it damage the wing?" I said.

"Probably not," he said, "but we'll be okay if I shut it down to save it."

We started a slow climb. "Altitude is our friend," he said, "just in case the other engine quits, and have to glide toward shore." He called Miami Central to request 12,000 feet.

I let him concentrate. He feathered his prop, shut down the port engine, then switched frequencies and identified himself to Sarasota-Bradenton. "We'll be coming in with only one engine on line," he said. "Two aboard. I don't foresee a problem."

The tower came back: "We'll keep an eye on you. Consider RSW, Fort Myers."

"I have it dialed in, thank you," said Sherwin.

"What's that, a rescue service?" I said. "Are they going into emergency mode?"

"Southwest Florida International Airport," he said. "RSW is their identifier."

"How far away?"

"We'll fly within twenty miles of it," said Sherwin, "but Sarasota's only another forty-five from there. There's also a smaller airport, Page Field, in Fort Myers, which they should have told me about first."

"You think anyone could have monkeyed with the motor or..."

"No," said Sherwin. "We can't be thinking like that. It's a minor stroke of shit luck, that's all. A little extra work for the hired help."

He showed that work by the shifting in his seat, using his rudder pedals to hold our course, to control yaw, the pull to one side. "This can't be right," he said. "I'm seeing the same movement on the starboard engine's gauges. Temps up, pressure down, but not as bad as the port side engine."

"And it's not a gauge malfunction?" I said.

"I don't know... No, no," he said.

"Do we want altitude now?" I said, "or do we want to turn toward land?"

"Oh, umm, land... but I don't think I'm shutting down that right engine."

I sensed his absorption of our situation, his mind hurrying to sift the chances of a gauge malfunction versus the loss of both engines. He eased our heading eastward but his mouth hung ajar as if his brain had shut down with the port side engine.

"Life jackets aboard?" I said.

"Right behind your seat. There should be four inflatables."

I reached to pull out all four. No harm in doubling up the Day-Glo orange. "How about safety pamphlets or procedures to review?"

Sherwin pulled a sheaf of photocopied pages from the back of his log book. "I've got to pay attention. Can you read this to yourself and tell me what pertains?"

I skimmed the printout titled *Offshore Ditching Procedures*. Its

intro paragraph gave basic stats on survival, facts meant, I supposed, to be encouraging. Odds were better in a high-wing airplane. Not us, so I had no need to share that with Sherwin. The 82
percent survival rate of blue-water ditching rose to 88 percent in
coastal and inshore waters. Comforting.

"We can survive a splash landing," I said, "but we could die trying
to reach land and save the plane. What's our stall speed?"

"Right at 90 miles per hour," said Sherwin. "If we crapped out,
I'd add twenty to that until I saw the beach. Read me some more
from those pages."

"Best to touch down into the wind and parallel to swells," I said,
reading almost word for word. "Most airplanes don't flip, but dig in
one wing, turn and settle upright or settle straight ahead with a bit
of nose under the surface. Once in the water, stick with something
big and visible. Search and Rescue can't see swimmers. Don't
inflate your vest until you're outside the plane. If you can see land
from down in the water, swimming for it is okay."

"I'll race you to the beach," he said.

"Unless there's a coastal rip," I said. "Does this plane have an
automatic EPIRB?"

"It's called an ELT, an Emergency Locator Transmitter. It sends
out an automatic 406 MHz beacon to GEOSAR."

The plane twisted right. I felt a surge, then heard a deep, crunch-
ing vibration. A rush of wind replaced the throbbing engine that
had hauled us to altitude.

Sherwin spoke the obvious. "We just lost starboard." He pushed
forward on his yoke, aimed us downward for about fifteen seconds,
played it like a stall to ensure we could hold airspeed, then raised
the nose to a glide angle.

"Will your port side restart?"

He checked his gauges, shook his head. "The temps are higher
than when I shut it down. Right now it wouldn't last two minutes.
I'll try it when we're closer to land." He punched buttons under the

radio and keyed his mike. "SRQ, zero-six-foxtrot-foxtrot with both engines gone, squawking seven-seven-zero-zero."

"Roger, Foxtrot. Do you have enough electrical power to stay with us?"

Sherwin said, "Affirmative."

"Redirect to Page Field, FMY, sir. Glide flaps up. Vector zero-seven-two, range twenty-two miles." SRQ closed out by giving us the FMY tower frequency.

"Thank you," said Sherwin. He switched his radio transmitter, checked in with Page Field and repeated his emergency status info.

The FMY tower came back, "We have your squawk, sir. Vector zero-seven-three, range twenty miles."

We stopped talking. Sherwin worked to streamline the fuselage, to monitor his rate of descent as the aircraft crept closer to the coast. I peered at the seawater of different colors and depths, different temperatures, and tried to judge the height of waves. It was essentially the same water I had looked into behind the Hogfish Grill three days earlier. I had watched fish glide under the liquid shimmer, bugs skate across the surface. This time it was no different than a sheet of concrete to the horizon, ready to claw and shred the King Air like a massive cheese grater. And I would bounce against hard objects inside the craft, not caring, technically dead long before I became liquid and part of the sea. It sure would end my career in crime photography, but it was a screwed-up way to do it.

What had Liska called it? A quick adiós.

On the chance that I was riding the 80 percent survival rate, that I wouldn't be crumpled like an old banana skin, I pulled the unused Ziploc bag from my pocket. I borrowed a pen from Sherwin's notebook, scribbled a note, stuck it in my wallet and stuck the wallet, my house keys and my cell phone in the plastic bag. There was no room for my small camera, a replaceable item, but I tucked its memory card into my wallet. I had to loosen the belt to stuff the bag into my Levi's front pockets. It would've been easier with cargo shorts, but I succeeded.

I had placed, in effect, all my valuables in the same cabinet.

I went back six days in my mind. Was this Pepe's bar nude sending me away? Or some payback from the past that I hadn't seen coming? That lovely young woman I left with one last look when I reported aboard ship for a four-month Navy deployment? Square away, sailor, I thought. If there was a time to get spiritual, it's a little damned late. More important were lessons I had learned in the damage control school's USS Buttercup or the Navy's helo-dump tank. Make a mental list of survival techniques, escape procedures, methods to draw rescue. If you're underwater, follow the bubbles. Work as a team and, if that's impossible, get your teammate out when you go.

"Isn't it amazing how few Harleys and sirens you hear up here?" said Sherwin. "Right now I could really use that road map that you mentioned."

I glanced sideways. Sherwin looked almost too calm, and for some reason the odd timing of his remark took me back to my photo job for Malcolm Mason, my pictures of the boat that sank and was salvaged. The boat owner, in spite of his experience, had panicked and drowned. His passengers kept their calm, lashed together all the wreckage that floated to the surface, and made themselves a raft of trash.

One survivor had said the boat owner's last words were, *"I can't think of what to do next."*

I caught the familiar smell of the salt water below us, for the first time in my life a worrisome odor. We were closer to the beach or to death. Then came a waft of body odor from the pilot's seat and a stink that told me Sherwin had pissed himself.

He ignored his drainage issue and asked me to swap headsets. "They're going to fire questions at me, but I need to pay attention to my airspeed. Press this button if you want to talk to me without them hearing you."

I heard: "Foxtrot-foxtrot, this is FMY. We have you heading zero-six-five at 900 feet. Please confirm."

"That's us," I said.

"You are cleared to land at FMY, runway five, elevation thirteen, wind zero-eight-zero at ten. Emergency crews standing by."

I said, "Thank you."

"I don't like that," said Sherwin. "I've gone into Page Field a few times. We have Cape Coral on our left and Ft. Myers on the right. We have to clear some condos on approach."

FMY Tower came back about ninety seconds later. "We have a King Air 90 pilot in the tower. Calculating your airspeed and rate of descent, you will not reach Page Field. We have alerted the Cape Coral Marine Rescue Unit and Lee County Sheriff. They are clearing the Caloosahatchee River of all recreational boat traffic."

"Got that," I said. "We have the river mouth in sight."

"Lay it down easy, sir."

Sherwin ran through an abbreviated landing list. "Undercarriage, seat belts," he said. "Is your belt tight?"

I checked. "Yes."

"Make it tighter, as tight as you can stand," said Sherwin. "Will you join me in asking for a blessing from God?"

"I'd rather just have you steer."

"I want to copy the Hudson River guy," said Rodney. "I can't think of his name. Every pilot in the world knows his name, and I can't think of it when it might inspire me. I think it starts with an E."

He wagged the wings, leaned to the right, then to the left. Was he checking how much control he still had? What if he discovered how little he had while we were leaning over? We'd be mincemeat if we cartwheeled or did a nose-over flip.

I glanced once again at his profile, trying not to stare. His indecision showed in his jaw movements and his squinting right eye. He was committed to a fast-moving event but baffled by it.

"His name starts with an S," I said, "but it isn't coming through to me, either."

"Right you are, and it's a long name," said Sherwin.

"It'll come to us, Rodney. Right now think about a plain old belly flop. You want to be level as a pool table. You want to put it on the water like you're landing on soft-boiled eggs."

The last thing I heard in the headset was faint as if the man speaking from the tower wished he didn't have to say it: "We have lost radar contact."

We entered the river mouth almost at treetop level, too fast, much too fast. The stall buzzer squawked, loud and adamant. I knew what it meant.

We were riding in a grand piano.

"If I don't make it and you do," said Sherwin, "kill Beeson for me, okay?"

The right wing dipped and I prepared for massive pain. But the tail touched first. It felt as if we were riding on a vast field of concrete rumble strips. No brakes, no shocks, no sense of deceleration. If anything, the sensation of going faster and faster made worse by the pounding spray, our loss of visibility. If we kept skidding without slowing, we could run ashore, become a traffic accident instead of a ditched aircraft. Would I rather swim ashore or T-bone a tractor-trailer? I heard a window crack and fall inward, but it was safety glass and it didn't shatter. In spite of my restraints, my head hit something hard. The aircraft spun 180 degrees and I wondered if my feet on the rudder control pedals had caused our spin. I heard flashes of old conversations, someone yelling at me, laughing, then an angry voice. Then, except for the pitches and wallowing on the surge of our wake, all movement stopped.

I recall awakening to a wetness in *my* pants, but it wasn't piss. It was seawater. I heard gurgling noises as the plane rocked slowly on the inshore waves. Had I been out for two seconds or thirty? Unfastening my harness, I tried to speak but my breath had been knocked from my lungs. A moment later I said, "Sullenberger."

Rodney Sherwin was catatonic. I realized we had bumped heads on the abrupt U-turn. Then he slurred the magic words. "What do we do now?"

I unfastened his harness. "Let's get out and walk on the wings."

20

A SMELL OF STRONG disinfectant woke me and I felt so cold my toes hurt, so cold I feared that I had been declared dead in error, then heaved into a stainless horizontal locker in the coroner's frozen basement. The only proper payback might be to open my eyes just before the autopsy and say, "Fish sandwich, small fries and a Coke."

The examiners wouldn't laugh because they knew the inquiry would be a son of a bitch. I would insist on state-funded warming therapy in St. Barth's.

I had a hazy memory of hearing far away sirens and Harleys, and of trying to see in mist lifted by the downwash of chopper blades. I was pulled through sea grass and bait fish and petroleum scum, examined for spinal damage and broken bones, strapped into a harness, hauled through intense brightness to the foredeck of a powerboat, wrapped in a thermal blanket and fed Snickers bars. The chocolate still in my mouth caused a sensitive tooth to ache. If the tooth and my toes were my only pain, I thought, it was either good news or very bad.

It's not your whole life that zooms through your mind just before death. It's more like selected short stories, random fragments of memory, chronology be damned. I can tell you no more about them right now than I could had I croaked. The hospital, like all others, I assure you, was too frigid and bright. Much better to heal in a dim night club with soothing West Coast jazz and VSOP cognac in a snifter. A lukewarm bottle of San Pellegrino on the side. On second thought I wished I was five yards off Woman Key with a striped umbrella stuck into the sand, flat out on a float mattress, a chilled beer resting on my belly and my raft tethered to the umbrella post so I didn't drift off to Texas.

"Off the record, an FAA tech is already calling it sabotage," said Sam Wheeler.

"What are you doing here?" I said, surprised more by the sound of my own voice than Sam's presence in the room.

"Came to pick you up. They told me I had to go to baggage claim."

A flannel shirt and long trousers? I had never seen Sam dressed for cold weather. He looked ready to shoot darts and arrows at Bambi. He looked older as well, as if I had been asleep for a long time, and held a well-worn John D. MacDonald paperback in his hand.

I had no desire to sit up, but I wasn't hooked up to monitors. There were no tubes in my nose, no IVs in my arms. I saw twilight outside the blinds and asked what time it was.

"Five-thirty in the afternoon," he said, "exactly one year later."

"Oh, kiss my ass. What stinks?"

"Alcohol we can't drink."

"Why do I need picking up? Can't I take myself out of this meat locker?"

Sam shook his head. "Liska got a call from a Bradenton cop who monitored your flight. He called Beth and she called me. All we knew was that you and the pilot had survived a crash. No grim details."

"Answer my question," I said.

"An adjuster repping the aircraft liability policy is trying to get you discharged as soon as possible. He'll ask you to sign release forms. If he makes a cash offer, I would, as your agent, advise settling for the value of five lost days of work. It'll pay for our celebratory supper tonight."

"What's with the American Eagle bag?"

"We heard when we landed that you'd probably be able to leave today. Beth made us stop at Edison Mall so she could buy warm clothes for you."

"Please don't tell me you chartered a flight."

Sam shrugged. "Beth's in the lobby with a bunch of law enforcement officers. The nurses gave her everything you had in your pockets. She read a note that was sticking out of your wallet and got right on her phone. I heard her ask for Mr. Fecko, and she started making notes to herself."

"How can they already know sabotage?"

"You had the Lee County Marine Task Force on scene in ninety seconds. You were pushing your pilot out the emergency exit, but he was dead weight. After the team got you both aboard the Cape Coral S&R Team's 33-foot Aronow steel hull, they attached floatation to the King Air. They towed it into a marina, steadied it with a yacht club boat hoist, brought over a crane and had it ashore in forty-five minutes. The FAA guy was in town on some other case. He pulled both engine cowlings right away."

"A leak in the oil coolers?"

Sam canted his head, gave me a strange look.

"The pilot guessed, when he was still thinking straight."

Sam nodded. 'The coolers had been drilled and the pinpoint holes patched with something that would melt at a certain temperature, after you'd been up in the air awhile."

"Why so many cops in the lobby?"

"Count the cops, count the reasons," said Sam. "The plane is evidence, parked in a special hangar. They won't let anyone near it."

"The pilot okay?" I said. "Rodney Sherwin?"

"Concussion, two broken ankles. He's four rooms down the hall. He keeps staring at the ceiling and saying, 'Chesley, baby,' over and over."

243

"That was Rodney's zone before we splashed down. At least he pulled it off. I tried to keep him talking so he could fly by instinct. I didn't want him to be distracted by actual thoughts."

"A big Cape Coral cop named Eric said it was picture-perfect," said Sam.

"Rodney told me before our flight that fear keeps him alive."

"Probably copped that line from the TV."

We stared at each other. Sam's expression screamed that I had been lucky.

"Please don't offer to fly me back to Key West," I said. "I would rather skateboard the length of Alligator Alley..."

"When you almost drown, you're supposed to jump right back in."

"I'm tired of looking down at it," I said. "For a week or two I want to appreciate the ocean at sea level."

"I'll swap my budget rental for a van so you can stretch out."

"Thanks. Any chance of looking at Beth's face instead of yours?"

A smiling, energetic nurse walked in, knocking on the door as she passed it. She looked about fifty, stocky with light brown hair, her eyes full of mischief, cute from the day she was born. "Awake now, sweetie?" she said.

"Why am I here?"

"Gotta check you for internal bleeding, disorientation. Were you in another plane crash a couple of days ago, too? Some of your torso injuries, discoloration..."

"I was run into by a police officer," I said.

"That explains all them officials in the reception area," she said. "You have a good nap, honey? You had a good dream seventy-five minutes ago, I'm here to tell you. We had a state fair tent pole for a little while."

Sam raised his eyebrows, stood to leave. "I'll send in Beth."

"I got him for four minutes," said the nurse. "The doctor will be here in ten. After that he's a free agent."

BETH CARRIED IN A plastic shopping bag. "Hello, my lover, the survivor." She gave me a sad smile and bit her lower lip. I smelled jelly doughnuts.

"Thank you for coming," I said, "wherever we are."

She kissed my forehead. "Twice in the almost two years I've known you."

"You've come? Or kissed me on the forehead?"

"Hundreds of times, those. I was talking about how often EMTs deliver you to an emergency room. You could inspire hospitals to build drive-thru lanes."

"Not until they start providing electric blankets. Sam said you stopped at a store. If you bought socks, could you put them on me right now?"

"This is action I view as extremely romantic..." She found them in the Nike bag, lifted the sheet, began to rub my feet and ease on the socks. "You're at Lee County Memorial in Fort Myers."

"I haven't helped you much this time around," I said. "Hell, now I've pulled you away from an active case."

Beth covered my feet, sat where Sam had been and looked me in the eye. "When Liska called six hours ago, I was afraid you were dead. When he said you were hurt, I wanted to get on my motorcycle. I didn't want to waste time arranging a flight. Sam called and convinced me that I couldn't see to drive if I was crying."

"How does that change..."

She held up her hand to shush me. "You know I appreciate your advice, Alex. But I didn't take my job with the idea that you would always be standing behind me. I took it because it's what I dreamed of doing. I didn't even know you then. I didn't know how much you would boost my spirits or give me great ideas. I love you and I want you to support me, but I've never wanted to recruit you. It's for damn sure I never expected you to put yourself in danger."

I stared at her, waiting, expecting more. But that was the whole speech. She had opened up to me, offered a rare moment. It was almost a scolding, but it was what I had wanted to hear for months, regardless of circumstance.

"You steered me to Wiley Fecko," she said, "and he had a little more for me."

"Am I permitted to ask what Wiley gave you?" I said.

"First a message for you. He said that Gamble represented Caldwell years ago. Is this something I need to know about?"

"Yes," I said, "but it's not urgent. What else was there?"

"Greg Pulver and Ocilla Ramirez were definitely moving money through clients' computers. But Ocilla had something else going with large amounts of cash. Even if she was a hooker..."

Distracted by scuffling steps in the hall, Beth turned toward the door.

Manatee County Detective Glenn Steffey peered into the room. "Mind if I join the party?" He entered in clothing identical to what he had worn the morning Tharpe found Amanda's body. Dark slacks, an open-collar blue button-down shirt and a tan sport coat that had missed a trip to the cleaners.

I introduced Steffey to Beth Watkins, and each pretended to be impressed by the other's job.

"I'm sorry your trip turned out the way it did, Rutledge," said Steffey. "But glad, of course, that you came away intact. By the chatter out front, the aircraft's engine failures are now top priority."

"You drove this far down I-75 just to say that, detective?"

"It was only seventy-seven miles," he said, "but you're right. I bring ironic news. Just before noon, due to new evidence, our prosecutor postponed the grand jury. Our need for your help is not as urgent as it was yesterday. Justin Beeson, I would expect, feels the same way. It's not because of your accident and, please be assured, if we need you in the future, a commercial air ticket will be provided."

"Does the new evidence have anything to do with Beeson?" I said.

"The victim was his ex-wife so, indirectly, everything links to him," said Steffey. "Analyzing this case is like unraveling a fist-sized knot of fishing line."

"Are you here because the plane crash might tie in…"

Steffey held up both hands to stop me. "Justin Beeson didn't want you dead. We determined that he knew about your law enforcement work before he hired you. He knew your rep for being good, for helping to solve several crimes. If he was part of a conspiracy, a plot to kill his ex-wife, he wouldn't want you at that scene. No killer in his right mind would invite you along. I have no doubt that you complicated things for Amanda's murderer."

"I can't believe my reputation carries beyond a ten-foot circle."

"Well it does," said Steffey, "and… I don't mean to blow breeze out of your sails, but your photo expertise offered Beeson credibility with the IRS. It allowed him to write off that first flight."

"He expensed the plane because of me? The bastard said that?"

"He stressed that he needed your artistic input. The second flight, he needed your truthful and respected testimony. He paid for the air charter as a defensive move."

"Artistic input, my ass. I'm a frigging tax deduction. Also, for what it's worth," I said. "Just before we hit the water, Rodney Sherwin, the pilot, said, 'If I don't make it and you do, kill Beeson for me.'"

"Whoa," said Detective Steffey. "I'll definitely follow up on that. He didn't provide a basis for that threat, by any chance?"

"He mentioned Beeson only once, before we took off. Said he was afraid to fly, and that tied into something Anya told me the night before Amanda's body was found. She said a friend of his had died in an air crash thought to be sabotage."

"So maybe he was the target, is that what you're saying?"

"I'm saying only what you just heard, detective. I'm not a cop and it's not up to me to make assumptions."

He glanced at Beth, then at me. "I have another question to ask."

"Why are you suddenly looking at me like I have ten previous convictions?"

"And why," said Beth, "are you acting like you want me to leave the room?"

Steffey made calming hand movements. "You don't have to answer my question, and if right now is a bad time..."

A low-calorie Miranda warning if I ever had heard one.

"I've got all evening, apparently," I said. "You're welcome to discuss anything in front of Beth. Go for it."

"Little kink up in Bradenton, which I'm sure you can easily explain. You told me yesterday that Luke Tharpe owned a Ram pickup, right? Said you saw it the morning Amanda Beeson's body was found."

"That's right. It's dark green."

"We appreciate your letting us know about that truck. Problem is, we found your fingerprints inside and outside of it."

"Did you find that clump of clothing alongside I-75?"

"You bet. A pair of cut-off shorts and a sweatshirt. We figured they belonged to one of the bums that live back in those woods. But they were Tharpe's. He told us that he kept extra work clothes in a locker at Beeson's auto shop. Said he wondered why they were gone. So we wondered if you maybe had..."

Beth was looking back and forth between us, not understanding a bit of it.

"Right you are, detective," I said. "I *did* borrow Tharpe's truck that morning. He arrived at 23 Beeson Way when I was out on the road trying to take photographs. I asked if there was a ladder inside the building. He drove over, brought one back to me, then he left me his truck. He walked back to the building so I wouldn't have to carry the ladder all that way."

"Kind of what he said, Rutledge. Glad we settled that." Glenn Steffey relaxed a notch or two, but he didn't look convinced.

Beth said, "How did the clothing get tossed by the road?"

Steffey smiled, shook his head. "The shorts had flecks of foam sealant stuck to them, which ties into our murder scene. We think the killer dropped them there, possibly to implicate Tharpe. While Mr. Rutledge's attention and insight have been a great help to us, we have no idea who the bad guy might be."

"I saw something in Key West just before I left," I said to Steffey. "I don't know if this has anything..."

"What sort of thing?"

"The human sort. Anya Timber's twin sister Sonya."

"Damn, said the detective. "Are they identical?"

"Damn near," I said. "She got into an SUV that I saw Luke Tharpe driving two days ago. I didn't see the driver this morning. I mean, for what it's worth..."

"It joins the stack of meaningful yet useless clues we have assembled so far."

"Could I ask a question?" Beth said, then asked it before either of us responded. "Why did a grand jury need Alex's testimony?"

"Formal verification," said Steffey. "In his photos of the crime scene there was something different from what my scene team found."

"I didn't know that," I said.

"Well, it may be meaningless," said Steffey, "but they will open your photos in a program that will show the exact moment you pressed the shutter button for each shot. All you'll have to do is acknowledge the fact that you took the picture."

The nurse ducked in the door long enough to say, "Wheelchair departure, got to go by the rules. Your limo will be here in five, if you want to get dressed."

"I brought the Manatee County voucher for your hotel tonight," said Steffey. "Maybe you can arrange for a rollaway bed to save you all some money."

"Which hotel?" I said.

"We usually use one near our offices but, with the shift in your itinerary, I put you in the Holiday Inn a quarter-mile up the road. There is, however, one more topic to discuss, a result of a talk I had today with our mutual friend, Fred Liska. There is a man who would like a few minutes of your time. He's in a Starbucks about four minutes from here. Sheriff Liska said that it may clarify a lot of things for you. I'll show you how to find the place, but it doesn't concern me, so I'll roll on up the road. Your friends, Mr. Wheeler and Detective Watkins, are welcome to join you."

"Give me a few moments with Beth," I said. "See you in the lobby?"

Steffey didn't want to go, but he did.

Beth checked the hallway to make sure, then turned back to me. "What?"

"Blow job."

"Pardon me, Alex?"

"Please kiss me on the forehead one more time and help me get dressed."

"I certainly will do that," she said. "Then I will call Chicken Neck's private cell number and verify this clarification malarkey."

AN ORDERLY WHO LOOKED like a recovering car thief pushed my wheelchair to the hospital lobby. The first person I saw was Edwin Torres in his brown UPS uniform, the mechanic from Justin Beeson's auto shop. He stood and walked toward me.

"You were on the news an hour ago," he said. "I wanted to come wish you well."

"That's great, Edwin, but you force me to ask. Why do you give a shit?"

Torres looked at the orderly and Beth then flung his arms wide. "You didn't treat me like scum. Most folk, they look at my neck tat, check out my mud-color uniform, they think I'm a dirtbag. That morning what's-his-face found Amanda's body, you talked to me like I'm a human. So I came to tell you in person because I think my phone is bugged. I think I'm being followed, and Beeson is trying to set you up. For what, I don't know. Why do I think that? I'm not

250

sure. But I've seen that nasty-ass choo-choo come down the tracks a few times in my life."

"Thanks, Edwin. I sure am glad you caught me before I left the hospital."

He turned to leave. "Be seein' you."

"Can I give you a few bucks for gas?" I said. "Or you can put it toward that GT-350 you want to own."

"We're okay right now, Alex Rutledge. I may come to you for car-buying advice in a few years. For now, we're slick."

21

SATURDAY NIGHT IN A riverside Florida town, twenty miles from the Gulf of Mexico, the mid-fifties in January and damp enough to soften your bones. I had been given pain meds, but a few aches began to fight their way through. After the antiseptic sting of hospital air, it felt great to inhale the poisonous diesel fumes of a passing bus. Seven hours earlier I had wondered if I would ever catch another deep breath.

Beth Watkins and I rode with Detective Glenn Steffey in his Manatee County unmarked Impala, and Sam Wheeler followed us into downtown Fort Myers in his compact rental car. In deference to my supposed injuries, Beth sat up front, allowed me room to stretch out in the rear seat. The car's interior colors were a combo of green, brown and gray—like the puke-proof carpeting in airport walkways. Its stale upholstery smelled of body odor, aftershave, mildew, fast food, and hair tonic.

We rumbled over slick modern bricked streets until both drivers found parking spots on Broadway, then regrouped and entered the Starbucks at the corner of First. A man in the seating area stood, waved us over, tapped his tablet screen on the table. He looked to be in his late-forties, just under six feet, with thick salt-and-pepper hair, his face taut and tanned as if he lived full-time in Florida. He moved like he stayed in shape, and he smiled like a man who kept secrets and had plenty.

"Max Saunders, FBI," he said, extending his hand. Beth and Steffey accepted his greeting while Sam and I fumbled to arrange chairs around two tables that Saunders had pulled together.

Beth had called Sheriff Chicken Neck Liska and verified Steffey's claim that this meeting would "clarify" things for me. But, if anything, Saunders's self-introduction had slammed me with confusion. While Beth was a law officer, a member of the club, I couldn't imagine why Sam Wheeler and I might be made privy to FBI matters.

Saunders asked if we wanted coffee. I wanted to walk back to the car. Sam gave me a look I knew. He agreed with my misgivings.

The agent started with me, no surprise. "Understand you've had a rough day, Mr. Rutledge."

"More or less got my blood pressure checked," I said.

"Naturally, we're working with the FAA on the aircraft sabotage. We think that someone wanted to kill you."

"Arrest Justin Beeson," said Beth.

"Probably not," said Steffey. "Agent Saunders and I have discussed the fact that Beeson had no interest in Alex's being dead. Also, he simply had no opportunity to set it up."

"I disagree," I said. "There are at least three possible co-conspirators whom I've seen in Key West over the past couple of days. I wouldn't know about their access to the plane...."

"We'll work on it when we get back," said Beth Watkins.

Agent Saunders looked her in the eye. "Yes, I'd be willing to bet you'll make the first arrest in the Keys."

A barista arrived at the table with a tray full of selections that Max had ordered ahead of our arrival. Lattes, regular and iced coffee, plus several bottled drinks. She placed the tray on our table and departed.

Beth twisted the cap off a green tea. "What else do you know about my future actions, Agent Saunders?" she said.

"That remark was pure speculation, detective," said Max, attempting a tone of assurance. "It's just a hunch. I'm not holding hard info, or holding out in any way, believe me."

"Why would I not believe you?"

Max let her question slide and turned to Steffey. "Were you going to stick around for the rest of this, Glenn?"

His inflection made the question sound like *"It's time to go away."*

Surprised, Steffey mumbled something about being due back in the office. He made sure we knew our way to the Holiday Inn, explained that only one room was covered, but that Manatee County wouldn't quibble over a surcharge if we requested a roll-away bed for Sam. Looking deflated, Glenn shook hands all-around and left the coffee shop.

Max said nothing until Steffey was gone, then turned to me. "Mr. Rutledge, I've been asked to provide you and Ms. Watkins some background on a case we're team-pursuing with Pinellas, Polk and Monroe Counties. The FDLE is facilitating, but we've asked our local colleagues to assume day-to-day ops so that our hand won't be tipped. We don't want the operation's prime managers to suspect that both we and Homeland and the Royal Canadian Mounted Police are on to them. They might fold their tents, kill anyone who could testify against them, and vanish into Paraguay or Bolivia."

"This mess started with drugs?" I said.

He shook his head. "Nothing so glamorous, but its low-profile nature may be its brilliance. They've been methodical and, because of that, long-lasting. I was being facetious when I mentioned Paraguay and Bolivia. We're dealing with a small but efficient check theft ring working primarily out of Toronto with links to six states. In Florida, they operate in Largo, next to St. Petersburg, Bartow in Polk County, and in Key West. They're pretty slick and they've been slowly, carefully growing. The only reason we've been able to get close to them is luck. But we're almost there."

"Is this about Emerson Caldwell?" I said. "Our dead Canadian in Key West?"

Saunders splayed his hands like a politician asking for patience. "Stay with me here, Mr. Rutledge," he said, then knocked back an espresso before he continued. "Our first break was to bust a man from Largo in a suburban Tampa bank this past July, cashing a stolen check. He told us that he met his only contact, Herman, at a card game in the back room of a Madeira Beach restaurant. During a play break, Herman took him aside, pitched his offer, and the fellow went for it. Herman gave him two checks to endorse and cash and told him that was the tip of the iceberg. He met Herman four days later, handed over the wad of money. Herman rewarded him with fifteen percent of the cash. After that Herman called him on throwaway cell phones and met him in coffee shops like this one. Our contact would give him all of the cash from the checks, then Herman would hand back twenty percent and a few more checks. Our contact was forging and cashing two checks every week. It was adding up, but so was the risk. They warned him to play by the rules if he got caught. Keep his mouth shut, do his jail time, and get paid a reward when he walked out of prison. He plain didn't believe the last part."

"Surely someone's missing some money by now," I said.

Max Saunders shook his head. "We're talking millions, though it's only a couple hundred thousand so far in Florida. The crack in the wall is enough to worry the tax and regulatory agencies. This group is clipping relatively small payments made by large American companies to residents of Canada. Those disbursements were already written off the books of the corporations. If someone up north missed a check, they might have been issued a replacement, or they never missed it either. We don't know. The red flags are waving because they can pull it off without scrutiny—they think. We believe it's about to escalate."

"Okay, back to Herman." I said. "Sorry I interrupted."

"When the man from Largo told us his story, we asked him to keep on working for them. We also managed to get a picture of

Herman meeting him up in St. Pete. We passed that picture around to our agents and caught a break two weeks ago when one of them saw Herman meeting with Ocilla Ramirez in a Key West bank parking lot, of all places. A goddamn bank parking lot. Only his name wasn't Herman in Key West. As you guessed, it was Emerson Caldwell."

"How did you identify him?" said Beth.

"Hé was driving a rental car, a Toyota Corolla. We traced the tag. He checked it out in Miami under his own name, but gave a fake address in St. Petersburg."

According to Wiley's earlier text message, I thought, Fonteneau also had given a St. Pete address when he rented the bronze Hyundai. Had they used the same fake location?

"Surely you followed him in Key West," I said.

"Unfortunately, Caldwell knew the island's back streets better than the team that tried to keep up with him. The rental was never returned, and the leasing company has reported it stolen. We did, however, make progress. By tracing Caldwell's calls and emails, we found that his name was Walter in Macon, Georgia, and Arthur in Savannah, and Howard in Monroeville, Alabama."

"Did he stay in Key West after that meeting?" said Beth. "Go back to his condo?"

Max shook his head. "We think he returned to his Tideline apartment before we learned that address. Someone used the security entry key pad in his condo that day. He didn't log on to his computer nor did he take it with him. We think he drove or got a ride out of town. The tag on that Toyota Corolla didn't pop up on any of the Florida Turnpike toll gates south of Miami."

"Where was Caldwell getting all these checks?" I said.

"The Mounties have narrowed it down to a dozen possibilities, seven post offices in Ottawa and another five in Montreal. They think the inside bad guys have found a way to detect the magnetic ink on checks inside envelopes. They haven't figured out where the checks go when they leave their post offices, or how they're cross-ing the border back this way, but they think they're close, too. We still need to find the black hole. No one knows where the cash went once it was delivered to Caldwell."

"Did Ocilla bring Greg Pulver into the scam?" said Beth. "Is that why he's dead now?"

"Nope, that's not it. When we discovered her part in the check scam, he was already working for her, cleaning houses. He had no part in the check scam. With Monroe County's help, however, we enlisted his assistance."

"You set him up," I said.

"Brought it on himself," said Max.

Beth looked disgusted. "What was he arrested for?"

"Trying to score two pounds of weed on Ramrod Key."

She said, "Liska oversaw the bust and the flip?"

Max shrugged and nodded. "We requested that he monitor things."

"You turned Greg Pulver so he could report back on Ocilla," I said, "and he was murdered. Did no one on your team foresee the possibility?"

"We warned him," said Saunders. "He didn't see any danger and he wanted the dope distribution charge to fly away."

"Except you knew more about the potential danger than he did," I said.

"What was he supposed to watch?" said Beth, calming the dialogue.

"They started a new pattern. Ocilla began opening new accounts, depositing the checks she got from Caldwell, then pulling the money out in cash either inside the banks or at ATMs. That one has the FBI baffled, but we began to wonder if she wasn't turning the scam into her own venture. Maybe she was going to build a nest egg and boogie to Bolivia herself. Anyway, he was helping us keep track of the banks and her daily schedule, near as he could tell and when he wasn't occupied elsewhere. He held another job as well, at some restaurant."

I looked at Sam, we locked eyes, then he looked down at the table, focusing on nothing. I read his passive reaction as distrust with a touch of loathing.

"How often did Caldwell visit and leave Key West?" I said to Max. "Did you track his air flights for the past few months?"

"His schedule was so random, it could've been generated by a computer," said Saunders. "He came and he went, but never back to Canada."

"What got Greg Pulver killed?"

"We have no idea. For all we know, he broke into Emerson Caldwell's computer. Or spilled his guts to Ocilla. We know they became lovers, though his track record in that regard was right up there with the rock stars. He could put Tiger Woods in the minor leagues. We certainly wouldn't put him in place to be murdered."

"Why are we being made privy to this information," I said, "aside from the fact that Liska hasn't found the courage to include us?"

"Two reasons," said Max. "One, Ocilla Ramirez came to your home twenty-four hours ago."

"Right," I said. "She followed Detective Watkins so she could plead her innocence in the deaths of Pulver and Caldwell."

"She told me that she had been followed and observed," added Beth.

"Yes," said Saunders, "we figured she was onto us when she dropped out of sight two days ago. At the time she also was being shadowed by two private investigators dressed as street people." He looked at me. "We assumed they were working for the individuals who engineered the scam."

"They weren't," I said.

"Thank you for being forthright," said Max.

"Does that mean you're happy that I didn't bullshit you?"

Max nodded. "Liska has explained the men he calls the Bumsnoops, which gave us a little relief. And that brings up our second reason to invite your help." He faced Watkins. "We need to separate Sheriff Liska from the Caldwell case. It's time to arrest Ocilla. For that, Beth, we need you."

"Now you're setting up Fred Liska?" I said. "If you don't already know, I'll tell you that he's not just an associate of mine, he's a personal friend."

Sam, without looking up at anyone, dropped his clenched fist on the table. A well-controlled exclamation point.

Max hesitated then said, "We know that, Alex, and we respect Detective Watkins's allegiance to both you and Sheriff Liska. We're not trying to sully his name, but we need, for prosecutorial reasons, to distance him from Emerson Caldwell. Liska has been aware of this from the moment the bodies were identified."

Just then, no one had a comeback for Max.

"Our associates have been watching the man in Bartow," said Max. "Watching him cash checks and meet with Caldwell. He's been acting normally this week, so he may not know about these deaths. I plan to make him a guest of that county tonight."

"Under what statute do I arrest Ms. Ramirez?" said Beth.

"Charge her with too many hangnails, whatever," said Max. "This is to save her life, not harass her. She's our last link to a resolution, at least from the American end. If the people at the top understand this, and they ordered the whack on Greg Pulver, Ocilla's walking under a very dark cloud."

"Okay," said Beth, "I arrest her. She bonds out in forty-five minutes, you lose your witness, she takes a bullet. What have we accomplished?"

"You hold her for a warrant check," said Saunders. "We already have her on video cashing one of those checks and accepting fifties with random serial numbers. We've got the bills photocopied, you compare them to money she's carrying and continue to hold her at our request."

Beth said, "What if someone shows up at our cop shop, wants to see her?"

"She moves to the county at the city's request. Visiting hours prevail. If shit goes wrong, I can bring in our equivalent of a Seal Team."

"That'll play poorly in Key West," I said.

"What?" said Max. "Will someone accuse us of cheating?"

"How will I find this woman?" said Beth. "Look under every bush in the Lower Keys?"

"You'll fly back in the morning, right? We'll know where she is by noon. Let's talk around eleven-thirty. Please let me know before then if you decide not to help us." Saunders pulled a business card from his shirt pocket, handed it to Beth, stood and crossed his arms to signal that our discussion was over.

Beth remained seated. "This will backfire if you arrest the man in Bartow before I find Ocilla. If he calls his handlers, they might find a way to take him out and Ocilla, too."

"Excellent point, detective," said Saunders. "We will wait for your move."

I stood to leave, and Max turned toward me, a solemn expression on his face.

"Hemingway survived two air accidents in one week in 1954, in Africa," he said. "The residual pain fueled his alcoholism and led to his suicide."

"I guess I'm just lucky," I said. "I have a friend who is a one-woman pain clinic. It's drug-free, and she gives me discounts."

He patted me on the shoulder, an attempt to be my pal. "Of course," he said, "the old buzzard might have driven himself nuts figuring out who fucked with the planes and tried to kill him twice in one year."

"That's perceptive, Max," I said, stepping away. "Where did I get the stupid idea that Ernest took himself out because J. Edgar Hoover's shadowing tactics drove him crazy?"

WE WALKED OUT OF Starbucks and stood beneath the mist-shrouded streetlights of downtown Fort Myers. The meeting with Max had aged me more than the airplane crash.

Sam said, "Company man, vaguely unclear."

"You stayed two steps ahead," I said.

Beth pulled her coat tighter. "You gents talking in code here?"

"Why did we just hear an FBI agent admit that their only success came through luck? Since when does the FBI cut civilians into their operation, their confidence? They don't even let local cops know what they're doing."

"Thank you, Alex," said Beth. "That last idea was raising its hand in my brain, trying to get attention the last five minutes we were in there."

"Finally, call me a wussy, but I don't want to stay in a hotel room that a detective has arranged for me. He may have visited the room to make sure it was suitable. May have left small devices in place to listen to my praise of the accommodations, my TV selections, and my snoring."

"Our pilot should be okay to fly," said Sam, checking his watch. "I asked him to get a room anywhere he wanted, chill out for the afternoon. He said he'd be happy to leave anytime before ten o'clock."

Beth looked at me, my eyes and face.

I felt a distinct need to head south. I looked up again at the streetlights, noticed that even trees sway differently with a cold wind. I nodded.

"Excellent," she said. "We'll stop at a Wendy's for six fish sandwiches then sleep in Key West and wake up in our own beds."

"Food," said Sam. "The detective reads minds."

THE RENTAL CAR COURTESY van dropped us at the flight service center. I could tell how cold it was by the sound of its tires on the pavement. Our pilot was ready to fly. Sam and Beth had chartered a Cessna 340A, a plane similar to but smaller than the King Air now quarantined in a hangar in Cape Coral.

As we walked to the aircraft, a phone in Beth's handbag rang a familiar tone. She extracted the Ziploc bag that held my wallet, house keys and cell. My phone had survived the crash and the water. Beth handed it to me. Its touch screen told me the call was from Glenn Steffey.

"Detective," I said.

"Just wondering what time you were going to check in to the hotel," he said. "I still haven't left town and I had two or three more questions for you."

"Sam and Beth wanted to leave so they wouldn't have to pay for their pilot to stay in a hotel, and I wanted to be closer to my doctor and my own bed. Sorry if I'm wasting Manatee County's money, but I'm flying back with them."

"Gotta say, I wasn't counting on that," said Steffey.

"I'm sure we can talk tomorrow, or you can email me the questions, right?"

He didn't respond.

"But one other thing," I said. "I can pass along something I've just learned, and you may find it helpful."

"Anything, please."

"Amanda was Beeson's second wife," I said. "His first wife was murdered many years ago, somewhere in your part of the state, and it's still an open case."

The silence on his end weighed a ton. I was sure that he knew the case and knew that his father had been removed from the investigation. Sounding exasperated, he said, "You came up here this week just to take pictures of Beeson's building?"

"That was the job description, detective."

"One guy is barfing, Rutledge, the other man is screaming with grief, and you're taking pictures like a walk in the garden? Do you ever worry about yourself?"

"Good night, detective."

I switched off my phone and looked at the January sky, blacker and colder than the tarmac. Orion's Belt looked back down from ten o'clock in the east-southeast. It was the constellation that had guided my night sails in the Bahamas years ago, in the days when I really got to know myself, when the elements tested my judgment and strength, when I pledged never to stop being curious and to quit worrying about me and to get on with my life, full speed ahead.

22

I WOKE ON THE twin-engine Cessna with no idea how long I had napped. I could see a band of lights in the distance and guessed I was looking at Big Pine and a few islands to its west. The sooner we reached the island the better. I needed sand in my shorts and beer in my shoes, and a year's worth of second thoughts about returning to the mainland.

After our departure from Page Field in Fort Myers, fatigued, not wanting to fight the engines' hum, we had escaped into silence. Sam sat next to the pilot, a fishing client he had known for years. Beth leaned back in her seat, staring out, studying the darkness, the back of her head illuminated by the instrument panel's pastel glow.

Over the years I had been fortunate to find photo jobs that paid well and lucky to work for low-stress repeat clients. In the past few months, however, I had felt jealous of Beth Watkins's regular paycheck. Every fifteen days her checking account caught a deposit, minus a lump for insurance and the state retirement flim-flam. It wasn't so much the amount of her salary as its regularity.

Then I would think again. If all she had to do was show up at work, put in her hours and leave, that would be glorious. But the job came home with her each day without fail—much as mine had haunted me for the past six days. Early in our love affair I had chosen not to pester Beth about moments when she would drift off in thought, distracted by cases in progress, the workload and the legal finesse it took to secure an arrest, then a conviction. A relative new-comer to Key West, she was not bogged down by local politics, not impressed by big money and the established families of the island. She wanted only to be effective, to do her job and make a difference.

Not that she wasn't effective at home, in every room. Early in our relationship, realizing that we could practically read each other's mind, we promised ourselves that we wouldn't let that limit our talking, our interaction. She was my fourth lover in twelve years, though I hadn't broken up with any of them. The women had moved off the island or become restless and strange. While I knew that nothing was certain and everything changed in big or small ways, I wanted this one to work. She pleased me more than any of the others, I trusted her completely—and I didn't want to be on the hunt for the next twenty years, if I lasted that long.

She had great taste in motorcycles. And dimples on her bottom.

Beth turned her head, saw my eyes open, and smiled.

"You didn't get a chance to tell me," I said. "What did Wiley Fecko have for you?"

"A mid-level criminal named Bobby Fuck No."

It took me about ten seconds, but she waited me out.

"Robert Fonteneau?"

"The Aristocrats did some very good work on the Internet," she said. "They found his former address in a gated community on the outskirts of Toronto, Ontario. Ten years ago, when he lived there and got his nickname, it was called Mimico Detention Centre. It was recently expanded to include a maximum security building constructed of stackable prefab concrete cells. It's now the Toronto South Detention Centre."

"In for what, this Bobby Fuck No?" I said.

"Multiple motor vehicle theft, and he made the most of it. His incarceration was his free ticket to the equivalent of a master's degree. He now owns a small chain of Canadian auto parts stores, and they specialize in repairing alternators, generators and small engines. His employees are all ex-cons and parolees."

"Skills they learned while basking in the Mimico glow," I said.

"Fonteneau now works with a private prison outfit to teach skills inside and he employs only parolees outside. He coordinates with a group of halfway houses and rehab operations. Canadian magazines and newspapers write praise-filled articles about him. He ships a lot of alternators into the States."

"Where did Wiley go, inside an Ontario Provincial Toshiba?"

"No," said Beth, "he found the jail records and he gave me some background on Caldwell's business activities—info he discussed with you three days ago. I found more this afternoon while the doctors assessed your condition. I think Fecko already told you that twenty-five years ago Caldwell and two partners formed a company in Ottawa called Currie Forms. The firm owned plastic manufacturing plants in Canada and in the States. Twelve years ago Caldwell bought out his partners and quickly sold Currie to a huge company called Branchdale. He made a fortune. The partners didn't see the sell-out coming, and both sued Caldwell. One case was settled out of court. The other partner committed suicide, and that case eventually was dropped."

"Convenient," I said.

"Yes. That partner's name was Richard Fonteneau."

"Richard? His brother?"

"No, he was Fuck No's father."

"We should invent a game called Information Whiplash."

"Follow it up with a game called Cold Revenge."

"If that's his game, he's got huge balls to show up in town to close out Caldwell's affairs," I said. "Especially since Mrs. Caldwell is here in town, talking with the same lawyer who took Fonteneau to breakfast on Thursday."

"Name?"

"E. Carlton Gamble, the man we spoke about this afternoon."

"I can't wait to speak with him," said Beth. "I also can't wait to speak with Mr. Fuck No."

"On another subject," I said, "my brother called this morning with an opinion."

"Two bits says he believes Darrin Marsh killed Teresa Barga."

"He strongly suggested it," I said. "He thinks that she was more than capable of giving him reasons to be jealous."

"An argument for which you had no argument?"

"Correct. You said there were two 911 calls, right?"

"Yes," said Beth. "The first was a hang-up and the second was from Marsh."

"From Caldwell's landline?"

Beth nodded. "Both calls came from Caldwell's phone."

"And he reported only two bodies?"

"I'd have to double-check, but I think that's right. He hadn't seen Pulver yet."

"But he saw Greg's body at some point. He told me... Today's Saturday, right? He told me that yesterday afternoon."

"That stands to reason," she said. "He may have looked around after he placed the call."

"I don't buy it," I said. "Walk through it in your mind. He's just come across the body of his neighbor slumped on the floor, then found Teresa dead in the kitchen. He knew for sure that she'd been killed within the past however many minutes. Let's say thirty minutes. And it's his day off. He probably wasn't walking around the condo's interior hallway with a weapon on him. Any cop worth a shit would have gone back to his own condo, called 911 from there, returned to Caldwell's with a weapon, and made sure the murderer wasn't still around. At that point he might have found Pulver. Then he would have backed out of the place and waited for the responders. Above all, he would have armed himself as quickly as possible."

"I have no problem with your reasoning," said Beth, "except you're assuming that Marsh, as a cop, is worth a shit."

"I have no knowledge of that," I said, "but I think he's a bad murderer."

"Because he killed Teresa in a condo with two other bodies?"

"We made a point of not discussing Marsh twenty-four hours ago," I said, "so let me preface my string of logic with something he told me yesterday. At some point in the past few months, Marsh sneaked into Teresa's belongings and read her diaries. He found proof that she'd had a fling with some tourist, but he didn't confront her about it because he was afraid she'd go ballistic about his snooping. He said he was afraid of losing her, and I believed him. Now I think it was all a half-truth. I think he wanted to go ballistic but was too ashamed to admit that he was a sneak. I think he was looking for another way to prove her infidelity, and he happened to discover that Teresa and Greg were a secret item. I think he killed Greg Pulver first. I think Teresa discovered Greg's body and accused Marsh, threatened to expose his crime, so he had to kill her too. I have no idea how Emerson Caldwell fits into any of it."

Beth didn't respond immediately, but after a minute of thought said, "I have to think like a cop and combine theories with facts and proof. You've just given me a first-rate scenario."

"Without a speck of proof, I know," I said. "How about a little more depth that may lead you to proof?"

"Please."

"Pulver had been dead two days. With this check-cashing scheme going down, if Ocilla or Emerson learned that Pulver was reporting back to the Sheriff's Office, they might have killed him or found someone else to do it. But not in Caldwell's condo. A dead man would draw police attention, exactly what they didn't want. Even if one of them had killed Pulver in the condo, none of them would want his body found there. They would have figured a way to get him out of there."

"Okay," said Beth. "I feel a punch line coming."

"Darrin Marsh is the only one on your radar who wouldn't care if a murder victim was found in Emerson Caldwell's condominium."

"That's a strong point, Alex. I wish I could take credit for it. The only problem I have with that takes us back to Fonteneau. If he was coming south from Canada the evening you returned from Sarasota, he couldn't have killed Pulver two days earlier. But what if he arranged for someone to kill the guy so we could blame the murder on Caldwell? That would be a nasty damn revenge, wouldn't it?"

"Except that Fonteneau would gain nothing financially. A perfect revenge would be to clean out Caldwell's life savings, not send him to prison."

I said, "Maybe he hired Pulver to rip off Caldwell, then... Hell, this is getting far too complicated."

Beth reached to the armrest behind her, raised a plastic bottle, unscrewed its cap and chugged down half the water. "I came up with an idea while Max related his version of the background story," she said. "I checked the Caldwell condo security keypad for the day the bodies were found and each of the three days before that. But you told me that Marsh had been an electrician, and I didn't check how many times the system went down. How did you learn that about him?"

"Carmen told me."

"Right," she said. "Are you thinking that he could have disabled the system or just Caldwell's keypad?"

"The company that monitors the system would know."

"And they wouldn't tell anyone," she said. "It would be bad for business if their customers found out."

"You just solved a murder case."

"Maybe so, and thank you," said Beth. "Who was that weasel who spoke to you in the hospital lobby?"

"His name is Edwin Torres," I said. "He's a mechanic who works for Beeson, the man that hired me in Sarasota. He wanted to warn me that Beeson was trying to set me up for something."

"Is he a flake?"

"I wouldn't have thought so until today. As of now he's either correct or crazy."

OUR APPROACH INTO KEY West International was quick and deliberate. The runway lights came on when our pilot clicked his radio mike five times. Simple automation. He explained while we taxied to his tie-down that the tower had been closed for forty minutes.

I asked if that meant that the airport was empty except for us.

"No," he said, "the security in that terminal would make the Secret Service proud. Someone knows we're here because I called ahead, but they still would know, even if I hadn't."

We descended the ladder to a chill breeze, the wind direction and scent promising cooler weather for the next couple of days. After Sam's friend locked the Cessna, we hiked three hundred yards to the flight service center where he had parked. Rather than waiting and paying for a taxi, we had accepted his offer of a ride.

"Someone knows we're walking out here, too?" I said. "Are we being observed though night-vision goggles?"

"I can't imagine so," said the pilot. "I doubt if they're up in the tower, but you never know. When the answers don't concern me, I don't ask the questions."

I said, "How can you..."

Beth elbowed my arm, a shut-up signal.

Sure as hell, we drove past The Tideline on our way into town but my memory spared me another replay of time spent with "the late" Teresa Barga. Perhaps the throng of ideas in my head had crowded out my grief and nostalgia.

Or postponed it all until a murderer was found.

23

ON SUNDAY MORNING BETH and I rose early at her house on Passover Lane and walked around the cemetery to Sandy's Cafe on White Street. It was cool, bright and not too breezy—the sort of day that paid back locals for the past year's nor'westers, tropical waves and hurricane watches. A day that was sure to piss off every tourist whose vacation was ending, who had to head back north that afternoon. We ordered two cafés con leche, split a ham and cheese breakfast wrap, then sat on red vinyl-padded stools on the sidewalk and watched joggers, bike riders, dog walkers and traffic.

I had left my phone back in her kitchen. Beth brought hers in case Max Saunders called with news on Ocilla Ramirez's location. Just when we had reached the point of flipping a coin for the last bite of food, Beth's phone rang. It was Marnie giving us a one-hour warning of a mandatory brunch of colby lasagna and pinot noir.

"Perfect," said Beth. "We'll be starved."

BACK IN BETH'S KITCHEN my phone was rattling on the countertop. A text message awaited me—from Wiley.

R U Dead? Just saw on internet you survived crash. Where R U?

I also had missed a phone call from Justin Beeson. I decided that returning to his world would spoil a good mood. For that matter, Wiley knew I wasn't dead. I didn't feel like confronting humanity's problems. I pocketed the cell, and Beth and I walked to our fashionable lunch. The whole town had come outside, and the sun, right there in January, made me wish I had worn SPF 30.

MARNIE DUNWOODY AND SAM Wheeler's home on the south end of Elizabeth Street smelled like a fine Italian restaurant. I heard Jesse Winchester on the stereo, noticed that Marnie was drinking a tall iced coffee. She handed us half-full wine glasses and sent Sam and Beth to the back porch to roast veggies on the grill. She waved me into the kitchen to chat while she toasted English muffins.

"See the paper this morning?"

"No offense, since it's your employer," I said, "but I've succeeded in avoiding it since I woke up."

"E. Carlton Gamble issued a press release on behalf of the estate of Emerson R. Caldwell," said Marnie. "We agreed to print it as a letter to the editor. It calls into question the offensive actions of the FDLE, the Sheriff's Office and the city police in ordering an autopsy for a gentleman with a history of age-related health issues. It was heartbreaking for the family and a financial burden because they had to postpone a funeral and burial in Toronto. While the family conceded that Mr. Caldwell's fatal heart attack took place at a tragic crime scene, the autopsy was a waste of taxpayer money."

"Excellent," I said. "He perfectly ignored the fact that the Canadian consulate asked for the autopsy. Now I will turn off my brain again."

"You've had a bitch of a week," she said.

"It's weird to think that twenty-four hours ago I swam out of a plane wreck."

"Sam said that Sherwin has two broken ankles. That ought to slow him down a notch."

"You know Rodney, my ace pilot?"

"Not until the night before you flew with him," said Marnie. "He was on the verge of rockin' the night away at Captain Tony's. I was there around six, having a beer with Rob O'Neal while Rob pissed and moaned about not being able to join in my multiple-murder scoop."

"Why was that?"

"When that call came on Monday morning, the boss had already sent him to Boca Chica to shoot a change-of-command ceremony. That's why I needed you. Anyway, the night before last, your pilot was right next to us at the bar when he got the call. He repeated your name as he wrote himself a note, then hung up and complained about having to stop his happy hour so he could fly in the morning. The guy drinking with him checked out the note and read your name aloud, said he knew you. He thought you were a fine person, and the island needed more like you."

"Who is my new best friend?" I said.

"His name was Fontaine." She knocked her knuckles on her forehead, tapped her memory. "Robert Fontaine."

"Please say it wasn't Fonteneau," I said.

"Right, that's it. You gave him the names of three great local lawyers because he's here to close out some real estate matters."

"Fonteneau and I shared a taxi from the airport on Tuesday night. He said that he'd come to town to settle the estate of a colleague who had died of a heart attack, a Canadian businessman."

"Oh, damn," said Marnie. "Emerson Caldwell?"

"I assumed that, but I didn't ask," I said. "I didn't give him names of attorneys, either. I told him to find one who'd been in town a while... Son of a bitch. He knew at least twelve hours ahead of time that I was going to fly on that plane. Did you tell him that you knew me?"

"I did not offer that information."

"How could he have known that I knew diddley about Caldwell?"

Marnie pointed toward the back porch. "Your connection to the investigating detective?"

"Okay, it's possible. What would he gain by killing me?"

Sam walked inside with a plate of hot squash, peppers and mushrooms. "Kill who, kill what?" he said. "Will it wait until after we eat? I'll help you kill this afternoon."

It got weirder after brunch.

AFTER WE PITCHED IN to rinse dishes, we returned to their open front porch where Marnie showed off her new pocket-sized Nikon. She returned my camera along with a bottle of contraband Havana Club Añejo Reserva Rum. "A shot of appreciation," she said. "You saved my ass, I'll attack your liver."

"Wish I'd had this in Starbucks last night."

"Sam told me about your awkward meeting in Fort Myers," said Marnie. "Now, I have a couple of questions about the shots you emailed to me early in the week." She handed me a print, and I recognized the scene. "This one's no big deal, Alex, but why did you take a picture of my car on Josephine Street?"

"That's where I parked my Triumph. I always fire a random before I begin work. Make sure my camera's functioning okay. Your Jeep happened to be there."

"I just wondered," she said. "That's not the real question I had."

I looked closer at the print. The car in front of Marnie's Jeep was Ocilla Ramirez's green Honda Element. I handed the photo to Beth, told her what it was.

"Do you still have this on your computer?" I said. "I'd like to see it blown up to full resolution."

"Sure, let me boot it up." She started into the house.

"What's your real question?" I said.

Marnie stepped back outside. "One thing at a time. It'll be simpler if I point to another picture on the screen."

A minute later she opened my Josephine Street "random." Helped by the glow of the laptop's screen, we saw the outlines of two people inside the Honda Element. The driver sat low in the seat, a match for Ocilla's stature.

"Oh, shit," said Beth. "It's the victim's business partner."

"Murderers who've returned to the scene of the crime?" said Sam.

"Or never left," said Beth.

Looking through the glass of the Jeep's windshield and the rear window of the Honda, I couldn't tell if the passenger was a man or a woman, but it was someone at least six inches taller.

"Nice hit, Marnie," I said. "What's next?"

"After that discovery, this may not be so remarkable." She selected and opened another image. "When you were taking photos for my story, why did you aim at cars across the street? You documented fifteen or twenty cars and vans in visitors' parking at the 1800 Atlantic condo. This filthy white van is particularly artistic. Let me zoom in closer..."

It was a fairly new van mottled with dried road dirt, its Ontario rear tag speckled by the salt employed to melt ice on northern roads. It wasn't unusual to see Canadian plates in the Keys, all year long, but if its owners could afford to stay at 1800 Atlantic, why hadn't they driven though a car wash south of the Snow Belt to rinse off the corrosive grime? Even rainstorms during the previous week would have washed away some of the salt, so the van must have been new in town.

"Two for two, Ms. Reporter," I said. "We're Canada-sensitive this week."

Marnie grinned with pride. "You think your new best friend Fonteneau has other friends in town?"

"I don't know about that," I said. "It could be Caldwell's van."

I gave Sam and Beth my version of Marnie's story from Captain Tony's about the pilot and my new friend and my new friend's elegant nickname.

Beth wagged her cell phone at the laptop. "I need that tag number."

I read it aloud while she repeated the numbers to a colleague in the police station who promised to call back when they had identified the vehicle's owner.

"You asked about airport security last night," said Sam. "Could Fonteneau and his possible friends have gone onto the airfield and messed with the King Air?"

"Someone got to the plane," I said. "Rodney Sherwin was adamant about never losing two engines for the same reason. He told me not to think about sabotage, but later he said, 'If you make it and I don't, kill Beeson for me.'"

"There's another possibility," said Beth. "Didn't you tell me that this Luke Tharpe from Sarasota is an ace mechanic?"

"Old carburetors are a world away from turbojets," I said, "but there's aptitude. Maybe he went to night school."

"We left through that key-coded gate last night," said Sam, "but it's a big, fenced-in airport."

"How about a Google satellite view?" said Marnie. She was already pressing buttons on her keyboard. "Zooming on Key West International and the Salt Ponds..."

"There's a north-side road parallel to the runway?" I said. "What's it leading to, a baseball stadium?"

"Government Road?" said Beth.

"I've never heard of it," I said.

"It runs south off Flagler like an extension of 7th Street," said Marnie. "It runs past the Cuban airliner and leads to the Little Hamaca nature trail. A few homeless people hide in the woods. That stadium-looking area is the old Hawk Missile Bravo Battery. These days it's a paintball field, so the war goes on."

"A missile battery, a Cuban plane and a paintball field? I feel like a stranger in my own city."

"A lot of water hazards around that airport," said Sam. "But someone could get to those planes between the runway and A1A."

"That's where the King Air was parked," I said. "In the middle of that group."

Sam nodded. "Must be dark and lonesome out there in the wee hours."

"Before you shut your laptop, Marnie," I said, "can you see if it snowed in Toronto early this week?"

"Getting off-topic here, Alex?" said Beth.

"Fonteneau said something on the plane Tuesday about having to shovel his way to his car so he could drive to the airport. I wondered at the time why he hadn't taken a taxi."

Marnie clapped her hands. "It hasn't snowed in Toronto since December 30th."

Beth read my mind, stood and patted my belly. "We've had our good eats. We're sure that Fonteneau's full of shit. Let's walk back and take a ride."

"Please let me set the pace this time," I said. "I'm starting to feel like I survived a freak airplane crash yesterday."

BETH AND I HIKED up United and wove our way through the back streets toward Windsor and Passover Lanes. A car drove by, music flowing from its open windows. For once it was classic Steely Dan instead of a bass-thumping mindless rant. As we crossed Olivia, no more than four hundred feet from Justin Beeson's elegant cottage, my phone buzzed: it was another call from Beeson.

"Maybe he's right down the street," said Beth.

"Or in Paraguay." I took the call. It was Justin's daughter, Eileen Beeson.

"I need your address, Mr. Rutledge. I heard that you were in a plane crash and I painted you a get-well card. Can you guess? It's a tropical tree limb, so don't guess too many times."

Beth and I had started past the Key West Cemetery, its discolored crypts and sad, plastic flowers. "Eileen, I'm thinking right now that you're the one who might need to recover."

"Oh yeah," she said, "but I'm okay."

"How is your father getting along?"

"Not so good. He cries. He started going through my baby clothes yesterday like it was me that died."

279

"Have either of you talked with Anya?"

"I have, twice on the phone. She's in Key West. I don't know about my dad."

"How about a detective named Steffey? Has he talked with you?"

"Oh, God, yes. He couldn't, you know... He asked about the men who delivered my mom's cars from Daddy's workshop."

"The mechanics, Luke and Edwin?"

"Yeah, those guys. My mom told me that Luke was okay but Edwin was nervous around us. She could tell because he always rubbed his thumb against that tattoo on his neck."

"How did you like those men?" I said. "Were you okay with them?"

"Oh, Luke was just another man. I didn't think about him, even when my mom said she liked him okay."

"How about Edwin?" I said.

"He creeped me out. One time I tried to draw his face and the drawing looked really scary. I tore it up right away."

"Why did you draw his face?"

"It's an exercise I do. I draw faces from memory. I draw my own face at least once a day, but I usually look in the mirror. Everyone else, I try to remember."

"Does anything else feel scary to you?"

"No, I'm just afraid that someone will hurt my dad."

BETH DROVE ME TO Dredgers Lane so I could change my shirt and grab my camera bag. Her white Audi A5 coupe is a stunning car. I had a ball driving it to Orlando to visit my brother before Christmas. Even Corvette drivers stared at it, and pedestrians would stop to let it pass so they could grab a second look. I wasn't sure it was the car we needed for a low-key clandestine run.

Stuck at the light at White and Virginia, in front of Sandy's Café where we started our day, Beth's phone rang.

"Another brunch," I said.

She handed her phone to me. The call was from PRIVATE NUMBER. I gave my name and explained that Detective Watkins was driving and couldn't talk just then.

"This is Max Saunders, Rutledge. We've got a puzzler on our end. We can't find the woman, but my squad is on the move. You two will know the minute we see her."

"Agent Saunders, we've pulled together some fragments of information since we saw you. We think a man named Robert Fonteneau is mixed up with Ocilla Ramirez. His nickname in a Canadian prison was Bobby Fuck No."

"Thank you, Mr. Rutledge. Where would the FBI be without citizens like you?" The call went silent.

Screw you, too, I thought.

I EXPLAINED MAX'S MESSAGE as we rolled east on Flagler, in style.

"I have an idea," I said. "Keep going and take a left just past Grace Lutheran."

"The fundamental premise of this idea?"

"We'll take Dubbie Tanner's car instead of yours."

"I get it," she said. "My car stands out in certain neighborhoods."

We found The Aristocrats doing yard work. I wanted to whip out my camera to gather evidence of their labors, but I knew they were embarrassed to be found with hedge clippers and a push-it-your-damned-self lawnmower. We chose to ignore their chore and they chose to help us out.

"You have made a wise decision," said Fecko.

Wiley Fecko dug into their wardrobe archive to find us suitable camouflage for cruising. Dubbie Tanner had to remove four cardboard boxes, a few stained towels, many empty soft drink cans, and a bulging black plastic garbage bag from the back seat of his Caprice. He spent most of five minutes in there with a wet/dry Shop-Vac, paper towels and a squirt bottle of Windex.

From that point onward the game got dirty.

24

WE ROLLED WEST ON Flagler for four blocks, turned left onto Government Road, then passed the entrance marker for KEY WEST SALT PONDS - LITTLE HAMACA CITY PARK.

"We get complaints from back in here," said Beth Watkins. "Homeless dudes in drunken fights, and they use sharp objects. Ironically, all the 911 calls come from cell phones."

"Blood brothers at noon," said Wiley Fecko. "Broken bottles and mortal enemies by midnight. I lived the booze opera too long."

"There was one brawl at the paintball field," said Beth. "A man was tagged during a war scenario, but he refused to vacate the field. The war turned into fists and rocks. One of the brawlers was an Eastern European already on probation for a bar scuffle. He was deported."

"Does that make me feel safer?" I said.

"Wasn't my decision, Alex."

"Sorry about this heat in the car," said Dubbie Tanner. "I've got the A/C on four-thirty."

Beth turned up her palms. I explained about four windows down and thirty miles-per-hour.

A blue bandanna was wrapped around my head and Beth wore a backward flat-brim ball cap. We hunkered down in the back seat of Tanner's four-door Caprice, and tried to look as deadbeat as possible. Every time we hit a bump, a cloud of dust mites escaped from under the front seats. The open windows were life-savers. We passed the Cubana passenger plane, an Antonov An-24 that Dubbie said had been hijacked in March, 2003.

Somehow I missed that event. I must have been ass-deep in somebody else's problems. Or off taking promo photos on a breeze-swept Caribbean island.

Fecko turned to check on us. "I'm going to play Phil Collins for a short time. It sets our roll tone, if you follow my reasoning. If it's too loud, tell me."

I was their guest, so I held my tongue.

A quarter-mile along and just beyond a barbed wire-topped fence on our right, we saw ponds and water weeds—enough to make entry to the airport a pain in the ass or worse. Only two hundred yards farther down we could see dry-looking silt clear to the runway, beyond which was the line of parked single- and twin-engine small planes where, thirty hours earlier, Rodney Sherwin and I had boarded the King Air 90.

"Along here, in my humble estimation," said Wiley, turning down the CD player, "this is your best access point."

Dubbie, at the wheel, spoke over his shoulder: "My able partner sounds far too desperate to prove that you need us."

"We need you," I said.

Airport security also believed that this stretch offered the easiest access. Every fifty yards they had posted signs: NO PARKING WITHIN FIVE FEET OF FENCE. The shrubbery in a couple of areas might help with cover, but not much, and it might not matter at night.

"That's cheesy barbed wire," said Wiley. "One twin mattress, a step ladder, and it's up and over. You pull the mattress over behind you so it's available for escape. Your only risks would be tripping an infrared alarm or being spotted by someone with night vision goggles. If security caught something on their monitors, they could flip on the runway lights, illuminate the entire area. You would turn into a cue ball on black velvet."

"Were you in Iraq?" I said.

"Kuwait," said Wiley. "Four-point-six months, civilian tech advisor. Okay, right along here, if you got over the fence, you would run for that windsock because they wouldn't place sensors near an object that moves around as much as it does. This spot gets eight points on a scale of ten."

"Another risk," said Dubbie, "would occur if a weed sleeper like the former Wiley Fecko figured a way to liberate the mattress."

"Are you seeing what I'm seeing?" said Beth.

I turned my head to look through the windshield. "Now I am."

We were witnessing a pizza delivery to a homeless camp.

"Homeless doesn't mean broke," said Wiley. "They garnish Social Security only for child support and back taxes. Not for alimony, thank God."

"What's up around the corner?" I said. "The defunct missile site?"

"First we'll pass the entrance to Little Hamaca, the indigenous hammock. It's a city park. This road goes all the way back to the old radar towers and the paintball field. Do you want me to chat up these boys during their lunch?"

"Not yet," said Beth. "Let's keep going."

Wiley turned up the music, waved to someone gathered around the pizza, then waited until we had followed the road northward to finally turn off the music .

"Tell you what we'll see," said Tanner. "Out by the paintball area there's ponds of water like we just saw back there. Too much water for a sneak intruder to navigate."

We drove into an alternative twilight zone. Twenty-foot fences, earthen and poured cement bunkers, grass gone to seed, weed shrubs gone to hell, radar dishes, five tall communications towers, and rundown buildings covered with graffiti. It was also a dumping ground for old city recyclables as evidenced by park benches, stacks of barricades and lumber, and a SIDEWALK CLOSED sign. I caught a glimpse of myself in the rear view mirror, mouth agape like a rube staring up at tall buildings in a big city.

"Welcome to the mean streets of Key West," said Beth. "Or street, singular."

The slum scenery changed only slightly as we drove along. Two grocery buggies, one without wheels, toppled onto a spindly bush. A scattering of concrete blocks—enough to build a missile shelter. Two junked vehicles under a flimsy carport.

"Holy shit, there's your white van, Alex," said Beth. One of the vehicles was the Ford Econoline covered with dried slush. Not junk, just dumped.

"It's lost its Canadian license plate," I said.

"Please stop right here, Mr. Tanner," she said. "Don't go any closer to it."

The car next to the van tripped a memory switch. "Didn't Max Saunders say that Emerson Caldwell was driving a Toyota Corolla rental when he ditched the agents that were tailing him?"

"So much for hunting down an aircraft saboteur's access point," said Beth. "Our scouting mission has taken a fresh direction."

Fecko reached over to the ignition key and turned off the car's engine. "Do you hear what I hear?"

We all looked more closely at the van. Blow flies swarmed the half-inch opening of the driver's-door window.

I said, "Oh, no, could that..."

"Don't even start to speculate," said Beth. She swung open the car door. "We'll find out soon enough. I'm staying here and I will wait ten minutes before calling in the forensic team. I want you three to drive back to the pizza party to ask questions."

"It might require token bribery to secure cooperation," said Wiley.

Beth didn't approve, but understood. She said, "What works best?"

"Pre-packaged sushi from Fausto's or Publix, either one, doesn't matter to these fellows."

"They're already eating and we don't have time..."

Wiley stopped her. "I'll need all the one-dollar bills we can pool together."

FECKO LEFT DUBBIE AND me in the car and ambled toward his former brethren. Our first hope was that no one had noticed Beth in the back seat, that none of them would ask why we had left her back by the paintball. Our second hope was that a slice or two of pizza remained so that Wiley could pay far too much for them. After the deal was complete, his questions would appear as mere afterthoughts.

The ploy worked—up to a point. Wiley bought two skinny slices for the price of the whole pizza, brought them to us in the car, then returned to speak with the four gentlemen of the sidewalk who slouched around a liberated picnic table. Dubbie and I watched the conversation, animated and punctuated by hacks and coughs, pointed fingers, waving arms. Finally Fecko walked slowly back to the Caprice, smiling slyly as he neared the car. Grinning smugly as he told us what he'd learned. He repeated it to Beth a minute later when we returned to the carport.

The crew figured that we had found the van that smelled of death, and speculated that the woman we had left behind was a detective. But only after Fecko promised to speak to the detective, to do his best to shield the vagrants from being hauled off to the county lockup, did they give him the information we wanted.

Two of them saw the Toyota arrive, at four in the morning a week ago, followed by a darker car, a new four-door. The Corolla smelled so new, they took it for "bait," a GPS-equipped car dropped by the cops to catch thieves. The van came in three or four nights later, also followed by the darker car. Again, the hobos kept their distance and told newcomers to do the same. When the stink began to waft from the van, they all knew to stay away.

"Did you pose the bonus question?" I said. "Did anyone use a mattress to go over the barbed wire?"

"Almost got that right," said Wiley. "They showed me the chaise lounge cushion, rips and all. Whoever it was didn't come back out the same way. Good thing, because the cushion was already someone's bunk."

"Did they steal his step ladder, too?"

"He didn't use one. He jumped from the roof of a light-colored SUV."

Dubbie turned to face me. "Like a silver RAV4?"

"I was thinking a silver BMW X3," I said. "I saw Fonteneau riding in one that belongs to the attorney, E. Carlton Gamble."

"They're not experts in current model years," said Wiley, "and it was night. All they could say was it wasn't white and it wasn't black or a dark color like navy or maroon. It was in-between."

Beth gave Wiley a soft jab on the chest. "You're a fine investigator. Keep at it."

Wiley turned to me. "One last thing. Do you think maybe the darker car was that Hyundai we've been seeing? The one leased to R. Fonteneau of St. Petersburg?"

AFTER THE SCENE TECHS arrived and opened the unlocked van, Beth was the first to look. Holding firm on her cop demeanor, she peered into it but refused to react to the body. She turned away and walked straight to me.

"Ocilla Ramirez," she said, "with a hole in her forehead just above her left eye. She looks absolutely peaceful, power-napping on the van's sheet metal floor."

Another quick adiós, and I wondered if Ocilla's battered daughter, Angel Baby Dobbins, might have wished for a match to her childhood, an uglier, more drawn-out ending.

Beth said, "Alex, please call Agent Max Saunders for me?"

"Please tell me I don't have to take pictures."

"You don't. For all we know, you might be on a witness list. Why did you mention a silver RAV4?"

"Justin Beeson's girlfriend drives one, so it popped into my mind. The last time I saw it, on Caroline Street, one of Beeson's car mechanics was driving it. Beeson, of course, like Robert Fonteneau, knew I'd be flying with Rodney Sherwin."

"That gives us two possible conspiracies," said Beth. "I'm going to have a busy afternoon."

"Do we keep Sheriff Liska up-to-date starting now?" I said.

Beth looked at me. "Any idea why he's been cut out of the loop?"

"Yes, and we should think of it as ninety percent voluntary," I said. "Let's do him the favor of keeping it that way, for now."

"There's a problem with that. Someone will call him in the next hour or so, even if it isn't Max or one of us."

"Probably, but that chain link fence is the borderline. The airport is his territory, and this road is inside the city."

"If he hears it first from us, at least he can decide not to answer the phone until tomorrow."

"Good point, my lover with a brain," she said. "I'll call him."

"What's Max's number?"

"Use my phone. I'll call Chicken Neck when you're done."

I TOLD FBI AGENT Saunders about Ocilla's death. He said, "Oh," as if having just been told why his newspaper hadn't been delivered that morning. He didn't offer me a sarcastic thank you, as he had done when I told him about Bobby Fuck No. He did, however, confirm the Vehicle Identification Number of the Toyota Corolla—the rental car that Caldwell had used to outrun the agents on his tail.

I closed the call and handed off the phone to Beth. Before calling Fred Liska, she phoned her office, spoke for a half-minute and clicked off.

"Two things," she said to the three of us. "The autopsy results were on my desk. Emerson Caldwell had a heart attack, but it might have been drug-induced. Outside Auto Parts Corporation, a Canadian company, is the van's registered owner."

"That's Fonteneau's chain of repair shops," said Fecko. "Its name probably refers to *outside* of prison."

Beth let us know that it was time for us to leave. She needed to stay with the city cops to wait for Ocilla's body to be removed and the tow trucks to arrive. She said, "I will spend the rest of my afternoon tracking down and speaking with E. Carlton Gamble, attorney for the dead and suspicious."

"And driver of nice cars," I said. "Fonteneau was riding in Gamble's BMW X3 when I saw them at Azur on Thursday. That's two silver SUVs in the game."

I RODE IN THE Caprice back to Wiley and Dubbie's home, to finally retrieve my motorcycle. None of the pizza gang was in sight when we took the bend in the road just past Little Hamaca Park. They were taking no chances on being questioned or implicated.

"Which of you two can explain the missile battery to me?" I said.

Wiley threw up his hands, but Dubbie sat up straighter in the driver's seat. "The Cuban Missile Crisis of October 1962," he said. "It lasted exactly two weeks, and it could have ended our world as we know it."

"Let's go hardware instead of drama," I said.

"Our Hawk Missiles were sent from the mainland, immediately installed and, as I've heard it, fully operational the day after the crisis ended. They remained in place from 1962 until sometime in the late-1970s."

"I never knew," I said.

When we arrived on Staples and parked behind Beth's Audi, I asked Wiley if, by chance, he had come across the middle or maiden name of Beeson's first wife, the murder victim from twenty years ago.

"I saw it once and... damn... I'll go look inside."

He came back out holding a sheet of paper. "A Latina. Maria

Rodriguez."

"Oh, man. That's a name like Mary Johnson or Linda Jones. She didn't have a middle name?"

Wiley checked the paper. "She did. Maria Torres Rodriguez."

I had him spell the middle name to make sure. But I knew.

GLENN STEFFEY TOOK MY call on the second ring. "What?"

"Sorry for blowing out of Fort Myers in such a hurry. My ride was leaving."

"I owe you an apology, too, Rutledge, my crack about gruesome photos."

"That wasn't out of line," I said. "I wonder about myself, too. What questions did you have for me?"

"Do you remember what Beeson said to you when he asked you to fly up for the meeting yesterday, the meeting that never happened?"

"He said he wanted to convince everyone that he wasn't involved in the crime. I was the only non-family member that could confirm his timeline and state of mind. He said my being there could make a difference."

"How did you feel about that?" said Steffey. "I mean, you agreed to come up here. Did he offer to pay you?"

"He offered to pay for my time, and I didn't have a schedule conflict. I was being asked to tell the truth, not to tell lies or make assumptions."

"I'll accept that," said the detective. "You may have answered all of my questions."

"Can I ask if you've turned up any solid leads?" I said.

"We knew this from your photos, but we've confirmed that Beeson totally fouled the crime scene cubicle with his fingerprints. I'm still trying to get my mind around the fact that he lied to us about the recycle time on his building's security videos. He told you seventy-two hours, and he told me one week."

"Major confusion factors," I said.

"Especially if we consider that she was brought into the building in the trunk of her own car," said Steffey. "Luke would not have moved that Mercedes-Benz into the building if he thought that we would find hard evidence of her presence in the trunk. The man knew he was on camera."

"Did you find evidence?"

"Start with urine stains and drops of blood," he said. "She cut the back of one leg on something sharp in the trunk, maybe on purpose."

"Hell of a start," I said. "What came next?"

Steffey gave a sniff of hesitation then said, "Amanda had cocaine in her system and she had sex just before she died."

"Consensual sex? With her killer?"

"No way to answer either question," said Steffey.

"But someone dropped off the Benz with Amanda inside it, alive."

"Correct," said the detective. "Then Luke moved the car into the garage without knowing she was along for the ride. He certainly had no reason to check the trunk. She may have been alive when you were in the building that first evening you were in Sarasota."

"Let me guess," I said. "The last person to leave the building that night was Edwin Torres."

"Let's say that's true."

"Isn't it about time for you to spend a day or two in the Keys?"

"What are we talking about here, Rutledge?"

"Go pick up Edwin," I said, "and tell him he won't do life without parole if he identifies his co-conspirator. I'm betting I'll see you down here in shorts and flip-flops by noon on Tuesday."

"Tell me more."

"Someone with building access trussed up Amanda Beeson and killed her," I said. "That whittles it down to the real estate people and Edwin Torres. If she was the real owner of that building, as I believe she was, no real estate broker or salesperson in their right mind would want her dead. She meant income to those people. She meant something else to her killer, but Edwin Torres doesn't have the gumption to pull it off by himself."

"Gumption like balls?" he said.

"Yep. I think someone gave him a push, and I also think that Justin Beeson knew that Edwin had killed her within minutes of discovering her body. That makes him an accessory after the fact, correct?"

"Who pushed him, Rutledge, if it wasn't Beeson? The saucy girlfriend?"

"I may not be 100 percent correct, so if I said a name, it would screw up your questions for Edwin. Show him some sympathy and understanding. He's had a rough life. Take my word, Glenn, the man will explain everything. Call if you need me to recommend a good hotel."

DUBBIE TANNER HAD DISAPPEARED inside his house and Wiley Fecko was folding the tarp that had covered my Triumph. One of them had brought my helmet outside and placed it on the porch chair.

"Do we need to bring your fee invoice up to date?" I said to Fecko.

"We know where you live. What's next on our list of impossible deeds?"

"Only one that I can think of right now," I said. "Darrin Marsh was working for an electrical contractor, maybe more than one, before he became a cop. Can you find out who employed him and the types of jobs they did? Maybe we can find out if he ever did wiring work at The Tideline."

"I'll get on it."

I STARTED THE TRIUMPH, snugged my helmet strap and watched the city's crime scene van stop in front of Southernmost Aristocratic Investigations. Beth Watkins exited the passenger-side door, clicked the locks on her Audi A5, and sat inside the car long enough to lower the windows. Then she walked over and hugged me while I removed my helmet.

"Home run on the white van," she said. "One of our forensic techs used to work for the Border Patrol in Arizona. They dealt with a constant stream of dope, and he's good at finding secret compartments. He found a stash in a vertical support pillar."

"Empty?"

She shook her head. "About three hundred in loose fifties and twenties and one uncashed check stuck in a seam. It was a refund check from a U.S. phone company sent to an address in Montreal, maybe to an American who had moved."

"If that's how they brought the checks into the country, why would they risk using the van to move cash back out?"

"That's someone else's problem," said Beth. "More important to us is that the van passed through Miami heading south on Sunday. It's too bad there's no way to know who was in it."

"How did you..."

"The Turnpike's tolls are paid either by SunPass or direct billing to the license tag holder. Cameras read every tag and every number goes into a database. That's why they bust so many people southbound in the Upper Keys who are driving with expired tags, revoked licenses or canceled insurance. Searching and cross-matching data is simple."

Amazing, I thought. "Big Brother is alive and well."

"As is Robert Fonteneau, unless he met the same fate as Ocilla."

"There are too many vehicles and too many arrivals," I said. "He flew down here on Tuesday, we know that. Did he also drive his van down here two days earlier? And let's not forget, both the Corolla and Hyundai were rented in his name. Is he aware of that fact and has he driven either of them?"

"I want to thank you and hug you, Alex. Then I want to put a bag over your head and beg you to stop thinking long enough for me to catch up."

"Give me one more thought," I said. "I can't believe that Fonteneau killed Ocilla and dumped her in his own truck. If he did that he would give up the check-cashing scam, taint his Canadian company, and make himself a murder suspect. I don't think he killed her. I think someone's trying to screw Bobby Fuck No."

"Now he's scrambling?" said Beth.

"He'd be a fool to stay in town. Even if he had to hitchhike... Unless he's waiting for some kind of payoff."

"He's probably gone," she said, "but I'll put a BOLO on the Hyundai and a watch at the Key West and Miami airports."

"The Greyhound Bus and the Ft. Myers Ferry?" I said.

Her eyelids drooped slightly. Not sultry at all. Slightly pissed.

"Maybe if we can find Christi Caldwell, we'll find him," I said. "They could be the masterminds at the top of the check-cashing operation."

She made the "T" sign with her hands.

"The last time I saw her, she was face down in a bottle of wine with E. Carlton Gamble."

Beth lunged for my throat. She stopped only to see if there were witnesses.

25

I LOCKED THE MOTORCYCLE in its designer shed and eyed my back yard shower. If I couldn't have forty minutes of slippery playtime with Beth Watkins, my next choice would be Little Feat full blast on the outside speakers until I ran out of hot water.

Indulgent, sure, but I could blame my plane crash aches. Or the weirdness of the past six days. Or incessant phone calls, not including the one that interrupted my idyll under the mango tree.

"Marnie drove somewhere to write about a dead woman," said Sam.

"The other housekeeper. They found her inside the white van from that photo. Beth's trying to find the van's owner, Bobby Fuck No."

"Some people come by their nicknames easily. Where was he last seen?"

"Captain Tony's," I said. "Two days ago, when Marnie overheard his chatter."

"Would he keep going back to the same saloon?"

"Criminals aren't always the smartest humans in the world. Ready for a beer?"

SAM DROVE AND PARKED in the Hilton garage, and we hiked up Greene Street.

"Like we did with that city cop on Thursday," he said, "I'll go in first."

I dawdled on the corner at Duval long enough to give him time to order a beer. Our precaution was meaningless. The place was half-full of weekend tourists having one for the road, and Fonteneau wasn't in sight. Every time I walked into Captain Tony's, with all the photos, flags, business cards, license plates and nautical artifacts plastered about, I thought about "All Up on the Wall," a song I particularly enjoyed. I joined Sam at the far end of the bar, a vantage point back toward the bandstand.

Sam began to talk about hanging out in there when he first got to town. He told me about sitting at a table right behind us while "The Captain" talked about losing the election, the first time he ran for mayor, and about losing Stacey Loux, the woman Tony called the love of his life.

"The only time I ever saw Tony get misty-eyed," said Sam. "How we doing?"

"This isn't working. Fonteneau's not here. He's probably in Toronto."

"It was a good try and the beer is cold."

"That's all the excuse I need to sit right here for the next two hours," I said. "Turn a hectic Sunday afternoon into a lazy Sunday afternoon."

No such luck. My phone buzzed.

I thought quickly about which callers I could ignore and which might prompt me to answer. The name that flashed on the screen made it easy. It was Malcolm Mason, the boat broker.

"The noise tells me you're in a bar," he said. "I'm sorry to disturb your hometown holiday. I've got a favor to ask."

"Anytime, Malcolm. Especially right now."

"Alex, I didn't tell you this when that man agreed to buy the boat the other day. I guess I didn't want you to get a big head and boost your prices. When he told me he was interested in buying it, I told him you were outside taking pictures. That seemed to make up his mind. He said that Alex Rutledge wouldn't bother to take pictures

298

of junk. He bought the boat without inspecting it."

"Sounds like I might be in line for a salesman's commission," I said.

"There may be a problem, Alex. When he and I shook hands on the deal, he gave me four thousand bucks in cash as down payment. Ten minutes ago he called me here at home. He wants to meet in the morning for a quick shakedown cruise, then close the purchase. But he warned me that he would pay the rest of the money in cash. That's forty-one thousand dollars."

"That sounds a bit shaky to me," I said. "What did you tell him?"

"I told him the boat wasn't in the water, which is true, so I had to check with my hoist operator, which is not. I really needed to call you. He knew your name, Alex, so I figured it goes both ways. I was wondering if you could vouch for him."

"Name?"

"Fonteneau," he said. "Robert Fonteneau. Do you recognize his name?"

"Have you got a number for him?"

"No, he was calling from a pay phone. He's calling me back in ten."

"Can I get back to you, Malcolm? I'll have to check something myself."

"Please don't leave me hanging," he said. "I want this sale."

I SPEED-SPOKE AN EXPLANATION to Sam while I thumbed Beth's number. She didn't answer—no surprise. She was into an interview, or looking for E. Carlton Gamble or chasing down leads in Internet caves accessible only to badge holders. Which left me playing solo with the knowledge that a person of interest, my possible murderer, was still on the island. He was trying to schedule a meeting with a boat broker who wanted the deal but knew nothing of Bobby Fuck No's background.

"All I know are five details," said Sam, "but here's the punch line. He called your friend on Sunday. He needs the boat. The man's desperate, in a hurry."

"Afraid of being killed or caught," I said.

"The instant he gets a toehold, he'll want to reschedule. You should start thinking that it's going to happen tonight." Sam checked his watch. "Just under two hours to sunset."

I have learned never to doubt Sam Wheeler's instinct. I tried again to reach Beth's cell. It went to voicemail, and I asked her again to call because Fonteneau was still in town and potentially available. I hung up and pushed my beer away.

Come on, come on.

The young woman who had served our beers wore a bright orange T-shirt that said in block letters, SHE AIN'T RIGHT. She reached under the bar, tapped her phone, read a message and cracked a big grin. I waved her over and handed her my cell.

"I know how to receive a text," I said, "but not how to send one. Could you please do me a..."

"To this last number you called?" she said. "What do you want to say?"

"'Call right now about Fuck No.'"

She began tapping with both thumbs. "You are so golden with the words." She handed back my phone, gave me a flirtatious but skeptical smile. "Done, dude. Are you really expecting an answer?"

"What have I got?" I said to Sam. "Three minutes to call Malcolm? It's too noisy to think in here. I'll meet you around the corner at the Smokin' Tuna. Tip the woman an extra five, okay?"

Thirty seconds later I was walking down Telegraph Lane, thinking fast. I needed to keep Malcolm Mason clear but I didn't have time to explain the danger. I needed to keep Fonteneau inside the city limits so Beth could arrest or detain him without involving Sheriff Liska. If someone started shooting, I didn't want innocent victims.

My phone buzzed: it was Malcolm.

"If I have to hang up," he said, "it's because he's calling me back."

"I understand," I said. "Where do you bank?"

"The, um... You know... The tall one behind Key Plaza."

"Okay, Malcolm, your sale to Mr. Fonteneau is a done deal. The shakedown ride, we understand that, so let's get your money first. Tell him to meet you at the bank because you don't want to be walking around with forty-one grand in your pocket."

"I've got a safe in my office."

"I'll explain later why that's not a good idea. He's also a very demanding person. Since it's a cash deal, I'm guessing he'll want to move fast and meet you this evening before sundown."

"Of course, the bank won't be open," said Malcolm.

"Right, but tell him to meet you there right away," I said. "Take a big envelope and a deposit slip for the night deposit drop box. Do not tell him you've called me to vouch for him. For absolute sure, don't tell him that."

"What the hell's going on, Alex?" he said. "Shit, there he is, calling now."

"Do what I said, Malcolm. Call me right back."

SAM WHEELER FOUND ME sitting on the curb on Charles Street, inside that gray area between pensiveness and puking. Half-fearing his judgment, I told him what I'd said to Malcolm Mason.

"Off to a good start," he said. "What can we do without Beth?"

"Stall Fonteneau, I suppose," I said. "Keep him in one place until Beth comes to our rescue. We can't let Malcolm near him."

"That works," said Sam. "Let's get the car."

In the near-darkness of the Hilton parking garage, I noticed that Sam had fresh white decals on his old Bronco's tailgate, silhouettes of fish with a year under each one.

"What are those?" I said. "I thought I knew my native species."

"You've seen those death notices on the back windows of cars, right? Rolling obits and memoriams? I did it for the fish. Those are local extinct ones."

So dependable in so many ways.

"Why are the streets so empty?" I said.

"NFL Playoff games today. Where are we going?"

"Key Plaza, and please step on it, driver."

"My foot will go through the floor."

WE WERE COMING OFF Eaton onto Palm Avenue when my phone rang. I answered and told Wiley Fecko that I couldn't talk.

"This is hot, so don't hang up," he said. "Marsh worked for Rafael Mendoza Electric when they rewired the security system at The Tideline. He had plans and codes."

"Jesus. Thank you," I said, trying not to think about Teresa. I clicked off.

Malcolm called back. "You were right, Alex. He wants to do the deal today. He wasn't happy but he agreed to meet me in the bank parking lot near the drive-through."

"Good," I said. "Will he recognize your car?"

"I forgot to tell him, I'm in my wife's car today. She took mine to Miami."

"Okay, Malcolm, I want you to meet me first in Key Plaza, at the front door of Office Max. I'll be there in three minutes."

"What the hell is going on, Rutledge?"

"You'll understand everything right away."

"FONTENEAU KNOWS YOU, RIGHT?" said Sam. "Your face will scare him off."

"Shit, I hadn't thought that far ahead."

"I'll go in with some kind of excuse, like I'm Malcolm's assistant."

"No," I said. "you're the substitute hoist operator, because his full-time guy is out of town. That's good, but where is he? Where are the NFL Playoffs being played this year?"

"I don't have to know that. I don't have to be a football expert. Just a hoist jockey working overtime."

"He'll probably be in a bronze Hyundai," I said, "parked a good distance from the bank's security cameras. Mispronounce his name at first. He'll jump all over that, give us an extra minute or two. Talk about your forklift career."

"Didn't you say that somebody might be trying to screw with the criminal?"

"Beth and I thought so. You don't, by chance, have your weapon..."

"Under your seat," said Sam, "but that's a good idea. You and Malcolm can bring his car the long way around."

"Am I going to protect you with your gun?"

"I'm not Wyatt Earp. If he has a weapon, I'd rather depend on your aim than my quickness. You and Malcolm drive around and south on Kennedy, pull in the row just beyond that line of utility trucks that's always there. Put up the hood, mess with the distributor cap. Do something to make yourself credible. Park at an odd angle as if you just broke down."

"Hell," I said. "I'm going to park where I have a clear shot."

We pulled into the shopping center and rolled over the speed bumps. My phone buzzed: Beth, finally. It took fewer than ten seconds to tell her what was going down.

"I hope this is good, Alex," she said. "God, I hope this is good. Don't let him out of your sight!"

She ended the call.

"She's rolling," I said. "There's Malcolm over there, getting out of that Subaru. Let's try one more thing." I called Sam's number and we both heard it ring. He took the call and dropped his phone in his Velcro-flap shirt pocket.

He said, "The code word is, 'Oh shit.'"

His voice came through to my phone, at low volume but clearly. I left the Bronco and started toward Malcolm Mason. Sam drove toward the rear entrance to the big bank's drive-through slots.

Sam's voice came through my phone: "Wave if you can hear me."

I waved. His taillights flashed twice.

"Here we go..." he said.

I EXPLAINED THE CONFUSION to Malcolm the best I could while I monitored what I barely heard from the phone in Sam's shirt pocket. On my directions, Malcolm drove east out of the Key Plaza parking area, turned right and headed toward the Florida Keys Aqueduct Authority Building, south of the bank's drive-through. Through the phone to my ear I could tell that Sam already had begun to speak with Fonteneau. This was happening too fast.

I heard: "Right, pal. Are you Fontaine?"

The muffled response to Sam's question came through faintly.

Sam again: something about meeting Mason five minutes ago.

Now, more clearly, Fonteneau: "I don't know who the hell you are. What is this, a rip-off attempt?"

"Fuck that," said Sam. "I wouldn't know your name if Malcolm hadn't told it to me. Why would he want to rip you off when he can just sell you the boat? Here's my wallet. You can see who I am."

We drove past them on Kennedy, perhaps sixty yards away. I watched Sam hand his wallet to Fonteneau.

Fonteneau said, "Why isn't the boat being put in the water right now?"

"I don't have the keys to the hoist," said Sam. "I don't know which boat it is, and when I work on Sundays I get paid cash in advance. Mr. Mason didn't explain all that to you?"

"Am I paying you or is he?" said Fonteneau.

"I don't care," said Sam. "It's all green on one side and black on the other."

Malcolm angle-parked farther away than I would have liked, but we were stuck. We couldn't move again without drawing attention. Our view of the two men was partially obscured by a decorative line of sabal palms native to the Keys but not to that parking lot. Sam, for a moment, looked toward the palms, allowing himself to be distracted by a scampering cat. His chat with Fonteneau had stopped, or our phones had lost contact. I was down between parked vehicles, creeping closer to Fonteneau with Sam's gun in my hand.

I heard the Ducati before I saw it. Beth pulled her motorcycle into the drive-through and attempted to open the night deposit drop box. She rattled it roughly, gave up, stopped her engine and let the cycle rest on its kickstand. Pulling off her helmet, she walked toward a cashier's window and peered around inside. Pretending to read an off-hours number, she tapped her phone.

My phone buzzed in my pocket. I crouched, put Sam on hold to take the call and said, "I'm in the line of utility pickups to your south."

I watched her look at her phone and shake her head, as if not getting an answer. I switched back to listening to Sam.

"Ma'am, it's not like a FedEx box," yelled Sam. "You might need a key."

Sam Wheeler walked toward Beth, offering to help with the drop box. In my peripheral vision I saw two city squad cars pull into the lot from the direction of Office Max. Then two more blurs to my right.

"Thank you, but it's that other man…" She slipped her phone into the carrying case on her belt and turned toward Fonteneau with her pistol drawn.

Bobby Fuck No had seen the squad cars and was one step ahead of Beth. His gun was aimed right at her chest. I raised Sam's weapon and aimed at Fonteneau's back, began to squeeze the trigger.

I heard a gunshot and a shrill woman's voice. "Mister Triple Deal, like your slimy old father. Now you die like him." Then another gunshot. "There's your suicide, cheap shit."

Robert Fonteneau went down ass-first on the concrete then toppled, dead on the spot.

I heard a Taser pop and a man yelled, "Clear."

Sam's voice came through my phone: "Oh, shit."

"What the fuck just happened?" yelled Beth. She had crouched alert, her weapon pointed upward and held with both hands.

I ran closer, still ready to dive to the pavement. Near the Kennedy Drive sidewalk I saw Officer Darrin Marsh waving a Taser, its wires dangling. Next to his police car was Carlton Gamble's silver BMW X3, and on the ground, in spasms, then trembling and whimpering, was Christi Caldwell. She had dropped the weapon she had used to shoot Fonteneau.

Beth stood and ran to Christi, kicked away the gun then stopped to catch her breath, assess the scene. I had run close enough to hear the ring of her cell phone. She looked and took the call. "Positive?" she said. "Thank you," and hung up.

"Good Taser shot, Officer Marsh," she said, putting her phone away. "Not just good but great, and timely, thank you. That woman needs to wait right there for the EMTs. Please cuff her to that sign post."

Sirens approached us from at least two directions, perhaps three. Chatter came from three or four compact shoulder-snapped radios. Marsh and I looked at each other without speaking while Beth stepped away to speak quietly with a lieutenant and three other officers. With a nodding of heads they gathered, surrounded Darrin Marsh for an impromptu sidewalk ceremony. Marsh stood in the middle, puzzled, his broad chest huge in contrast to Beth's head.

"Okay, JD, Carson and Steve," she said, "you'll be getting letters in your upcoming fitness reports. This thing could have gone messy, so I appreciate your quick response to my backup request. Officer Marsh, a permanent commendation will be attached to your file for action in defense of a fellow officer. As you know, we have a procedural formality since you fired a weapon in the line of duty. You'll have forty-eight hours' relief of duty and the mandatory shrink chat, but that's it." She smiled and continued, "If you'll make yourself available for a few pats on the back... I noted your wide stance and two-handed grip, like they taught us all in school.

You didn't burn your wrists on the backfire, did you?"

"Backfire?" Baffled by the question, Darrin Marsh extended his arms and turned his palms upward. "There's no backfire on a Taser, detective."

"There is this time," said Beth. She and the lieutenant snapped their handcuffs onto his wrists. One of the other officers knelt to clamp on an ankle chain. "I don't expect this to get ugly, Marsh, because if it does, I'll be the first one to shoot you. You're under arrest for the murder of Greg Pulver."

"No goddamn way," said Marsh. "No fucking way."

"We discovered traces of Greg Pulver's blood on the underside of your cruiser's trunk lid. You did a fine job bleaching out the trunk, Marsh, but you failed to realize that blood can splatter upward when a body shifts. Even when it's been dead for a while. That was the call I just got, about the blood match."

The first group of EMTs hoisted Christi Caldwell onto a stretcher. They wheeled her past our group just as Beth Watkins began reciting the Miranda Warning.

"You the cop that killed the wrong dude?" said Christi, laughing at Marsh. "Your girlfriend was fucking my husband, not the boy."

THEY TOOK AWAY ROBERT Fonteneau's body, then found a briefcase in his car with seven grand, a pistol and three nautical charts for Florida's west coast. There was no forty grand. He was going to rip off Malcolm Mason, perhaps kill him for the boat.

"How did Christi Caldwell happen to show up?" I said to Beth.

"I went to Gamble's home on Von Phister to question him about his car and his clients. Driving up his street, I saw the X3 parked about ten houses away from his and, for an instant, saw movement. Someone was hunkered down in the front seat. I ignored it, stopped and parked on the sidewalk and knocked on Gamble's door. I'd been inside for maybe five minutes, learning that Gamble had loaned his vehicle to Mrs. Caldwell, when I got your message about the bank. I drove the wheels off that Ducati to get here. Somehow she kept up with me."

"You let her follow," I said.

"Maybe so."

Two other city detectives showed up to deal with Darrin Marsh. The crime scene team had yellow-taped the area and the city's official police photographer was hard at work.

"You brought this together, Alex, but now it's time," said Beth. "Show me a badge or get the hell out of here."

I got the hell out, asked Malcolm Mason for a ride. We didn't say much until he turned into Dredgers Lane. I wasn't sure how to bring up the lost boat sale.

I opened the car door and said, "We needed to catch this bastard."

"No problem, Alex," he said. "You probably saved my life."

"Too much drama, Malcolm. No matter what, we both suffered short-term memory loss."

Mason looked at me, confused.

I said, "What four thousand dollars?"

He grinned, shrugged and nodded. "I've got plenty more boats to photograph, whenever you're ready."

I felt like I'd been in a plane wreck.

Or watched a gunfight.

I went inside, called the Aristocrats, said a simple "Thank you," drank two beers and went to bed.

26

THE NEXT MORNING, AFTER only thirty minutes of daylight, it was 72 and sunny. I had planned to sleep late but birds woke me, or maybe the fresh air fluttering the crotons and wafting through screens. Perhaps I emerged early to make sure that the past seven days were really behind me. The radio promised an imminent cold snap, nights in the fifties and days only in the high sixties, but I was comfortable for the moment. If Key West was a board game, this kind of morning would cancel out three days of flooded streets, power outages and sewer-work street detours within a block of the house.

I was barefoot in fishing shorts and a T-shirt, forsaking my usual Bustelo for a coffee called La Llave suggested by a recent Havana transplant named Mercedes. I was using a dinner knife to open a week's worth of mail that had stacked up on my porch table.

Marnie Dunwoody's headline story about the shooting of murder suspect Robert Fonteneau and the arrest of Officer Darrin Marsh dominated the *Citizen*'s front page. As she had promised to do, Marnie had taken credit for one of my exterior photos of the ten-unit Tideline condominium building. Banished to below-the-fold was the paper's story about over-zealous post-Playoff game celebrations downtown, and the arrest of six men for group-urinating on a losing team's jersey in the middle of the intersection of Duval and Greene. I was in no hurry to read the articles.

I heard a vehicle drive slowly down the lane. I didn't even look up. Nothing could be worse than the treachery and violence already in my rear-view mirror. I heard a car door shut in front of the house, then a second door. I gave up and looked.

Liska stood back by the lane's pavement, his arms crossed, a stern expression on his face. Manatee County Detective Glenn Steffey approached the porch, a badge held high for visibility's sake.

"Why are you waving your authority at me, detective?" I said. "I remember you from way back thirty hours ago."

He stopped walking six feet from the porch door. "If you look closely you'll see that it's not my badge, Rutledge. It's yours."

"I would sing for you the Buddy Holly classic, 'That'll Be the Day,' except I can't stand my voice in the morning."

Steffey opened the door, walked in and sat. He placed the Manatee County Junior Deputy badge next to my coffee cup. "You were wrong about Edwin Torres being Justin Beeson's son, but not too far off the mark."

"Coffee?" I said.

"Had mine at four a.m., thanks," he said. "Beeson's first wife, the murdered one, was Edwin's older sister, and he and his family have held for years what they thought was evidence of Beeson's guilt. It was information her family kept to themselves because they were afraid of bringing up unresolved immigration issues."

"Have you arrested Justin?" I said.

Steffey shook his head. "Unfortunately, the evidence was bogus. It was similar to a tip we received way back when, and our office disproved it. It's sad, but we may never solve that case, unlike the current one which I wrapped up forty minutes ago."

"Edwin's revenge—or attempted revenge?"

"Right," said Steffey. "Except it's complicated and incredibly greedy."

"Did the twin sister, Sonya, push Edwin to kill Amanda?"

Glenn nodded but raised an index finger to make a point. "Anya researched the previous dead wife, Maria Rodriguez. I suspect you

310

already know that name. Anya concluded that Edwin was Justin's brother-in-law and told her sister. Sonya crafted the plan for the four of them to kill Amanda and take over Justin's world. Each had a different motive but, as I said, the fundamental stimulus was greed."

"And the chief selling point was seduction."

"You bet," said Steffey, "in stereo. They double-teamed both mechanics. Sonya was the creative one, for sure. She taught Edwin how to truss up Amanda to make it look like a sex crime. They all thought it would be an unsolved crime, like the killing of Maria Rodriguez. Anya insisted that Beeson hire you, by the way. She thought your rep as a sleuth would bolster everyone's alibi."

"Is anyone in jail?"

"Edwin stayed with us last evening in Manatee, and Sheriff Liska's team grabbed the other three on Olivia Street first thing this morning. What Key Westers might call 'the last thing last night.' They're being processed into the system right now. Oddly enough, they were not all in the same bed. Nor will they be again for twenty years, minimum."

"After all that effort," I said, "was Justin's world even worth two cents?"

"It would be huge after he and Eileen inherited Amanda's personal wealth. Her money financed Beeson's projects, including 23 Beeson Way. That's why she kept all her cars there. Part of the divorce settlement was that Justin would oversee Eileen's trust."

"It sounds like you're going to overlook the idea that Justin suspected Edwin from the start," I said.

"Tough to prove in court," said Steffey, "especially given the relationship, the brothers-in-law thing. Also, the girl needs her father, which brings us to..."

"What's her status?" I said.

"I spoke with her last night and mentioned that I might come down here to the Keys." He reached to hand me a small envelope. "She asked me to give this to you, if I saw you."

I extracted and unfolded a piece of copy paper. The message read:

> I guess I will always miss my mommy but I missed her alot when she was alive, too. Writing this note to you feels good so if it's okay I will send you postcards or whatever. The school called Ringling just said I could start taking college courses next year. I'm not sure, I don't think I have to pay. If you find any more books like that one you gave me on the airplane, I would like to borrow them, okay? That would be cool. Your friend, Eileen.

Steffey was standing, ready to leave, when I looked up again.

"Amazing resilience," I said.

"One last thing," said the detective. "I asked Edwin Torres if he had any reason other than revenge to murder Amanda Beeson. He explained that she didn't appreciate what she had. He couldn't get out of his mind the fact that she left the top down on one of her cars during a rainstorm. The dampness shorted out her electric seat warming circuitry, and every time she started the car while wearing shorts, the seat shocked her thighs. He didn't think that was enough punishment."

I WENT INSIDE TO drink the last of the coffee and clean out the pot. I was staring downward, studying the grounds when Wiley and Dubbie arrived on their bicycles.

Dubbie was first onto the porch. "Would have been here a half-hour ago," he said, "but we saw mucho officialdom in the lane. Nice to see you still sitting here. Are we off the hook, too?"

I patted the *Citizen*. "See your names in the paper?"

"I read it twice," said Wiley, shaking his head. "Didn't see your name, either."

"That's one sign of a successful operation," I said.

Tanner said, "We continue to blend into scenery like two blades of grass in left field. But we still need camera advice and a couple of favors."

"And some work," said Fecko. "To generate a continuing cash flow."

"Obviously our approach requires credible introductions," added Tanner. "You know, referrals for word-of-mouth growth. Given the fact that we intend to work more or less undercover, we can't exactly advertise."

"We need to start building rep by word-of-mouth," said Wiley. "We need someone like you to front for us."

Dubbie grinned. "Put our best monkey on the front of the train."

"Me?" I said. "Be your agent?"

"That would be great, thank you," said Dubbie, "though 'representative' has a more solid ring to our ears."

Wiley agreed. "You could say it implies a flexible fee structure."

"Appreciate your acceptance," said Tanner. "We need to be at a meeting in ten."

AN UNPLANNED TWO-HOUR RETURN to napland was shortened by a knock at the door. A cab driver delivered a tray of chilled seafood from Malcolm Mason identical to the one that had caused me to drool four days earlier. Conch seviche, steamed shrimp, salmon mousse, thin-sliced ahi tuna, smoked fish dip and water crackers plus two chilled bottles of Willamette Valley Pinot gris.

As if on cue, Marnie and Sam approached the porch.

Sam carried a booze-heavy paper sack. "We're celebrating a transition," he said, "if that's the word I want. Marnie got called on the carpet today."

Looking glum and afraid, Marnie shrugged. "We're looking, or trying to look, at the positive side of things."

I did not want to hear this news. If Sam and Marnie were leaving the island, they would create a huge gap in my life. Their friendship would never disappear, but their companionship would take the form of twice-annual road or business trips. Sam had been my primary source of strength and sanity and laughs. He had given direc-

313

tion to my soul-searching, pulled me through a lot of crap. Marnie had tolerated our antics, our ventures to the edge of peril. She and Beth had found a trusting friendship.

I waited for the bomb.

"The best way to describe the change," said Sam, "is that Marnie's been asked to cut down on her reporting tasks, as such."

"Such what?" I said.

"The publisher and my boss sat me down this afternoon," said Marnie.

"Get to it," said Sam. "You'll have to admit this fifty times in the next week."

Marnie bit her lower lip, radiated worry, then smiled. "I've been promoted to assistant managing editor. It's pretty good. The managing editor gets stuck with a lot of meet-and-greets, club luncheons, that kind of thing. I get to run the newsroom."

Sam pulled three bottles of Perrier-Jouët champagne from the bag, and I heard Beth's Ducati roar away from the light at Grinnell, then turn into the lane.

"Perfect time and reason for a celebration," I proclaimed.

"Time, yes," said Sam. "The real reason is that Marnie got a book deal and the newspaper okayed it."

"I thought non-fiction required visual proof of truth and all that," I said. "How can you sell a book without pictures?"

"Some of yours weren't bad," said Marnie, "as you saw on the front page today. I dug up old mug shots on everyone but Christi Caldwell. I've been assured a copy of hers, too. All I have to do now is sit on my personal-time ass and write."

"What about those two small planes over The Tideline?"

"They weren't shooting stills. They shot video only. One guy had incorrect camera settings, and the other got 14 seconds on TV once an hour for less than one day. That was it. The story wasn't the building, it was inside."

WE CELEBRATED AND ATE things that used to swim and raised toasts to Marnie's new job and Beth's having scored two major arrests in five minutes. It came down to four full bellies, eight bare feet and eight droopy eyes.

"I haven't even left my house," I said, "and today has been a perfect day."

"What's on your schedule for this evening?" said Beth.

"A personal investigation of police tactics."

"Aren't you supposed to wait an hour after eating?"

Sam looked away to mask a grin while Marnie called a taxi to take them home.

WHILE WE CLEANED UP enough to discourage an infestation of insects, I asked Beth if she had learned anything more from Christi Caldwell.

"Start with this fact. Christi and one of her several lovers, a Canadian post office employee, invented the check scam. Emerson Caldwell was their 'coordinator,' as she termed it. They recruited Robert Fonteneau, another of her boyfriends, because he had trucks crossing the U.S.-Canadian border both ways on a regular schedule. It worked for over two years."

"That FBI man, Max Saunders, said that his crew had seen Emerson and Ocilla Ramirez in a bank parking lot," I said. "If she was running checks for him, why didn't they meet in his condo?"

"It was when Emerson and Christi and Fonteneau first discovered that Ocilla and Greg Pulver were starting to steal as much money as possible. The housekeepers had big plans to bolt, leave the country. But they got stupid about small things like not paying the condo rent and cable bill in Emerson's place. If Marsh hadn't killed Pulver first, Fonteneau would have done the job."

"Marsh killed the wrong man and screwed up the larger scam," I said.

"He blew two scams," said Beth. "Christi and Fuck No planned to push Emerson out of the check-cashing scam so they could take over everything."

"Teresa Barga died for screwing around. Harsh penalty."

"Are you okay?" said Beth. "You knew her quite a while."

"Her death opened up a few memories," I said. "There were good moments, certainly a few bad ones. I don't miss the relationship. Memories are for sharing, but I can't imagine that she and I would ever have reminisced. Memories for one person are like a slow, bluesy electric guitar melody without even a hint of reverb."

Beth's phone buzzed.

"I've got to take this call. It's Chief Salesberry, probably calling to congratulate me."

"I'm going to go out back for three minutes."

"Okay," she said. "I took a shower before I rode over here."

When I walked back into the house, clean and nearly sobered by the evening air, Beth was off the phone. She was standing in the kitchen in her underwear eating an Entenmann's raspberry danish twist. A dot of sugar was on her upper lip.

"Plans for the rest of the night?" I said, stealing the sugar with my tongue.

"Have we dated before?"

"I'm Alex. You don't remember?"

"Yes, but I still need to check your user name and password. Make sure this is a valid approach."

"How about I show you my love when the towel drops," I said.

She wagged the danish at me. "You will show me better if it gets snagged and doesn't fall."

"When confronted with pastry, I've been known to eat the muffin top first."

Beth said, "Not tonight, mister."

••

316

About the Author

Tom Corcoran is a photographer and former journalist and the author of the Alex Rutledge novels set primarily in Key West. He has created "Key West in Black and White," a book of retrospective Key West images; and "Key West Point of View," a collection in DVD format of over 400 recent color photographs of the island. Acoustic guitar and steel pan background music was created for the 40-minute DVD by musicians John Frinzi and John Patti.

A resident of the Florida Keys for fifteen of his thirty-five years in Florida, Corcoran was an early collaborator with Jimmy Buffett, providing photos for seven of his album and CD packages and lyrics for the songs "Fins" and "Cuban Crime of Passion."

Corcoran's photographs and articles have appeared in *Rolling Stone, Southern Boating, Cruising World, Car & Driver, Esquire, Look* and *Outside.* For seven years Corcoran edited *Mustang Monthly,* a magazine for restorers of classic Ford Mustangs.

In addition to continuing the Alex Rutledge Series, Corcoran has co-written song lyrics for several recent John Frinzi CD releases.

The Alex Rutledge Series

The Mango Opera
Gumbo Limbo
Bone Island Mambo
Octopus Alibi
Air Dance Iguana
Hawk Channel Chase
The Quick Adiós (Times Six)

ALSO BY TOM CORCORAN

Key West in Black and White
Jimmy Buffett—The Key West Years
Key West Point of View (Photo DVD)

www.TomCorcoran.net
www.DredgersLane.com